This was no accident.

Isyllt wrapped a concealment around her, and a ward against the flames, and crossed the street.

Her ring blazed as she entered the shop, pushing back the crackling heat—no survivors inside. Flames consumed the doors and wall hangings, rushed over the ceiling to devour the rafters. Lamps melted on shelves, brass and silver charring wood as they dripped to the floor. Witch-light flickered around her in an opalescent web, holding guttering flames at bay. But it wouldn't keep the ceiling from crushing her when it came down.

The smell of charred flesh and hot metal seared her nose, and something else. The air was heavy with intent, with sacrifice. The magic that turned the shop into an inferno had been dearly paid for.

A spell so powerful must have left a trace. She nearly stepped in a puddle of brown-burnt blood, nudged a body aside with her toe. The man's eyes melted down his charred cheeks and Isyllt frowned; intact, he might have shared his dying vision with her. Not that she had time to scry the dead.

By Amanda Downum

The Necromancer Chronicles

The Drowning City

THE DROWNING CITY

THE NECROMANCER CHRONICLES
BOOK ONE

AMANDA DOWNUM

www.orbitbooks.net

New York   London

Copyright © 2009 by Amanda Downum
Excerpt from *The Bone Palace* copyright © 2009 by Amanda Downum
All rights reserved. Except as permitted under the U.S. Copyright Act of 1976, no part of this publication may be reproduced, distributed, or transmitted in any form or by any means, or stored in a database or retrieval system, without the prior written permission of the publisher.

Cover art by Larry Rostant

Orbit
Hachette Book Group
237 Park Avenue, New York, NY 10017
Visit our Web site at www.orbitbooks.net.

Orbit is an imprint of Hachette Book Group. The Orbit name and logo are trademarks of Little, Brown Book Group Limited.

Printed in the United States of America

First edition: September 2009

10 9 8 7 6 5 4 3 2 1

For New Orleans

Drowning is not so pitiful
As the attempt to rise.

—Emily Dickinson

Hope lies in the smoldering rubble of empires.

—Rage Against the Machine
("Calm Like a Bomb")

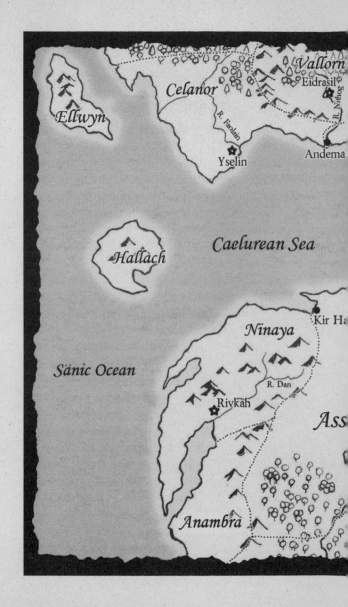

Veresh

Vrana

Ashke Ros

The Steppes

Kiva

Sarkany

Selafai

Temes

Zaratan
Sea

R. Mori

R. Herodis

Iskar

Kehribar

Erisin

Inle

Skarra

Sherazad

sh

Khitoum

Khejuan

R. Mir

Ta'ashlan

R. Ash

Symir

R. Nilufer

Sivahra

Khebari
Strait

r

Archeon Ocean

Iseth

PART I

Waiting for the Rain

CHAPTER 1

Symir. The Drowning City.

An exile, perhaps, but at least it was an interesting one.

Isyllt's gloved hands tightened on the railing as the *Black Mariah* cleared the last of the Dragon Stones and turned toward the docks, dark estuarine water slopping against her hull. Fishing boats dotted Ka Liang Bay, glass buoys flashing in the sun. Cormorants dove around them, scattering ripples as they snatched fish from hooks and nets.

The west wind died, broken on the Dragons' sharp peaks, and the jungle's hot breath wafted from the shore. Rank with brine and bilge, sewers draining into the sea, but under the port-reek the air smelled of spices and the green tang of Sivahra's forests rising beyond the marshy delta of the Mir. Mountains flanked the capital city Symir, uneven green sentinels on either side of the river. So unlike the harsh and rocky shores of Selafai they had left behind two and a half decads ago.

Only twenty-five days at sea—a short voyage, though it didn't feel that way to Isyllt. The ship had made good time, laden only with olive oil and wheat flour from the north.

And northern spies. But those weren't recorded on the cargo manifest.

Isyllt shook her head, collected herself. This might be an exile, but it was a working one. She had a revolution to foment, a country to throw into chaos, and an emperor to undermine with it. Sivahra's jungles and mines—and Symir's bustling port—provided great wealth to the Assari Empire. Enough to fund a war of conquest, and the eyes of the expansionist Emperor roved slowly north. Isyllt and her master meant to prevent that.

If their intelligence was good, Sivahra was crawling with insurgent groups, natives desperate to overthrow their Imperial conquerors. Selafai's backing might help them succeed. Or at least distract the Empire. Trade one war for another. After that, maybe she could have a real vacation.

The *Mariah* dropped anchor before they docked and the crew bustled to prepare for the port authority's inspection; already a skiff rowed to meet them. The clang of harbor bells carried across the water.

Adam, her coconspirator and ostensible bodyguard, leaned against the rail beside her while his partner finished checking over their bags. Isyllt's bags, mostly; the mercenaries traveled light, but she had a pretense of pampered nobility to maintain. Maybe not such a pretense—she might have murdered for a hot bath and proper bed. Sweat stuck her shirt to her arms and back, itched behind her knees. She envied the sailors their vests and short trousers, but her skin was too pale to offer to the summer sun.

"Do we go straight to the Kurun Tam tonight?" Adam asked. The westering sun flashed on gold and silver earrings, mercenary gaud. He wore his sword again for the first time since they'd boarded the *Mariah*. He'd taken to sailor fashions—his vest hung open over his scarred chest, revealing charm bags around his neck and the pistol tucked into his belt. His skin was three shades darker than it had been when they sailed, bronze now instead of olive.

Isyllt's mouth twisted. "No," she said after a moment. "Let's find an extravagantly expensive hotel tonight. I feel like spending the Crown's money. We can work tomorrow." One night of vacation, at least, she could give herself.

He grinned and looked to his partner. "Do you know someplace decadent?"

Xinai's lips curled as she turned away from the luggage. "The Silver Phoenix. It's Selafaïn—it'll be decadent enough for you." Her head barely cleared her partner's shoulder, though the black plumage-crest of her hair added the illusion of more height. She wore her wealth too—rings in her ears, a gold cuff on one wiry wrist, a silver hoop in her nostril. The blades at her hips and the scars on her wiry arms said she knew how to keep it.

Isyllt turned back to the city, scanning the ships at dock. She was surprised not to see more Imperial colors flying. After rumors of rebellion and worries of war, she'd expected Imperial warships, but there was no sign of the Emperor's army—although that didn't mean it wasn't there.

Something was happening, though; a crowd gathered on the docks, and Isyllt caught flashes of red and green uniforms amid the blur of bodies. Shouts and angry voices carried over the water, but she couldn't make out the words.

The customs skiff drew alongside the *Mariah*, lion crest gleaming on the red-and-green-striped banners—the flag of an Imperial territory, granted limited home-rule. The sailors threw down a rope ladder and three harbor officials climbed aboard, nimble against the rocking hull. The senior inspector was a short, neat woman, wearing a red sash over her sleek-lined coat. Isyllt fought the urge to fidget with her own travel-grimed clothes. Her hair was a salt-stiff tangle, barely contained by pins, and while she'd cleaned her face with oil before landfall, it was no substitute for a proper bath.

Isyllt waited, Adam and Xinai flanking her, while the inspector spoke to the captain. Whatever the customs woman told the captain, he didn't like. He spat over the rail and made an angry gesture toward the shore. The *Mariah* wasn't the only ship waiting to dock; Isyllt wondered if the gathering on the pier had something to do with the delay.

Finally the ship's mate led two of the inspectors below, and the woman in the red sash turned to Isyllt, a wax tablet and stylus in her hand. A Sivahri, darker skinned than Xinai but with the same creaseless black eyes; elaborate henna designs covered her hands. Isyllt was relieved to be greeted in Assari—Xinai had tutored her in the native language during the voyage, but she was still far from fluent.

"Roshani." The woman inclined her head politely.

"You're the only passengers?" She raised her stylus as Isyllt nodded. "Your names?"

"Isyllt Iskaldur, of Erisín." She offered the oiled leather tube that held her travel papers. "This is Adam and Xinai, sayifarim hired in Erisín."

The woman glanced curiously at Xinai; the mercenary gave no more response than a statue. The official opened the tube and unrolled the parchment, recorded something on her tablet. "And your business in Symir?"

Isyllt tugged off her left glove and held out her hand. "I'm here to visit the Kurun Tam." The breeze chilled her sweaty palm. Since it was impossible to pass herself off as anything but a foreign mage, the local thaumaturgical facility was the best cover.

The woman's eyes widened as she stared at the cabochon black diamond on Isyllt's finger, but she didn't ward herself or step out of reach. Ghostlight gleamed iridescent in the stone's depths and a cold draft suffused the air. She nodded again, deeper this time. "Yes, meliket. Do you know where you'll be staying?"

"Tonight we take rooms at the Silver Phoenix."

"Very good." She recorded the information, then glanced up. "I'm sorry, meliket, but we're behind schedule. It will be a while yet before you can dock."

"What's going on?" Isyllt gestured toward the wharf. More soldiers had appeared around the crowd.

The woman's expression grew pained. "A protest. They've been there an hour and we're going to lose a day's work."

Isyllt raised her eyebrows. "What are they protesting?"

"New tariffs." Her tone became one of rote response. "The Empire considers it expedient to raise revenues and has imposed taxes on foreign goods. Some of the local merchants"—she waved a hennaed hand at the quay— "are unhappy with the situation. But don't worry, it's nothing to bother the Kurun Tam."

Of course not—Imperial mages would hardly be burdened with problems like taxes. It was much the same in the Arcanost in Erisín.

"Are these tariffs only in Sivahra?" she asked.

"Oh, no. All Imperial territories and colonies are subject."

Not just sanctions against a rebellious population, then, but real money-raising. That left an unpleasant taste in the back of her mouth. Twenty-five days with no news was chancy where politics were concerned.

The other officials emerged from the cargo hold a few moments later and the captain grudgingly paid their fees. The woman turned back to Isyllt, her expression brightening. "If you like, meliket, I can take you to the Silver Phoenix myself. It will be a much shorter route than getting there from the docks."

Isyllt smiled. "That would be lovely. Shakera."

Adam cocked an eyebrow as he hoisted bags. Isyllt's lips curled. "It never pays to annoy foreign guests," she murmured in Selafaïn. "Especially ones who can steal your soul."

She tried to watch the commotion on the docks, but the skiff moved swiftly and they were soon out of sight. A cloud of midges trailed behind the craft; the drone of wings carried unpleasant memories of the plague, but the natives seemed unconcerned. Isyllt waved the biting insects away, though she was immune to whatever exotic diseases they might carry. As they rowed beneath a raised water gate, a sharp, minty smell filled the air and the midges thinned.

The inspector—who introduced herself as Anhai Xian-Mar—talked as they went, her voice counterpoint to the rhythmic splash of oars as she explained the myriad delta islands on which the city was built, the web of canals that took the place of stone streets. Xinai's mask slipped for an instant and Isyllt saw the cold disdain in her eyes. The mercenary had little love for countrymen who served their Assari conquerors.

Sunlight spilled like honey over their shoulders, gilding the water and gleaming on domes and tilting spires. Buildings crowded together, walls of cream and ocher stone, pale blues and dusty pinks, balconies nearly touching over narrow alleys and waterways. Bronze chimes flashed from eaves and lintels. Vines trailed from rooftop gardens, dripping leaves and orange blossoms onto the water. Birds perched in potted trees and on steep green- and gray-tiled roofs.

Invaders the Assari might be, but they had built a beautiful city. Isyllt tried to imagine the sky dark with smoke, the water running red. The city would be less lovely if her mission succeeded.

She'd heard stories from other agents of how the job crept into everything, reduced buildings and cities to exits and escape routes, defenses and weaknesses to be exploited. Till you couldn't look at anything—or anyone—without imagining how to infiltrate or corrupt or overthrow. She wondered how long it would take to happen to her. If she would even notice when it did.

Anhai followed Isyllt's gaze to the water level—slime crusted the stone several feet above the surface of the canal. "The rains will come soon and the river will rise. You're in time for the Dance of Masks."

The skiff drew up against a set of stairs and the oarsmen secured the boat and helped Adam and Xinai unload the luggage. A tall building rose above them, decorated with Selafaïn pillars. A carven phoenix spread its wings over the doors and polished horn panes gleamed ruddy in the dying light.

Anhai bowed farewell. "If you need anything at all, meliket, you can find me at the port authority office."

"Shakera." Isyllt offered her hand, and the silver griffin she held. She never saw where Anhai tucked the coin.

The she stepped from the skiff to the slime-slick stairs and set foot in the Drowning City.

The Phoenix was as decadent as Xinai had promised. Isyllt floated in the wide tub, her hair drifting around her in a black cloud. Oils shimmered on the water, filled the room with poppy and myrrh. Lamplight gleamed on blue and green tiles and rippled over the cool marble arch of the ceiling. She was nearly dozing when someone knocked lightly on the chamber door.

"Don't drown," Adam said, his voice muffled by wood.

"Not yet. What is it?"

"Dinner."

Her stomach growled in response and she shivered in water grown uncomfortably cold. She stood, hair clinging to her arms and back like sea wrack, and reached for a towel and robe.

The bedroom smelled of wine and curry and her stomach rumbled louder. The *Mariah*'s mess had been good enough, as sea rations went, but she was happy to reacquaint herself with real food.

Adam lit one of the scented-oil lamps and sneezed as the smell of eucalyptus filled the room. The city stank of it at night—like mint, but harsher, rawer. Linen mesh curtained the windows and tented the bed. The furniture and colorful rugs were Assari, but black silk covered the mirror, true Selafaïn fashion.

Adam sat, keeping the windows and doors in sight as he helped himself to food from the platter on the table. He'd traded his ship's clothes for sleek black, and the shadows in the corner swallowed him.

"Where's Xinai?" Isyllt asked, glancing at the door that led to the adjoining room.

"Scouting. Seeing how things have changed. The curry's good."

She tightened the towel around her hair and sat across from him. The bowls smelled of garlic and ginger and other spices she couldn't name. Curries and yogurt, served with rice instead of flat bread, and a bowl of sliced fruit.

"We should find our captain tonight." She stirred rice into a green sauce. "The Kurun Tam may take all day tomorrow."

The *Black Mariah*'s legitimate business would keep her in port at least half a decad, but Isyllt wanted to make sure their alternate transportation was resolved before anything unexpected arose. She scooped up a mouthful of curry and nearly gasped at the sweet green fire. A pepper burst between her teeth, igniting her nose and throat.

The sounds of the city drifted through the window, lapping water and distant harbor bells. Night birds sang and cats called to one another from nearby roofs. Footsteps

and voices, but no hooves or rattling carriage wheels—
the city's narrow streets left no room for horses or oxen.

"You don't want to be here, do you?" Adam asked after
a moment. Shadows hid his face, but she felt the weight of
his regard, those eerie green eyes.

She sipped iced-and-honeyed lassi. "It isn't that,
exactly."

"You're angry with the old man."

She kept her face still. She hadn't cried since the first
night at sea, but emotions still threatened to surface when
she wasn't careful. "I know the job. My problems with
Kiril won't interfere." Her voice didn't catch on his name,
to her great relief.

"I hope not. He'll skin me if I don't keep you safe."

Isyllt paused, cup half raised. "He said that?"

Adam chuckled. "He left little room for doubt."

Wood clacked as she set the drink down. "If he's so
bloody concerned, he could have sent someone else." She
bit her tongue, cursed the petulant tone that crept into the
words. The side door opened with a squeak, saving her
from embarrassing herself further.

Xinai slipped in, feet silent on marble. "I found Teoma.
He frequents a tavern on the wharf called the Storm God's
Bride." Izachar Teoma had made most of his wealth and
notoriety smuggling along Imperial shores, but sailed
north often enough to have encountered Kiril's web of
agents before. A ship quick and clever enough to escape
harbor patrols would be useful if they had to flee the city.

Xinai tossed a stack of cheap pulp paper onto the table.
"News-scrawls, from the past decad or so. The criers will
have stopped spreading those stories by now."

"Thanks." Isyllt flipped through the stack—wrinkled

and water-spotted, and the ink left gray smears on her fingers, but the looping Assari script was legible. The latest was three days old. She took a moment to adjust to the Assari calendar; today was Sekhmet seventh, not the twelfth of Janus; 1229 Sal Emperaturi, not 497 Ab Urbe Condita.

She often found the pride of nations silly. Trade and treaties between Assar and Selafai had to be twice dated, because the founders of Selafai had abandoned all things Imperial when they fled north across the sea five hundred years ago. But if not for the pride of nations, she'd be out of a job.

She sipped her drink again, watery now as the ice melted. Moisture slicked the curve of the cup. "Did you hear anything about the protest we saw?"

"Not much. The guards ran them off not long after we arrived, it sounds like. There were arrests, but no real violence." From Xinai's tone, Isyllt couldn't tell if she was disappointed in that or not.

Adam rose, taking a slice of mango with him. "Finish your dinner, Lady Iskaldur." The title dripped mockingly off his tongue. "We'll leave when you're ready."

Night draped the city like damp silk. Heat leaked from the stones, trapped between close walls; sweat prickled the back of Isyllt's neck. The end of the dry season in Symir, but the Drowning City would never be truly dry. Insects droned overhead, avoiding the pungent lamp-smoke, and rats and roaches scuttled in the shadows. Charms hummed around them, soft shivers from doors and windows. *Safe*, some murmured, *home*. Others pulsed warnings—*stay back, move on, look away.*

Shadows pooled between buildings, leaked from narrow alleys; the glow of streetlamps drowned the stars. Voices drifted from taverns, floated up from the canals as skiffs passed. Water lup-lup-lupped against stone and wind sighed over high bridges, rattling the chimes that hung on nearly all the buildings. Hollow tubes and octagonal bronze mirrors flashed and clattered—in Erisín, Selafai's capital, no one left mirrors uncovered and even still puddles were avoided, but here it seemed they were lucky.

The crowds had thinned after dusk, stores closed and shuttered, the last clerks and shopkeepers hurrying home. More than once they passed guard patrols, green uniforms edged with Imperial red—a whispered word kept the soldiers' eyes off them.

A cool draft wafted past Isyllt, and a whisper light and hollow as reeds. Her bare arms prickled and the diamond chilled on her finger. She smiled—the touch of death was comforting, made the city feel less foreign.

She studied Adam's easy stride, the roll of Xinai's hips as she kept pace with him, the dangerous grace with which they moved. At home she worked alone more often than not—probably more often than she ought—but Kiril had insisted she bring backup this time. She could have brought someone familiar, but it was better this way. Too many people in Erisín knew her bitter history with Kiril, offered her sympathy and sad glances. She preferred the quiet solace of strangers. And, she admitted to herself, in this strange place she was glad of their presence.

They crossed a wide canal into the dock district—Merrowgate, the map named it. The Phoenix lay in Salt-lace, the tourist and market quarter. The night grew louder as they neared the docks, bare and sandaled feet slapping the stones, laughter and music echoing from taverns, bells tolling to guide ships in the dark. The cloying spice-sweetness of opium drifted out of an alley mouth.

As they passed a narrow walkway along the water Isyllt heard a soft cry, like a child's muffled sob. She paused, searching for the source. It sounded like it came from the water.

Xinai laid a hand on her arm as she leaned toward the black offal-reek of the canal. "Don't. It's a nakh."

"A what?"

"A water spirit. Like your sirens in the north. They mimic children to lure people close to the water, then pull them in."

Isyllt frowned down at the black water. "Then what?"

Xinai shrugged. "Eat you. Drown you. I don't know. I doubt you'd care once you were at the bottom of the bay. The inner canals are warded, but they slip in around the edges of the city sometimes." She leaned over the railing and called out in Sivahran; the word shivered with a weight of magic. Something below them croaked, then splashed and was still. Xinai turned away and Adam and Isyllt fell in behind her.

The Storm God's Bride lay on the far side of the district, nestled between storehouses, with cheap rented rooms stacked above it like a child's precarious block tower. The sound of flutes and drums drifted through the door and firelight fell from the windows in oily-gold streaks.

Isyllt was glad to find the Bride little different from the disreputable dock taverns at home. Smoke and sweat and spilled beer thickened the air, and the tiles were cracked and sticky. Dried plants hung from warped rafters, wards or decoration or something else entirely.

Xinai twisted through the crowd in search of the captain; Isyllt stayed close to Adam, careful not to foul his sword-arm. She ran a surreptitious hand over the hilt of her own knife, though the mood in the room seemed pleasant enough.

Musicians played on a low wooden platform against the far wall, mostly ignored by the custom. Sailors and dockworkers, Isyllt guessed, watching the people slouched on low benches or gathered loudly around the gaming tables. Wiry men and women, scarred and wind-scoured and plainly dressed, bronze skin and ocher, shades of black and brown. Ninayans and Sivahri and Assari alike laughed and gambled and drank bowls of beer, and none seemed less welcome than the others. She even saw a few fairer heads, from Hallach or lands farther north.

Xinai reappeared soon and led them across the room, toward a door beside the stage. As they moved down a narrow corridor, Isyllt heard the rattle of dice. They entered a cluttered storeroom and found a man sitting alone, rolling bones across a scarred table.

She'd known Teoma was a dwarf, but the leather cuff that capped his missing left forearm was a surprise. Dark eyes gleamed under heavy black brows as he glanced up at them.

"Good evening. Here for a game of chance?"

Adam's lips curled. "Since when is there chance in your games, Izzy?"

The dwarf's grin rearranged his creased face; lamplight winked off two gold teeth. "It's dangerous to accuse a man of cheating." He nodded toward his maimed arm. "Look what happened to me."

He turned his eyes to Isyllt. "But if you haven't come for the bones, what can I do for you?"

Isyllt twisted a red-gold ring off her finger and held it out. "Among blind men—" She gave the first half of the code in Selafaïn.

"The one-eyed reigns," he finished. He reached out to clasp her hand and palm the ring in one smooth gesture.

As his calloused fingers touched hers, a shiver ran up her arm. Isyllt barely managed to keep her face still; no one had mentioned the man was a sorcerer. The sensation vanished so quickly she almost doubted her instinct, but his eyes narrowed as he studied her.

"Well met, I hope. I'm Izachar Teoma."

"Isyllt Iskaldur."

His eyes flicked briefly toward her left hand. "What is it you wish of me, Lady?"

"I want to hire your ship."

"The *Rain Dog* can take you anywhere you need to go."

"Actually, I want you to stay in port. We'll be in Symir for perhaps a month—hopefully it will be a peaceful visit and we'll leave quietly. But it may come to pass that we'll need to leave the city very quickly, and we'll need a fast ship we can trust."

"Ah." Izachar ran a hand over his curling beard. His chair creaked as he leaned back. "I understand. But a month . . . My crew have families to feed, and I'll lose business." A gold tooth gleamed with his smile. "And with the new import taxes, my business is booming."

"We're prepared to compensate you."

Adam slid a purse across the table. Izachar hefted it, listened to the clatter of metal and stones. He loosened the ties and pulled out a coin. Silver gleamed smooth, unstamped.

"I'll keep the *Dog* in port for a decad," he said at last. "My first mate's daughter is sick, anyway, and she'd like to spend some time with the child. After ten days, find me again and we'll negotiate further."

Isyllt nodded. She'd expected no better. "A pleasure doing business with you, Captain."

"The pleasure's mine, Lady." The money vanished off the table.

The door swung open and a dark, scar-faced man leaned in. "Time to go," he said. His hand moved against his thigh, a sign Isyllt didn't recognize. Then he was gone.

Izachar cursed softly. "A raid's coming. Business is booming a little too well." He pushed off his chair and crossed the room, quick enough for his short legs. "We'll use the back door," he said, motioning them on. "It'll be clear for a few more minutes—Desh pays his bribes on time."

Isyllt and Adam exchanged a quick glance and followed the dwarf down the hall. From the main room she heard a door slam, then a flurry of curses and shouting and the clatter of an overturned table. They stepped outside into a dark alley, as empty as Izachar had promised; the last light caught his grin before the door shut behind them.

"Welcome to Symir," he called after them as they escaped into the sticky night.

Xinai moved through her exercises by the light of one guttering lamp. The flame gleamed on her knives, shattered on their razored edges. Her breath hissed through clenched teeth as she thrust and spun and stretched. Normally she flowed like water from one stance to the next, but tonight tension trembled her limbs, made her movements too quick and jerky.

The smell of the canals breathed across the casement: water and waste, eucalyptus and brine and citrus-sweet champa flowers. Beneath it her own sour salt sweat clogged her nose.

She'd thought she could do it. She'd thought she could come home after twelve years gone. On the voyage she'd told herself that the city would have changed, that time would have made her memories bearable.

She'd almost believed it.

The exercise wasn't calming her. She stopped, stretched, and put her blades away. Adam watched her from the shadows of the bed as she stripped off her vest and trousers. He'd asked if she could take the job, one of the rare times he acknowledged all the things she'd never told him about her past. In Erisín, spending the wizard's money on food and wine, she'd said yes. Even the necromancer hadn't deterred her, for all the woman's magic made her skin crawl.

She could do this. She didn't have a choice.

She threw herself down beside Adam and buried her face in a cushion. His familiar scent was a comfort—oil and leather, musk and iron. Nothing that reminded her of home.

He propped himself up on one elbow. "Is it so bad?"

"It's—" Pillows muffled her sigh. "It's the same. Things have changed, but it's still the same."

He knelt over her, running his hands over her shoulders. She grunted softly as he pressed against knotted muscles.

"They think they're lions," she muttered, thinking of

the customs inspector with her expensive coat and hennaed hands, her perfect Assari. The Sivahri soldiers in their red-trimmed uniforms. "Only dogs licking their masters' boots." She gasped as Adam dug his thumbs into her back.

He worked down, calloused hands strong and steady. She forced herself not to stiffen as he brushed the scars on her back. It had been a long time, even after they were lovers, before she let him touch them. Not until the nightmares faded and she didn't wake up gasping, expecting to find her skin slick with blood.

Years of partnership had left his touch as familiar as her own. By the time he reached the small of her back she could breathe easily again, the angry stiffness gone from her limbs.

"It's only a job." He leaned down to kiss her shoulder. "When it's over we'll go somewhere else. Anywhere you like." He caressed the unmarked skin on her sides and she shivered. "You want to be a pirate?"

She chuckled and rolled over, stretching out the last of her tension. "You might be able to talk me into it." But she pulled him down and kissed him before he could try.

CHAPTER 2

Isyllt and Adam crossed onto the mainland north of the Mir early the next morning and rented horses to carry them up the foothills to the Kurun Tam. Mount Haroun loomed above them, its shadow casting a false twilight over the western hills.

The sun burned away the dawn mist, embroidered the mountain's green skirts in gold and amber. Summer heat left leaves curled and drooping, baked the roads cracked and dusty and withered the ferns that grew in the shade.

Ward-posts lined the road, simple charms to keep predators away and something else, a spell to hold the stones steady if the earth shook. Isyllt wasn't sure she understood the intricacies of it, but the implication was unsettling. Far above the canopy, white smoke leaked from Haroun's summit. Liquid fire still bubbled in the mountain, but it hadn't erupted in the hundred and fifty years of Assari occupation. The mages of the Kurun Tam expressed nothing but confidence in their ability to keep the mountain quiet—since they'd be the first to burn if Haroun stirred, Isyllt tried to take comfort in their assurances.

The trail turned sharply and she saw the sluggish waters of the Mir below them, and the broader, gentler slope of Mount Ashaya on the far side of the river. The South Bank was home to politicians and merchant moguls, mansions and plantations. Whatever native families had lived there were long gone, driven out or bought off and their lands divided up for gifts to those who pleased the Emperor. The North Bank was poorer, home to Sivahri who couldn't afford to live in the city proper. From the ferry she'd seen clay and brick buildings, thatched roofs and packed-earth roads.

And between the two banks and the bay, Symir shone in the morning light, all colorful roofs and gardens and glittering webs of water.

Isyllt swallowed bitter dust and the smell of horse. This assignment was one others would have vied for, exotic and expensive. And important.

They'd lost three agents in Assar—clever, well-trained spies. Two had simply vanished from their posts, and the body of the third was found dumped near the Selafaïn embassy in Ta'ashlan. And in Erisín, Kiril had caught two Assari agents already—one trying to seduce a Selafaïn inventor whose clever designs would make wonderful instruments of war, and the other worming his way into the palace bureaucracy. The latter had fallen on a blade before Kiril could question him, but his presence was story enough—the Emperor was growing bolder.

In the five hundred years since refugees fleeing the al Sund dynasty's armies had crossed the sea and founded Selafai, several Assari emperors had tried to take the younger kingdom. Assar had never established a solid presence on the northern continent, and every other generation some general-prince with dreams of fortune and glory thought to be the first to do so. And now Rahal al Seth sat the Lion Throne, young and greedy and itching to match his grandfather's conquests—and backed by generals canny and greedy enough to give him a chance.

She pressed the tip of her tongue between her teeth and tried not to scowl. What Kiril said was true—she was his best student, his most trusted agent. And what he didn't say was true as well, that given a job as important as this she'd die before she disappointed him. He needed her here. But he'd sent her away, and it gnawed.

She tried to relax, but the jolt of hooves stiffened her back and shoulders. Adam rode more easily beside her, his eyes on the trees. The jungle clamored around them, screeching and chirping and rustling. Jewel-bright lizards and long-tailed monkeys watched them from tree branches, calmer than the birds that took flight whenever the clatter of hooves grew close. The trees hid all manner of exotic beasts.

And bands of desperate men as well. She just had to find them. Trade gold and weapons for warriors to wield them. To die for them. Thousands of Sivahri lives in exchange for Selafaïn ones.

She looked up and caught Adam watching her, pale eyes narrowed. She schooled her face and smiled at him. Then she shivered as they passed through a tingling web of wards. The trees fell away and they rode into the courtyard of the Kurun Tam.

The Corundum Hall. A long building of crimson granite, pillared and domed in Assari style. Faces watched them from the wall, bound spirits staring through stone eyes. Neat green lawns stretched within the walls, shaded by slender trees and pruned topiaries—all the jungle's wildness tamed.

A young stablehand appeared to take charge of their horses, and Isyllt dismounted with a wince and brushed at the dust on her clothes. The gray-green linen hid the worst of it, at least. She breathed deep, tasted magic like spiced lightning in the back of her throat. It tingled down her limbs and prickled the nape of her neck.

They climbed broad red steps and entered a columned courtyard. Isyllt sighed as cool air washed over them—a subtle witchery and a welcome one. A fountain played in the center of the yard and she worked her dry tongue against the roof of her mouth. The air smelled of flowers and incense and clean water.

Isyllt washed her face and hands in the basin beside the door, and she and Adam added their boots and socks to the neat row of sandals and slippers. She didn't hear the footsteps approach over the splash of the fountain until Adam spun around. She turned as a shadow fell across the stones at her feet.

"Roshani," the man said, bowing low. Light gleamed on the curve of his shaven head, set mahogany skin aglow. He wore robes of embroidered saffron silk, the hem brushing the tops of his bare feet. "Or should I say good morning?" he asked in Selafaïn. "You must be Lady Iskaldur."

"Yes." She lifted her ring in warning as he offered a hand. "I'm *hadath*." Unclean. Had she been born in Assar, she would go gloved and veiled and touch no one but the dead.

"Ah. It's not often we see necromancers here." He took

her hand and raised it to his lips; his skin was warm, his magic warmer still as it whispered against her. His smile was wry and charming. "I'm not devout. My name is Asheris. Vasilios mentioned that he was expecting you. I'll take you to him."

"Wait for me," she said to Adam, and followed Asheris down a shadowed arcade.

Zhirin was late again. The sundial in the Kurun Tam's courtyard told her it was nearly noon—she should have been at lessons an hour ago. But as Jabbor escorted her up the steps, she couldn't bring herself to care.

"You shouldn't come in," she said as they paused on the threshold. It might have been more convincing if she'd taken her hand off his arm.

"Why?" His smile crinkled the corners of his dark eyes. "Will your magic strike me down?"

"Hush." She stepped inside, toeing off her sandals. Two new pairs of boots rested beside the familiar row of shoes. "You'll get me in trouble."

"You'll get yourself in trouble, you mean." Jabbor stepped through the doorway, glancing about curiously. He didn't take off his shoes; Zhirin rolled her eyes but didn't chide him. It was progress enough that curiosity overcame his distrust of all things Imperial—politeness could come later.

He turned away from a stone face on the wall. "I haven't been struck down yet, and you're not in trouble." His flippancy died as he folded her hand in his broader, darker ones. "Zhir, are you sure—"

She shook her head sharply. "Not here. And yes, I'm sure. I'll know by tonight."

He nodded. "Be at the ferry by sunset, then. And thank you." He leaned down to kiss her, then froze.

"Jabbor?"

He spun, one hand falling to the hilt of his kris-knife. Zhirin followed his gaze across the courtyard and jumped. A man sat in the shadows beside the fountain, eyes half closed as if he drowsed. No one she recognized, neither Assari nor Sivahri. Her cheeks stung as she tried to remember what he might have overheard.

The man blinked lazily and brushed black hair away from his face. "Roshani."

If he spoke Assari, perhaps he hadn't understood anything. Not that she'd said anything she shouldn't. She'd done nothing to feel guilty for. Yet.

"Go on," she told Jabbor in Sivahran, shoving him toward the door. "I'll see you tonight."

She turned back to the man and bobbed a shallow bow. "Excuse me." He didn't look or feel like a mage; the cut of his clothes was foreign, as was the line of the sword at his hip. "May I help you?"

"No, shakera." Amusement colored his voice beneath the foreign vowels and she drew herself up straighter. Of course, she was blushing like he'd walked in on a tryst—which was very nearly true. "My mistress is visiting. I'm just waiting for her."

"Visiting whom?" She tried to mask the wariness with polite curiosity; letting strangers in unquestioned would get her in more trouble than tardiness.

"Vasilios Medeion."

"Oh!" Her cheeks flushed hotter as she remembered why her master had asked her to be on time today. "Excuse me." She bobbed a curtsy, then turned and fled down the hall.

*   *   *

Power soaked the walls of the Kurun Tam, residual magic steeping the elegant soapstone lattices and frescoes. It reminded Isyllt of the Arcanost in Erisín, though this building was much younger and less austere. That it was primarily a research facility and not a school made its beauty all the more impressive. The corridors around them were silent and echoed empty to her *otherwise* senses.

"Many have gone to the mountain today," Asheris said, catching her unspoken question. "They won't return till nightfall." He arched one dark brow. "Have you seen the mountain yet, Lady Iskaldur?"

"No, I only arrived last night."

"You must. I'd be happy to show you, as your time permits. It's a much more pleasant journey before the rains begin."

"Thank you." She caught herself studying his bright amber eyes, the planes and angles of his jaw, and forced her gaze elsewhere; she didn't need a pretty distraction.

He had more than pretty eyes to distract her—his presence lapped over her, warm and rich. A powerful mage, from the diamond he wore on a narrow gold collar. Spices and smoky incense clung to his robes, and his magic left the taste of crackling summer storms on her tongue. No doubt she smelled of bones and death to him.

The stones chilled underfoot as they left the sunlight behind and entered a corridor lit by golden witchlights. Elaborate arabesque friezes lined the walls, and the tops of the columns were carved in delicate lotus blossoms. Asheris stopped before a brass-studded door and rapped the polished wood lightly. Someone called out a muffled "Come in."

They stepped into a narrow study, lit by lamplight and tall windows. The air was thick with the scent of leather and vellum and wood polish; books and scroll casings lined the walls. An old man looked up from his book, forehead creasing in curiosity.

"You must be Isyllt," he said before Asheris could begin introductions. Wrinkles rearranged as he smiled. "It's not every day I see Vallish girls anymore."

Isyllt inclined her head with a smile. "Vasilios of Medea, I take it."

"I am he. Not that I've seen Medea in a good many years." He rose and moved around his cluttered desk to greet her, favoring his left leg. A tall man, but he stooped till he was barely of a height with Isyllt. Gnarled, ink-stained hands clasped hers affectionately. A benevolent tutor, his smile said, a kindly grandfather—not a spy.

"Welcome, my dear. Kiril has told me good things about you."

"He speaks fondly of you as well."

"Told you stories of our misspent youth, has he?" Pale eyes glinted under creased olive lids.

Hard to believe this bent old man was only five years Kiril's senior. Even after her master's heart had nearly given out a year ago, he hadn't aged so much. *He wants me to see this, to see what age has in store for him.* Her smile ached as she held it in place.

"Have you by chance seen my wayward apprentice?" Vasilios asked Asheris.

The dark man cocked his head. "No, but I think I hear her now."

Bare feet slapped the hall outside and an instant later a young woman appeared in the doorway, plump tea-brown cheeks flushed cinnabar. "Forgive me, master," she gasped. "I didn't mean to be gone so long."

Vasilios waved a negligent hand. "I'd be more concerned if you suddenly became punctual. This is our guest, Lady Iskaldur. Isyllt, this is my apprentice, Zhirin Laii."

"Roshani, Lady." The girl bowed low, one narrow braid uncoiling from its twist to bounce over her shoulder.

"Have you had lunch, Isyllt?" Vasilios asked, fetching a cane from beside his chair.

"No," she said, realizing that she'd forgotten breakfast as well.

"Come, let's remedy that, shall we? Asheris, would you care to join us?" And he herded them out the door.

It was a pleasant meal, though the presence of Asheris and Vasilios's wide-eyed apprentice left them unable to speak of Isyllt's true reasons for visiting. Not that she would have felt comfortable discussing such things inside the walls of the Kurun Tam—stone had a long memory, and clever mages could convince it to repeat what it heard. So they ate and lingered over tea, and Isyllt answered questions about Erisín and Kiril and Selafaïn politics and arranged to visit Vasilios the next day at his house in the city, before letting Asheris escort her through the library and halls and gardens, where he flirted with great charm and little sincerity.

Wheels and hooves rattled into the courtyard as they returned to the fountain. Isyllt glanced through the doorway to see an ox-drawn cart rolling through the gates, flanked by a dozen soldiers in full Imperial livery.

Asheris excused himself and stepped into a pair of

sandals before descending the steps to inspect the cart, counting crates and accepting a scroll case from an officer. The driver urged the oxen on, steering the cart to the back of the hall, while a man and woman not in uniform dismounted.

"Shipments from the mines," Asheris said as he returned to Isyllt's side. "We charge the stones here and ship them to Assar." His mouth twisted. "Nowhere as interesting as the mountain, I'm afraid. Though of course I'm happy to have stayed behind, since it meant meeting you."

She smiled at the graceful save, but her attention stayed on the cart as it clattered around the corner. Sapphires and rubies from Sivahri mines were one of the country's greatest assets to the Empire. That cart alone must contain a fortune's worth; after they were charged with energy, their value would more than double. Lesser stones couldn't contain as much power without fracturing, and diamonds such as Isyllt's—or the yellow stone around Asheris's neck—were saved for binding ghosts and spirits.

"Are you going to introduce us, Asheris?" the woman called, tethering her horse. She crossed the courtyard, graceful and light on her feet. Young and very fair for an Assari, with striking kohl-rimmed blue eyes. She pulled aside her riding veil and dipped a shallow curtsy. "It's not often we have visitors." Her eyes widened briefly as she saw Isyllt's ring; she didn't offer her hand.

"Of course," Asheris said, straightening his shoulders. "Lady Iskaldur, this is Jodiya al Sarith, one of our apprentices, and her master, Imran al Najid." He gestured to the man who had joined them. "Lady Iskaldur has just arrived from Erisín, to study with Vasilios."

Al Najid bowed, also not offering his hand. As he straightened, a stone gleamed at his neck—a diamond, also yellow-hued. The Kurun Tam didn't lack for powerful magi. She wondered what unlucky spirits lay trapped at their throats.

"Roshani. I trust Asheris has made you welcome." She guessed him near fifty, tall and lean. He should have been handsome, but all the lines carved on his long face were dour, and his greeting was more perfunctory than polite.

"I managed some degree of civility," Asheris drawled.

"Indeed he did," Isyllt said as Imran's dark eyes narrowed. "The hall is quite impressive."

"Shakera. Please excuse us, meliket, but we must see to the stones. Enjoy your visit." With a nod, he turned and strode away, Jodiya at his heels.

Isyllt tried to school her face but couldn't keep an inquisitive brow from rising. Asheris smiled faintly, but the corners of his eyes were tight. "Yes, his company is always so pleasant. We're as close as siblings here. I'm sure it's the same at your Arcanost."

Isyllt chuckled. "Of course."

He pulled on a more convincing smile. "Forgive me, but I too must see to the stones. I hope we'll meet again soon."

"I'd like that." As he bowed over her hand in farewell, she even meant it.

The last sonorous dusk-bells echoed across the water as the carriage finally rattled onto the ferry dock, and the sun sank into the sea, trailing veils of violet and carnelian. Zhirin worried the inside of her lip and tried to look unconcerned. She was late—again—but no magic at her disposal could have packed her master's books and instruments any faster.

The dock was empty, and for a moment she feared she was too late. But as the dockhands arrived to help unload the coach, she recognized two of them. Not Jabbor, and she swallowed a rush of disappointment, but likely he was already busy. Games and trysts were for drowsy afternoons—by night he and his people worked.

Instead Temel and Kwan came to meet her—silent Temel, whom she might call friend; and sharp-tongued Kwan, whom she wouldn't. She restrained the urge to smile at Temel and instead helped him unstrap a box from the carriage rack.

"Tonight," she whispered, leaning close as she fumbled at a buckle. "The dockside warehouse." Her palms were sweating, fingers slick on the rough leather straps. "Seven crates, three too flawed to use—those are marked.

"Be careful with that," she said, louder, as he lifted the chest free. "Our instruments are fragile." He nodded once as he handed the crate down to Kwan. The woman's lips curled in a sneer.

And as easily as that, she was a rebel. A traitor. She bit back a giggle; whatever would her mother say?

Blood rushed in her ears as she swung down from the carriage and followed her master onto the boat. Not the wide, flat-bottomed ferry that crossed to the South Bank, but a sleek-curved skiff to take them into the city. The familiar sway of the craft as they shoved off soothed her nerves. Worry and doubt were no use now—better to let the river take them.

"What's wrong?" Vasilios asked, settling himself beside her on the bench. He moved gingerly, and Zhirin regretted all the haste she'd wished for on the ride down.

The steersman kindled the prow lantern and its reflection glittered golden on dark water.

"I was thinking of my family," she said, not untruthfully. "I haven't seen them in a month. May I go home tonight?"

After a moment he nodded. "I don't see why not, as long as you're back in the morning for our guests." Thick eyebrows rose. "And I do mean morning, my dear, not some hour of the afternoon."

Her cheeks warmed and she glanced aside. "Yes, master."

They sat in silence for a while, surrounded by the rhythm of the oars and the drone of insects. Something heavy moved in the water and she brushed the coldly patient awareness of a kheyman. A glimpse of golden eyes and then it was gone, sinking into the silt-thick depths of the river.

The last daylight died before they reached the city, but Symir burned with a thousand lamps, a filigree of light and shadow. The scent of eucalyptus drifted across the water, clean and sharp. She missed the green and the wet when she slept at the Kurun Tam, the river's breath against her skin.

The skiff carried her through the winding canals of Heronmark to the landing at the end of Feathermoon Lane. Her family's boat was moored by the stairs, and another she didn't recognize, its oarsman drowsing at the prow; someone visiting in the neighborhood. She bid her master good night and climbed the damp steps.

A quiet street after dark. Someone practiced a flute on an upper story, running through scales. Someone new to the instrument, she guessed with a wince. Her own music lessons had been interrupted when she began talking to spirits, likely to her tutor's relief. If not for her magic, she'd be at the Imperial University in Ta'ashlan.

Lights shone in the front windows, falling like water across the steps and flower boxes. The door, engraved with the Laii heron crest, was unlocked. Zhirin smiled as she slipped off her sandals and glanced around the entryway—the hangings and mats had been changed, gold-patterned green now instead of crimson. Her father must have found a new geomancer, with new opinions on fortuitous colors.

She expected her mother's steward, Mau, or one of the servants to appear, but no one did. The ground floor was silent and Zhirin climbed the curving staircase, polished stone cool under her feet. They must have company; her mother would never leave so many lights burning otherwise.

Her mother's study door was cracked open, and voices drifted out. ". . . and hopefully we'll have no more unpleasantness like Zhang's," a man said.

"Of course not," Fei Minh Laii replied, in a softly rebuking tone Zhirin was all too familiar with. "What do you take me for?"

Too late, Zhirin wondered what the answer might be, but her hand was already falling to knock on the door.

"Mira, I'm home—"

The door swung open, and she froze as she recognized the man sitting across from her mother. "Oh!" She dipped a hasty bow. "Your Excellency, excuse me."

Fei Minh rose, setting aside her teacup. "Zhirin!"

Faraj al Ghassan, Viceroy of Symir, stood a heartbeat after his hostess, a chuckle erasing the startlement on his face.

"I'm sorry, Mira," Zhirin said as her mother kissed her stinging cheek. "I didn't realize—"

"Don't worry, Miss Laii," Faraj said. "I should be going anyway. Thank you for the tea, Fei Minh, and for your help."

He inclined his head to Zhirin, and it was all she could do to smile and nod. Her face burned as though her crimes were branded there for him to read. Rebel. Traitor. But he only turned away to clasp hands with her mother.

"It's my pleasure," Fei Minh said, following him down the stairs. "You must visit again soon. Bring Shamina and Murai."

"After the festival, perhaps." He stepped into his slippers and bowed again, silk coat whispering. "Good evening, ladies."

"What are you doing home?" Fei Minh asked as she shot the bolt behind him.

"Vasilios is staying in the city for the festival, and I thought I'd visit."

"About time you thought of that." She smiled to take the sting from the words, one cheek dimpling. Delicate lines fanned from her eyes and framed her mouth, but Fei Minh's skin was still soft as almond-milk and honey. "You picked a bad night for it, I'm afraid. Your father and Sungjin are visiting on the South Bank for a few days."

That was no surprise; her father and brother had started spending most of their time at Cay Laii when Fei Minh began her first term on the Khas thirteen years ago. Only propriety and habit kept him coming home at all, Zhirin suspected. And since her mother's last term had ended a year ago, she knew how bored and restless Fei Minh had been.

Zhirin's brow creased as she eyed her mother's hair, unbraided and held up loosely with sandalwood sticks. Absent servants, late visits . . . "Mother, are you having an affair?"

Fei Minh blinked, then began to laugh. "Oh, darling. With Faraj? Wouldn't that be a scandal?" She wiped delicately at one eye. "No, dear, I'm afraid not."

"What are you helping him with, then?"

"Just business. He's using some of our ships for a private investment." She took Zhirin by the elbow and steered her toward the kitchen. Her perfume was still jasmine and citrus; the scent was as much home to Zhirin as the smell of the river. "You missed dinner, but I'll make tea. And since you're here, perhaps you can look at the fountain—it's not flowing properly, and your father will rip it out and rearrange the whole garden if I give him half an excuse."

"You paid quite an apprentice-price for me to become a plumber."

Fei Minh snorted softly. "Think of it as part of your repayment—I want to see some return on my investment. Now, sit down and tell me about your lessons."

Zhirin woke to midnight bells, the bedside candle a puddle of cold wax in its bowl. She ran a hand over her face, knuckled gritty eyes. She'd only meant to lie down, but feather beds and the whisper of the canal had lulled her under. Jabbor had promised to meet her, after—

The bells kept ringing and Zhirin's stomach curdled. Not the solemn night bells after all, but brazen clashing chimes.

An alarm.

Let it be a coincidence, she prayed as she groped for her clothes. Her mother met her in the hall, robe hastily tied and night-braids unraveling over her shoulders. "What is it?" they asked on the same heartbeat, and chuckled breathlessly.

A few neighbors stood on their front steps, listening to the clamor. Blessedly distant—not Heronmark's watchtower but one farther west. Merrowgate, perhaps.

"What's happened?" Fei Minh called to the next house.

"We don't know. There've been no criers yet."

Zhirin descended the steps to the canal, stones cool and slick beneath her feet. Water soaked her trousers as she knelt and laid a palm on the surface. One breath, then another, and her heart began to slow as the river's rhythm filled her, deep and inexorable. She raised her hand, scattering ripples.

And the lapping water showed her colors, red and gray, gold and orange, dancing and twisting against the black. It took her a heartbeat to make sense of the distorted reflection.

Fire.

"Something's burning," she said as she rose, scrubbing her wet hand on her trousers.

"Ancestors," her mother whispered. "Not the docks."

The Laiis had been a southern clan once, tenders of marshy rice fields. But these days their money came from the sea, from swift trading ships and goods piled in dockside warehouses.

"I'm going to see what's happened," Zhirin said.

"No—"

"I'll be careful, Mira." She darted up the steps to kiss

her mother's cheek. Before Fei Minh could protest more, she unmoored the household skiff and pushed off.

She whispered to the river and soon the current caught her, swifter and more graceful than she could have rowed. But even with the water's help, she didn't want to risk the skiff dockside. She moored at the far edge of Jadewater and ran the rest of the way.

Her side ached by the time she reached Merrowgate's warehouse district and her breath ripped her chest like gravel and broken shells. Her feet throbbed, likely bleeding, and she chided herself for not putting on shoes. A sullen orange glow lined the rooftops, and bells and voices rang loud and raucous.

The crowd led her to the fire, and she skirted the edges till she could see. The street was mud-slick and cold despite the waves of heat. Rats and insects scurried for safety; Zhirin shuddered as a finger-long cockroach crawled over her foot. City guards surrounded the building, passing buckets down a line.

It wasn't enough. A canal ran behind the building, and a wide street in front, but only alleys separated it from its neighbors, narrow enough that even she could have jumped them. The wind off the bay was gentle, but enough to blow flames onto the next rooftop; already it had begun to smoke.

The whole district could be gone by morning.

The bucket lines moved faster, water glowing gold as it splashed the cobbles. Zhirin wanted to join them, but it was no use. She couldn't call a flood. Not even the Mother's temple could, since the river had been dammed. For all her tricks, she was useless against this.

Gongs echoed from the waterfront, warning ships to

lift anchor before the docks caught. That would take a while, at least, unless the wind shifted.

Another section of roof collapsed with a groan and roar and a flurry of sparks rode the wind like orange fireflies. Someone screamed as flames burst through the gap. Mirrors dangling from nearby roofs threw back the firelight in angry flashes.

A moment later she realized what the burning building had been. A government warehouse. She pressed a hand over her mouth and swallowed the taste of char. *Jabbor—*

She should run home, warn her mother since she was no use here, but she could only stare. Guards appeared on the neighboring warehouse's roof, splashing wood and plaster and tiles in a futile bid to keep the flames at bay. A shout rose from the back of the crowd, and she scrambled to keep out of the press as the mass of people parted to admit a man.

His face was a mask of flame and shadow, but Zhirin recognized the curve of his bare head. Her stomach tightened. She'd thought Asheris was sleeping at the Kurun Tam tonight; his rumpled clothes looked as though he'd only just woken. But he was here. He waved the guards away and kept walking, so close his skin must be crisping. If the building fell now it would crush him.

Pain spread down Zhirin's arm; she'd bitten her knuckle hard enough to break the skin.

Asheris extended a hand toward the fire, palm up. Flames flickered toward him, though the wind didn't change. Fire lapped his fingers like a curious hound, then twisted up his arm in a glowing spiral.

Her vision blurred, tears welling against the smoke,

and she watched through a crystalline glaze as Asheris called the fire into him. The blaze died in the warehouse as the flames ran like water away from wood and stone and into flesh. The last came in a rush, flaring around him like giant wings.

Then it was gone.

The rest of the roof fell in, billowing smoke and ash and sparks. But no more flames. The absence of light blinded her, and her eyes ached as they adjusted. The wind stung her face.

Asheris swayed and fell to his knees, head sagging. Steam rose from his skin. Not even the guards approached him.

Zhirin bit her lip; she might be useless, but she didn't have to be a coward. But before she could move toward the fallen mage, a hand closed on her arm. She started, then recognized the dark fingers.

She turned, his name on her lips, but Jabbor silenced her with a shake of his head and drew her away from the crowd. Down an alley she followed him, biting back questions as she dodged fleeing vermin. They ducked through a back door into a narrow lamplit kitchen. Temel and Kwan followed them in—Zhirin hadn't seen them outside. Soot smeared both their faces, and blood dried in a dull crust along Temel's brow.

Kwan vanished into the front of the house, returned a moment later. "It's clear."

Jabbor sank into a chair by the table and Zhirin sat beside him. Her filthy feet smudged clean tiles and she tucked her heels onto a chair-rung like a child. Sweat and tears dried stiff and itchy on her face, and when she scratched her cheek her nails came away dark with grime. Her finger was bruised where she'd bitten it.

"What happened?"

"We slipped in quietly—a few coins, drugged wine, and a little distraction. It should have been bloodless. But the Dai Tranh came right behind us."

Zhirin's stomach chilled. Jabbor's group, the Jade Tigers, were known for their peaceful—if not always legal—protests. It was part of what drew her to them. The Dai Tranh, however, was known only for violence.

His full lips tightened, carving lines around his mouth. Sweat glistened oily between the neat rows of his hair. "They outnumbered us. Killed the guards, looted the stones, and set the fire. We tried to put it out, but they left some of the rubies behind for fuel."

No wonder the blaze had been so fierce—Haroun's fire, harnessed into stone. "But how did they know?"

Kwan's eyes narrowed to angry black slits. "Shouldn't we be asking you that question?"

Zhirin's mouth opened, but Jabbor raised a hand before she could snap a retort. "No, Kwan." He caught her eyes and held them. "But I'll ask it anyway. Did you say anything to anyone else?"

She shook her head, cheeks stinging. He couldn't afford to trust blindly, she knew that. Not even her. Maybe especially not her. "I only told you."

"Then they have someone inside us, or a spy of their own in the Kurun Tam." He wiped a sheen of sweat off his face.

Kwan snorted softly but held her tongue. She found a pitcher of water and a rag on the counter and began to sponge the blood off Temel's face. True cousins, not just clan-kin, and the resemblance showed in the set of their cheekbones and short, flat noses. High forest people, the

Lhuns, before the Empire had claimed their lands for the
Kurun Tam and sent them to live by the river.

"We looked inside one of the crates," Jabbor said, "before everything fell apart. One of the boxes marked for
flawed stones. Do you know what we found?"

Zhirin shook her head.

Jabbor pulled something from his pocket and held it
out to her. A stone gleamed dully against his palm—the
size of her thumbnail, uncut, yellowish-white. A chunk of
quartz, she thought, until she reached for it and felt the
crystal's sharp pulse.

"Sweet Mother," she whispered, snatching her hand
back. "Is that—" She swallowed the foolish question; she
knew what it was. A diamond.

She'd never seen one in the rough before, only cut and
polished and gleaming on the hand or throat of a mage,
and very few of those. Unlucky, the uninitiated called
them, or cursed. For the spirits or ghosts who ended up
trapped in them, they must be.

And expensive. No question about that. The stone rest-
ing on Jabbor's palm was worth a dozen rubies in Assar.

"What's it doing here?" She caught herself leaning
back. Foolish superstition—it was just a stone, without a
mage to wield it. Her master would chide her for making
warding signs against a lump of rock.

"It came from the Kurun Tam, didn't it?" Kwan asked,
setting aside the bloody ash-smeared rag.

"No! How could it? We mine rubies, sapphires—"

"We?" the other woman snapped, but Jabbor waved
her silent.

Zhirin shook her head, pressing her stinging knuckle
against her lips again. Diamonds came from Iseth, or

lands far to the north whose names she could never remember. Places where people bound ghosts into slavery,
as well as spirits. She couldn't call it abomination—the
Empire accepted such practices and her own master wore
a diamond—but it still made her skin crawl.

"We need to find out where this came from," Jabbor said, closing his hand over the stone. "I need you to
investigate."

Zhirin nodded. All the energy had drained from her,
leaving fatigue and aches in its place. She wanted to lean
into Jabbor, to breathe in the smell of his skin and let
him hold her till the world felt right again. But weakness
wasn't what he needed from her. Her eyes stung.

"I should go," she said, wincing as she put weight on
her bruised and torn feet. Who would clean up the mess
they'd made? Perhaps whoever lived here was used to rebels tracking mud and blood across their floor. "I'll find
you when I learn something."

Jabbor rose with her and took her hand, tracing a gentle
thumb across her knuckles. "Thank you." And she would
have run twice as far barefoot for that smile.

The crowd had thinned when she limped past the ruined
warehouse, and guards roped off the shell. She didn't see
Asheris. Smoke trailed a gray veil across the city and ashes
drifted softly on the breeze.

CHAPTER 3

Isyllt and Adam found a tavern in Saltlace that night, an expensive one overlooking a broad canal. The sort of place where a bored traveler might come to waste time and money—Isyllt thought she could manage that ruse. She lifted her chin as she crossed the threshold, letting her hips roll. Midnight blue silk swirled around her ankles and a corset cinched her waist and kept her back straight. They drew glances like gnats to the paper lanterns as they crossed the room. Whether it was her bare white arms or Adam glowering at her back, she couldn't say.

They weren't the only foreigners. Symir had a reputation as a haven for expatriates—separated from Assar and the northlands, it was a place to escape local trouble and live in exotic decadence. If you had the money for it.

They claimed a table on the balcony and Isyllt let the waiter recommend food and wine. Skiffs paddled in the canal below and evening crowds drifted across bridges

and along the sidewalks. Xinai was out in the city somewhere—hopefully the mercenary would have better luck
finding insurgents.

Their food arrived and inside the tavern musicians
began to play, deep drums and a woman's ululating voice.
Blue lantern-light glittered on the cutlery and washed
Adam's face cold and gray.

"How did you meet Kiril?" Isyllt finally asked, picking at the arrangement of rice and fish on her plate. She
should have asked sooner, but she'd spent too much time
during the voyage hiding in her cabin. He studied her for
a moment, head tilted. She found herself mimicking the
gesture and distracted herself with a rice ball.

"I came to Erisín when I was young," he said. "Just a stupid orphan brat—I thought I could make a living picking
pockets, become as good a thief as Magpie Mai, or some
nonsense like that." He snorted and sipped his wine.

"I was damned lucky Kiril found me, or I'd have wound
up in a cell, or the bottom of the Dis. He helped me find
work I was better suited for." He touched the hilt of his
sword. "So I owe him."

Isyllt's mouth twisted. "He always did like taking in
strays." She glanced down and found her goblet empty.
Condensation glistened on the curve of the flagon—
chilled, but the wine burned going down and kindled a
pleasant warmth in the stomach. She refilled her cup, let
the sweet plum vintage ease the bitter taste in her mouth.
Adam watched her, waiting.

The next cup emptied the pitcher and the waiter appeared to replace it. When he was gone, her bitterness
began to leak.

"He found me when I was fifteen. Not thieving, but bad

enough. Selling charms to pay for a tenement room with three other girls. I was too stubborn to ask the temple of Erishal to take me in." She shook her head at half-forgotten pride. "But Kiril found me, offered me training without the temple vows. I've studied with him for twelve years." She drained the last of her cup in a single swallow. It was enough of an answer, but she couldn't stop the rest from spilling out.

"I don't think he ever imagined I'd fall in love with him. Neither of us did."

Adam blinked. "What happened?"

Her laugh was soft and ugly. But she might as well finish it now. "Three years ago I finally said something, when he realized I wasn't a child anymore." Though perhaps she'd been wrong about that. "And it worked. We were happy."

Adam sipped more wine and speared a twisted creation of raw fish and seaweed, finishing it in two bites. "But not anymore?"

The quiet curiosity of the question nearly undid her. She'd grown used to the feigned grief and relentless probing of the court gossips, and her friends had learned not to ask. She glanced aside, stared at the canal lapping gently below them.

"Did he tell you what happened last summer?" she asked. Her cheeks were flushed, from wine or embarrassment she wasn't sure. At least she wasn't going to cry.

Adam shook his head. "I heard of the plague, but I was in the north that season. Kiril didn't say anything about it."

"The plague, yes." Such a small word to hold so much horror and grief. "The bronze fever. It tore through the city, all the way to the palace. The queen fell sick. The king begged Kiril to save her, and he tried." Her voice felt cold and dead in her mouth. "He tried until his heart gave out, but she died all the same. I thought he was dead too—"

Lanterns swayed in the breeze, rippling blue and violet light across the balcony. Isyllt swallowed against the tightness in her throat, concentrated on the press of corset stays as she breathed. She hadn't told this story before, not in so much detail.

"He recovered, but he wasn't the same. We waded through death to the knees every day, but it finally came too close. And he said . . . He said I was too young to nurse an old man to his grave. I argued, but he put me aside. We fought for a year. And now he's sent me away, far enough that I can't play the termagant."

She smiled, bright and bitter, and shook her head. "And that's the whole of it, mawkish as a bad play."

They sat in silence for a time, music and laughter and water swirling around them. "I'm sorry," Isyllt said at last. "You didn't need to hear all that. But as I said, I know what we're here to do, and my feelings won't interfere."

Adam only nodded.

She glanced at the nearly empty flagon and blinked. "Black Mother. Lucky I haven't made more of a fool of myself than I have."

"Eat some more," Adam said, nudging the plate toward her. "Then we can walk it off."

Isyllt shivered in spite of the heat as they left the tavern, wrapping her silk shawl over bare shoulders. Wine burned in her blood, stung her cheeks. Corset stays pressed against her ribs, and she wasn't sure more food had been a good idea.

Moonlight shimmered on rooftops, glittered on the water. The city was full of spirits tonight. Or maybe it always was, and she only now heard them. Not ghosts, but water creatures, jungle creatures, flitting and whispering in voices she couldn't understand. She paused, eyes closed, and let the strange sounds wash over her. The ground spun beneath her.

Adam's hand closed on her arm and she opened her eyes. "Are you all right?" he asked. His calloused fingers were warm against her clammy skin and she fought not to sway on her feet.

Very lucky not to have made more of a fool of herself.

"Can you feel them?"

His smile stretched lopsided. "Some of them. Not like you do. I hear them sometimes, the louder ones."

She cocked her head, studied the play of shadows over his face. "Are you a witch?" she asked, even though she caught no hint of power under his skin. But the way he moved, alert as a mage . . .

"Not even a little. Charms are Xin's job. I just kill things."

She looked down at his hand, let her vision unfocus. Colors blossomed around him, deep forest greens and grays, swirled red and black around his hands and sword. "You're good at it."

"I am." For an instant his eyes gleamed green-gold like an animal's and a sharp-toothed shadow hung over his.

"What are you?" she whispered. "Not just an orphan brat."

He smiled a wolf's smile. "Tier Danaan. Half-breed, at least."

Isyllt blinked, colors fading. Adam was just a man again—a man she was leaning on drunkenly in the middle of the street. She straightened and took a step back. "I've never met one before."

"People in civilized places usually haven't." He started walking and she fell in beside him. "I wasn't raised among the Tier." The careful flatness in his voice warned her away from the subject.

They crossed an arching bridge over one of the broad canals that bordered the districts; someone sang from a passing skiff below. The breeze tugged strands of Isyllt's hair free of their pins, stuck them to her sweat-damp shoulders. And they called this the dry season.

Descending the bridge steps, Isyllt tripped on an uneven stone. Adam caught her before she fell. The streetlamp's glow revealed a crack in the rock, several inches deep.

"The street is sinking," Adam said, pointing down the side of the canal where the pavement sloped sharply toward the water.

"Lovely. Let's hope it doesn't finish the job tonight."

The streets in Straylight were narrow and cracked and the houses tilted drunkenly, some leaning so close their gardens grew together. Wards dripped from shop signs, shimmered in windows and doorways. Many lamps were out, only a few puddles of orange-gold glow marking their way. Someone stirred in the blackness of an alley, racked with a consumptive's cough. Isyllt heard death waiting in that wet rattle.

A trio of young men passed them, armed and swaggering. Isyllt felt their angry stares and her fingers twitched. Adam's hand settled lightly on his sword hilt. "I think we've outstayed our welcome," she whispered. She traced a careful charm in the air—*not worth it*. The men kept walking.

She and Adam turned a corner onto another well-spelled lane. The street marker had been broken off its post, an octagonal wooden sign nailed in its place. A lantern swayed above it, rippling light and shadow over Sivahran letters.

"What does that say?" Isyllt asked.

"Salt Street. I'd guess it also translates to *No Assari welcome*."

"Or any other foreigners."

The spirits were quiet here. Warded away, or frightened. Isyllt heard human voices instead, raised in emotion. A woman stood in the street, arguing in Sivahran with an older woman framed in a shop door. The old woman spat in the gutter and slammed the door as they approached.

"That," Adam murmured in Isyllt's ear, "was nothing polite."

The woman in the street sobbed angrily, shoulders slumping. She turned toward them and light fell over her face—the customs inspector from the *Mariah*.

"Miss Xian-Mar?" Isyllt stepped closer; the woman's eyes were swollen and shining, but she wasn't crying now.

She blinked, dragged a hennaed hand through her unbound hair. "Lady Iskaldur." She straightened, tugging at her coat.

"Are you all right?" Impossible not to feel the black worry that hung over the woman like a pall.

"My niece is ill. She needs help, but that *jhanda*—Forgive me. The witches won't help me."

"Is there no physician you can go to?"

"It's no longer an ailment for medicine." Her voice was calm now, but her face was ashen and her hands twisted together.

Isyllt paused for several heartbeats. "Can I be of some assistance?"

Anhai's eyes flickered toward Isyllt's left hand. "Lady, I couldn't impose on you for a family problem." Her voice cracked.

"What's wrong with your niece?"

Anhai stopped arguing and started walking, Isyllt and Adam trailing along. "It started as a simple fever. A common childhood complaint, rarely serious . . . I was taking care of her while her mother was away." She shook her head, a wealth of anger and fear in that gesture.

"And it's beyond the physicians now?" Isyllt shivered. "I'm a mage, but I have no miracles for you." Kiril had tried that, and she'd seen the good it did.

"Not beyond—outside. A ghost found her, slipped through my wards, and now I can't cast it out again."

Isyllt smiled. "Ghosts I can handle."

Anhai's house sat on the far side of Jadewater, in a quiet, well-kept neighborhood past the temple spires. Isyllt recognized the reek of illness and anger and death before the woman led them up the steps. She felt the ghost as they crossed the threshold, felt strength and madness. A shudder crawled down her back and her blood quickened.

An old woman opened the door for them, gray hair tousled beneath her scarf. She stared at Isyllt and Adam.

"How is she?" Anhai asked.

"No better. Her mother is with her now."

Adam caught Isyllt's arm, pulled her close. "How dangerous is this?"

She shrugged and tugged free of his grip. At least the hall wasn't spinning. "Take me to her," she said to Anhai.

The girl lay on a narrow bed, curtains and blankets pulled back. A pleasant cluttered room—toys piled on shelves and books and quills scattered across the low desk, but the specter's presence filled the room like rank fog, drained it of warmth and color. Salt lined the windows and door, but it was too little too late. Another woman sat beside the bed, gray and drawn, henna-streaked hair in tangles around her face.

"What's her name?" Isyllt asked, leaning over the bed. The girl looked no more than ten or eleven, darker skinned than the other women but ashen now. Sweat-damp curls clung to her face and sprawled across the pillow. Bruise-shadowed eyes were closed and her narrow chest rose and fell too fast.

"Lilani." The other woman looked up, eyes widening as she saw Isyllt. "Who are you?"

"A mage." She crouched beside the girl, brushed a hand against her fevered brow. The child twitched but didn't wake. "You're her mother?"

She nodded. "Vienh Xian-Lhun. Please, Lady, if you can help— The ghost is inside her now. She's fighting, but . . ."

Isyllt nodded. It lay like a seething shadow below the girl's skin. "Do you know who it is?"

Silence filled the room, save for Lilani's labored breath.

"My grandmother," Vienh said at last. "Deilin Xian."
She licked cracked lips. "We knew she hadn't had the
proper rites—her body was lost—but I never imagined . . ."
She shook her head angrily. "The house was warded, rot it!
The whole damned city is supposed to be warded."

"Do you have more salt?" Isyllt asked Anhai. The
woman nodded and darted down the hall. "Brush those
seals away," she told Vienh, jerking her head toward the
window and door. "They're worthless now."

The woman did it, fast and efficient, while Isyllt leaned
over Lilani again. The girl's skin burned dangerously hot,
and they had no time for ice and cold compresses. Ghostlight flickered in the black diamond and a chill washed
through the room. Lilani sighed, hair scratching on the
pillow as she turned her head. Her eyes flickered, showing
Isyllt bloodshot whites and amber irises.

She let out a breath she hadn't realized she held. Just a
fever. Not the plague. The room swam as urgency warred
with wine in her blood. She'd never tried an exorcism
drunk before.

Anhai returned with a jar of salt. Isyllt ran white
crystals through her fingers, letting their clean strength
reassure her. "Shakera. Anhai, Vienh, leave the room.
Please," she added as Anhai's eyebrows climbed toward
her hair.

"Why?" Vienh crossed wiry arms, dark eyes
narrowing.

"Because you're both the ghost's blood, yes?" They
nodded. "And when I draw her out of Lilani, she may try
this with either of you. And I don't want to do this three
times in a row."

They relented, retreating into the hall. "Adam, come

here." He came, warily. "Have you ever been part of an exorcism before?"

"Yes. I didn't enjoy it."

"I doubt this will be any more pleasant. Help me move the bed."

They dragged the heavy wooden frame away from the wall, until Isyllt had enough room to trace a circle of salt around bed and child. "Sit with her," she told Adam.

He propped Lilani up in his lap, leaning her head against his chest and stroking her hair when she moaned. He knew what he was doing, thank all the powers. Isyllt swallowed, her stomach clenching.

She pulled a leather pouch from a pocket in her skirts. Inside the silk-lined wallet lay a narrow surgeon's blade, a palm-sized mirror, a sack of salt, incense, and a silver chain. An exorcist's kit—years of habit had trained her to carry it always. They were past the stage for incense and cajoling. Instead she removed the knife.

The blade was well-honed. She didn't feel the cut until blood pooled in her left hand, feathering across the fine lines of her palm. The pain came a moment later, hot and sharp.

Isyllt crouched at the foot of the bed and stretched out her bleeding hand. "Deilin. Come out and talk to me."

Lilani tossed; Adam's hands tightened on her shoulders.

"What do you want with this child?"

The darkness surged inside the girl, drowning Lilani's own colors. Isyllt blew across her hand, stinging the wound and wafting the smell of fresh blood into the girl's face. Lilani moaned and licked her lips.

"Deilin Xian!"

Isyllt's voice cracked like a lash, and the child stiff-ened. Chapped lips parted and a rough, hollow voice let loose a stream of angry Sivahran.

"Let me guess," Isyllt muttered, "none of that is polite either?"

Adam chuckled. "*Kaixe* means 'frail,' if that gives you an idea."

"Charming woman." She met Lilani's eyes, and the wraith's lightless gaze behind them. Deilin's control was strong if blood wouldn't tempt her out. "Leave the child alone, Deilin. It won't work."

More cursing. Lilani twitched and writhed, but Adam held her fast.

Isyllt rolled her eyes. "Fine. Don't say I didn't give you a chance." She reached out, pressed her bloody hand against Lilani's chest. Flesh stopped flesh, but cold *otherwise* fingers stretched further, clenched in tangling souls.

"Lilani," she whispered, praying the girl could hear her over the ghost's invective, "hold on."

And she wrenched the ghost free.

Lilani screamed. Someone in the hallway screamed. Deilin lunged against Isyllt, icy dead fingers clawing for her throat. Just a pale shadow to Isyllt's blurring eyes, but strong with anger and desperation. The ghost fell against her, nearly as solid as flesh, and both women tumbled off the end of the bed.

The salt circle caught them like a wall of fire, and Isyllt twisted in time to keep from breaking it. Her arm was numb, breath a shuddering plume in the frosty air.

Deilin was strong, but Isyllt was a trained necroman-cer, student of the finest sorcerer in Erisín. She drew a breath, focused, and pinned the ghost flat to the floor. Her ring spat opalescent fire, burning with the presence of death.

Anhai trembled at the threshold, held back by her sister's arm.

"I can make sure she never does this again, to anyone." Isyllt's voice rasped through her frozen throat. "Will you give me leave?"

Anhai gasped, pressed a hand over her mouth. Vienh's eyes widened, then narrowed. "Do it," she spat. Anhai made a choked sound and turned her face away.

Isyllt stood, the ghost twisting in her grip like a cat made of gossamer ice.

"Deilin Xian." The spirit trembled, eyes wide now with fear, the madness leaving her. Too late. "By your name and your soul, you are mine."

The diamond blazed, bright enough to bring tears to Isyllt's eyes. Deilin screamed and screamed as the fire burned her, froze her, swallowed her whole. Then she was gone and the lack of sound echoed through the room. The screams lingered in Isyllt's head as the ghost pounded against the flawless adamant curves of her new home. Then the other ghosts who dwelled in the diamond found her, and there was only silence.

Lilani sobbed, clinging to Adam. At Isyllt's nod of invitation Anhai and Vienh rushed into the room, breaking the circle and snatching the child into their arms.

Isyllt leaned against a bedpost as the room spiraled queasily around her. Lamplight lanced through her head, sharp as a blade, and as the numbness receded pain rushed up her arm. Sweat and sickness clogged her nose and her stomach lurched as she stumbled into the hall.

Adam caught up with her in a few strides, holding her against him when she would have fallen.

She barely pulled free in time to vomit.

Isyllt accepted Anhai's tearful offer of tea, if only because she feared Adam would have to carry her back to the Silver Phoenix otherwise. The old serving woman boiled water while Anhai found bandages for Isyllt's hand. Afterward, she sat on a low couch, dignity and corset stays keeping her upright when she wanted to melt, and let hot spices wash away the taste of bile and wine and ease the lingering chill in her bones.

Anhai picked up her cup, but her hands trembled so badly she set it down again. "That you had to save my niece from her own blood . . ." She shook her head. "My family is in your debt, Lady Iskaldur, more than I can say."

"Isyllt, please."

"Then you must call me Anhai—"

"Iskaldur?" Vienh interrupted, coming into the room. "Isyllt Iskaldur?" Her eyes narrowed as she stared at Isyllt.

"That's right."

"Mother's bones!" The woman shook her head, undoing the hasty knot that held up her hair. "I'm first mate on the *Rain Dog*. I'll see that Izzy gives your money back."

Isyllt swallowed a chuckle, glanced at Anhai. The woman caught the look and smiled.

"Don't worry. I'm well aware of what my sister does on that boat of hers. But silence is the very least you may ask of me, La—Isyllt. After what you did for Lia, I would help you load a smuggling ship myself."

Isyllt nodded thanks. "Keep the money," she said to Vienh. "Just don't let him sail off in the night."

Vienh grinned wearily. "I'll flense him myself if he tries."

"Do you know why your grandmother was so angry? More than a lack of proper funeral rites, surely."

The sisters exchanged a glance, kinship plain in otherwise dissimilar faces. Vienh broke the silence first. "The rites would be bad enough for many Sivahri, but Grandmother— In her generation the Xians were rebels, fighting the Assari however they could. Deilin died in an ambush gone wrong—the Empire's soldiers got the upper hand. They left the bodies in the jungle for beasts."

"Things were less bloody by our time," Anhai said. "But for Grandmother, trapped in death, watching . . . The witch on the Street of Salt called me a filthy collaborator dog, and that is—was—Deilin's opinion as well." She pushed her hair back. "That a foreigner came to our aid when our own people would not is a shameful thing for Sivahra."

Silence welled in the room, until Isyllt heard the creak of leather as Adam shifted his weight behind her. Fatigue lapped over her, forcing out a yawn that she barely caught with the back of her hand. "Forgive me." Sivahri politeness must be contagious. Adam pressed a surreptitious hand against her shoulder, keeping her upright. "Thank you for the tea, but we should be going."

"Of course." Anhai rose, graceful in spite of her tangled hair and wrinkled clothes. "You have our blessings."

"Find a physician for Lilani, to be safe. Possession will drain her worse than any fever."

Anhai nodded and escorted Isyllt and Adam to the door. "If you need anything in Symir, anything at all . . ."

"Thank you."

The door closed, cutting off the light, and a lock clicked. Adam's hand lingered on her arm and Isyllt allowed herself to lean on him for a weary instant.

"You're not going to be sick again, are you?"

She snorted and pulled away. "I hope not." She rubbed her hands against her arms—her scarf must be somewhere in Lilani's bedroom. "Thank you for helping in there."

He shrugged it aside. "That was good work. The old man taught you well enough."

She was too tired for the thought to even ache. "He did."

They returned to the Phoenix in silence. By the time they reached the inn, the night had dissolved into a blur of shadows and lamplight and Isyllt's blood echoed in her ears. The wind gusted and Adam stiffened, raising his face.

Isyllt wrinkled her nose. "Smoke?"

"In the north. Something big is burning."

"Should we see—" But a yawn caught her mid-question, popping her jaw with its force. Adam chuckled.

"In the morning. I'll wake you if the city burns down."

The last thing she remembered before darkness took her was Adam catching her as she stumbled and carrying her to bed.

Xinai slipped in long after the midnight bells had sounded; the door squeaked as she closed it and Adam stirred. By the dim light through the window she saw him grope for his sword and fall back when he recognized her.

She kicked off her boots and unbuckled her belt. The smell of alcohol mingled with his sweat was familiar, but as she moved closer to the bed she caught another scent and frowned. Magic, cold and dark.

"You smell like death," she said, standing at the foot of the bed. He'd fallen asleep still dressed. Waiting for her—it made her smile, even after so many years. "Death and wine."

"The wine came before the death," he muttered, kicking off his boots.

"It usually does." The bed creaked under her weight. She leaned over him, wrinkled her nose at a trace of bittersweet perfume. "You smell like the witch too." She arched an eyebrow, though he probably couldn't see it. "I didn't know she was your type."

He chuckled and laid his hands on her waist. "If her magic didn't kill me, her hip bones would. No, we had an adventure."

Better than spending hour after hour in smoky bars, listening to disgruntled laborers mutter into their beer. Liquor might stir their tongues against the Empire, but in the morning they'd curse their hangovers and go about their lives without a thought of doing anything more. Even those who'd gathered to protest at the docks yesterday weren't likely to do more than shout. She needed warriors, not angry tradesmen and merchants. The stink of beer and smoke and other people's sweat still clung to her skin, and she had only a handful of names that might be of use. At least the fire in the dockyard had been a pretty distraction.

She forced her disappointment aside. "A story," she said, straddling Adam's hips and helping him undo his belt and shirt laces. "Tell me."

He pulled her down beside him, leaning his head on her shoulder as he recounted the trip to Straylight. A hollow feeling grew in Xinai's stomach as he told of the exorcism and the binding of the Xian ghost.

"How horrible," she whispered when he finished. "To die like that, unburned. To watch your family become collaborators." She might have died a hundred times in the north, and no one would have known the rites and songs. It had never worried her much then, when she thought she'd never see home again. Now the thought tightened her stomach with queasy dread.

Adam snorted softly and she stiffened. But it wasn't his fault. He couldn't know.

"Trying to steal your great-granddaughter's body is still a bit much."

"Yes." Just a child. A warrior's body would be more use. They lay in silence for a while and she felt Adam start to drowse. "I wonder how many of them are left," she mused aloud. "The rebel ghosts."

"We're only concerned with the live ones." He slid his arm around her waist and pressed his face against the crook of her neck. "Do you have any stories to tell? I smelled a fire."

"Yes, a warehouse by the docks." His breathing had already begun to roughen and she kissed his forehead, soothing a hand over his tangled hair. "I'll tell you in the morning. Rest."

A moment later he was snoring softly, but a long time passed before Xinai followed him into the dark.

CHAPTER 4

Isyllt woke to a hot swath of sunlight creeping across the bed and corset stays gouging her ribs and breasts. Dreams of ghosts and ice clotted her mind, cobweb-sticky, and for a moment she couldn't remember where she was, or why.

Then she sat up and clarity returned, gilding the spike of pain that stabbed her between the eyes. Bile burned the back of her throat, and for a nervous instant she thought she would retch. She swallowed it down, closed her eyes, and waited to make an uneasy truce with her stomach.

A truce that lasted until she staggered out of bed and breathed in the canal's stench through the open window. She reached the water closet just in time.

She'd lied, it seemed—drinking herself stupid qualified as letting personal feelings interfere with the job. She couldn't afford to do that again.

After a long bath and clean clothes she joined the mercenaries for breakfast, where she managed to sip lassi and nibble bread. She closed her eyes against the wicked sun-

light and listened to Xinai talk about insurgent groups and
warehouse fires. At the moment all she cared about was
letting the words sink into her ears—she'd try to make
sense of them when her head cleared.

"Wait," Adam interrupted in the midst of the report.
Isyllt opened one eye and winced as light shattered off the
table settings. "What was that name?"

"Jabbor Lhun?" Isyllt replied. At least her memory
still worked, even if the rest of her body contemplated
mutiny.

"He's the leader of a rebel group," Xinai said again.
"The Jade Tigers. They're one of the public ones, at
least."

"Is he Assari?" Adam asked.

"Half, or so I heard." She raised black eyebrows.
"Why?"

He grinned. "I think I saw our rebel leader yesterday.
Trysting with an apprentice at the Kurun Tam."

Afternoon settled hot and lazy before they left the Phoenix. A few criers still shouted the news of the fire, but
most had fled the heat. The wind from the north smelled
of ashes and char.

A skiff carried them to the eastern side of the city,
through wide canals and water gardens. The steersman
pointed out landmarks, including the shining walls and
gates of the Khas Maram. The House of the People, in
Assari, the name of both the domed council building and
the elected officials who gathered there. The councillors
were native Sivahri, meant to balance the imperially appointed Viceroy. In theory, at least—Isyllt doubted anyone not a wealthy loyalist sat in the people's house.

The emerald shade of the canals spared them the worst of the heat, but the long sleeves Isyllt wore to cover her bruised and salt-burned arms were no help. Insects buzzed loudly through fragrant balcony gardens and upper windows glittered in the sun; reflected light rippled liquid across the undersides of eaves. Raintree was a wealthier neighborhood than Jadewater or Saltlace, with fewer shops to ruin the line of expensive houses. No broken streets or sinking buildings here—police patrolled these streets, not gangs, and she doubted anyone slept in these alleys.

The skiff let them off at the circular tree-lined court where Vasilios lived, and Adam tipped the steersman. As they climbed the steps, Isyllt reached for the power stored in her ring, teasing out just enough to numb her aches and clear her head. No safer a remedy than a drunkard's morning wine, but this was the job and she couldn't muddle through it. The world snapped into crystalline focus and she swallowed a sigh.

Zhirin greeted them at the door, looking nearly as tired as Isyllt felt, and led them to an upstairs study. The windows stood open to the garden breeze and treetops swayed against the casement, framed by flowering trellises. A fat cream-colored cat napped in a stripe of sunlight, sparing the visitors only an amber-eyed glance.

Vasilios rose to greet them, setting aside a book. He must have noticed the reek of magic hanging on Isyllt; his eyes narrowed as he clasped her hand, but he said nothing.

"Good afternoon." He waved them toward chairs, settling back into his own. Isyllt winced as his knees cracked.

"This is nothing," he said wryly, catching the look. "When the rains come, all my bones try to catch the next fast ship for Assar." He glanced at the window, at the cascade of vines and flowers beyond it. "But I can't seem to leave Symir, no matter what old bones would like."

Zhirin returned laden with an elaborate brass tea set, and Isyllt smiled—brewing countless pots of tea was part of any apprenticeship she'd ever known. They waited in silence as tea was poured and pastries passed around. The rattle of saucers drew the cat, who threw himself against ankles indiscriminately until Vásilios shared a honey cake with him.

"It's pleasant to have new company," the old man said when everyone was served, "but I suspect you wish to speak of the real reasons behind your visit."

Zhirin glanced toward the door, but Vasilios waved her back. "Stay, my dear. This very much concerns you." The girl settled on a cushioned bench beside his chair, hands clasped in her lap. "In fact, why don't you explain to Zhirin exactly what you're doing here?"

The girl's face paled a shade, but she sat still and waited. Soft and pretty and demure, and brewed strong tea—prized qualities in apprentices the world over. Revolution would be a tempting hobby after a few years of that.

Isyllt took a sip of tea to drown her amusement; the heat stung the cut on her left hand. "Rumors of rebellion brewing in Symir have reached the court in Erisín. My master, who serves the king, sent me here to investigate those rumors."

"Why?" Zhirin asked. She flinched, then continued. "How does Symir concern Selafai?"

One corner of Isyllt's mouth curled. "The Emperor's eye turns north. If he does attempt to invade Selafai, Sivahra's wealth will finance it. Selafai has no desire to be subsumed by the Empire."

Zhirin's hazel eyes narrowed. "And Symir has no desire to be handed off to another master like a piece on a game board." She flushed, as if surprised by the vehemence in her voice.

"Not a piece. A power." Isyllt leaned forward. "The king of Selafai doesn't want to rule an empire any more than he wants to be part of one. All he cares about is keeping his kingdom secure."

In truth the king of Selafai was too distracted by grief over his wife to care about much else, even a year after her death. It was Kiril who saw the eyes of the Empire turning north, and Kiril who chose to act sooner rather than later.

"What does this mean for Symir?" Zhirin asked.

"It means that I'm here to find this rumored rebellion, to treat with its leaders. If there is a faction strong enough to take back Sivahra and hold it, Selafai would be willing to offer aid."

The girl's jaw tightened and she sucked in a breath through her nose. "Why are you telling me this? I'm just an apprentice—a collaborator, no less." She glanced at Vasilios with a rueful half-smile.

Vasilios's laugh broke the thickening tension. "Forgive me, Zhirin. But do you really think I don't know who you're with, all those times you're late for lunch or lessons?"

"Oh." And her brown cheeks burned crimson.

"The empire isn't the worst of it," Zhirin said later, after she'd stopped blushing and stammering. She paced in front of the window, despite her still-aching feet; at least the carpets were soft. The cat followed her circuit with slitted eyes, tail-tip twitching. "Not really."

"No?" Isyllt cocked an eyebrow. Hard to meet the woman's gaze for long, eyes paler than an animal's, clearer and colder than river water. "I had the idea that some Sivahri were none too pleased with things Assari."

"Some, of course. But the Assari's influence hasn't been entirely bad. They built Symir, if nothing else. It's the Khas Maram we fight." Not that *she* fought anything—Zhirin shrugged the thought aside like a biting fly.

"The Assari are conquerors, but at least they didn't betray their own blood. The Khas deny their clans, bleed the people with taxes." Taxes that paid her mother's government pension, taxes that had bought her clothes and childhood toys.

"They sacrifice our people in rice fields and mines. Many of the miners are prisoners, some arrested on ridiculous charges and forced into work camps. People die in the mines, more than the Khas will ever admit. Bodies are lost, never given burial rites. They disappear." She glanced at her master and the stones glittering on his gnarled hands. Did he know about the diamonds? She didn't dare ask, not yet.

The sorceress rolled her shoulders as if against a chill. Her companions—or bodyguards—watched silently. Zhirin couldn't place the man's features, but the woman was clearly forest-clan, though she hadn't given a clan-name.

The sky darkened to slate and silver as the light died. Shadows thickened in the room for a moment before the lamps sprang to life, witchlight kindling to real flame.

"The Khas doesn't care about the people," Zhirin

continued. The words felt awkward in her mouth—Jabbor
was the one who made speeches. A mimic-bird, she imagined Kwan would call her. "Their only concern is wealth,
theirs and the tithes that keep the Empire content."

"Would this faction of yours rather see Sivahra in-
dependent, or only replace the Khas with less-corrupt
officials?" Isyllt turned a cup of tea—doubtless long
cold—between her hands and her ring gleamed. Zhirin
had never seen a black diamond before, but she knew
what they meant.

She paused in her circuit, shifting her weight with a
rustle of cloth. "Of course we want to see Sivahra free.
But our first concern is the people. We don't want violence, not if there's any other answer. There's been enough
bloodshed in Sivahra's history."

The Sivahri woman turned her head, lips tightening.

"Can we meet Jabbor?" Isyllt asked, leaning forward.
By lamplight her face was an ivory mask; Zhirin wondered if her skin was cold to the touch.

"Yes. That is, I think so. I'll ask him." He hadn't spoken of it last night, but she knew how much they needed
the money they would have made from the stolen stones.
Hard for the clanspeople to rise in revolution when they
had farms to tend and no other way to eat.

She turned to Vasilios, who'd been silent for most of
the conversation. "How long have you known, master?"

"Quite a while, my dear." He smiled affectionately and
she smiled back, though her stomach was cold. If he had
noticed, who else might have?

Xinai couldn't sleep, even after Adam snored softly beside her. His arm draped over her stomach, hair trailing

against her cheek. Usually the press of warm flesh comforted her, but tonight she could barely breathe for the heat. Sweat-damp linen scraped against her skin, snagged on her scars.

Finally she rolled out of bed, groping for her clothes. Adam stirred, eyes flashing in the dark.

"I'm going out," she whispered. "Go back to sleep."

After a moment his breathing deepened again. She tugged on vest and trousers, stomped into her boots. Sandals would be cooler and less conspicuous, but she liked having a place for extra blades.

She leaned against the handle to keep the door from squeaking. Moisture warped the wood till nothing opened or closed smoothly. She turned her key in the lock and slunk down the shadow-thick hall.

She'd hoped—ancestors, how she'd hoped—but the witch's contact was nothing but a foolish child. Didn't want bloodshed. Xinai snorted softly. There was nothing without bloodshed, let alone tearing down the Khas and casting out the Assari conquerors. Freedom was measured in blood.

She pitied the poor dead woman, trapped now, forever cut off from her family and her homeland. She hadn't had the heart to ask what would happen to her spirit once the witch returned to Erisín. An ugly fate.

But no worse than her own family had known. Did their ghosts linger still, haunting the jungles or the mines?

The night was heavy in her lungs as she slipped out the servants' entrance to the street and turned toward the docks. But after a few streets she halted, frowning. She needed more than drunken complaints and rumors. She knew where she needed to go; she'd avoided it long enough.

Xinai turned and made her way to Straylight, and the Street of Salt.

Easy for the mageling to keep her idealism. No Laii ever lived in a tilting hovel that flooded with the rains, ever sent their children to the mines or fields to keep the lease on such a hovel. Easy for the mages to look down from their mountain and call Symir a jewel, when they were too far away to see the flaws at its heart.

She smiled at the missing signs and Sivahran writing, tried to imagine the whole city like that. No use. The city was Assari, from wooden pilings beneath the water to the rooftop tiles, even if it had been paid for with native blood. Perhaps it could be reclaimed, made Sivahri, but the jungle was her true home. She should go into the hills, find her family's banyan tree. If it still stood. The spirit might have withered with no one to tend it.

She touched one of the charms around her neck, the oldest. The last of her mother's work, containing bones and ashes of generations of Lins. She should have worn her mother's bones in that pouch, but they were lost.

A pack of young men loitered on the corner, lounging against crumbling walls. Prides, they called themselves, like hunting cats. Clanless children who banded together for safety, formed families just as tight as blood-kin. She had feared them when she was young, but now she understood. She nodded acknowledgment as she passed and the leader nodded back.

The smell of herbs and witchery washed over her as she walked down the street and her eyes burned. Time pulled away like the tide, leaving a different Xinai standing on the pitted stones. Young and scared, torn and bloody.

She stopped in front of a narrow shop-front, swallowing the taste of tears. The sign was nearly the same as it had been twelve years ago, faded now and weathered. Lamplight flickered through the windows. Too much to hope . . . But she climbed the worn stairs and knocked.

For a moment she thought no one would answer, but finally the door creaked open. A stooped woman stood silhouetted in the doorway, her face cast in shadow.

"What do you want?" she asked. A familiar voice, like a cold blade in her heart.

"Selei?" The name cracked in her mouth, nearly shattered.

Silence stretched. Finally the old woman moved, let the light fall through the door.

"Xinai? Xinai Lin?" Her wrinkled brown face broke into a wondering smile. "Oh, child—" And she stepped forward to clasp Xinai in her arms, and pulled her into the shop.

The room was much the same as she remembered, clean but crowded, walls warped and water-stained. Fragrant herbal smoke drowned the mold-musk that lingered in older buildings. The last time Xinai had crossed the threshold she'd been barely fifteen, desperate and alone, her back bloody and slick with grease to keep her shirt from sticking to open wounds.

Selei had paid for her passage on a smuggler's ship, sent her away before hate and grief poisoned her. It had saved her life.

The witch locked the door behind them and turned to study Xinai. Age clouded one eye milk-blue, but the other was dark and sharp as ever. Not blood-kin, but a friend of the Lin clan since before she was born, the closest thing to family she had left in Sivahra.

Selei's gaze took in her jewelry, the blades at her hips. One bird-light hand caught Xinai's, turned it over to trace the calluses. "You've done well for yourself."

Xinai nodded, throat tight.

"But you came home." Not quite a question, but her forehead creased in curiosity. Braids the color of steel and ashes rattled as she moved, woven through with feathers and bone beads.

Xinai felt the weight of age and experience in the woman's mismatched gaze, felt herself being measured. She nodded again and found her voice.

"I've come back to help."

CHAPTER 5

Waiting was always the worst part.

Isyllt sat in Vasilios's kitchen, sipping bitter green tea and resisting the urge to pace while stripes of sunlight moved slowly across the blue and orange tiles. She and Adam had left the inn this morning and settled into the mage's home. For all her flippancy about spending money, she still needed to fill out expense reports when she returned, and the Crown's accountants didn't believe in luxurious or glamorous spying.

Nothing to do now but wait for Zhirin to arrange a meeting, or for Xinai to uncover something else of use, some other faction in case Jabbor's people couldn't help them. Isyllt didn't remember the mercenary being so tense on the ship, spine stiff and brow creased. It hadn't, she guessed, been a happy homecoming.

Her parents had fled civil war in Vallorn when she was seven, but she had only vague memories of her parents' worry, her mother's tears in the night and their hasty descent from the mountains. Memories of their home were vaguer still. And after her parents died in the plague sixteen years ago, she'd moved from one shelter to another until Kiril found her. Until Kiril and the Arcanost, home was any tenement she could afford or anywhere she could hide, anything better than an alley. Nothing worth fighting for, or dying for.

She tried to picture it, foreign soldiers in the streets of Erisín, the house of Alexios cast out of the palace. Even though she'd spied and schemed and killed for Selafai—for Kiril—she couldn't imagine how Xinai felt, how the ghost of Deilin Xian felt.

She drew a breath sweet with spices and flowers in the garden. Across the kitchen, the housekeeper kneaded bread dough, gnarled brown hands slapping and shaping with practiced ease. Flour dusted her apron, smudged the scarf that held back her iron-gray braids. She was the only servant Isyllt had seen; the peace in the house was nearly soporific.

But still her nerves sang, like a child first sent to bazaar alone. Ridiculous.

Or not, perhaps. Her other assignments had been paltry things compared to this—an ear in the shadows, a knife in the dark. Nothing so grand as revolution.

Footsteps distracted her, light and uneven. She glanced up as Vasilios came in, his limp not quite hidden beneath his robes.

"I always did hate the waiting most of all," he said with a wry smile, pulling out a chair. "Kiril was the patient one. I always wanted to be *doing* something—it nearly got me killed a time or two."

Isyllt smiled; Kiril had told her a few of those stories. "When did you leave the service?"

"After the old king died. I married, and my wife wanted me to keep my skin intact. I still took an occasional job. It gets in your blood after a time."

She nodded.

His eyes narrowed. "My wife died ten years ago and I hadn't the heart to stay in Selafai. Memories are worse than ghosts. I told myself I'd retired, but when I learned of the rebellion here . . ."

Isyllt lifted a hand, palm up, baring the blue veins in her wrist. "In your blood."

More footsteps approached and Zhirin paused diffidently in the doorway. "Am I disturbing?" The cook slid a pan of dough over glowing coals before retreating to give them privacy. Zhirin waited till the slap of her sandals faded, then moved closer.

"I've sent word to Jabbor. We're to meet tomorrow, near the Kurun Tam. I'm sorry it can't be sooner—"

"I understand," Isyllt said, lips quirking. "Some things shouldn't be rushed."

The girl shifted her weight, slippers rasping on tile. "I'm going into the city today, meliket, to look for a costume for the festival. I thought perhaps you'd like to come."

"Yes." *Relax*, she told herself. *Play the tourist. With less wine.* "Yes, I'd like that."

Market Street was wider than most in Symir, more of a plaza, and packed nearly wall to wall with people. Assari and Sivahri voices tangled together as vendors haggled and hawked their wares. Silks and spices, brass and silver and steel, screeching birds and lazing lizards—Isyllt saw barely half the offered merchandise as she kept up with Zhirin, trying to find the rhythm of the crowd. Her height gave her an advantage but made her conspicuous as well. At least Adam had gone elsewhere to look around; an armed shadow would have drawn even more attention in a place like this.

She struggled not to flinch away from the careless brush of shoulders and arms. Erisín had its share of crowded places, but even the worst recognized the need for personal space. This was a thief's playground. Or an assassin's.

Zhirin led them out of the press eventually, into a narrow second-story shop. The crowds opened enough to move without touching anyone and Isyllt drew a grateful breath. Bolts of cloth piled on tables and shimmering swaths draped the walls.

"What sort of costumes do you wear to the Dance?" Isyllt asked, taking in the riot of colors and textures.

"Traditionally, people dress as spirits, to honor those that bring the rain. We give the masks to the river afterward. Though it's not as traditional as it once was."

"Selafai celebrates the winter solstice with a masque. It's meant to keep the hungry ghosts from finding you when they crawl through the mirrors that night." She smiled as Zhirin's eyes widened.

"Do you have so many ghosts in the north?"

"In Erisín, at least. The city is built on bones. I don't know your spirits—what do you think I should wear?"

Zhirin glanced around, turned toward a bolt of rough white silk. Rainbow luster danced along the edges as she lifted a fold. "You would make a good *kixun*."

"What are they?"

"Spirits of moonlight and fog. They take the shape of

foxes or women in white and lead men into the forests at night."

Isyllt cocked an eyebrow. "And eat them?"

"Sometimes. They're not very kind."

Isyllt stroked the silk; it ran cool and slick as water between her fingers. "What does that say of your opinion of me?" The girl flushed and Isyllt chuckled. "I'm only joking—"

She broke off as someone bumped into her. Immediately a steadying hand closed on her elbow.

"Excuse me."

She turned to face an Assari man, his hazel eyes crinkling in consternation. Automatically, her hand twitched toward her purse; his lips quirked as he caught the motion.

She gave him a crooked apologetic smile. "No harm—"

Thunder crashed outside the shop, rattling the floor. A scream followed, then another, till Isyllt's ears rang with panicked cries. Someone jostled Zhirin on their way to the window and the girl fell into Isyllt. The Assari man caught her shoulder, holding them both steady. Another crash followed and dust and plaster drifted from the ceiling.

Isyllt twisted, pushing Zhirin into the man's arms as she moved toward the window. With a whispered word she chilled the air around her, until the spectators retreated from winter's bite and gave her room. She pushed aside the mesh curtain and leaned out.

Smoke billowed from a building across the street and flames licked its doorway. The cacophony of the crowd nearly deafened her as shoppers fled, tripping over one another in their haste. Already people in the room were rushing for the stairs, shoving down the narrow hall.

"Is there another way out?" she asked the shopkeeper. Wide-eyed, he pointed toward a curtained doorway in the back wall. Isyllt ducked through it, heard footsteps following her as she darted past a storeroom and through the back door. It opened onto a narrow stair above a canal; the steps creaked and the railing left splinters in her palm as she rushed down.

She ducked down a narrow alley and emerged into the street across from the burning shop. People lay crumpled on the ground, knocked down by the blast or by their neighbors. The wounded were mostly Assari, but not all. Smoke and dust billowed, eddied to reveal a hole in the wall and the sidewalk littered with shattered stone. The wind shifted and Isyllt choked on the reek of smoke and char and sour magic.

This was no accident. She wrapped a concealment around her, and a ward against the flames, and crossed the street.

Her ring blazed as she entered the shop, pushing back the crackling heat—no survivors inside. Flames consumed the doors and wall hangings, rushed over the ceiling to devour the rafters. Lamps melted on shelves, brass and silver charring wood as they dripped to the floor. Witchlight flickered around her in an opalescent web, holding guttering flames at bay. But it wouldn't keep the ceiling from crushing her when it came down.

The smell of charred flesh and hot metal seared her nose, and something else. The air was heavy with intent, with sacrifice. The magic that turned the shop into an inferno had been dearly paid for.

A spell so powerful must have left a trace. She nearly stepped in a puddle of brown-burnt blood, nudged a body aside with her toe. The man's eyes melted down his charred cheeks and Isyllt frowned; intact, he might have shared his dying vision with her. Not that she had time to scry the dead.

There. A red glitter caught her eye, beside a body so mangled it must have been near the center of the explosion. She tugged a handkerchief out of her pocket—the silk insulated whatever magic was left in the crystalline shards as she scooped them up, and spared her hands the heat.

The ceiling groaned, loud even over the roar and rush of the flames. Isyllt uncoiled from her crouch and leapt through the door, gasping as the air outside rushed damp into her lungs.

The ringing in her ears drowned the noise of the crowd, but she caught sight of red uniforms forcing their way through the press. No more time to investigate.

Zhirin waited in the alley-mouth, one hand pressed tight over her mouth like she was trying to keep in hysterics. The man from the fabric shop stood beside her, holding her arm. Isyllt let her spells drop as she ducked off the street and they startled. Sparks crackled in her hair as she moved, stung her skin like wasps as the magic bled away. The humid breeze off the canal made her face tingle.

The man's eyes narrowed, measuring. He glanced at her hand, and his own twitched in a warding gesture.

"Are you all right?" Zhirin asked, her chin trembling.

"I'm fine, but I wouldn't mind getting away from the thick of things." Already she felt death lapping over her, cold threads swirling through warm air. Her limbs crawled with gooseflesh and sweat prickled her scalp. At least

a dozen dead, probably more, and one of the wounded
wouldn't survive.

So much senseless death. The kind she was here to
encourage.

Excitement hummed in her blood, dizzied her worse
than any wine. And that was the true reason she was here,
the reason she would go where she was sent, no matter
how ugly the mission. Not for king and country, not even
for Kiril, but because danger sang to her like a siren, and
after the first giddy brush with death, the rush of knowing
that she was still alive, she'd known she could never stop.

She ran a hand over her face, smearing ash and sweat.
Her fingers came away red; her nose was bleeding. "Excuse us," she said to the man, taking Zhirin's arm.

He stepped aside. "Be careful, ladies."

Isyllt nodded, wondering how many ways he meant it.
She led Zhirin down the alley, away from the smell of
smoke and death.

Isyllt wasn't sure how long she and Vasilios spent studying the shattered stone, but by the time Adam returned her
back was stiff from leaning over the table. She straightened with a wince as the mercenary slipped into the study.
Not yet sunset, but they'd drawn the shutters and stark
witchlights lit the room.

"What happened?" Adam asked.

"Someone blew up an Assari shop, and everyone in it."
Isyllt shook her head, hair crackling. "He blew himself
up too." Her face still stung from the fire and itched with
dried sweat. Adam's eyes narrowed as he studied her, and
she wondered how awful she looked.

He turned to the table and the pile of red dust and crystal shards glittering there. "A ruby?" He reached out a cautious hand; gooseflesh roughened his arm as he felt the heat still radiating from it.

Vasilios nodded. "They didn't let the news out, of course, but we'd just readied a shipment of charged stones to be shipped to Assar. They were in the warehouse that burned—whoever started the fire must have taken the rubies. This Dai Tranh was dangerous enough with gunpowder and flash bombs, but now—" He shook his head. "But this stone was flawed, and we never charge flawed stones. Too easy for things like this to happen. They must have a mage working with them."

"Zhirin?" Adam said, echoing Isyllt's thought.

The old mage's eyes narrowed. "I cannot believe that of her."

Adam shrugged eloquent skepticism, but Isyllt believed the girl's horror at the market had been unfeigned—if Zhirin had helped the rebels get their hands on these weapons, she doubtless regretted it now.

"Did they leave anything else behind?" Adam continued. "Today, I mean."

Isyllt frowned. "I hadn't the leisure for a proper search. I'll go back after the soldiers have gone. I didn't sense any ghosts lingering, but they might return." It was a scant hope, but her best one.

Vasilios ran a hand over his face; his skin was gray and drawn in the unflattering light. "I cast a tracing on the stone, but it must have been covered until it was used. If I could find something of the assassin's, I might trace it further."

"We'll see what we can find." Isyllt glanced at Adam, tilted her head inquiringly. "The sooner we go in, the better our chances."

"Tonight," he said with a nod. "After the soldiers have left."

Vasilios lowered himself into a chair. "You'll forgive me if I don't join you in sneaking around in the dark. I'll keep working with the stone. Maybe there's something I've missed. We won't have a proper dinner tonight, but you can ask Marat to make you something."

Isyllt and Adam left him to rest, following the scent of spices downstairs to the kitchen. All the houses in Symir seemed to follow the same pattern—tall and narrow, with the family's rooms on top and only the ground floor open to strangers.

Isyllt frowned as she watched Adam descend the stairs. "You're limping."

He glanced down, flexed his right leg. "An old wound. I landed on it badly during the mess at the market." He caught the question in her eyes. "I'll be fine by tonight. What about you?"

She ran a hand over her frizzing hair, wincing as her fingers brushed her tender cheek. "No worse than a sunburn. Did you have any luck today?"

He shrugged. "Xin will do better than me. Vienh Xian-Lunh might be helpful, though—within reason. She has no love for the Dai Tranh."

"Zealots are easier to use than to love. But maybe the Tigers will be use enough for us." In spite of the cold practicality she tried to summon, she couldn't be rid of the images of Lilani Xian's fevered face or the corpses in the market. Practicality could only excuse so much.

Covered plates sat on the kitchen table, and a sweating carafe of ginger beer. Marat arranged more food on a tray as they came in.

"I know what it means when he locks himself in his study that way," she said. "I'm amazed any of you sorcerers live so long, if this is how you take care of yourselves." She shot a narrow-eyed glance at Isyllt.

Isyllt waved Adam into a chair and served them both. "Where's Zhirin?" Her voice was steady, but her hands trembled, beer splashing too loudly into their cups. Now that she wasn't distracted with spellcraft, she could feel the strain and hunger stealing over her.

"Sleeping." Marat snorted. "At least someone in this house lets herself rest." She lifted the tray, balancing it easily on one hand; muscles shifted in her forearm as her sleeve fell back. "I'm going to force something down the master's throat now. If you need anything later, just ring."

"Will you be all right by tonight?" Adam asked as Isyllt slid a plate of bread and goat curry in front of him.

The sky outside was orange fading to gray; still hours left before it would be safe to return to Market Street. "Of course." She nudged his foot with her toe. "Let me see your leg."

He stretched out the injured limb and she crouched beside him, laying light hands on his knee. Closing her eyes, she sent tendrils of power lapping curiously through his skin. Nothing serious, but she felt the strain in the muscle, the tenderness in the surrounding flesh. The rest of him was healthy, save for the subtle-sweet song of decay that sang in all living flesh. Her magic rubbed against him like a friendly cat; death always recognized a killer.

"You're a healer?"

She chuckled at the skepticism in his voice. "Not at all. My magic is the absence of life." She glanced up at him through her lashes, smiled to see him blanch. "But you learn to work around the limitations."

She summoned cold, let it radiate from her hands into his flesh. He shuddered but didn't jerk away. Then he sighed as the chill soothed the inflamed tissues in his knee.

"Be careful," she said, uncoiling from her crouch. "It's pain I'm easing, not damage. Don't try any acrobatics for a while."

"Thanks." He flexed his leg carefully, shot her a curious glance.

She waved it aside and sat down to eat.

CHAPTER 6

Isyllt and Adam returned to Market Street late that night, after the guards and gawkers had left. The damaged shop had been hastily reinforced with spells and wooden beams to keep the roof intact. Isyllt lingered in the shadows across the street and watched the burnt ruin with *otherwise* eyes.

The street was silent, windows shuttered and dark, but she doubted she was the only one watching. Moonlight fell in pale stripes between buildings, shining on clean cobbles; death still echoed here, in spite of the fresh-scrubbed stones.

Adam crept up beside her, only the warmth of his flesh giving him away. "It's clear as far as I can see." His whisper ruffled the fine hairs above her ear.

"Wait for me," she whispered back, their faces so close she could taste his salt-musky sweat.

She slipped across the cobbles and into the shadow of the ruined shop. Red ropes were strung across the door and broken wall to keep intruders out. Isyllt paused when she felt the spell woven into the cord. Subtle magic, well-cast, meant to snare or mark an intruder. She knelt and twisted through the ropes, careful not to touch them.

The air still stank of charred flesh and seared blood; crusted gore marked where the bodies had lain. Isyllt closed her eyes and reached, listening to the stones.

The explosion had killed most instantly, leaving only shudders of shock and violence. Someone in the far corner had died slower, roasted by the flames. Pain resonated there, raising gooseflesh on Isyllt's limbs and stinging her fire-tender skin. But it was only the echo of agony blasted into the rock, not a soul left intact.

Even her mage-trained eyes could barely see in the gloom and she couldn't risk a light. Inching cautiously, she moved closer to where she'd found the shattered ruby. If the investigators had missed something, any scrap that had belonged to the saboteur—

A hand closed on her shoulder, another slapping over her mouth before she could gasp. She tasted spice-steeped skin and summer lightning. Isyllt cocked her leg for a backward kick when her assailant spoke.

"I admit," Asheris's low voice whispered in her ear, "you aren't what I expected to catch here, Lady Iskaldur." The hand left her mouth and he turned her around. A sliver of moonlight gleamed in amber eyes.

"What were you expecting?" She licked her lips, tasted the salt of his hand. Her heart hammered in her chest, and she fought to keep from trembling in the aftermath of shock. She'd felt nothing, heard nothing.

Asheris grinned, a pale flash in the darkness. He wore black and the shadows welcomed him. "A criminal foolish enough to return to the scene of the crime, perhaps. I hope that isn't what I've found."

His hand was warm on her shoulder, their bodies only inches apart. Nearly a dance step. He was only an inch or two taller. "Not a criminal, my lord, only careless."

He took a step back and Isyllt almost matched him. But this was another sort of dance entirely. "When I offered to take you sightseeing, this isn't what I had in mind."

She was glad she had no need to lie. "I was in the market when this happened. I wanted to have a closer look." She shrugged ruefully. "Habit, I'm afraid. I didn't mean to interfere in the investigation." She cocked an eyebrow. "Your investigation?"

"Yes. Forgive me, I neglected to mention it earlier—I'm the Imperial Inquisitor for the city." He stepped back to give her a shallow bow.

"I hope I'm not impeding you."

"No, my lady. There's little here for you to impede. Such attacks are no mystery in Symir. Unless—" Light caressed the curve of his head as he turned. "Are there any ghosts here for us to question?"

"No. They died suddenly—no time to seal themselves to this place. "

"Ah, well. Better for them, I suppose, if frustrating for us. We know who's responsible, of course, but without witnesses it's difficult to make a proper case."

"Have you scried the dead?"

"We have no necromancers on staff—they make the locals very uncomfortable. I've requested one, but the Emperor has none to spare." His eyes flickered toward her. "Unless I could beg your assistance in the matter."

Isyllt smiled. She trusted him no more than he trusted her, but this dance was far too entertaining to stop now. "I'd be delighted."

He offered her his arm. "I'm a poor host, to entertain you in a charnel house. Let me take you somewhere more pleasant." He helped her over a fall of rubble; the moonlight was bright after the shadowed ruin. "And perhaps you should tell your escort in the alley that I have no ill intentions. I suspect he's rather concerned at the moment."

Somewhere more pleasant, it turned out, was the police station in Lioncourt. Despite the late hour, the lobby was crowded, every bench full and more people pacing in the corners. Some wept, some cursed and pleaded with the guards at the desk, some stared at nothing with hollow eyes; the air was thick with the heat of lamps and bodies, and reeked of sweat and dust and old tea. As Asheris led her through the press, Isyllt caught snatches of conversation.

"Let me see the body, please—"

"I can't find my daughter—"

"My wife was arrested at the docks on Sabeth, and I've had no word since. Where is she being held?"

She glanced up at the last, saw the man's angry, desperate expression and thought of the disappearances and work-gangs Zhirin had mentioned. Asheris steered her past the cordons, and she didn't catch the guard's weary response.

A haggard-looking sergeant met them near the stairs and saluted Asheris, casting a curious glance at Isyllt. The guards at the desks were local police, but his rumpled sweat-stained uniform was Imperial poppy red.

"I need the morgue key, please," Asheris said.

"Of course, Lord al Seth." The man turned away to fetch it, just in time to miss the startled blink Isyllt couldn't control.

Al Seth—the royal house of Assar. That was a choice bit of information Vasilios had forgotten to share. Much more than a pretty distraction.

They left the noise and close heat behind as they climbed the stairs. The morgue was a narrow, windowless room, sealed by webs of spells to keep out heat and moisture and insects. Lamplight gleamed on metal and tile, everything polished and scrubbed, but neither the lingering tang of soap nor the sachets of incense could drown the smell of charred meat.

Isyllt rolled her shoulders, trying to ease the itch of gelling sweat, and eyed the bodies. Six of them, mostly intact. Isyllt recognized the eyeless man she'd nearly tripped over in the shop. Her ring chilled with the presence of death, but not the biting cold that meant a ghost lingered nearby.

Asheris lounged in the corner, giving her room to work. Still sleek and handsome, but all the lazy grace and charm she'd seen when they met was more purposeful now. More dangerous.

What was he doing here, she wondered, glancing at him out of the corner of her eye as she circled the tables. But she could worry about that later. The bodies in the room were of more immediate interest than the fit of his jacket over broad shoulders.

She turned her eyes back to the grisly corpses. The smell of roast pork filled her nose, with the sharper reek of burnt hair and clothing beneath it. "Were these the only dead?"

"Less than half. Some were too mangled to keep and some have already been claimed by their families."

"You let them take the bodies so soon?"

"Wealth has ever sped certain processes along."

She arched an eyebrow. "Wealth enough to demand retribution?"

"Oh, yes. There will be arrests."

"Appropriate ones?"

Asheris smiled with the not-quite-cruelty of a cat cornering a bird. "As appropriate as we can make them."

"Of course." Isyllt leaned against a cold metal tabletop, tracing the scratches where gore or rust had been scoured away. The corpse stared up at her, face eerily whole, though his body was a shriveled crisp. She touched his stiffened arm; skin cracked, char-black flesh flaking away to reveal seeping red tissue. But his eyes, milk-clouded and sunken, were still intact, and that was all she needed.

She leaned over the dead man, laying a careful hand on his face to steady herself. The heat had singed his receding hair.

"What did you see?" she whispered.

His dying vision unfolded in his eyes, wrapped around her.

A crowded shop, polished metal gleaming in the warm afternoon sun. Dust motes spark in front of the windows, swirled by the passage of customers. Outside the market's din blurs to a noise like squalling birds. She glances down at the lovely enameled lamp in her hands, then toward the counter. A man with long beaded braids brushes her shoulder. Muffled grunt of apology and a crystalline red gleam out of the corner of her eye as she keeps moving—no, no, turn back, look, but the vision was set, only one way to play out now—*toward the front of the shop, where the tired-looking shopkeeper glances up and smiles*—

And Isyllt stumbled, even the memory of the explosion enough to rock her on her feet.

Asheris caught her elbow. "You saw something?"

She leaned against him for an instant, trying to decide how much to tell him. But he'd led her this far—perhaps he could take her further still.

"Yes." She feigned a catch in her voice, let him steady her more than she needed. His shoulder was a pleasant warmth in the chill room. "I saw the man who did it."

"Can you show me?"

Her hesitation this time was real, but after a heartbeat she nodded. She had been trained by the best, after all.

Asheris laid a hand on the side of her face. Isyllt closed her eyes and summoned up the image of the shop, locking the rest of herself deep away where he couldn't reach. She expected him to intrude, to search, but his presence in her mind was controlled, constrained, as if he feared to touch her.

A brief contact and a deft one, but as he slipped away she caught a flash of something else—sand and fire and wind, the desert's fury. Her eyes flew open to see him recoil, dark face draining ashen.

"Forgive me," he said after a moment, inclining his head. "That was . . . unexpected."

Curiosity defeated tact. "What did you feel?"

"A great deal of nothing. I don't envy your magic, my lady." He straightened his coat, brushing imaginary dust off the embroidered sleeves. "But thank you for your assistance. Even though the man responsible is dead, this helps us track down his accomplices. Perhaps we can find them before anyone else dies." His tiny shrug spoke eloquent disbelief.

Every time Zhirin closed her eyes, she saw bodies crumpled on the street, smelled smoke and blood and fear. Before long she gave up and lay staring at the ceiling until night fell and the house grew quiet.

She should have tried to help Isyllt and her master, but she couldn't stand to watch them pore over details of the attack. As though it were a mathematical equation or a difficult translation to be solved. As though a dozen or more people weren't dead, for nothing more than deciding to buy a lamp today.

As if that was just something that happened.

Finally she rose and straightened her clothes. For a moment she contemplated counterfeiting a sleeping form with pillows and slipping out the window, like she and her friend Sia had done when they were young. She restrained herself; nineteen was old enough to come and go as she pleased. Better to save the sneaking for when she really needed it.

But she didn't find her master or Marat and tell them she was going either, only slipped down the stairs to the dim first floor and let herself out the back. Crickets chirped in the darkness of the garden and hibiscus bushes whispered in the breeze. The house-wards recognized her and stayed quiescent as she left through the garden gate.

She didn't know where to go. Not home—her mother would ask too many questions. Would make Zhirin ask herself too many questions. A councillor's daughter, rich and fattened on Khas money while people died, and what did she think she could accomplish by playing at revolution with the Tigers? Would she even have joined the Tigers a year ago, when Fei Minh was still a member of the Khas?

Zhirin shook her head, eyes stinging. Jabbor might have reassured her, but he was on the North Bank, and she couldn't go that far for comfort, even if she had remembered shoes tonight. She had few other friends in the city, and none she could trust with this. Not for the first time, she wished Sia had remained in Symir instead of attending the university in Ta'ashlan. But Sia could no more have stayed than Zhirin could have followed her.

As Zhirin crossed the soaring Bridge of Sighs, whose lace-carved stone drew voices from the wind, she realized she was going to the temple. It had been too long.

She walked the edges of the Floating Garden, where moonlight rippled silver over black water and night-blooming lilies glowed milk-blue in the darkness. Trees rustled in the breeze, bobbing in their anchored wooden tubs. Webs of moss embroidered the surface, soon to be washed away when the rains came and the river rose. The night was too quiet; the few people she passed moved quickly, hunched as if expecting a blow.

The River Mother's temple was always open, though at this hour it was all but deserted. The candles and lanterns had gone out, but witchlights glowed in the elaborate spiraled channels that covered the center of the floor. The drip and murmur of water echoed in the vaulted chamber.

A curtain rustled and a veiled priestess emerged from an alcove, lantern in hand. Zhirin curtsied and the woman inclined her head. Eyebrows rose above her veil, a silent question.

Zhirin had thought perhaps to light a candle and sit in peace for a time, but now she realized she needed more than that.

"May I use the pool?" she asked softly.

The priestess hesitated a heartbeat, then nodded, gesturing with her lantern toward the far end of the hall.

Zhirin still knew the way, though it had been years since she'd used it. She still dreamed of the temple some nights, dreamed of her imaginary life as a priestess. Her mother had been intent on sending her to university with Sia, the first of the Laiis to attend. Apprenticeship at the Kurun Tam had been their compromise.

At least she had met Jabbor.

The priestess opened the antechamber door and lamplight rippled across the low domed ceiling. A small room, with benches and racks for clothing and a shower; acolytes scrubbed the pool at least twice daily, but courtesy suggested one track in as little grime as possible. The veiled woman found towels and a robe in a cabinet and set them on a bench, and cocked her head in another question.

"That's all I need, thank you."

She nodded and closed the door, leaving the lantern behind.

Zhirin paused as she unbuttoned her shirt—for a moment she feared she'd have to hurry after the priestess to beg a comb, but no, she still had one tucked into her pocket. She set it aside as she stripped and folded her clothes. Her toes curled against the cold marble floor, gooseflesh crawling up her legs.

The water from the tap was cold too, and she stifled a yelp as it splashed over her shoulders. She worked the braids and knots from her hair, watching long strands slither down the drain. When all of her was cold and wet and clean and her hair clung like lace-moss to her arms and back, she shut off the tap.

Leaving the lantern in the antechamber, she took her comb and padded dripping to the inner room, footprints shining behind her. As she shut the door she conjured witchlight; the steps were slick already and she had no wish to miss one in the dark. If she listened, she thought she could hear the river's pulse through the stone.

The pool filled the center of the room, deeper than a man was tall. Only a foot of water stood in the bottom now. No taps or faucet in this room—either the river came to you here or she didn't.

Zhirin descended the shallow steps into the pool, water lapping gently around her ankles as she reached the bottom. The wooden teeth of her comb bit her palm, and her own nerves saddened her. Once she'd never have doubted that she could call the river.

She raised the comb to her dripping hair and began to hum softly.

For a moment she feared she'd been gone too long. Then the water began to ripple, welling from tiny holes in the stone. Cool but not biting, it slid up her calves, over her thighs and hips, lapping higher with every stroke of the comb.

Once, the stories said, before the Assari built their dam, the reed-maidens would sit on the banks combing their long green hair before the floods came. They said the river had been wilder then, more dangerous. The gentle inexorable rush of the bound Mir was all Zhirin had ever known, all she had ever needed.

When the water reached her shoulders, she left off combing and lay back, floating in the river's embrace. The Mir's voice filled her head and she sank, and listened, and let it take her pain.

Xinai crossed the river after sunset, as shadows chased the last vermilion light into the west. Her heart was a stone in her chest—she was surprised the skiff didn't sink under its weight.

The steersmen poled in silence, lanterns doused. Insects droned across the water and frogs and night-herons splashed along the shore; an owl's deep *bu-whooh* echoed in the trees. Sounds she'd heard only in dreams for the last twelve years. She'd seen a dozen rivers in the north, but none of them sounded like the Mir.

She raised a hand to the charm around her neck, the leather pouch that held her great-grandmother's ashes, and her mother's before her. The bag thrummed softly against her skin. *Tomorrow*, she promised them. *Tomorrow I'll take you home*. The wall of trees rose above them as they neared the shore, eclipsing more stars.

She touched another charm, a beaded owl feather, and the darkness fell away. Colors faded to ghostly hints, but the river became a road of moonlight and the stars lined the treetops with gray and pierced the canopy with slivers of light. Her charms could best even Adam's keen senses, though she had no way of making the effect permanent. As the skiff scraped onto the muddy bank she leapt ashore, avoiding rocks and tangled reeds easily.

Selei snorted quietly. "Always the show-off, eh,

child?" The old woman stepped off more carefully, leaning on a steersman's arm. The ground squelched beneath their feet.

"Shall we wait for you, Grandmother?" the man asked.

"No. We'll find our own way back."

He nodded and bowed, and the boat moved away with a slurp of mud.

"Where are we going?" Xinai asked softly. Selei had been withdrawn ever since the explosion at the market that afternoon, her good eye distant and unhappy. Xinai had wanted to listen to what the city had to say about it, but the witch had kept her close all day.

"Cay Xian." She raised a hand when Xinai would have spoken. "From here we go in silence. The Khas watches these hills, and it will be worse after what happened today. We'll speak when we reach the village."

Xinai nodded, swallowing a frown, and followed Selei into the trees.

They climbed twisting hill-paths for more than an hour, or so Xinai guessed from the few glimpses of the moon she caught. The shadows under the canopy were thick enough to strain even her owl's eyes. Xian lands bordered her family's holdings, and the sounds and scents of the jungle welcomed her home.

She'd taken what comfort she could in the cold forests of the north, but it was never the same.

The path widened and the darkness ahead gave way to brighter grays. Cay Xian was close. Dust itched on her feet, grated between her toes. Boots were fine in the city, but in the jungle toes would rot in closed shoes. She missed the extra blades.

Something rustled in the trees and Xinai's hands dropped to her belt knives even as Selei called for her to stop. She recognized the squeal of a lantern hinge a second too late. Light blossomed blinding-white in front of her and she cursed, turning away as tears leaked down her cheeks. Selei's calloused hand closed on her wrist, trapping her knife in the sheath.

"They're with us," she said. "And hood that lantern, you fool. Do you think we're not watched?"

"Not at the moment, Grandmother," a man said. "Phailin distracted the Khas's soldiers."

Grandmother—not the honorific, but a kinship. Xinai hadn't realized Selei had a grandson.

The lantern dimmed and Xinai released the charm. Red and gold spots swam in front of her eyes. Rubbing away tears, she let Selei lead her toward the lights of the village.

By the time they reached the walls of Cay Xian, Xinai could see again. Torchlight glowed over the carven parapets, flickering as sentries moved along the walls. The heavy wooden doors swung open quietly, just wide enough for the three of them to slip through.

As soon as she stepped onto the yellow dirt of the courtyard Xinai knew something was wrong. This was the heart of the Xian clan, and the heart of Xian mourned angrily.

The clan's tree grew in the center of the courtyard, dwarfing the houses around it. In the flickering torchlight its cluster of trunks seemed to move, root-tendrils writhing toward the ground. Charms and mirrors hung from the branches, rattling softly even though there was no wind. People watched them from the shadows of its trunks.

Xinai glanced at Selei's grandson, seeing him clearly for the first time. Tall and lean, he wore a warrior's kris-knife at his side, the long, curving blade sheathed in silver and bone. His clothes were mourning gray and ashes streaked his long braided hair.

Others in the yard wore gray as well, if only scarves or armbands, and tears and ashes marked several faces. But the village was silent. If the clan mourned, they should have wailed and sung their grief to the trees and sky.

"What's happened?" Xinai asked softly.

As the door was bolted behind them, Selei's calm mask cracked, letting grief and anger show. Her shoulders slumped.

The man answered. "The explosion in the market today? The man who did that was Kovi Xian. His body is lost, and we can't even sing his spirit home." He spat in the dust. "If we mourn him the Khas will arrest the whole clan as accomplices. They may do that anyway."

"He was a fool," Selei said softly. "A proud, hot-blooded fool. I told him he would better serve his people alive, but his honor demanded it of him." She glanced up at her grandson. "Do you have honor, Riuh? Will it take the last of my grandchildren from me?"

His smile bared a chipped front tooth. "Don't worry, Grandmother. I'm a scoundrel—honor won't be what sends me to the twilight lands."

She smiled back wearily, then glanced at Xinai. "Forgive me, I grow forgetful in my age. Xinai Lin, this is my scoundrel of a grandson, Riuh Xian. Xinai has returned to us from across the sea."

Riuh's eyes widened. "The last Lin? Welcome home."

"Has the funeral feast begun yet?" Selei asked.

"We were waiting for you."

She nodded and took Xinai's arm again, this time for support instead of guidance. Xinai hid a frown as the old woman's bird-fragile weight settled on her. "Come, child. Tonight we feed the ghosts."

CHAPTER 7

Isyllt stands in the shop again, clutching a lamp, unable to move as shoppers swirl around her. The light streams gray and metallic through the window, like a storm threatens.

A man brushes past her. Kiril. She tries to call to him, but her tongue is numb. Her master pauses and stares down at her, his dark eyes tired and sad. He opens his hands to show her a ruby. It pulses against his palms like a heart, light scattering off faceted edges. The stone is flawed deep, and the crack spreads even as she watches.

Kiril shakes his head and the dream explodes.

And Isyllt woke gasping in the dark, the smell of smoke and charred flesh thick in her nose. She raised a hand to her face; her cheek was smooth, unburnt, damp.

Trees rustled outside her window, rippled moonlight and shadow across the floor. She sat huddled in the dark, weeping silently until sleep stole over her again.

She rose early the next day and joined the others for a hasty, silent meal before the trek to the Kurun Tam. No one looked like they'd slept well—Vasilios moved as though all his bones ached and dark circles branded Zhirin's eyes.

Wind blew sharp and salty off the bay, ruffling the canals and swirling dust and leaves. Everywhere they passed people hung colored lanterns and garlands, erected awnings along the streets. The rains were coming soon.

And everywhere they went Isyllt saw green-clad guards and soldiers red as poppies patrolling the streets and watching the ferry crossings. An uneasy hush hung over the city.

Thin white clouds veiled the sun but couldn't stop the heat, and the humidity was worse than ever. By the time they neared the Kurun Tam, Isyllt dripped sweat and the backs of her hands were baked pink. She sighed happily as they stepped into the spell-cooled walls of the hall and stopped to rinse the dirt off her face. In the courtyard, Zhirin helped Vasilios down from the carriage. Isyllt watched the old man lean on his apprentice's arm and swallowed the taste of dust. There but for the whims of fate . . .

A shadow fell across the stones at her feet and she turned to see Asheris.

"Good morning," he said with a bow. He wore riding clothes today, shades of rust and ocher that would hide dust. "I hope you slept well."

"Hello, Lord al Seth." Her smile felt too sharp and she tried to school her expression. "I'd thought the investigation might keep you in the city today."

"I had a previous engagement, but I have good people keeping their eyes on things. I'm glad you're here," he went on. "We're going to the mountain. You must join us—this may be the last chance before the rains come."

"Thank you, but I intended to study with Vasilios today."

"Bah." He waved a dismissive hand. "Study tomorrow. I promise the mountain is far lovelier than the library." He turned to Vasilios as the older mage entered the courtyard. "You'll forgive me, won't you, if I steal your companion for the day?"

Vasilios snorted, leaning on his walking stick. "I know I can't compete with your charms, Asheris. Just don't expect my bones to endure such a trek." Behind him, Zhirin stiffened but kept her face pleasantly blank.

Asheris turned back to Isyllt and his smile was beautiful and implacable. "Come, Lady."

"As you wish." She shot Zhirin a quick glance, praying the girl understood, and that she could contact Jabbor. It would take at least an hour to reach the mountain—who knew how long the meeting would be delayed.

A crowd assembled in the courtyard, including a great many soldiers. At Asheris's word, a stablehand brought Isyllt a fresh horse. Her thighs ached just looking at the saddle.

"Let me introduce you to our companions on this expedition." Asheris took her elbow and steered her toward the center of the knot of horses, where a mounted woman and young girl spoke to a man on the ground.

"This is Faraj al Ghassan, Viceroy of Symir. His wife, the Vicereine Shamina, and their daughter, Murai. Your Excellency, this is Isyllt Iskaldur, of Erisín, who was gracious enough to assist with my investigation last night."

Isyllt dropped a low curtsy, awkward though it was in

trousers. "Your Excellency." A short man, with golden-brown skin and a hooked nose too large for his face. His wife was a tiny Sivahri woman, for all her Imperial name and dress.

Faraj smiled. "Well met, Lady. Asheris tells me you did us a valuable service. The Empire appreciates your efforts. But we must speak again later—I have business in the hall, and my daughter is impatient to see the mountain." He nodded politely and touched his wife's hand in farewell before turning toward the hall.

Adam caught her as Isyllt set her foot in the stirrup. "Do you want me to come?" he asked in Selafaïn.

"If he decides to murder me on the mountain, I doubt you could save me."

His eyes narrowed as he glanced at the smoking mountain. "I don't trust that thing. I don't trust anything here."

"Good. Don't start."

His mouth twisted. "I'm doing a lot of waiting for you."

She gave him an arch smile. "But you do it so well." Feeling Asheris's eyes on her, she swung into the saddle before he could reply.

The ride up the mountain was an easy one, despite Isyllt's aching back. The road was cleared wide and paved, the horses sure-footed. The same ward-posts lined the way. She caught sight of other buildings scattered behind the hall that she hadn't visited on her first tour—lapidaries' offices, and servants' quarters.

No matter how sure-footed, horses couldn't climb the steep upper slopes. They dismounted at a way station a third of the way up and began the rest of the climb on foot.

Soldiers led the procession, with the Viceroy's family just behind. Murai, whom Isyllt guessed to be near twelve, skipped up the road, tireless and nimble as a goat. Isyllt walked beside Asheris, the rest of the guards trailing a polite distance behind.

The path was broad and smooth, but stable footing didn't lessen the unnerving whistle and tug of the wind around the rocks, or the sight of dust and pebbles rolling away into nothingness. The wooden railing seemed far too fragile for the fall beneath it.

The forest stretched below them, draped like velvet across the hills. The Mir glittered as it rolled to the sea and the bay shimmered with gray-green iridescence, shot with blue and gold where sunlight fell. Across the river lay the green slopes of Mount Ashaya, a jewel-bright lake nestled in her cauldron. Unlike her sibling, Ashaya slept, her fires cold and dead.

Isyllt glanced down and frowned. They must make a lovely target, strung like beads against the mountainside. Would rebel arrows reach so high? Sweat trickled across her scalp and stuck strands of hair to her face.

"How is it that a member of the royal house came here?" she asked Asheris, to distract herself from calculating assassinations.

"Barely a relation. But the bonds between us were enough that the Emperor trusted me to oversee things here." His voice was a shade too bland as he wiped his brow. He wore no hat—which seemed unwise despite the color of his skin—and moisture glistened across the curve of his skull and darkened his collar. "Sivahra is a valuable asset to him."

"Are attacks like yesterday's common? We hear only rumors in the north."

"They become more common, though yesterday's was worse than usual. This Hand of Freedom grows bolder, or madder. They kill their own with every such strike."

"Have you made any arrests?"

He glanced up at the sun, amber eyes narrowing against the glare. "I suspect that's being taken care of even as we speak." His smile was hard and cold, and Isyllt turned her gaze back to the path in front of her.

Xinai woke to sunlight dappling through a window, memories and dreams so tangled she couldn't tell where she was. *Home.*

But not truly, though the room with its clay walls and woven mats was nearly twin to the room she'd slept in as a child. She swallowed, the taste of last night's spiced beer sour now on her tongue. Outside, the familiar sounds of daily work drifted in the air.

The door creaked softly and her hand neared her knife hilt. Riuh Xian ducked his head into the room.

"Good, you're awake." He'd washed the ashes from his hair and replaited his beaded braids. In better light he was younger than she'd thought, not far past twenty.

"What time is it?"

"Nearly noon. You missed breakfast."

She wrinkled her nose at the thought; last night's feast still sat heavy in her stomach.

He tossed a folded bundle to her. "Grandmother says I'm to take you to Cay Lin, if you wish."

"I know the way." It came out harsher than she meant, and he began to turn away. "But I don't mind the company. Thank you."

She bathed in the clan bathhouse and dressed in hunter's clothes—calf-length trousers and loose tunic under a snug vest. In traditional clothes, she was suddenly aware of her shorn hair. Practical, but out of place among clansfolk's long beaded braids. Such a ridiculous thing to worry about, but she tugged a cap over the damp spikes anyway.

A group of girls led by Riuh's lovely cousin Phailin left the village for the stream and Xinai and Riuh went with them, ducking quietly into the woods along the way. No telling how many eyes the Khas had watching Cay Xian.

They crossed the stream—a narrow tributary of the Mir, but wide enough to survive the dry season—and headed northeast toward Lin lands. They walked in silence, but she felt Riuh watching her. She tried to ignore it, to ignore the way his hand lingered on her arm when he helped her up steep slopes and over fallen trees. Think of Adam, she told herself, think of the job, but the forest swallowed such things, filled her head with warmth and jade-colored light and the smell of sap and earth.

She nearly missed the marker. The stone had fallen, half-covered by mud and vines. Crouching, Xinai brushed away dirt and leaves, bared the carved bear clan-sign. Cay Lin was only a league away. Whatever was left of it.

Riuh stopped, wiping a thin sheen of sweat off his brow. "Would you rather go on alone?"

"Yes. Thank you."

"I'll be here."

He didn't tell her to be careful and she liked him more for that. She smiled, quick and clumsy, then turned and began to climb the bramble-choked slope that led to the village.

The woods weren't empty; all around she felt watchful eyes. Not soldiers, but ghosts and spirits. Her charms shivered around her neck. Wise to be gone from here before nightfall, though the thought galled. She should have nothing to fear on her family's lands.

Should or not, she knew she *did*. Many spirits resented human incursion into their lands, or simply found them good eating. And a clever spirit was more cunning than a tiger when it came to stalking prey, and had more than claws and teeth to bring it down.

Trails were long overgrown, landmarks reclaimed by the jungle, and it took her more than an hour to reach the stone walls. The sight of them struck like a blow in the pit of her stomach and she stumbled to a stop.

The wooden gates had rotted away, only a few moss-riddled timbers fallen in the opening. Vines crawled the walls, crumbling the arches. Wind rustled the leaves of the canopy and spears of light danced across the ground.

Cay Lin. The clan-heart. Her home. Home to nothing but ghosts now.

She crossed her arms to still her shivering, then forced them down again. Lifting her chin, Xinai stepped through the ruined gate.

The emptiness was a solid thing, a weight in her chest. Nothing dwelled here, not even animals. Shutterless windows stared like accusing black eyes; she couldn't meet their gaze. Somewhere in these leaf-choked streets was her house, the houses of her friends, the shops they'd frequented. The well she'd drawn water from, the pool where she'd tossed wishing stones—dried now. She saw no bones, though she could still remember where the bodies of her kin had lain untended. Time and weather had erased them, or the earth swallowed them.

The banyan still lived, though its leaves curled and drooped in the dry heat. Its root-tendrils had spread, stretching throughout the walls, dripping through broken roofs and pulling down houses. A forest made of one tree. Yellow dust puffed under her feet as she crossed the root-tangled yard. The slap of her sandals echoed like hammers.

A charm shivered warning a heartbeat before she walked into the trap, but she couldn't stop in time. Magic enveloped her in a rank miasma, a net of pain and suffering distilled with time and purpose. Xinai tripped on a root and fell, bruising her hands on dry earth. The gentle cacophony of the jungle vanished as long-walled-off memories broke loose to swallow her.

She shudders as the lash falls. She lost count of the strokes after the fifth, can't even feel the individual blows anymore, only the twigs that gouge her stomach, her nails cracking as she claws the ground. Pain is a red sea and she so much flotsam.

She only realizes that it's stopped by the absence of the whip-crack over her sobs and roaring pulse. Booted feet rush around her; she feels them through the yellow earth beneath her cheek. Muddy now with blood and tears and sweat. Others still cry and curse and scream. At least they're alive.

Xinai pries open her good eye and blinks away a film of tears. The other is swollen shut—she feels that pain clearly, and it nearly makes her laugh.

"Is she dead?" one of the soldiers asks. A boot lands in front of her face, leather dull with dust. She wonders if he'll kick her, but she has no strength to flinch.

"Not yet," another answers. "Do you want her for the work-gangs?"

The boot nudges her shoulder, flips her over. The blur of leaves and sky washes black as her back strikes the ground. She means to scream, but all that comes out is a teakettle whine.

"No." The man above her is a blur of Imperial crimson. Red as poppies, their uniforms, red as blood. "She'd be dead before we reach the mines. Let her rot with the rest."

She tries to roll over but only manages to turn her head. Through the forest of boots and red uniforms she sees other bodies limp on the ground, the earth trampled and soaked dark. Other villagers are roped together and dragged through the broken gates—neighbors and friends, clan-kin all of them.

"Mira," she whispers, scraping uselessly at the dirt. "Mira."

"What's that?" the soldier asks in Assari. He crouches beside her, hands loose between his knees. His tone is nearly genial now that she has no fight left.

Another man's shadow falls over her and she squints against the glare of sky through banyan leaves. Not a red-coat, this one. He wears green, with red stripes on his sleeves. Sivahri—a local guard. She closes her eyes against his traitor's face.

"She's asking for her mother," he says, his Assari barely accented.

"She's the leader's brat, isn't she? Your mother's right over there, girl. You want to see her?"

"Captain—"

"What? She made her choice, didn't she? She should see the cost." He slides a hand under her shoulder and hoists her up. Not roughly, but she shudders as his fingers brush a weal. Her braids swing across her back,

snagging on blood and torn flesh. "There." The captain points toward the heart-tree.

No, Xinai told herself, struggling for control. *It's not real. It's over.* But she couldn't break free.

Her mother slumps against the root-trunks, chin against her breast, long black hair wild over her shoulders. Her hand curls as if to hold her kris, but the blade is gone.

"Mira—" She rocks forward, catching herself on one forearm; the other arm crumples when her weight hits it. Like a three-legged dog she creeps forward on hand and knees. Pity the Assari should see her crawl, but she has no strength left for pride.

Her mother's flesh is still soft, not even cold, only drained to pasty yellow-gray. Blood spills down her chest like a necklace of rust and garnets. The air reeks of raw meat and bowel and she can't tell the smell of her mother's death from her own sour metallic stink.

If the captain laughs, she knows she'll throw herself at him, fight until he kills her and she joins her mother in the twilight lands. But he turns away, indifferent to her grief as he is to her life, and begins overseeing the removal of the last prisoners.

The Sivahri guard watches her, weary lines carved on his face. Forest-clan, she guesses. He could be kin to any of the bodies that litter the dust. His uniform is damp with blood and sweat.

"I'm sorry," he says softly in Sivahran.

She was wrong—she does have some pride left. Xinai spits. It strikes the dirt yards from his boots, but he flinches as if it hit him. She lowers her head to her mother's lifeless shoulders and closes her eyes, waiting for the darkness to claim her.

And as it had twelve years ago, darkness waited for her. Not the shallow red-lined black of exhaustion, but a deep and icy pit that fell forever.

"Leave her alone!"

She flinched at the shout and opened her eyes. A mottled gray-green face hovered close to hers, white hair tangling in an invisible wind. A gangshi. She might have known—spirits that feed on suffering would love the site of a massacre. What a feast she must be. Xinai flinched again, stronger, jerking awkwardly away from the gangshi's gaping hungry mouth and empty eyes. A charm bag pulsed and throbbed around her neck.

A woman lunged between her and the spirit, a blur of black hair and shining kris-blade. Xinai scrambled back on all fours, fetching up against a twist of banyan trunks. Her dagger trembled in her hand and she coughed as she drew a deep breath. A few more heartbeats and the gangshi would have drunk down all her pain and fear, and her life with it.

Her vision grayed and she leaned against the tree for strength. Her face was slick with salt and snot and her back burned with phantom wounds.

"It's gone now," the woman whispered, turning back to Xinai. And then, even softer, "You're back. I knew you would come home." Her voice was wind in leaves, water through river-reeds; the sound sliced through Xinai, deeper than Assari whips could ever reach.

The woman stood over her, watching with lightless eyes. Her hair hung in snarls around her narrow face, her clothes in tatters. Her skin was ashen, paler than the earth beneath her feet. Xinai's charm bag hummed against her chest.

"I knew you'd come." The ghost stepped forward and

passed through a hanging root. Xinai couldn't speak as the dead woman knelt before her. Her throat was slashed; the wound gaped when she moved, flashing bone white as pearls amid ruined flesh and crusted blood.

"Don't you recognize me, child?"

Xinai's dagger dropped to the dust. Her vision blurred again, glazed with fresh tears.

"Mother—" The word broke on a wet hiccup.

Shaiyung Lin smiled a sad, terrible smile and stretched out a cold gray hand to stroke her daughter's cheek.

"They showed me— They made me see—" She choked on snot. The gangshi's trap had undone all her defenses and she could only sob, helpless as she'd been twelve years ago.

"Don't worry," Shaiyung whispered, wrapping her icy insubstantial arms around Xinai. "You're home, and we're together, and it will be all right. We'll put things right."

The sun dipped into afternoon by the time they reached the last landing. Isyllt slumped against the carven cliff-face, trying not to double over from the sharp stitch in her side and the burn in her thighs. Stone benches circled the small platform, but she feared if she sat she'd never stand again. Wind keened around the crags, threatening her hat and tugging at her sweaty clothes.

More wards ringed the upper slopes, different from those along the road. "What do these do?" she asked, moving closer to the nearest post.

"If too much pressure builds inside the mountain, it will erupt," Asheris said. "These shunt the energy aside, bleed it off into the air."

"Or let you channel it into the stones."

"Exactly."

She reached out, not quite touching the ward-stone. Its magic shivered warm through her fingers. The edges shimmered, like the air around a flame. An intricate spell, cunningly wrought. It would be the envy of half the Arcanost—they prided themselves on being at the forefront of magecraft.

"Ingenious."

"Thank you," Asheris said, lips curving. "We are rather proud of the technique. No one has ever done this before, to the best of our knowledge."

"Be careful, Lady Iskaldur," the Vicereine called, securing the veil pinned over her hair. "Once he starts talking about his mountain, you'll be hard-pressed to silence him."

Asheris chuckled. "Her Excellency has no ear for the music of the mountain. But come, my lady, we aren't at the top yet. You must see the cauldron." He gestured toward another narrower stair leading up.

Isyllt sighed and promised herself a long bath when they returned to the city. "Of course I must."

"And me," Murai said, springing up from her bench. Isyllt felt even wearier just watching her.

"Of course, little bird. Your Excellency?"

"I've seen your mountain often enough," Shamina said. "Be careful up there, Murai."

"I always am, Mama."

"I won't let her come to harm," Asheris promised.

He took the lead as they ascended the final stair, Murai walking in the middle, sedate until they were out of sight of her mother. Then she hurried ahead, following on Asheris's heels.

Sivahra stretched below them, forests and rivers and hills, patchwork fields in the south and buildings like grains of salt scattered on a tablecloth. Isyllt took off her hat, letting the wind unravel her braid and dry her sweaty hair. The air was cooler here, without the jungle's heat and the river's damp. Then the wind shifted and she tasted hot stone and ash, the breath of the mountain.

"Isn't it beautiful?" Asheris called over his shoulder.

"Yes." She returned his smile, and the honesty of it surprised her.

He offered her a hand and helped her up the last uneven step. The wind buffeted her and she leaned on his arm as she found her feet.

Then she looked down, into the mountain, and her breath left on a wondering gasp.

A cauldron of char-black stone—the smell of it reached her even against the wind, burnt and bitter. And deep within the well a pool of molten rock bubbled gold and orange, leaking smoke.

"Can you feel it?" he asked. "The strength of it? I thought I'd never love anything as much as the desert winds, until I came here. I'd stay up here forever, if they would let me."

"Would you really? Or would you miss it, before too long?"

He didn't need to ask what she meant. "I don't know. It's not an option I can explore." He turned his head, but not before Isyllt saw the longing and bitterness naked on his face. She looked down in turn.

She took a few careful steps away, thinking to circle the cauldron's rim, but Asheris raised a warning hand.

"Please, don't. We know the rock here is stable, but I can't vouch for the other side. And if you fell there, it's a very long drop with no one to catch you. I'd much rather not spend the night searching for your body."

Isyllt glanced down the steep face and nodded. As she looked up, she found Murai watching her. The girl ducked her head.

"I'm sorry, I know it's rude to stare. But I've never seen anyone so pale before. Are you from Hallach?"

"No, I was born in Vallorn, which is farther still north. But I haven't lived there for a long time."

"Are they pirates there too?"

Isyllt smiled. "No. Vallorn has no sea, only mountains. All the pirates have to go to Hallach or Selafai."

"I was born at sea, while my parents were coming back from Assar. My mother's time came early. That's how I got my name."

"Murai?"

The girl nodded. "In Sivahran it means bird's nest"— she wrinkled her nose—"but it's really from Ninayan. Mariah. It means the sea. It was the captain's idea." She ducked her head again. "I talk too much. Asheris, will you show Lady Iskaldur the birds?"

"Of course, meliket." Asheris looked toward the cauldron, where magma cooled in ash-gray veins only to crack and melt again. He raised one hand, letting the wind billow his sleeve theatrically. A red-orange bubble swelled and burst, spitting fire that flared into golden wings. Birds wrought of flame soared from the pit, spiraling up until they hovered in front of Isyllt and

Murai. Tiny beaks opened soundlessly and sparks rained from their wings. The girl laughed in delight, and Isyllt echoed her.

After a final swoop the birds flew higher, till they vanished against the sun. Murai applauded, bouncing on her toes. Isyllt grinned at Asheris and he smiled back, and for a moment there was only the wind and the fire and the taste of magic like spiced wine on her tongue.

She wished she could have met him somewhere else, somewhen else.

Asheris's smile dimmed, and the moment with it. He glanced at the sun and straightened his shoulders. "It's time to go down. Lady Shamina will be waiting."

The light deepened and streamed sideways between the trees when Xinai finally returned to Riuh. His eyes widened and she wondered what he saw in her face. She'd wiped away the dirt and tears as best she could, but she was too light, spinning; shock still tingled in her hands and cheeks.

She didn't speak on the way back, despite Riuh's attempts to draw her out. Her head was too full of questions, all the things her mother had told her, all the things she had to ask Selei.

They heard the noise before they saw the village walls. Shouts and screams, metal on metal, the sound of clumsy feet through the brush nearby. Her pulse surged with shock and panic—for an instant she thought it was another memory-trap. For an instant she thought the memories were real.

Riuh caught her arm and pulled her behind a bank of ferns. Her knife was in her hand, blind instinct, and it was all she could do not to cut him. His attention was turned toward Cay Xian, though.

"Ancestors." She read the word on his lips—her heart raced too loud to hear it. Her hand tingled against her dagger hilt, and her back stung and itched with sweat.

Riuh drew his own knife. "We've got to help them."

"No."

They both spun at the voice. Phailin Xian stumbled out of the trees, clutching her bloody arm to her chest. "Cay Xian is overrun. You're not enough to change that." She staggered and went to one knee; blood trickled down the side of her face.

Riuh knelt beside her, wrapping a careful arm around her shoulders. "What happened?"

"Khas soldiers. They came with warrants, demanding Kovi's accomplices, members of the Dai Tranh—they named you, Riuh. We . . . resisted."

"You should have let them have me. I can take care of myself."

She shrugged, winced. "We won't lose anyone else, not without a fight."

"What happened to Selei?" Xinai asked.

"She escaped, with most of the other elders. But we paid for that."

Xinai forced her nerves aside, tugged off her cloth belt, and began to wrap Phailin's wounded arm. The cut was deep into the flesh of her upper arm, but she had at least some use of it. The girl's lips pressed white, but she made no sound.

"We have to get out of here," Riuh said as soon as Xinai tied off the bandage. He helped his cousin to her feet.

"Where?" Phailin nodded toward Cay Xian. "The soldiers are between us and all our safe houses."

"Cay Lin," Xinai said, before she could consider it.

Riuh's throat worked. "It's haunted."

"Better spirits than Khas swords." Shaiyung had driven away the gangshi, and her own witchcraft was enough to best lesser spirits.

After a heartbeat's hesitation, he nodded. "Let's go."

CHAPTER 8

Zhirin watched the procession ride toward the far gate and swallowed. The Viceroy and Imran al Najid strode across the courtyard and up the steps. There was still time to salvage their plans, and perhaps more.

"I'm going to find Jabbor," she said to Adam and Vasilios. "Wait for me inside." Her cheeks warmed as she heard the tone of command in her voice, but Vasilios only smiled and nodded.

She circled past the stables, around the library wing of the hall, but didn't head for the fig tree by the wall where she often left messages for Jabbor. Instead she waited in the shadow of the building until she saw Faraj and Imran emerge from the eastern hallway. Isyllt and her plans had distracted Zhirin from the mystery of the diamonds, but now she had a chance to investigate.

The two men walked toward the lapidary hall; the Assari mage topped the Viceroy by a head, stiff-spined and square-shouldered. Zhirin followed, keeping to the grass and shadows, a whisper of concealment hanging off her. Not that it could hide her from a mage as strong as Imran, but it made her feel better.

She felt better knowing that Asheris was gone too. Imran was a humorless and disapproving man, but he didn't make her skin crawl. Lesser spirits fell silent when Asheris passed, the way small animals cowered away from predators. No matter how charming he was, she still shivered when she met his eyes. It was the diamond he wore, she suspected—something fierce and unsettling bound in it.

The two men spoke as they walked, but she couldn't make out their words over the crunch of gravel. Her own slippers on the grass sounded ridiculously loud and she didn't dare move closer. She often enjoyed the soporific peace of the grounds, but now it thwarted her.

When they finally stepped inside the lapidary she sped up, slinking around the gray-white trunk of a neem tree and toward the back of the building. She nearly sighed out loud when she found a window open to the breeze. Crouching amid hibiscus bushes, she forced herself to ignore her racing heart and concentrate on sharpening her hearing. After a moment voices came into focus.

"It's not enough," Faraj said. Sandals scuffed against tile. "Half our tithe was in that warehouse, or more. The Emperor won't be pleased."

"We'll redouble our efforts in the mines," Imran replied. "Empty the Khas's prisons—we need every body available if you wish to collect the tithe on time."

The Viceroy sighed. "Very well. They'll be full anyway, after today." His voice faded as he paced away, loudened again as his circuit brought him near the window;

Zhirin held her breath. "But what about the rubies? Not all of them could have been destroyed in that fire. Can you locate them?"

"We can try. If we have some stones cut from the same vein, it will be easier."

Between their voices, she heard someone else breathing, and the scrape of a chisel. The old lapidary Hyun, she guessed. The man was long deaf—Zhirin had never suspected they kept him on because he couldn't overhear their plans.

"Tell the overseers—they'll help however they can." Faraj paused. "What about the other stones?"

"Again, we can try. Those will be easier, perhaps. There are less of them about to muddle our scrying."

Faraj sighed. "No wonder people say they're cursed— the wretched things are more trouble than they're worth."

Zhirin drew a sharp breath through her nose. It was true. Pain stung her mouth and she realized she was chewing her lip.

"The Emperor doesn't agree."

"The Emperor doesn't have to manage this operation. Not to mention deal with these insurgents."

"His Majesty has more than enough to concern him. But I'm sure we can recoup our loss soon enough. With Asheris's help—"

"No." Faraj's voice hardened. "Asheris is too valuable to me in the city. I need more than geomancers to govern Symir."

"You rely too much on Asheris." Disapproval colored Imran's sonorous voice. "And trust him too much. The man is dangerous—"

"The Emperor appointed him personally, didn't he—just as he did you? And Asheris has proved more valuable to me than half the members of this hall. If Ta'ashlan cannot part with more inquisitors, then I have no choice but to use the one I have to his fullest capacity."

Zhirin could imagine the stern lines of Imran's face in the silence that followed. The soft scratch of chisel on stone continued. "Very well," he said at last. "We shall make do, I'm sure."

Their footsteps—Faraj's sandaled and Imran's booted—moved away, and a moment later the door opened and shut. Hyun's chisel kept up its rhythm. Zhirin's breath left in a rush, loud as thunder to her heightened hearing. She leaned against the wall until her pulse slowed.

And she'd thought the ruby mines were bad enough. She moved out of the shrubbery, scuffing a footprint out of the soft earth of the flower bed. Did Vasilios know, she wondered, and cursed the thought. But what if he did—?

Movement in the corner of her eye distracted her. Turning, she found Jodiya watching her from the far end of the building.

Sweet Mother, had the girl caught her spying? But Jodiya didn't approach and Zhirin forced herself to keep walking. She didn't trust her voice if she had to speak, and they weren't friends, for all they were the same age and the only female apprentices. She'd made a few shy overtures, missing Sia, but Jodiya was too sly, silent most of the time and sharp-tongued the rest. Being Imran's apprentice was likely a thankless occupation, but it couldn't entirely explain Jodiya's coldness. But if she was an Imperial agent as well, that might.

Now that she thought of it, the girl reminded her of

Isyllt. Swallowing nervous metallic spit, she glanced over her shoulder; Jodiya had gone. Zhirin rubbed her arms, shivering in the warm sun, and hurried to find Jabbor.

By the time they returned to the Kurun Tam, the sun hung orange and swollen in the western sky and the meeting with Jabbor was hours past. Isyllt wanted only to sink into a bath or a comfortable chair. Instead she rinsed the taste of the road from her mouth and slipped away to find the others in Vasilio's study.

The old mage squinted over texts while Adam studied maps and Zhirin sat by the window and fidgeted. As Isyllt slipped in, the apprentice sprang to her feet.

"There's still time," she whisper-hissed as soon as the door swung shut. "He'll wait until sunset."

Isyllt sighed. "All right. Let's go, then. Where do we meet?"

"Past the fourth ward-post, on the eastern side of the road, there's a game trail. Follow it a mile and you'll find a clearing. He'll be there." Before Isyllt could turn away, the girl laid a hand on her arm. "Your ring— I didn't tell them you were a necromancer. They . . . wouldn't like it."

Isyllt nodded and twisted the ring off her finger; a ghost-band remained beneath it, a strip of white on her sun-reddened hand. She slipped the diamond into her pocket, where its weight settled cool against her hip.

Vasilios gathered his things and the four of them made their way back to the courtyard. "I'll wait for you by the ferry," Vasilios said as he stepped into the carriage.

The fourth ward-post lay half a league down the hill,

the game trail a shadowed gap in the trees. Isyllt and Adam dismounted and let their horses follow the carriage. She tried not to think of her aching feet, or the walk to the ferry.

As they stepped off the road, Isyllt stopped to scoop up a handful of dirt and pebbles. With a word of confusion, she scattered them across the trail. Then she ducked into the green and violet shadows of the jungle.

The last of the sun bled through the canopy when they reached the clearing and she feared they'd missed their chance. Then the trees rustled and Adam's sword hissed free.

"No need for that," a voice said. "If you're who you say you are." A Sivahri man stepped into the clearing, his face half-hidden by a scarf. "Are you the foreigners who wish to treat with me?"

Adam's hand brushed her arm, a warning pressure.

"We're here to treat with Jabbor Lhun."

"I am he."

She laughed softly. "Don't you know better than to lie to a mage? Send out Jabbor."

He hesitated; Isyllt folded her arms under her chest and waited. A moment later leaves rustled again and another man stepped out. Dark-skinned, his black curls twisted into nubs against his scalp. Adam let go of her arm.

"Hello, Jabbor. Did Zhirin tell you why I'm here?"

"She did. Come with us, Lady Iskaldur, and we'll speak further." He gestured toward the southern slope. "The jungle is no place to linger at night."

Isyllt blessed her mage-trained senses as she followed Jabbor's masked companion through the trees; without them she'd have killed herself falling over rocks and roots. Even Adam moved with less silence than usual. Others slipped through the shadows beside them—at least four.

Night had settled thick and black by the time they reached the village, a tiny collection of clay-and-thatch buildings gathered around a river. Not the Mir, but some smaller tributary. Isyllt waved aside a thick cloud of gnats.

"Here," Jabbor said, pointing to a building that rose on stilts at the water's edge. A tavern, from the smell.

A few people sat quietly inside; when they saw Jabbor they either vanished quickly or drew closer. They claimed a table in the back and Isyllt sat gratefully. A girl brought them a pitcher of beer and clay mugs and left without a word. Half a dozen other men and women sat down around them.

"Now, Lady Iskaldur," Jabbor said, filling their cups. "Tell me what it is you propose."

Her cup was empty by the time she finished, and her mouth was dry again. Silence settled over the table, broken only by the pop and sizzle of a gnat flying too near a lamp.

"She isn't lying," one of the women said at last.

A murmur circled the table and died. Jabbor frowned, full lips twisting. She couldn't read his slanting dark eyes.

"You want our blood to buy your freedom."

Isyllt shrugged. "If you're going to bleed anyway . . ." Someone muttered behind her; Adam tensed. "You wear a yoke. We can help you remove it. If you want idealistic fervor instead of practicality, then I'm sorry—I have none. But I do have gold."

After a moment, Jabbor nodded. "Fair enough."

Isyllt reached for the pitcher, refilled her cup. "Zhirin says you don't want bloodshed."

Someone laughed, but a glance from Jabbor silenced him. "Zhirin has all the idealism you lack. And of course we don't want bloodshed—we're not madmen like the Dai Tranh. But we want our freedom, or at the very least the equality the Empire claims to offer to all its citizens. And if that takes a war, then so be it."

She sipped enough spiced beer to wet her tongue. "The Dai Tranh. Those responsible for the attack in the market?"

"Yes. The Khas calls us all radicals and murderers, but only the Dai Tranh goes to such extremes."

"You don't ally yourselves with them?"

"They wouldn't have me." He raised one dark hand. "I'm not pure enough for their cause. Though my father was Isethi, and that country has forgotten more Assari oppression than Sivahra has ever known." He shrugged. "Anyway, I don't approve of the Dai Tranh's methods."

"Do we have an arrangement, then?"

Jabbor looked around the room—none of his people spoke. "It seems we do."

She held out a hand to Adam, who pulled a purse from inside his shirt. The bag chimed and rattled softly as she took it. "A gesture of good faith. More will follow."

Jabbor opened the pouch, poured coins and gems carefully into his hand. Unstamped gold and silver, garnets and amethysts—not mage stones, but still expensive.

"I could only carry so much, but I can have a ship sent. Gold, weapons, medicines—tell me what you need and I can arrange it."

"Good luck," he said with a humorless snort. "Perhaps you noticed the new port tariffs? Only foreign goods," he went on when she nodded, "because everything we need we can get from Assar. It's also a convenient excuse to search foreign ships, or the ships of merchants who don't toe the Khas's line."

She nodded. "I understand. Let me worry about that."

"And what happens if you're discovered? Zhirin says you've already drawn the attention of the Emperor's pet mage."

Isyllt smiled. "If the Empire captures me, my master will disavow me and I'll be left to the mercies of the Khas's soldiers. It would be some time before he could send another agent, if at all."

"Then I'll give you advice, since you're worth more to us alive. Walk carefully around that mage, no matter how charming he seems. And stay away from the Dai Tranh. They have no love for foreigners, even ones bearing gifts."

She nodded. "We will."

Jabbor stood, ending the meeting. Chairs scraped the floor as the other Tigers rose as well. "Follow the river—it joins the Mir by the ferry dock." He offered her a hand to clasp. "We'll speak again soon, Lady Iskaldur."

When they finally reached Vasilios's house, Isyllt indulged in a long bath, but not yet in sleep. Instead she pulled on a robe and combed her wet hair, then removed the shroud of black silk from the tall mirror in her chambers. An old one—the tarnished silver backing mottled her reflection, made her a wraith by shadows and candlelight.

The night was late in Erisín as well, though not quite so late as here, but she doubted Kiril would be asleep. She hesitated for a moment, then laid her left palm against the glass and whispered his name.

The mirror clouded, darkened till it matched her diamond, and she fought not to sway as the spell leeched strength from her. Perhaps she should have waited for morning after all; the distance made it difficult, and the vast salt-thick ocean between them didn't help. But she tightened her jaw and held on.

At last the mist cleared, revealing a room she knew as well as her own. Lamplight and gloom, a worn brocade chair and a desk cluttered with books and quills and empty teacups. Atop a stack of papers lay a pair of spectacles that would never leave the room—magecraft could hone the senses keen as a beast's for a short while, but couldn't undo time. No matter how much anyone prayed otherwise.

"Kiril."

A moment later he appeared, sinking into the chair and turning to face the glass. "Isyllt." Heartbeats slipped by as they watched each other. "You look well," he finally said.

"You look tired. You should rest." His hair had been streaked with gray as long as she'd known him, but now it was paler still, and white peppered his auburn-black beard. The shadows beneath his dark eyes had become permanent in the last year, the seams around his mouth starker.

He smiled, spiderweb wrinkles deepening around his

eyes. "Maybe later." An old argument, more a joke by now. Isyllt swallowed. "But how are you? How goes the trip?"

"I've spoken to the people I needed to, and made arrangements."

"Wonderful. I knew you would."

She admonished herself for the warm rush of pride in her chest. "Vasilios and Adam send their regards."

"How are they?"

"Well. Adam's upset that he hasn't got to kill anything yet."

Kiril chuckled. "Likely better if he doesn't. I'll find him bloodier work when you get back. How long do you plan to stay?"

"We need to make arrangements for supplies, and a fast ship with a clever captain. I'll stay until the ship arrives. I'll contact you when I know where it should put in to port."

He nodded. One long, ink-stained hand twitched, as though he meant to raise it to the glass. "Just be sure to bring yourself safely home."

She swallowed all the things she might have said, only nodded instead. Before she could change her mind, she pulled her hand away and let the vision fade. The glass showed her own face again, pale and stiff as a mask. She draped the mirror and turned away, praying for a dreamless night.

The night was full of ghosts and spirits. Xinai leaned against the crumbling doorway and listened to their fluting whispers and soft animal noises. She had no salt, but the firelight kept them away for now. Or perhaps they were afraid of Shaiyung; her mother lingered in the shadows of the room, watching with sunken eyes.

Not their family's house—Xinai hadn't the heart to find it yet—but another small clay building, one that had best survived the years and the banyan tree's stretching roots. Phailin dozed by the fire, her breath rough with pain.

Xinai wasn't sure how long it had been since Riuh had gone; it seemed hours, but she couldn't see the stars. She turned away from the night, leaned against the wall and watched the fire instead.

Heat and jungle noises lulled her. She woke with a start and berated herself for drowsing. Phailin still slept, but the spirits had quieted. Xinai drew her daggers and listened through broken shutters. Footsteps, stealthy through the brush. Then Riuh whistled their all-clear signal, and she sighed.

He stepped into the light, Selei and a handful of warriors with him. Xinai sheathed her blades.

"I feared—" She paused, and Selei smiled.

"You feared I'd be no match for soldiers." The woman knelt beside the fire and kindled a lantern. "Don't worry, child, I'm neither toothless nor helpless quite yet." She drew Xinai aside as Phailin's relatives entered the room. "Let them tend her. I need to speak with you." Her milky eye flickered toward Shaiyung. "Both of you."

They followed Selei into the thicket of the banyan tree, and the light cast their shadows wild and writhing amid the branches. Shaiyung stood close to Xinai, a line of cold down her left side.

"You can see her?"

Selei snorted. "I've been speaking to ghosts since before your mother first propositioned your father, girl."

"You knew she was here."

"Yes. We've talked, Shai and I." She smiled at the ghost. "She's been waiting for you."

"I'll do the rites, if you'll teach me. I'll sing her on—"

Shaiyung shook her head, twisting the gash in her throat wider. "No," she hissed.

"That isn't what she's been waiting for."

Xinai crossed her arms against the chill. "What, then?"

"She's been waiting for you to come and free her, so she can join our cause."

Shaiyung nodded.

"A ghost?"

"She's not the only one in these woods." Selei brushed dry fingertips over Xinai's eyes. "Do you see?"

And there, pale in the darkness, stood half a dozen ghosts, lurking among the tree roots. Xinai sucked a breath through her teeth. Most looked more substantial than her mother, but still gray and hollow-eyed, bearing the marks of their deaths.

"You haven't sung them on?"

"And lose allies? This is their war too, and they've already paid a higher price than any of us."

"But they should rest."

"We'll rest when the land is free again," one of the ghosts whispered, nearly lost beneath the distant song of crickets.

Shaiyung nodded again. "There aren't many us of us," she whispered. "It's hard, hard to stay awake, to stay sane in the Night Forest. So many have faded or wandered on, or been trapped in their bones."

"You're a good omen," Selei said. "The last Lin child returned. Hope for the clan again. Maybe other clans might live again too."

Xinai didn't know what to say to that—bad enough when the living pinned their hopes to her, let alone the dead. "Does everyone know of this? Riuh and Phailin and the rest?"

"Phailin does," Selei said. "But not everyone knows of the Ki Dai."

The White Hand. Xinai's eyes widened. "Rebel ghosts."

"Ghosts and witches, yes. Not all our warriors can see or hear the dead, and some wouldn't understand why we don't sing them on. The Dai Tranh works in the land of the living—the Ki Dai works in the twilight lands as well."

"So Deilin Xian—"

"Was one of us, yes. We tried to keep her away from that child, but the madness took her." Selei's eyes narrowed. "You know what happened, then? What your companions did to her?"

She nodded. "I heard."

"Can we free her?"

Xinai heard the rest of the question and swallowed. "I don't know. But the necromancer wants to treat with you, with the Dai Tranh."

"We fight for a free Sivahra, not to trade one master for another. We won't be snared in webs of foreign gold. Nor can we barter for Deilin like a fish in a market. She would understand."

Xinai's shoulders sagged. "So it was all for nothing."

Selei clucked her tongue. "We won't treat with foreigners, girl. You're kin. If you want to fight with us, we welcome you."

She glanced from Selei to Shaiyung. The ghost nodded. "Stay," she whispered.

"What about my partner? He's saved my life more times than I can count. We're . . . close."

Selei shook her head. "He may be a good man, but he has no place with us. If you care, send him away. Will you stay?"

Her chest felt too tight. Years of partnership, of friendship. It would hurt him. But she only hesitated a moment; she was home.

"I will."

"There's one thing I must ask of you first."

Xinai waited; there was always a test, a cost.

"Shaiyung is bound to this place, to the tree. You're the only one who can set her free."

She swallowed. "What do I need to do?"

"Bleed. Shed Lin blood for the tree and take a piece of its wood in return. Shaiyung will be able to leave the walls, and to find you if you're ever in need."

"All right." Xinai drew her knife, tested the edge with her thumb; it wanted honing but would serve for the moment. She touched a young tendril that hadn't reached the ground and glanced a question at Selei. The old woman nodded.

"That will do."

She pushed back her sleeve and nicked the smaller vein running down her left thumb—the first mercenary witch she'd met in the north had laughed her out of the habit of taking blood from her palm. Pressure, then the flash of pain, then beads of blood welling black in the darkness.

She tilted her arm, let the drops trace a dark rivulet into her palm.

Harder to pierce the tree's skin, and by the time she'd sawed through the tendril tip the last of the edge was gone from her blade. Sap smeared sticky on steel. She pressed her palm against the root, mingling her blood with the tree's.

Shaiyung sighed like wind in the reeds.

"Is that all?" Xinai's bloody hand tightened around the sliver of banyan root.

Selei smiled. "Welcome to the Ki Dai, child."

PART II

Downpour

CHAPTER 9

O n her eighth day in Symir, Isyllt woke in the ash-gray dawn to thunder and the hiss and rattle of rain on the leaves.

That morning the normally quiet neighborhood echoed with splashes and laughter as children scrambled outside to play in the puddles. Adults showed more restraint, but many descended their steps and lifted their faces to the rain. Marat's gray scarf was spotted with damp as she laid out breakfast dishes.

After the meal Zhirin went to the temple district for her devotions and Isyllt and Adam went with her. They'd spent the last two days sorting out arrangements for the supply ship; Isyllt thought they'd earned another day's vacation. Vasilios—whose discomfort in the increased damp was plain to see—retired to his study.

The sky hung low and dark over the city, the rain gentle but steady. Despite the umbrella she carried, the hems of Isyllt's trousers were sopping by the time they

crossed the first bridge, and the back of her shirt damp.
The canals had already risen, flowing faster and cleaner.
Tiny wooden boats and garlands of flowers rushed toward
the bay, the blossoms filling the air with their bruised-wet
sweetness. Mask-sellers hawked their wares in the streets,
cheap last-minute choices nothing like the elaborate cre-
ations she'd seen in shops.

The temple district was in the southern half of Jadewater, facing Lioncourt across the wide expanse of water
called the Floating Garden. Today the Garden swarmed
with barges and workers. The smell of incense mingled
with the rain, and coils of smoke rose from the domed and
pillared churches.

Adam lifted his head as they neared the temples, nostrils flaring in the shadow of his hood. "Xinai is here," he
said when she cocked a brow. "I'm going to look for her.
I'm not feeling especially pious today anyway."

Isyllt nodded and he melted into the eddying crowds.
Zhirin watched him go out of the corner of her eye.

"Is he as dangerous as he looks?" the girl asked
quietly.

"I hope so. It's what I'm paying him for." She tilted her
head. "Are you fond of dangerous men?"

Zhirin blushed. "Only Jabbor. And it's not the danger,
so much as his . . ."

Isyllt swallowed several teasing responses. "His passion? His conviction?"

"Yes. Ever since I met him I've wanted to be . . . more.
Cleverer, more useful. I want to help. Do you know what
I mean?"

"All too well." She smiled and shook her head at
Zhirin's curious glance. "But that's over now," she lied.

She looked away, turned her eyes toward the churches instead.

A half-dozen or so temples stood in a wide horseshoe around a fountained courtyard. Some she recognized— the Ninayan sea lady Mariah, the Assari Sun King, Sela- fai's dreaming saint Serebus—others not. In the center of the half-circle rose a tall, domed cathedral of blue-green marble. Vines trailed from high eyelet windows, spread- ing wild and green across the walls. Water flowed down either side of the wide steps and disappeared below them, perhaps back into the canals from which it came. It was toward this temple that Zhirin led them.

"Whose house is this?" Isyllt asked.

"The River Mother's. The Mir's."

They climbed the rain-slick steps and left their drip- ping umbrellas and mud-grimed shoes on a rack in the care of a young acolyte. The floor was cold underfoot.

Inside was nearly as damp as the day without. Water dripped in shining streams from holes in the roof, sluic- ing over smooth-polished pillars and swirling into curv- ing channels in the floor, filling the vaulted chamber with the music of rain and river. Flowering vines clung to the ceiling, shedding petals onto the water. People sat in si- lent prayer on benches that lined the room, or knelt beside the spirals of the water garden. Some lit candles and set them in floating bowls, while others waded quietly into a deep pool in the center of the room.

"It's meant as a place of peace," Zhirin said, her voice soft. "Of solace. We give our pain and troubles to the river, and she washes us clean."

"It's beautiful." She was gawking like a child, but the place was worthy of it.

An old woman passed them, smiling at Isyllt's expression. She wore a scarf nearly identical to Marat's, even to the pattern embroidered on the hem. Several others in the temple wore them too, mostly the elderly.

"Those scarves, the gray, do they mean something?"

"They mark the clanless. Those who've lost all their kin. To many Sivahri, it's the worst thing that can befall someone."

"So Marat—"

"Yes. Many of them end up as servants. It's a sad thing, to have no one to look after you. I'm going to leave an offering, and light a candle. Afterward I'll show you where the festival will take place."

The girl took a coin from her purse and walked toward a stand of votives. Isyllt stepped out of the way of the doors, moving into a green-shadowed corner. A place of solace indeed, and gentler than the sepulcher peace of the cathedrals in Erisín. No one built temples to the black river Dis, and that was likely for the best; it claimed enough sacrifices for itself.

As she glanced around the room, she saw Anhai Xian-Mar hunched on a nearby prayer bench. She wasn't going to interrupt, but the customs inspector looked up and met Isyllt's eyes, trying to soothe her face.

"Is something wrong?" Isyllt asked softly as she moved closer. "It isn't Lilani, is it?"

"No. No, Lia's well, and my sister too." She sighed. "It's nothing serious, truly. Only an indignity."

Isyllt hesitated for a heartbeat. "May I ask?"

"I have been suspended from my position." Anhai's lips twisted; the unhappy set of her shoulders made her look older. "The Khas arrested several members of the

Xian family for involvement in the market bombing. The port authority suggested that I take time off until the matter has been settled."

"Surely they don't suspect you?"

"Not me personally. But as all know, in Sivahra family means more than anything." The last words were so bitter Isyllt thought she might spit. Anhai glanced at Isyllt's ring and ran a hand over her face. "Forgive me. You find me at unpleasant times."

She stood, tugging her coat smooth. "I seem unsuited for meditation today. Perhaps I should see if my sister has a place for me on her boat."

Across the room, Zhirin set her tiny flame adrift and rose, the knees of her trousers damp-darkened.

"Would you like to have tea with us?" Isyllt asked. "We're only sightseeing before the festival."

"Thank you, but I should go home. Lilani and Vienh will want to attend the Dance and I should find something to wear. Perhaps we'll meet again on a happier day." With a farewell nod she turned away.

Xinai's first mission with the Dai Tranh took her and Riuh into the city, where a Xian clansman poled them through the twisting back canals of Jadewater. They leaned together like young lovers, clasping hands and laughing. Sometimes her throat tightened when she met his eyes— black instead of green.

Rain misted cool against her face, glistened in Riuh's braids. A common sight, couples walking or boating in the rain, making wishes. An ancient custom adapted to the city, when once they might have walked through the forest or along the riverbank. Most couples today hoped

only for a child or good business, not for the overthrow
of the Assari.

It's only a job, she tried to tell herself when Riuh's
thumb stroked her knuckles. But that was a lie. It was a
job, it was home, it was clan-ties and blood-ties and her
mother's fingers brushing her cheek, soft as memory. It
was freedom and revenge and other memories hot as coals
in her breast, and she couldn't tell one from the other anymore, couldn't tell where she stopped and everything else
began.

All she could do was smile back and try not to think
of Adam.

The skiff drifted close to the canal bank, where flowers
overflowed their window boxes. The water had already
risen, but not all the way. The low waterline bared wards
carved in the stone.

Riuh leaned close to shield her movements as Xinai
drew a slender chisel from her sleeve. She tensed as his
lips brushed her shoulder, but managed a giggle. With one
careful motion she dragged the blade across the stone,
gouging through crusted moss and grime to mar the sigil
beneath, then palmed the chisel and reached up to pluck a
violet blossom from the vine. She barely felt the shiver as
the ward-spell broke. With an aching smile, she threaded
the flower into Riuh's hair.

Something splashed softly beside them. Xinai looked
down, and found herself staring into the flat face of
a nakh. She stiffened; she'd never been so close to one
before. Skin pale as a snake's belly, hair a weed-tangled
cloud. Black eyes blinked, flashing white as pearlescent
membranes slid sideways. Xinai's hand dropped to her
knife.

The nakh grinned, baring rows of bone-needle teeth, and lifted one webbed hand from the water. A ruby glistened blood-black in its palm. It hissed softly, then sank beneath the surface.

Riuh touched a charm-bag at his throat. "Ancestors," he whispered. "I hope my grandmother knows what she's doing."

"So do I." The nakh had no love for the warded city, or the invader mages who had driven them out of their delta, but they weren't allies Xinai would have sought out. Gold skin or brown made no difference once someone was at the bottom of the river.

The steersman pushed farther into the city. They'd finished their section of canals and now there was nothing to do but wait for the others, and for the nakh.

The skiff neared the Floating Garden, which was full of barges and workers swarming to set up platforms and hang lanterns. As Xinai watched the construction, movement on the far bank caught her eye. A flash of white skin and a familiar cloaked shape. Adam and the witch. Her stomach tightened painfully and she swallowed. She brushed a charm, vision honing, and watched the Laii girl lead them toward the temples.

"Let me off here," she said, before she could think better of it.

"What is it?" Riuh asked.

"Something I need to take care of. Wait for me behind the temples."

The steersman pulled up to the nearest steps. Riuh reached for her arm as she rose, but she dodged easily. "Don't worry, I won't be long."

She waited for Adam in an alley beside the canal.

Rain dappled the murky green water, and low clouds cast an early twilight between the walls. Marks covered the stone, children's pictures drawn in charcoal and chalk, scrawled names and vows of love. A handprint stood out in the midst of the smeared scribbles, red brick dust not yet streaked by the rain—another of the Dai Tranh had already been here.

Rain dripped cold against her face and hair, warmed as it trickled down her neck. She didn't have to wait long, as she'd known she wouldn't. Adam could always find her. He'd thrown his hood back and tendrils of hair clung to his cheeks. He grinned when he saw her, but her own face was stiff and numb.

"What's wrong?" he asked.

Her control slipped, brows pulling together. Nothing was easy now that she faced him. "I'm sorry."

"Xin? What is it?" He glanced around, hand dropping to his sword hilt. Afraid of an ambush, and that left a bruised feeling in her chest. Voices drifted from the temple yard and rain pattered against the water. He moved closer, laid his hands on her shoulders. She fought a flinch, but his eyes narrowed and she knew she'd failed.

"I'm sorry," she said again. "I'm staying here." A clean break was always best.

"Here?"

"In Sivahra. I won't become a pirate with you after all." Her mouth twisted.

"I'll stay with you—"

She shook her head, short and sharp, and shrugged off his touch. "No, you can't. I'm sorry." The words fell like stones from her mouth, but she kept on. "Please, stay away from the festival tonight. I don't want you hurt."

Wariness diluted the pain on his face. "What's going to happen?"

She didn't answer, only reached up and unhooked a heavy silver hoop from her ear. "It's been . . . good." She pressed the earring into his palm, the metal warm as flesh, and let her hand linger against his for a heartbeat. "Thank you for bringing me home."

She leaned up and kissed him, tasted rain and salt. Then she turned and fled toward the canal. The red hand-print dripped down the wall.

Adam returned as they left the temple. Isyllt frowned at the grim lines of his expression, and Zhirin flinched.

"What's wrong?" Isyllt asked in Selafaïn. Zhirin drew back to give them privacy.

"I found Xinai. She's left us, left the job." *Left me*, she read in the unhappy set of his shoulders. "She's joined the rebels."

"The Dai Tranh?"

"Looks that way. She warned me away from the festival."

Isyllt's eyes narrowed. "Lovely. So we'll get a better show than masks and lanterns tonight. So much for our day off. We need to know this part of the city by tonight," she said to Zhirin, repeating it in Assari after the girl gave her a blank stare.

As they followed Zhirin toward the far side of the plaza, Isyllt slowed and laid a hand on his arm.

"Are you all right?"

He shook his head, scattering raindrops. "Just stupid." He tried to smile—or maybe it was a grimace. "I won't let it interfere with the job."

She nodded wry acknowledgment. "If you don't want to go tonight, I understand." He turned away from the sympathy in her voice.

"And let you get killed?"

"I can take care of myself."

"You've forgotten the part where Kiril skins me if you get hurt. It's the job—I've got your back."

She smiled. "Good. I bought you a mask."

CHAPTER 10

I'll be half-blind in this thing," Adam said, glaring at the mask in his hands.

Isyllt chuckled as she unwrapped her own costume. "But very menacing."

He snorted, running a finger over the black molded leather. A jackal's head, stylized like paintings of the *ghulim* that haunted the Assari deserts. Gold paint outlined wide slanted eyes and tall pointed ears.

"You pay me to be effective, not just menacing."

"Tonight I'm paying you to be both."

He looked the part at least, all in black, sleek northern clothes instead of the billowing southern styles. He'd make a charming counterpoint to her own white silk.

Her costume was simple, loose trousers and a long Sivahri coat that fit snug to the waist and belled from hip to calf. The fabric made it beautiful, rippling with lustrous rainbows, opalescent as moonlight and fog. The mask was white as well, a sharply pointed oval with slanting eyes and fur-lined ears. Her hair hung loose down her back and between the mask, the high-collared coat, and her soft white gloves, the only skin that showed was her eyelids.

The sky had deepened from ash to slate by the time she finished dressing, and already shouts and music drifted down the street. Zhirin waited for them in the front hall. Her mask was a simple domino, but the rest of her costume made up for it. Green and silver ribbons threaded her hair and iridescent scales gleamed on her skirt and vest. Blue-green malachite dust shimmered on her bare arms and throat, over the soft curve of her stomach.

When she saw Isyllt, the girl's mouth gaped and she brushed a hand across her left eye in a warding gesture. "Lady . . . It suits you."

"Thank you. I think."

"Are you sure you want to stay, master?" Zhirin asked Vasilios as he walked them to the door.

"I'll be fine. I'm getting too old for drunken revelry." His limp was more pronounced and he rubbed his swollen hands. "And without Marat here to force meals on me, perhaps I'll get some work done. Have fun. Be careful." He patted Zhirin's shoulder fondly and shooed them out.

The night was bright with music and lanterns, thick with the smell of wine and incense. A few mask-sellers still cried their wares, but nearly every face they passed was already covered. Herons and owls, lions and hounds, sea monsters and spirits, all dancing and laughing in the streets. The rain had paused, as if in encouragement, but clouds still rode the rooftops and Isyllt's face was soon damp and sticky beneath her mask.

The guards were out in force as well; red uniforms

marked nearly every street corner, stood like pillars adorning alleyways. None wore masks.

They followed the crowd toward the water plaza. Banners and garlands hung from roofs and bridges, and candles bobbed like fireflies in every canal. The crowd thickened when they reached the streets around the Floating Garden, till they couldn't move without brushing arms and shoulders or tangling in someone's costume.

"This is madness," Adam said, their masks bumping as he leaned in. "We have to get out of this. If something happens—"

She nodded and tried to push her way to the far side. They hadn't reached the next building when drums rolled nearby and half the crowd began to dance. Someone grabbed Isyllt's hands and spun her around. She laughed in spite of herself, but by the time she slipped free she'd lost sight of Adam and Zhirin.

A new partner seized her, a man with a raptor's wicked beak, his mask a glorious crown of red and gold feathers. Gold thread gleamed on fluttering sleeves and topaz and garnet chips rattled as he moved. Wings hung lovely and useless down his back, two pairs. A jinn.

He caught her hand and bowed over it, graceful even in the unwieldy mask. His magic crawled against her skin and she knew him.

"Lovely, my lady," Asheris said. "But too plain. You should be hung all in opals."

"We can't all burn as bright as you, Lord al Seth."

"No, I suppose not." He twirled her and pulled her out of the flow of the crowd. Someone jostled her in passing and she steadied herself against his shoulder.

"I keep running into you," she said, leaning close to

his ear. "I might suspect you were following me." Foolish to tease him, but the heat and energy of the dance stole away her caution.

His lips curled in the shadow of his beak. "This isn't a night for suspicions."

"Then why so many guards?"

"That, my lady, is caution, and sadly well-founded."

She nodded, fighting the urge to pass on Xinai's warning. But he knew as much as she did, doubtless, and she needed no more attention.

Before she could speak, Zhirin appeared, laying a light hand on Isyllt's arm to keep them from drifting apart.

"My escort," Isyllt said, nodding farewell to Asheris. "Perhaps I'll see you again tonight."

"I suspect you shall." He bowed again and Isyllt let Zhirin lead her away. He was dangerous, she reminded herself. But that never stopped her as often as it should.

Wooden platforms covered most of the Floating Garden, firmly lashed together and to the banks. Some were stages for musicians, some dance floors, others bridges. Lanterns bobbed in a web of ropes overhead, their reflections like colored moons in the night-black water. Theater boxes had been erected around the plaza, raised and sheltered vantages from which to watch the revelry.

"Adam's on the other side," Zhirin said, pushing her way through.

Isyllt stepped onto the rocking boards, but a new song started and she was caught in another dance. She dodged reaching hands, balancing on the edge of the platform as dancers spun, trading partners as they twirled. Feathers and sequins littered the wood.

When she neared the far side, a man in a fox mask—copper and black instead of white—offered her a hand from the bank. As she reached for it, the barge trembled under her feet. A dancer stumbled drunkenly beside her and his companion giggled. Isyllt's stomach tightened and she tensed to leap for the shore.

Too late. Her fingers brushed the man's and the water erupted in a violent fountain, flinging flowers and candles into the air. The barge surged up, snapping its moorings as it capsized. Someone screamed, and then the water closed over Isyllt's head.

All around she heard frantic splashing and muted shouts from above. Water seeped into her mouth, bitter with silt. Her coat weighed her down, fouled her legs as she tried to swim. A hand caught her arm, rescuer or fellow victim, and she reached for it.

But the flesh she touched was nothing human and whatever held her was dragging her deeper.

She ripped off her mask and summoned a sickly white ghostlight that glowed through the murk. Black eyes paled to pearl in the sudden glare and the creature bared needle teeth in a silent hiss. No seductive siren, this—webbed hands and sea-wrack hair, a mouth twice as wide as a man's. A finned tail like a sea serpent's lashed the water, coiling around Isyllt's legs.

A nakh. She groped for her knife but found only wet silk and scales. Already her chest burned and she fought to keep her mouth shut. Claws scored her flesh. *Just take a breath*, she thought, wild and reckless. The river will take the pain.

She rallied her scattered wits, abandoned the knife in favor of better weapons. Her ring blazed through her

glove, shards of light aimed at the creature's eyes. It recoiled, letting go of Isyllt's arm.

It wasn't alone—at least half a dozen sinuous monsters
moved in the water, dragging down other hapless cele-
brants. Black ribbons of blood twisted on the current.

She kicked up, but the nakh recovered too quickly. Its
wide hand closed on her ankle and jerked her down so
hard that she nearly gasped. Air leaked from her nose and
mouth and dark spots swirled across her eyes.

A splash broke the water above them, a burst of silver
bubbles as someone dove into the canal. Isyllt kicked at
the nakh, slammed her heel against the side of its head
and wished for heavy boots. It snapped at her and she
barely jerked her foot away in time to keep all her toes.

A voice carried through the water, clear and echoing
with magic, though Isyllt didn't understand the words.
The nakh flinched and released her leg. Its kin let go of
their prey as well. Another shout and they turned and
glided down, vanishing into the darkness below.

Isyllt's light faltered and died; the current had her now,
pulling her on. Then someone grabbed her hand and she
began to swim, clawing the water in desperation.

Her head broke the surface and she gasped a heartbeat
too soon, swallowing a bitter mouthful. Someone else
caught her, dragged her onto stone steps and let her collapse in a sodden, coughing heap.

She raked her hair from her face, blinked grit from her
eyes. Adam stood beside her, still mostly dry. The current
had carried them away from the plaza, but she could still
hear the screams and sobbing.

"Who went into the water?" she asked.

"Zhirin. She's still in there."

As he spoke, the choppy surface of the canal bulged, and the girl rose, water and magic sluicing off her in shining streams. The water cradled her, carried her to the steps.

Isyllt pushed herself up and winced; her ankle ached where the nakh had yanked on it. "How did you do that?"

Zhirin smiled. "I am the river's daughter." For a moment her voice was changed—older, deeper. Isyllt shivered.

"What happened to the nakh?"

"I sent them away, back to the bay." She shook her head, and the echo of the river vanished. "They should never have been here—the inner canals are warded."

"Not any longer, it seems. The Dai Tranh knows its business."

Footsteps approached, and she turned to see the fox running toward them. "Do explosions always attend you?" He lifted off his mask, revealing sweat-sheened tawny skin and tangled curls. The man from the fabric shop. Kohl smeared around his eyes, trailing black tears down his cheek.

"Not usually. I think the city has a sense of humor." As if in answer, the clouds opened with a sigh and warm rain misted down. At least the city wouldn't burn.

"If this keeps up, one might suspect a connection."

Isyllt's eyes narrowed. "One might say the same to you."

His smile stretched, wry and crooked. "One might. I only wanted to make sure you didn't drown." He bowed, his coat glittering with bullion. "Perhaps we'll see each other again, meliket."

"Will the city survive if we do?"

"We'll find out." He turned into the shadow of an alley and was gone.

They took a longer route back to Raintree—some streets were still clogged with frantic people and all the skiffs had vanished. Isyllt's wet shoes rubbed a blister as she walked.

"Do you know that man?" she asked Zhirin, cursing herself for not asking after the market.

"No. I thought I saw his mask near one of the boxes, though. He may be from the Khas."

That would be all she needed, attracting the attention of yet another Khas agent.

Lights burned in windows all down Campion Street—people up late celebrating, or worrying over the news? But Vasilios's house was black and cold.

Isyllt paused. She'd never seen the house without some sliver of light. "Could he have gone out?" she asked as they climbed the steps.

Zhirin frowned as she found the key on her belt. "So late, in this weather—it would be odd." Isyllt nearly stopped her as she slid the key home, but the lock turned with no burst of flame.

But as they stepped across the threshold, Isyllt's ring chilled. Her jaw tightened. "Something's wrong."

"What?" Adam asked.

"Someone's dead." She reached, listening, but heard nothing. Weak light spilled past her and she glanced down. No wet footprints marked the tile, no mud stained the rug but what clung to their shoes. "Adam?"

"I can't tell. It smells like it usually does."

She followed the chill upstairs to the study. A flutter of

movement in the shadows made her tense, but it was only the curtains dancing in the damp breeze from an open window. The lamps were out and she conjured witchlight as they entered the room. Eyes flashed in the sudden glare and the cat hissed and vanished in a pale blur. Zhirin gasped.

Vasilios lay sprawled facedown across the carpet beside his chair, one arm twisted behind his back, the other reaching for his throat.

She moved closer to the corpse, the light floating in front of her. A length of silk circled his throat and his face was dark and swollen. Zhirin let out a choked sob.

Isyllt willed the light closer. The silk was blue, familiar. "Black Mother," she whispered, stiffening. Her scarf, that she'd worn their second night in the city; she'd forgotten she lost it.

"Adam, check the house, and the back."

He nodded and vanished down the black hallway.

Tugging her wet coat-skirts aside, she knelt beside Vasilios. No trace of a lingering ghost, of course—that would be too easy.

"What are you doing?" Zhirin asked as she reached for his face.

"Finding out what happened."

The vision came quickly: *She sits in the chair, a book in her gnarled and spotted hands, reading by the steady golden glow of a witchlight. No sound of footsteps, but a breath of displaced air warns of a presence in the room. She looks up, too slowly.*

Only a flicker of darkness as the scarf loops over her head, then crushing pain as it draws tight. So strong—

cutting off blood, crunching the windpipe. The light sput-
ters and dies as she claws for her attacker. Or maybe
that's just her vision blacking . . .

Isyllt jerked away with a gasp, one hand flying to her
throat. Her light flickered with her speeding heart.

As her pulse slowed, she realized Zhirin was gone. Then
she heard the footsteps. Heavy booted feet rushing up the
stairs. A lot of them. Lantern-light flooded the room as
she spun.

And found herself facing an eagle-headed jinn and a
troupe of red-clad soldiers. In front of the procession, Zhirin hugged herself, her face sickly in the unsteady light.

Asheris took off his mask and handed it to the closest
soldier. He stared at Vasilios, then back at Isyllt.

"I hoped," he said softly, "that they were wrong. We've
had enough unpleasantness tonight."

Isyllt rose, damp cloth peeling off her skin. "That who
was wrong?"

"The anonymous person who reported a disturbance at
the Medeion house."

"And you came yourself? Aren't you needed in the city
right now?"

"The city guards have things in hand, as much as they
can. More must wait for morning. And if you were involved in any trouble, I thought it best to come myself."

She cocked an eyebrow. "You think I was part of
this?"

"I think someone wants me to believe you were."

"We just returned," Zhirin said, fear a shrill edge in
the words. "You can't think—" Her voice broke and she
rubbed a hasty hand over her face.

"Forgive me, Miss Laii. This has been a very unhappy

night, and it's cruel of me to prolong it. I'll arrange for an escort to take you home to your family. Until I learn who's responsible for your master's death, I don't feel it safe to let you travel unaccompanied. Or you, Lady Iskaldur— you'll be under my protection until this is resolved."

Trapped, as easy as that. "You're too kind, my lord."

"Where is your companion?"

"We were separated at the festival. I'd expected him to return by now." A cautious stretch of *otherwise* senses found Adam lurking in the garden below the open window. She pushed as hard as she dared, not taking her eyes off Asheris. *Away, go!*

"I'll leave men stationed here. When he returns, they'll bring him along."

"What about our luggage?"

"I'll have that brought too, when we're done searching the house. I trust you'll forgive the inconvenience."

"Of course."

She accepted his offered arm and his hand closed on her, gentle and inexorable as shackles.

From the shelter of a fern bank on the northern shore, Xinai watched the lights of the city. Lukewarm rain misted around her, whispering against the leaves, gleaming as it rolled off fern fronds.

No point in watching, she knew. Even her night-charmed eyes couldn't see so far, couldn't watch what happened in the city's heart. There would be no fires tonight, no plumes of smoke to mark their success. The scattered groups of Xian revolutionaries made offerings to the spirits tonight, but there would be no masks or dancing in the forest camps.

This was not the kind of death one should celebrate, even if it was necessary. It left her stomach cold, and she wasn't sure why. She'd witnessed crueler things. She'd done crueler things.

The air chilled and her skin crawled with gooseflesh as Shaiyung appeared beside her. "Don't mourn them, gaia. They made their choices, as we made ours."

Xinai nodded, shuddering as her mother draped an icy arm across her shoulders. The ghost was clearer now, her touch stronger.

"I've waited so long for this," Shaiyung whispered. "Soon we'll have what we've dreamed of, what we've bled for." She raised a pale hand to the wound in her neck; Xinai nearly mimicked the gesture.

"What will you do then? Will you go on?"

"And leave you again? I want to see the land remade, cleansed. I want to see my grandchildren. All their whips and knives won't take that from me again. Your children will rebuild Cay Lin."

"Ch-children." Xinai drew her knees close against her chest, tried to rub warmth into her hands. "I've never thought of that. Of a family." A mercenary camp was no place for a baby, and neither she nor Adam had ever wanted to settle down.

"I've seen the way Riuh looks at you," Shaiyung said with a smile.

"Ancestors!" Her teeth chattered as she laughed. "No need to matchmake yet, Mira. Let's win the war first."

"We will." Shaiyung pulled her closer, and the familiarity of the embrace made Xinai's eyes sting. "They bound the mountain and the river, but they can't bind us."

Leaves rustled nearby, almost quiet enough to be the wind's work. Shaiyung vanished, leaving Xinai shivering in the damp. She reached for a blade, but it was only Riuh.

"How did you find me?" she asked as he crouched outside her shelter.

He grinned crookedly. "You walk softly, but not so soft that I can't find your trail." He ducked under dripping fronds and knelt beside her.

"I'll have to practice." The warmth of his flesh lapped at her, feverishly hot after Shaiyung's embrace.

"What's wrong?" he asked after a moment's silence. "It's not just what we did today, is it?"

"No."

"Was it the man you met in the city?"

Her eyes narrowed. "You followed me?"

He shrugged. "I see how much my grandmother cares about you. I'm not going to let something happen to you out of carelessness."

"Or courtesy?"

"That either."

She snorted. "He was my partner for years. I thought I'd never come home again. It's hard to leave a life behind, even for a better one."

"What was it like, the north?"

"Strange, at first. Different. Mountains sharp as tiger's teeth. Seasons so cold everything freezes, even your breath. People pale as ghosts. The forests taste different."

Riuh shook his head. "I don't think I would have been so brave. The elders used to rail at me for being wild, traditionless, but I don't know if I could have left Sivahra."

"I had nothing here. Aren't you wild anymore?"

"Sometimes." He grinned again, but it faded quickly. "But it's not the same. I never cared much about the Dai Tranh, about the cause. I ran with the prides in the city, stayed away from Cay Xian."

"What happened?"

"My father was arrested after a raid. They said he would be sent to the mines, a three-year sentence. Grandmother tried to find him—she knows people everywhere—but he wasn't there. He was just gone. No body, no rites, no songs. We've never discovered what happened."

Xinai laid a hand on his; he squeezed her fingers and frowned. "You're freezing." He shifted closer, his warmth burning against her shoulder, and pressed her hand between his. "It hit Kovi hardest of all, but even I couldn't ignore that. We can't let the Khas keep doing this to us."

"No," she whispered. Her head spun and she closed her eyes. Riuh's arm settled over her shoulders, warm and solid. He touched the short hair at the nape of her neck and she shivered.

"Not very traditional, I know," she said with a wry smile.

"I like it. We can do with a few less traditions."

This was wrong. The smell of his skin, the fit of his hand around hers. She needed time . . . But she was so cold, a northern winter gnawing at her bones. He could make her warm again.

Riuh's calloused fingers brushed her cheek, tilted her head toward his. His thumb traced her lower lip and her pulse throbbed like surf in her ears. She should say no, but his lips brushed hers, soft and tentative, and she couldn't speak. Her hand rose to his shoulder—her body felt like a stranger's. Like a puppet.

"No—" she whispered against his mouth. He pulled back, and she shuddered with the absence of heat. Clumsily she jerked away, hand slipping in mud as she landed on her hip. Her chattering teeth closed on her tongue and the taste of pain and blood filled her mouth.

"What's wrong?"

She shook her head, scrambling to her feet; her flesh was her own again, but she couldn't stop shaking. "No," she said again, more to her mother than to Riuh, but she couldn't explain that to him. Instead she turned and fled into the night and the rain. He didn't follow.

CHAPTER 11

The room was pleasant enough, but still a prison, no matter how decorative the bars on the window. Isyllt paced a quick circuit after Asheris and the guards left—a bedchamber and a bath, all the amenities courtesy dictated, but nothing that might easily become a weapon. Nothing resembling a mirror.

She paused in mid-pace as the weight of her kit swayed against her thigh. At least that wasn't at the bottom of the canal. She slipped it out of her coat pocket; the leather hadn't taken well to water and the silk wrappings were sodden, the salt dissolved, but her tools were still intact. The mirror lay cold and quiescent in her palm as she wiped off water spots with a corner of the coverlet.

The black surface showed her pale and weary face, her hair hanging in knots over her shoulders. At least no spirits waited on the other side—she was in no shape to fend off anything deadlier than a gnat.

"Adam," she whispered, leaning close to the glass.

But the mirror remained still. Wherever he was, she couldn't reach him through the reflected world.

Isyllt sighed and wrapped the mirror in its soggy silk. She was too tired for clever plans. The best she could hope was that no one killed her in the night and quietly sank her body into a canal. One more missing spy. She stripped off her damp and soiled clothing, tucked her kit beneath the pillow, and crawled into the feather bed.

The bed, at least, was soft. She didn't dream.

The creak of the door woke her. Isyllt blinked sticky eyes as a woman dressed in servant's clothes slipped in. Apricot dawnlight trickled through the leaves and puddled over the casement.

The woman dipped a curtsy and laid clothing on top of the dresser. "Good morning, Lady. Lord al Seth has requested that you join him for breakfast at your convenience." She stepped into the bathroom and water gurgled and splashed into the tub. "And he says the rest of your luggage should arrive later today. Do you need any assistance?"

"No, thank you. Tell Lord al Seth I'll be with him soon."

The maid nodded and ducked out the door, giving Isyllt a glimpse of the armed guard standing in the hall.

For her own protection, of course.

She washed her hair twice and combed it with oil, and still had to rip out several knots. The dusty-sweet scent of lavender soap clung to her in a cloud, like a stranger leaning over her shoulder. She pinned up the damp length of her hair and dressed in the trousers and long blouse the maid had left. They were too short, but at least clean and dry. The slippers were hopeless and she wore her own, wincing as they pinched the fluid-filled blister on her right foot.

The guard led her down a long corridor. Mostly other living quarters, she guessed, perhaps guest rooms; the floor was quiet, and she felt no one else nearby. The third-story windows looked over rain-soaked grounds and gardens, the rooftops of Lioncourt blurry beyond the Khas's walls.

The guard waited outside Asheris's suite as the mage led her into his sitting room. Light filled the northeastern windows, cool and gray. The air smelled of food, but also of disuse, and dustcloths draped some of the furniture.

"Excuse the mess," he said as he waved her toward a chair and poured coffee. "I hadn't planned to return so soon. How are you feeling?" Plates covered a low table, bread and hummus, honeyed nutcakes, sliced boiled eggs, and cold poultry with fruit preserves. She usually had little appetite so early, but her mouth began to water at the sight of food.

"Well enough, considering." Brocade rustled as she sat, and she nearly sighed as her weight left her feet. Nothing like weeping blisters to slow an escape attempt. She accepted a cup of coffee, inhaling the rich, bitter steam happily; Assar taxed the beans heavily and the drink was rare and costly in the north. "How is the city?"

He frowned, dipping a slice of bread into the hummus. "The structural damage isn't too bad—a few canal walls fractured, but nothing sinking. So far we've found eighteen dead in the canals, drowned or killed by nakh. More are still missing."

Isyllt took a bite of pastry, honey melting across her tongue. Yesterday's breakfast seemed years past. "Do you think the people responsible are the ones who murdered Vasilios?" She cocked an eyebrow. "Or do you think I killed him?"

"I don't," he said after a moment's pause. "But someone wants me to think you did. The simplest of spells will link the scarf that killed him to a gown in your luggage." He sipped his coffee. "Do you know why anyone would want to implicate you?"

She met his eyes over the rim of her cup. "A foreigner— a necromancer, no less—who's already been seen snooping around? I imagine it was too much to pass up. I'm told the natives aren't fond of my sort of magic."

"No." He glanced toward her ring. "It's quite anathema." She finished the last bite of pastry and he pressed a saucer of eggs and meat on her.

"But why kill Vasilios at all?" she asked, salting the eggs.

"That I don't know. And that's why I'd prefer you stay here until I find out. What do you think has happened to your bodyguard?"

She swallowed carefully. "I don't know. I hope he's not one of those missing in the canals. But he is a mercenary— perhaps he decided I'm not worth the trouble. How long should I plan on staying here?"

"We'll make every effort to find those responsible. Of course, if you'd prefer to leave immediately, I could find you passage on an Imperial ship . . ."

"You're too kind. But no, I'd rather stay and learn who's responsible. My master wouldn't wish me to leave with an old friend's death unsolved."

"Of course. You may explore the grounds as you wish—
the guards can direct you. The gardens are quite lovely—"
Even as he spoke, the light dimmed and grayed and rain
rattled the leaves. Asheris glanced at the fat raindrops
rolling down the windowpane and sighed. "But perhaps
not this morning. We're having a ball tonight, however,
safely indoors. I'd be delighted if you would attend."

"A ball? After what happened?"

He shrugged. "The Khas always holds one to celebrate the rains. I imagine it will be more subdued than
usual this year. Will you come?"

"If my luggage arrives." She tugged at one too-short
sleeve. "I'm not very presentable like this."

"I'm sure we can find you something."

The pigs were a long time in dying.

Of all the sounds of Sivahra, that was one Xinai hadn't
missed. She lay curled on the floor of a hunter's blind,
trying to concentrate on the snores of her companions
and the rain on the roof, while pigs died shrieking in the
valley below.

Cay Xian had emptied overnight; elders and children
and women too pregnant to fight slipped away to neighboring towns, while warriors scattered into the forest.
By now the village stood empty as Cay Lin.

Selei slept beside her, snoring softly, and Riuh drowsed
on the far side of the room. He hadn't spoken about last
night, thank all the small gods. Shaiyung hadn't spoken
of it either, hadn't spoken at all, though Xinai occasionally felt the cool draft of her presence.

Bad enough trying to keep your living mother from
meddling in relationships, let alone a ghost.

A birdcall sounded in the trees outside, was answered a moment later. No real birds, but Xian warriors keeping watch.

One high squealing shriek faded and another began. Xinai winced and tugged her blanket tighter around her shoulders. As a child, she'd wondered if men screamed like that as they died. Funny how inured she'd become to the sounds of a battlefield, but animals being slaughtered could still upset her so.

As the sky paled to a gray ceiling behind the lattice of leaves, Xinai gave up on sleep. She slipped outside to relieve herself, and when she returned Selei was awake and folding their blankets.

"What's the plan?" Xinai asked.

"I'm going to talk to the village. We need food and supplies, safe houses. But I have another task for you two." She gestured them closer, tsking when she looked at Xinai. "I hoped you'd at least get a good night's sleep before I sent you off."

Xinai and Riuh sat beside Selei, their knees not quite touching, both carefully not looking at each other.

"We thought people were disappearing in the ruby mines," Selei said, "that the Khas was lying about accidents and deaths. It's worse than that." She pulled a pouch from her pocket, unwrapped it carefully. A stone lay on the cloth, rough and pale. It glittered in the light, color sparking in its heart.

"What is it?" Riuh asked.

"A diamond. They're mining diamonds somewhere in Sivahra, using our people to harvest their soul-stones."

Xinai reached out a hand, pulled it back again. "Where?"

"We don't know. They've kept the secret well. We might never have known, but we found this stone in a raid on a government warehouse."

"Part of the tithe?"

"I don't think so. They were stored with the flawed stones, the ones the Khas sells. I don't know what game al Ghassan is playing, but I mean to find out."

"What do you want us to do?" Xinai asked.

"Find the mine. From the routes we've seen the soldiers take, we guess it's somewhere to the west, between the mountain and the mines. I've charmed this stone as best I can to seek out others of its kind. Just be careful it doesn't lead you straight to a Kurun Tam mage." She wrapped the diamond again and handed the pouch to Xinai, who slipped it carefully around her neck. It hung quiet among her other charms.

Selei's joints creaked as she rose and Riuh steadied her. "You need a proper bed," he said.

She snorted. "In what house? The jungle is the safest place we have now."

Xinai hesitated, but Riuh was right—the old woman looked exhausted and moved stiffly. "You could use Cay Lin." She waited for Shaiyung to offer protest, but none came. "It has walls, if nothing else," she went on. "Even a few roofs."

Riuh made a warding gesture. "But the ghosts—"

"I'm not afraid of ghosts," Selei said. "But the Khas soldiers are, and everyone knows the ruins are haunted. A good idea."

Xinai tried to ignore the warm rush of pride. It was sacrilege, but she doubted any of the Lin ancestors would begrudge their allies a little succor.

They rolled the blankets into their packs, took rations of salt pork, cassava root, and fruit leather from the blind's stores, and descended the hill to the village. Xao Par Khan, Selei had named it, one of the dozens of tiny communities that dotted the forest, away from clan-seats. The Khans, like the Lhuns, had lost lands to the Empire, but had never been slaughtered wholesale like the Lins and Yeohs.

Xao Par sat in one of the myriad narrow valleys that fanned away from the mountain, a collection of simple wood-and-thatch buildings beside a rain-swollen stream. Children were already out tending plots of yams and lentils. The pigs had finished dying by the time they reached the outskirts. Dogs barked as they approached, rusty brindled beasts the same color as the mud. Soon some of the villagers leaned out their doors.

"We've come from Cay Xian," Selei called. "I need to speak with your elders."

A few moments later an old man emerged, leaning on a young woman's arm as he descended the steps of his house.

"Xians." He glanced at Riuh's kris-knife, at Xinai's daggers. "You're the ones calling yourselves the Hand of Freedom, aren't you?"

"We are. The Khas's soldiers have driven us from Cay Xian."

The old man cocked his head, eyes glittering beneath sagging lids. "And you've come here for help."

"That's right. We need food, shelter. If any of your warriors wish to join us, we would welcome them."

"There are no warriors here. Only farmers and woodsmen. And certainly not murderers." He lifted a curt hand when Selei tried to speak. "I know what it is your people do."

Selei lifted her chin. "We fight for Sivahra. A free Sivahra."

"A Sivahra watered in blood. We want no part of your cause, and we won't harbor murderers. The Khas leaves us in peace here, and we intend to keep it that way."

"How long do you think that will last? How long before they decide they need your land, or need your children in the mines?"

"They'll decide that much sooner if they find you here. Go on—take yourselves back to Xian lands. We want none of you."

Selei's eyes narrowed. "As you wish." She turned, shoulders stiff, and waved Xinai and Riuh toward the jungle. When Riuh would have protested, she cut him off.

"No. It's their decision."

As they walked, she glanced over her shoulder and whispered something Xinai couldn't hear.

"Go on," Selei said. "The sooner you find that mine, the better. I wish I could go with you, but I'd only slow you. I'll wait for you in Cay Lin."

Riuh stooped to kiss her cheek. "We won't let you down, Grandmother."

The air chilled, prickling the back of Xinai's neck. She looked for Shaiyung, but saw nothing except a light mist curling across the ground.

"Selei, what's happening?" Tendrils of fog writhed toward the village.

"They made their choice, child. You should go. Don't turn back, whatever you hear."

"But what—"

"Go. There's nothing left here you need to see."

Xinai hesitated, but Riuh caught her elbow and steered her gently toward the path. Gooseflesh roughened her arms and legs as the cold intensified. They were deep into the jungle when she heard the first scream. Riuh stiffened but kept moving. She tried to pretend it was only another pig.

CHAPTER 12

Zhirin paced. Her head was still achy and muddled from crying, and movement didn't help, but she couldn't sit still. Every time she did, the images caught up with her: blood in the water, drowning screams, Vasilios's black and swollen face. She scrubbed a hand across her eyes as fresh tears welled.

But she couldn't hide in her room forever either. Her mother had knocked three times already and eventually she'd demand Zhirin answer.

She paused beside her window, leaned her forehead against the cool glass. Raindrops trickled down the pane, fat beads of rain darkening the stone and trickling through the gutters before eventually joining the river. Zhirin wished she could lose herself in the water so easily. Already the current rolled on, washing away the blood and corpses, easing the shock of shattered stone; the river took all the pain.

She straightened, wiping the oily smudge of her skin

off the expensive glass. Nearly noon—she had to go downstairs sooner or later. She rubbed her eyes again and opened her wardrobe, wafting the fragrance of imported cedar into the air. It had been a long time since she'd worn her mourning clothes, but they were still tucked inside, gray trousers and long blouse. Her mother would never let her leave the house with ashes in her hair.

After dressing and twisting her tangled hair up in sticks, Zhirin eased open her bedroom door. The third floor was quiet, no lamps burning against the rainy gloom. Rain-streaked windows cast rippling shadows over the tiles at the end of the hall.

On the second floor she heard soft voices from her mother's study. She shook her head at the familiarity of it—had it been only seven days since she'd last come home? This time, she paused outside the door and listened.

"When will your next shipment be ready?" Fei Minh asked.

"At this rate, who knows?" Porcelain clinked and Faraj sighed; Zhirin was becoming far too familiar with the sound of his muffled voice.

"I can't just order my ships to sit in harbor all season. People will talk. Not to mention the money I'd lose."

"We'll lose more than money if this fails. And we only need one ship."

Zhirin swallowed; the pit of her stomach chilled, but she was too tired for true shock. *Oh, Mira. Not you too.*

"The *Yhan Ti*," Fei Minh said after a moment. "She's dry-docked anyway. I'll tell the captain to take her time with the repairs." A cup rattled against a saucer. "You have to do something about these terrorists, Faraj. My daughter could have been killed."

The fierce protectiveness in her mother's voice made Zhirin's eyes sting again. She pressed a hand over her trembling mouth to stifle a sob. Swallowing tears, she knocked on the door and pushed it open.

Her mother rose, and Faraj set aside his cup.

"Darling—" Fei Minh raised a hand, let it fall again.

"Do you know yet?" she asked Faraj. "Who murdered Vasilios?"

"No. Asheris is investigating. Do you know anything that might help him?"

"They asked me that last night. No. He was . . . a good mage. A good master. An old man." Her voice sounded hollow; she was hollow. No blushing now, no stammering. Was this how Isyllt did it? Scrape out everything that mattered, leave nothing but the cold?

"I'm sorry," Faraj said, not meeting her eyes. He rose, straightening his coat. "Will you come to the ball tonight?" he asked Fei Minh.

Zhirin's brow creased. "You're still having a ball?" The festival usually lasted for days, but after last night she couldn't imagine anyone celebrating.

He spread his hands and shrugged. "It's a victory for them if we don't. We can't let them grind us down so easily."

She swallowed half a dozen answers, pressed her lips tight.

"I don't know yet," Fei Minh said, carefully not glancing at her daughter.

"I understand. Again, Miss Laii, I'm sorry for your loss." He waved Fei Minh back as she stepped toward the door. "I can see myself out."

Zhirin waited till she heard the front door close to

pour herself a cup of tea from the cooling pot. Fei Minh watched her carefully—afraid she'd start crying again, perhaps. Tea washed away the taste of tears, bitter replacing salt; leaves clung to the sides of the cup, swirled lazily in the dregs.

"Your business with Faraj," she said at last, "your personal investment. It's stones, isn't it? It's diamonds." A tea leaf stuck in her throat and she fought a cough.

Fei Minh blinked, dark lashes brushing her delicately powdered cheeks. Pale as any pure-blooded mountain clan, and she had always taken care to show it, instead of counterfeiting bronzen Assari skin as some tried.

"How—" She smiled fleetingly. "My daughter."

"Diamonds, Mira! Soul-stones. How can you have any part of that?"

Her mother's jaw tightened. "Now you sound like your father. Aren't mages supposed to know better than foolish superstition? As for how—" She sat again, crossing her legs and straightening the seam of one trouser-leg. "Those diamonds are the reason Faraj is Viceroy, and not some politician from Ta'ashlan. Those diamonds are the reason I sat on the council, and that all the other clans have their representatives."

All the loyalist clans, you mean. Zhirin held her tongue.

"It's our arrangement with the Emperor," Fei Minh continued. "He gets our diamonds, unregulated by the Imperial Senate, and we get home-rule. If these Dai Tranh madmen keep interfering, we'll be awash in Imperial soldiers again."

"What happened to Zhang, exactly, that Faraj was afraid to repeat?"

Fei Minh cocked an eyebrow. "He lost ships in a storm and panicked. Thought the stones were cursed. The man couldn't guard his tongue—he was going to make a spectacle of himself."

"And what happened?"

"I don't know," she said with a shrug. "He'd been drinking too much, perhaps, and fell. Accidents do happen, especially to the foolish." Black eyes narrowed. "Zhirin, have you spoken of this to anyone?"

"No, no one. Why—am I likely to have an accident as well?"

"Of course not!" Fei Minh stood, caught Zhirin's arm. "You're my daughter and I won't let anything happen to you. But for the love of all our foremothers, hold your tongue. Especially around your father. Do you understand how important this is to everyone?"

"Yes, Mira."

Her mother pulled her close and she didn't resist, though she couldn't relax either. "I'm worried about you, gaia. What was that master of yours mixed up in? What are you mixed up in?"

No more than you, at least. "I don't know," she said again, and the lie still came easily. "I don't know who could have killed him, or why."

"And you're sure it's not that foreign witch? I don't want you getting involved with such dangerous people."

It was all she could do not to laugh. "I know it wasn't Isyllt, Mira. I was with her, after all. You sound like a Dai Tranh, blaming all our troubles on foreigners."

Fei Minh snorted softly. "I want you to be careful, darling."

"I will."

"Oh, a message came for you this morning." She picked up a folded piece of parchment from the table. The seal was broken, and Zhirin didn't bother to complain. Plain red wax, on solid but inexpensive parchment. The sort anyone might use for a quick note.

Miss Laii, the looping Assari script read in a fine scribe's hand.

It grieves me to learn of Lord Medeion's death, and I extend my deepest condolences.

I know how hard this time must be for you, but I beg a favor nonetheless. My associate Lady beth Isa was also close to your master, but I have lost track of her recently, and don't know where to reach her with this terrible news. I would hate for her to learn of it through the criers. If you have any way to reach her, please do so. I stand ready to offer any aid or support that I can in our time of mutual grief, if only she will send word of her wishes.

I shall await a reply from either of you, at your convenience.

Yours in sorrow,

Asa bin Adam

Zhirin blinked stupidly at the paper for a moment.

"What is it?" her mother asked, as though she hadn't just read the message herself.

"A friend of Vasilios," Zhirin said, lowering the letter. "He wants me to take word of . . . what happened to someone else they knew, but I don't think I can help him."

"News travels fast."

"I'm sure police and Khas were swarming all over the house." That brought a fresh lump to her throat—unknowing, uncaring feet tramping through the house, rifling through her master's belongings. "Everyone in the neighborhood must know by now."

She swallowed. So much for staying at home with her grief. "Are you going to the ball?" she asked after a moment.

"I'd planned to, but I won't leave you here alone."

"I could come with you."

Fei Minh frowned. "Are you sure? After everything that's happened?"

"I don't want to sit here all night and think about it over and over again." That much was true at least, nor was the catch in her voice feigned. "I need lights and music and distraction. And besides, it's the Khas—where else would be safer?"

"I suppose you're right," her mother said after a moment. She laid a soft hand on Zhirin's. "So brave," she said, and the unexpected gentleness of her smile tightened Zhirin's chest. Then it vanished, replaced by her usual cool good humor. "But you certainly can't go dressed like that."

Rain or no, Isyllt intended to explore the palace, but the arrival of her luggage early in the afternoon distracted her. Everything was intact save for her blue gown; insurance, no doubt, in case Asheris decided to charge her with murder after all. He'd even left her knife, though a white ribbon delicately spelled with a peace-bond looped the hilt.

By sunset she and her newly assigned maid had her clothes steamed and ironed, and by dusk she was dressed in a skirt and bodice of rough pewter silk. Even laced tight, the corset was loose at her waist; she needed to eat more than just breakfast for a few decads. The maid, Li, couldn't entirely conceal her discomfiture at the sight of Isyllt's ribs. The fabric was stiff enough that the mirror in her pocket didn't ruin the line of the skirt.

After pinning up her hair, Li helped her line her eyes with kohl and smoky amethyst powder. The woman's hands were sure as a physician's, and the fatigue shadows around Isyllt's eyes soon vanished beneath brushes and creams.

A knock sounded at the door as Li put up the cosmetics, and she turned to answer it. Isyllt rose, shaking out her skirts, and slipped her feet into her slippers. And hissed as her blister pinched and pain shivered the length of her body, tightening her jaw and leaving a sour taste on her tongue. With a careful thought, she numbed the ball of her foot, stopping as the deadening cold tingled along her instep. Not an ideal solution, but it would let her dance.

Li opened the door and Asheris stepped inside, dark and vivid in burnt orange. Gold thread gleamed on his sleeves and collar. He smiled as he straightened from a bow, shaking his head slightly. "Did you know that gray is the color of mourning in Sivahra?"

Isyllt paused. "I didn't, no. Should I find something else?"

He cocked his head, studying her. "No. It suits you. And under the circumstances, the color is not inappropriate." His gaze slid down her throat and across her bare shoulders. "Opals, I still say. A pity I have none at hand."

She glanced at the clothes still strewn on the bed; she'd contemplated a jacket or shawl, to spare the Assari the sight of so much death-tainted flesh. But the night was too muggy, and Asheris's smile too encouraging. Instead she tugged on a pair of long gray gloves as a concession to tact. Pearl buttons gleamed against the insides of her wrists.

Outside it rained again, gleaming silver-bright past windows and columned arcades. Lanterns glowed green and gold and crimson, cast wavering pools of color on polished floors. Asheris led her downstairs and through a series of corridors and covered walkways.

She expected a grand entrance, but instead they slipped through a narrow side door. The great hall wasn't unlike the throne room in the palace at Erisín, though instead of the malachite throne the dais held a crescent of chairs, all the same size. Red-and-green-striped cloth draped the seats, and the lamps on the platform were unlit, though the rest of the hall blazed. Garlands of lotus and gardenia and hyacinth coiled around the columns and swayed over the doors. Petals already littered the floor.

"Normally this is a masque," Asheris said, "but this year Faraj decided that was inappropriate."

Isyllt snorted softly. Perhaps forty people had arrived so far, though the room could hold many more. Conversations buzzed and chattered, mingling with the quiet music. Occasionally laughter rose above the flutes and strings, only to die swiftly. This had none of the festival's frenetic energy. Gaudy silks and flashing jewels, but the guests were too subdued. She saw the Viceroy among the crowd, his wife and daughter beside him. The tall mage al Najid was there as well, dour as ever.

Asheris made no move to join the conversations and Isyllt was content to lurk, but it wasn't long till someone noticed them.

"Asheris." An Assari man approached. "When did you sneak in? And who's your companion?"

Isyllt fought to keep her face politely blank. The man from the fabric shop, the fox from the festival. Taller than Asheris, but slender and narrower of shoulder; tonight he wore elegantly draped green linen. Gold flashed in his ears and on his long brown hands.

"Isyllt," said Asheris, "meet Siddir Bashari, of Ta'ashlan. Lord Bashari, this is Lady Iskaldur, of Eri-sín." Perfectly polite, but his voice and manner cooled, stiffened. She read a challenge in Siddir's hazel eyes, one Asheris had no desire to take up.

Siddir bowed over her hand. "So you're the foreign mage Asheris is protecting." He made the last word sound like a euphemism for something besides house arrest. "My condolences on the death of your colleague."

"Thank you."

He looked as though he might say more, but smiled instead. "Excuse me," he said, the curl of his lips sharpening as he glanced up at Asheris. "I should finish making my rounds. Perhaps you'll save me a dance later this evening. Always a pleasure catching up, Asheris."

She cocked a curious eyebrow at Asheris when Siddir was gone, but he studiously failed to notice. Instead he claimed two cups from a passing servant's tray and offered her one. The liquid inside was clear and warm—she frowned at the pungent aroma.

"*Miju*," he said, smiling at her expression. "A local rice wine. It may be an acquired taste."

She took a sip and coughed as the liquor evaporated on her tongue and seared her throat. "I can see why."

They sipped their drinks, watching the growing crowd.

"Are you going to *protect* me all night?" she asked, mimicking Siddir's inflection. "I don't want to keep you from the party."

He waved a dismissive hand. "I don't mind being kept. Faraj expects me to attend these things, but I don't have much taste for it tonight."

The quiet music trailed away, so softly it took a few heartbeats to notice its loss. Conversations faltered and stilled, and a moment later drums rolled.

"The dancing is about to begin," Asheris said.

The guests retreated to the edges of the room, leaving Faraj alone in the center. "Good evening," he said, his voice carrying through the vaulted chamber, "and welcome. I'm glad that so many of you could attend tonight, especially after yesterday's tragedy. In light of recent events, the Khas will be convening early this season. Official notices will go out tomorrow, so try to enjoy yourselves tonight. And if you enjoy yourselves too much, we can always roll you into your session chambers." Polite laughter rippled and died.

"Our original entertainers are unable to perform tonight—"

"Because they ended up in a canal last night," Asheris whispered dryly.

"But luckily," Faraj continued, "the Blue Lotus troupe has agreed to dance for us, accompanied by the Kurun Tam's own Jodiya al Sarith." An expectant murmur rose in the crowd.

The drums began a steady throbbing rhythm as Faraj stepped aside. A side door opened and five masked dancers stepped out, two men and three women. Centermost among them was al Najid's young apprentice. She wore blue, the others green, loose trousers and short snug vests. Scarves trailed from their wrists and Jodiya's chestnut hair hung loose and shining. Their masks shimmered with sequins and peacock feathers. Flutes and strings joined the drums.

They moved like water, rushing and gliding and rippling. Every motion seemed effortless, seamless as they dipped and twirled and leapt—Isyllt knew how much effort such grace required. All professionals, but Jodiya was the best. But for all their skill it was still choreographed, just a performance, with none of the wild celebration of the dancers in the street.

The music ended with a flurry of drums like thunder and rain and the dancers sank to their knees, faces upturned, masks discarded. Applause filled the hall; as soon as it quieted, a lively dance tune began and guests crowded the floor. A woman took Asheris's arm and he followed her, giving Isyllt a rueful glance.

She retreated from the press, exchanging her empty cup for a goblet from a sideboard. A Chassut red, the sort of vintage that sold for griffins in Erisín. One of the privileges of Imperialism, she thought, rolling herbs and tannin across her tongue.

"Good evening, Lady." She looked up to find Siddir smiling at her. He claimed a cup of wine and stood beside her. "I'm still waiting for the explosion."

"It's early yet. I've always thought explosions would enliven most government parties."

He chuckled, his eyes on the dancers. His curls were oiled, but stray strands frizzed in the humidity. Beneath the wine, he smelled of amber and spices.

"You certainly seem to find trouble, my lady."

She shrugged. "Perhaps I'm a storm-crow."

"Storm-crow, or spy."

"An interesting accusation, my lord." She sipped her wine, wishing now for something stronger.

"Not an accusation, simply an observation. A foreign sorcerer with a knack for being at interesting places at interesting times. And I've heard of your master and his role in Selafaïn politics. What in Sivahra interests Lord Orfion?"

Before she could answer, a Sivahri matron dripping silk and jeweled bangles slipped free of the crowd and seized Siddir's hand.

"Lord Bashari, how wonderful to see you."

"Good evening, Madam Irezh."

"My daughter is here tonight, the one I've told you about. I must introduce you." She glanced at Isyllt then and blinked.

"Go on," Isyllt told him sweetly. "I'm sure we can talk later."

When they were gone she finished her wine and set the goblet aside, stopping herself when she nearly reached for another. Getting drunk wouldn't help, no matter how pleasant it sounded. As soon as she got home she would buy a bottle and charge it to the expense account.

She retreated farther from the crowd and lights, looking for Asheris's dark head above the crowd. After a moment, she spotted him.

Jodiya had steered him away from the dance, into the shadow of a column near the dais. She slipped one hand beneath his jacket and the other rose to his jeweled collar. He didn't touch her, not even to push her away, but Isyllt could see the tension trembling through him from yards away. The girl tilted her face to kiss him and his lips blanched.

It was none of her business, and Asheris doubtless knew how to close his eyes and think of the Empire.

But his hands shook like frightened birds and she couldn't walk away.

Isyllt moved toward them, tugging her gloves off. "Excuse me," she said too sweetly, leaning close. "May I steal Asheris for a dance?" She reached out her left hand, the diamond leaking bitter chill. Jodiya recoiled just in time to keep Isyllt from touching her shoulder.

"Of course." She recovered quickly, but her smile was brittle, kohl-darkened eyes narrow. A stray sequin flashed on her cheekbone. Blue silk hissed as she strode away. Brazen for an apprentice—what other services did she perform for the Kurun Tam, or for the Empire?

"Am I interrupting?" Isyllt tucked her gloves into a skirt pocket, shaking her hands lightly to dry her palms.

"Yes, and I thank you for it." Asheris laid a hand against her waist, the heat of his flesh soaking through cloth and stays. "Your timing is wonderful." She could still feel his tension as he took her hand, but the tightness in his jaw eased.

The dance was a simple one, measured steps that required little thought. They moved in silence for a time. Asheris smiled pleasantly, but his eyes were hooded, unreadable.

"Does it bother you not at all to bind ghosts?" he asked at last. His thumb slid across the knuckles of her left hand, not quite touching the ring. "To enslave them? Not even spirits, but the souls of your own kind."

"Every ghost I've bound committed crimes that would

see living men imprisoned or executed. You wouldn't let a living man who tortured or murdered his family go free—why let him do such things in death?"

His lips twisted. "I know many torturers and murderers who walk free, and I suspect you do too. Even so, it still seems . . . cruel."

She reached up, breaking the form of the dance, and brushed his shirt away from the golden collar. The yellow diamond burned at his throat, much too fiercely to be empty. "Do you think it less cruel to trap spirits?"

He caught her hand, hard enough to hurt, and his eyes narrowed. A heartbeat later his face smoothed and he kissed her knuckles apologetically. "Every bit as cruel. Believe me, Lady, I take no pride in this stone."

The music ended and he released her too quickly for courtesy. "Excuse me a moment. I need a drink."

Isyllt let him go. The musicians struck up a livelier beat, and she turned to find Siddir weaving toward her through the crowd. She let him claim her hand, not yet sure if she should be amused or worried, and they spun into the dance.

"For someone who thinks I attract ill-luck," she said as the steps brought them close, "you seem quite willing to keep my company."

"You never answered my last question."

"What makes you think my presence here has anything to do with Kiril? If you know so much about him, you might know we had a falling-out last year."

"Arguments are easily counterfeited."

She twirled, skirts spinning, and touched his outstretched hand. Her slipper clung damp and sticky to her foot; the blister had broken. "Let me assure you, Lord

Bashari, there is nothing counterfeit in the unpleasantness between me and Lord Orfion." Truth, raw and bitter, straining her voice. His pleasant expression faltered.

"Then I'm sorry for your grief." They drew together, nearly breast to breast. "I know you have no reason to trust me and a dozen not to, but I think our goals may lie in similar directions."

That pulled her eyebrows up. She met his eyes—green-and-gold-flecked and terribly earnest. She envied him; she doubted she'd looked so innocent since she was ten years old.

"What if they don't?" Another step apart, another twirl. "We've only just met—are we to become enemies so soon?"

"I hope not. But perhaps the risk is worth it."

She stepped back into his arms, wishing she could scent deception as some mages claimed they could. All she smelled was wine and sweat and the cloying mix of a dozen perfumes. "Are you prepared to tell me you're plotting against the Khas?" she whispered.

"No." His breath warmed the side of her face. "I'm plotting against the Emperor."

She drew back, struggling to keep up with the dance steps while she looked at his face. If he was lying, she couldn't tell. Choices dizzied her. But she had to do something, so why not risk?

"We aren't enemies, then."

Zhirin and her mother arrived unfashionably late, after the dancing had begun. Their argument over the proper amount of mourning-wear had lasted nearly an hour. In the end Fei Minh lent her a sari, deep green silk shot with

gold and orange thread, still trimmed in gray since the
death of Zhirin's great-aunt two years ago.

Lanterns and garlands dripped from the trees of
the Pomegranate Court; rain bruised the flowers and
decay tainted their waxy sweetness. Usually the court
was open to guests, but now soldiers patrolled amid the
trees and no couples sat in the rain-sheltered alcoves.
They passed the wide lion fountain, twin to the one in
the Kurun Tam, and climbed the steps to the council
hall. The smell of sweat and wine and perfume wafted
through the doors, mingling with the cloying flowers
and the sharpness of the rain. Zhirin swallowed nervous spit.

"Are you sure you're all right?" Fei Minh asked.

Zhirin forced a smile. "Of course."

It wasn't much of a crowd, she told herself as they
stepped inside. Much smaller than other parties she'd attended here. But still too many; her vision blurred, marble
rippling like water, the guests a shimmering haze of gold
and silk and gems. No one else wore gray. How many of
these people would feel like dancing if they'd watched a
nakh sink its teeth into a man's throat?

Her courage nearly fled, but her stomach rumbled and
the sharp edge of hunger cleared her head. She hadn't
eaten anything today but tea, and her body no longer
cared about her grief. She grounded herself in the practical concern; she'd survived last night, she could survive
a party.

"Oh, look," Fei Minh said. "Lu Zhin is here." She
waved to the matriarch of the Irezh family, bracelets
chiming softly. "And Min is back from the university."

Zhirin barely stopped her eyes from rolling. That was

a conversation she planned to stay far away from. "I'm going to find something to eat. I'll join you later."

"Good idea." Her mother's eyes narrowed. "You're looking a bit sallow—not that the color helps." She flicked a fingernail against a gray ribbon.

Zhirin pushed Fei Minh lightly toward the Irezhs. "I'll see you later, Mira."

The dancing distracted people from the food, and Zhirin filled a plate with cakes and century eggs wrapped in pickled ginger. The finer red wines were nearly gone, but plenty of chilled white Mareotis remained, goblets sweating on the linen tablecloths.

She found a chair against the wall and balanced her plate on her knees, nibbling a cardamom cream-cake and watching the dancers circle. She had no idea if Isyllt would be here, she realized. For all she knew Asheris had locked her in a lead-lined cell somewhere.

Then the crowd shifted and Zhirin saw her. She nearly choked on a bite of cake and washed it down with wine. More specter than living woman, with her gown the color of ashes and bone-pale skin. Like something out of a play, the White Bone Queen stalking a ball for her next victim. It took a moment to recognize her dance partner—the man from the festival. At least he didn't look as though he'd fall over dead anytime soon.

Across the room servants opened the terrace doors; the heat of so many dancing bodies threatened to overcome the building's cooling spells. Almost at once couples began to trickle out in search of privacy.

The song ended and Isyllt and her partner moved toward the refreshment tables. Zhirin rose to join them—

she nearly set her plate down, but the sight of Isyllt's shoulder blades rippling beneath too little flesh made her hold on to it.

Color burned in Isyllt's cheeks and she smiled at something the man said as they collected wineglasses, but it seemed strained. The pleasant expression fell away when she saw Zhirin.

"How are you?"

Zhirin shrugged. "All right. Considering. You?"

"The same. Excuse me—Zhirin, meet Siddir Bashari."

Not a name she recognized—maybe her mother knew who he was. She nodded politely. "Excuse me, but I need to speak to Lady Iskaldur for a moment. Come outside with me?"

Isyllt nodded and bade farewell to Bashari.

The rain had stopped, save for the steady drip of the gutters. Lanterns swayed lazily, tongues of light lapping across the wet grass. Whispers drifted from shadowed corners. Zhirin left the terrace, moving toward a covered bench on the lawn. Damp seeped between her toes and stray blades of grass clung to her sandals.

"Adam sent me," she said softly. "He wants to know what he should do."

Isyllt sighed a little, as if in relief. "Tell him to get a mirror, a small one that will fit in a pocket, and carry it with him. Glass if he can manage, but brass or bronze will do. Beyond that, we'll have to see. I don't know yet if I need a daring rescue or not."

Across the yard, a stone platform shone pale in the darkness, each corner marked by a column. Zhirin grimaced at the sight.

"The execution yard," she said when Isyllt raised a

questioning eyebrow. "The stones will be blooded soon, my mother says."

"Oh?"

"Three members of Clan Xian have been linked to the Dai Tranh and will be charged for the attack on the festival. Never mind that they were arrested days before it happened." She put her back to the square as they reached the bench. "What happened with Asheris?" she asked, testing the stone for dampness before she sat.

"He's keeping me close. It's all very polite, but I can't leave the Khas."

"What will you do?" Zhirin set her plate on the bench, nudging it toward Isyllt.

Shadows rippled across the woman's face as she frowned. "I don't know. Escape would only give him reason to arrest me."

"You could leave, couldn't you? Go home. You've done what you came to do."

"Not until the supply ship arrives and Jabbor has the cargo. I won't leave the job half finished." Isyllt took a pastry, tearing off a bit of crust.

The job. Zhirin picked at a black-marbled egg. Revolution must be easier if you didn't have to stay to watch. If you didn't have to live in the ashes.

"What is it?" Isyllt asked, watching her.

She almost held her tongue, but she'd trusted the woman this far . . . "It's more complicated than we realized." Haltingly, she told Isyllt about the diamonds, about the warehouse raid and the conversation with her mother.

Isyllt whistled softly when she was finished. "That's quite a thing to keep hidden. And why bother, when the Emperor could simply claim the stones as tithe?"

Zhirin shook her head; her mouth was dry and tepid wine did nothing to help. The sour smell of the eggs turned her stomach.

She nearly dropped the goblet as Isyllt grabbed her arm, cool fingers digging into her flesh. She followed the woman's nod in time to see a man and a woman cross the terrace; lantern-light flashed on long brown hair and the man's familiar hook-nosed profile. They walked to a shadowed corner and the hedges blocked the sight of them.

"Can we get closer?" Zhirin whispered.

"I have an easier way." Isyllt reached into her skirt pocket and pulled out a silk-wrapped shape. A mirror— black glass gleamed as she unwrapped it. "Be quiet. Sound travels both ways." She turned toward Zhirin and held the mirror between them.

The surface shimmered like water and images rose and vanished one after another—strangers' faces, lights and ceilings and floors, a dizzying series of angles and views. Finally one remained, a scattering of darkness and light. After an instant Zhirin realized it was water dripping into a puddle, as seen from below the surface. Looking closer, she saw a man's outline reflected in the rippling pool.

"What is it?" Faraj's voice drifted faintly from the mirror, dull with annoyance or resignation.

"The Laii girl has been snooping around." Jodiya. "She may already know about the mine, and she keeps company with the Jade Tigers. I can make sure she doesn't talk."

"No. I need her mother's ships, and if Fei Minh even suspects we hurt her daughter, she'll make more trouble than Zhang could have dreamed of. I'll tell Fei Minh to keep her quiet, but you don't lay a finger on the girl."

"What about the foreign witch, the necromancer? She's taking more interest in Asheris than I like."

"Her you can dispose of, if you need something to keep yourself occupied. But for the love of heaven, not here. The last thing I need is an international incident. Make it quiet, and quick."

"They'll never find the body."

A moment later they were gone, and Isyllt wrapped the mirror again.

"What are we going to do?" Zhirin whispered. Her hands shook and she clenched them tight in her lap.

Isyllt shrugged. "Be careful. Watch our backs."

"I could go into the forest with Jabbor."

"And that will be exactly the excuse that little assassin needs to kill you when she finds you and blame it on the Tigers. And we still don't know who murdered Vasilios. If it wasn't Faraj or his killers, then even more people want to put knives in our backs." Her expression softened. "Stay quiet and don't draw attention to yourself."

Zhirin shook her head hard enough to shift a braid in its pins. "How do you do it? How do you live like this?"

Isyllt smiled, quick and rueful. "I don't remember any other way."

Clouds rode the jungle canopy, blurring the tops of the trees in gray. Not yet heavy enough to rain, but the air below was thick and sticky and clung to Xinai's skin in a clammy false sweat. The ground was soft with rain, the soggy leaf-litter crawling with beetles and centipedes. Already plants half-dead from summer heat greened again, and the smell of jasmine and satinwood flowers threaded through the richer scents of wet earth and leaves, rot and moss.

Shaiyung returned an hour or so after they left Xao Par Khan, her chill presence stronger than ever. She didn't speak, and Xinai was happy not to be distracted. So many years away from home had dulled her sense of the jungle, and she struggled to keep up with Riuh as they moved through the dense vegetation.

They took game trails when they found them, but much of the going was scrabbling up muddy slopes and slipping down the other side. More than once birds took flight at their passage, and once a long-tailed macaua flung a half-eaten pomelo at them in startlement. At least the lands north of the mountain were scarcely populated—most of the clansfolk had gravitated toward the river and the city, or fled to the northern highlands where the Assari rarely ventured. Xinai couldn't remember which clans had lived in these hills, and shook her head at her own ignorance. How many villages lay in ruins, choked by the jungle? How many ghosts haunted dying heart-trees?

They followed the ward-posts that circled the mountain, but gave the markers a wide berth. Xinai couldn't read the nature of all the magic woven into them and didn't want to risk tripping any alarms. Her lip curled at the sight of the things.

They kept on till dusk settled and even tracker's eyes strained against the gloom. The familiar fatigue of a forced march dragged at her, but the diamond's pulse was stronger against her chest and she knew they were going the right way. Anywhere from two to five more days, she guessed, depending how far around the mountain they had to go.

They slept in watches; neither had caught any sign of pursuit, but they'd crossed several sets of three-toed claw marks in the mud. Kueh tracks—flightless birds taller than a man and vicious if startled. And there were always tigers in the mountains.

In the middle of the rain-soaked third watch, Xinai slipped out of their woven-leaf shelter to relieve herself. When she returned, the air beside her cooled. A nearby nightjar fell silent, though insects and frogs continued their songs; only animals large enough to attract attention feared ghosts and spirits. Only men were brave enough—or stupid enough—to seek them out.

She crouched in a tangle of hibiscus shrubs and listened to the rain and distant thunder and Riuh's soft snoring. Hunger sharpened in her stomach, till she fished a strip of jerky from her pouch. Dry and salty, but she always craved meat before her courses came and they had no time to hunt. The silence stretched and she shivered as her wet hair chilled.

"Hello, Mother," she murmured at last.

Shaiyung materialized, shimmering and pale. Stronger now, clearer, the color of her skin less sickly. The wound in her throat still gaped—the unsung dead would always bear their death-marks while they lingered.

"That stone you wear," she whispered. "It's an ugly thing."

"I know. I hope I won't wear it long." Xinai swallowed salt and a dozen questions. "Can you scout ahead for us?"

Shaiyung shook her head. "It's still hard for me to see when I'm not with you. Hard for me to leave the Night Forest. I can find spirits and ghosts, but not works of man."

"What's it like, the twilight lands?"

"Strange," Shaiyung said after a pause. "Even after all these years. Before you came home, there was only the dreamtime. I saw things . . . distant cities . . . I can barely remember now. I hear the songs of our ancestors on the eastern wind."

"Will you go to them?"

"One day, perhaps." Her smile was kind and ghastly. "When Cay Lin is rebuilt. When I see your children playing by the tree."

"Mother—" Xinai shook her head, frowned at the half-eaten piece of meat in her hand. "I know how much this means to you, but what you did by the river—" Even now she couldn't force the word past her teeth. Possession. "You can't do that again."

"It would have been good luck, a child conceived with the rain."

"Worry about the Khas first. I won't be much use in a fight if I'm pregnant."

Shaiyung's eyebrows rose. "The northlands made you soft. I was leading raids a month before you were born. My mother still had enemy blood on her hands when I came. Your foremothers are warriors, child."

Xinai turned her head, cheeks warming. "I haven't forgotten."

"It's not the fighting, is it? You're still thinking about that foreigner of yours."

She pulled a knee close to her chest, her heel digging a rut in soft earth. "I know I shouldn't—"

"Oh, darling." A cold hand stroked her back. "I know. Your father wasn't the first man I cared for. I know what it's like to lose, to let someone go. You can't help what you feel. But you can't let it cloud your thoughts either, or dull your blades."

"I know, Mama—"

Leaves rustled and Xinai stiffened. But it was only Riuh. He rolled over, propped himself up on one elbow. "Who are you talking to?" He blinked sleepily, but his knife was in his hand.

Xinai let out a breath. "Just ghosts." Her mother's coldness faded.

Riuh stared at her for a moment, the question—*Are you joking?*—plain on his face. But finally he rolled over and tugged the blanket back over his head.

She wasn't sure if she was grateful for the reprieve.

CHAPTER 13

Thunder came in the dead hours of morning, with wind to rattle the windows and arcs of blue lightning. Despite her bravado with Zhirin, Isyllt barely slept. Twice she woke from nightmares of faceless assassins and cold blades, of seeing her body lifeless in the street as uncaring crowds stepped around her.

As the storm eased into a gray dawn, she finally started to doze again, only to be startled awake by a knock at the door. Louder and more insistent than Li. Fumbling for her robe, she rose to answer it. Assassins didn't usually knock first.

"I'm sorry to wake you," Asheris said when she opened the door, "but I have a favor to ask." He wore riding clothes and carried two oilcloaks over his arm.

She stepped aside and waved him in. "What is it?"

"I've had reports that something's happened in one of the villages on the North Bank."

"Something?"

He shrugged wryly. "They're sketchy reports. But I'm told people are dead, and that ghosts or spirits may be involved. You've no obligation to help, but I still don't have a necromancer on staff."

She blinked sleep-sticky lashes. *They'll never find the body.* "I'll come."

They collected half a dozen soldiers before they left the Khas, and horses from the stable by the ferry. As they climbed the high road they left the rain below, a shifting sea of gray covering the city and harbor. Rainbows shimmered along the tarnished edges of the clouds as the sun rose, and Isyllt soon shed her cloak as the day warmed.

They turned off the road to the Kurun Tam onto a narrower trail and met a group of local soldiers waiting at a bend in the path. The captain straightened, saluting Asheris. His skin was ashen and sweat stained his uniform.

"What happened?" Asheris asked.

"The villagers in Xao Par are dead, sir."

His eyebrows rose. "All of them?"

"I'm not sure—we can't see through that damned fog. Things are moving in the village, but I don't think they're alive. Forgive me, my lord, but we couldn't stay in there."

"What fog?"

"Up the road. You'll see, my lord."

Asheris cocked his head, and Isyllt turned her horse up the path. One of the soldiers rode first, then Asheris, and Isyllt followed close behind. The trail sloped into a narrow valley, shadowed like a wrinkle in a velvet skirt.

The jungle rose up on either side, damp and green and much too quiet.

Her ring chilled first. An instant later the wind gusted, pricking gooseflesh on her arms. Tendrils of mist snaked between the trees. Above and below the day was clear, but inside the valley a gray brume gathered. She didn't entirely understand the science of weather, but she knew it took cold and heat combined to produce a fog, like breath misting on a winter day.

Or a hot day and something very cold. Her ring burned like a band of ice; the bones of her hand ached with it.

Within a few yards the fog enveloped them, damp and algid. The horses balked, tossing their heads and sidling. Isyllt could barely see past her mount's nose.

"Go on foot," she called, drawing rein. "We'll be trampled if the horses panic."

The animals were all too happy to comply and cantered down the hill as soon as their riders released them. Isyllt moved closer to Asheris, whose warmth was a beacon in the chill. The soldiers gathered around them, swords and pistols drawn. She hoped none of them were nervous on the trigger.

Things moved in the fog, flickering shapes that set her neck prickling. The diamond sparked and glowed, and every breath drew the taste of death into her mouth. Something white and faceless wafted past, and one of the soldiers whimpered softly.

"Ghosts?" Asheris asked softly.

"Oh, yes." The mist was full of them; their hunger pressed on her. The souls in her ring stirred restlessly and she stilled them with a thought. Water flowed close by, the rush and splash of a narrow rocky stream. A few paces more and they reached a bridge, boards echoing beneath their boots.

"The village is close now," one of the soldiers said, voice soft as if he feared something would snatch it away.

As they reached the far side, a shape solidified out of the haze. A woman with skin like buttermilk, dressed all in white. She smiled and beckoned; a soldier moaned.

Not a ghost, just an opportunistic spirit. "Not today," Isyllt said. Did Sivahri spirits understand Assari?

Maybe so—the woman smiled and winked at her, then turned and vanished into the fog with a flick of her white fox tail.

The mist was thicker on the other side and Isyllt's teeth began to chatter. The ground squelched underfoot; they'd wandered off the path. A soldier shouted and a pistol shot echoed. Isyllt spun, tripped over a rock, and landed on hand and hip in wet earth. Furrowed wet earth—a garden.

"Something touched me!" the soldier gasped. His gun smoked, mingling with the fog. "A hand—"

Isyllt pushed herself up, scrubbing mud onto her trousers. Something moved beside her, retreating as she turned toward it. Not cautious—mocking. She took a step back and her foot hit something more yielding than stone. She glanced down at a slender dirt-streaked arm and swallowed.

"Can you clear this?" she asked Asheris.

He hesitated. "I'm no weather witch, but maybe I can manage something. Step back and brace yourselves," he called to the guards. "And cover your eyes. You too, meliket."

Isyllt raised a hand to her face, peering through her fingers. Asheris cupped his hands and blew gently into them. His breath steamed, and the diamond flared at his throat.

The breeze spiraled away from him, strengthening into a tame whirlwind. Isyllt winced as the heat of it struck her and gooseflesh stung her skin. Leaves rattled, ripped free of branches; dirt and twigs filled the air and Isyllt closed her eyes against the stinging debris. Something hissed and wailed—nothing human.

She opened one eye and saw the fog receding, the air around Asheris shimmering with heat. Then the wind died, leaving only a thin gray haze clinging to the ground, and morning sunlight washed over the village.

Bodies littered the ground, curled like womb-bound babes or sprawled prone, fingers clawing at the soil as if to crawl. Isyllt knelt beside the nearest corpse, a boy no older than thirteen. Dirt and weeds stained his hands, dark crescents under his nails and sap green and sticky on his fingers. Beneath the garden grime his nails were blue, as if he'd frozen to death. Perhaps he had; she couldn't see a wound. He lay on his side, and blood had settled dark and purple in one cheek and outstretched arm. His flesh was stiff as wax, colder than the air.

"What happened?" Asheris asked.

"Ghosts. The dead are hungry. They drained his life away. Does this happen here often?"

"No," one of the guards said. A Sivahri man, face drained pasty and yellow. "We sing the dead on, to guide them to the twilight lands. We burn offerings and prayer-sticks, and in exchange the ancestors watch over us."

"And no ancestors ever decide they want more?"

His throat bobbed. "It happens, but not often. I've seen the madness take a ghost, but an exorcism usually puts things right. I've never seen anything like this."

"This was more than one ghost." She stood, moved farther into the village. She'd seen slaughter before, villages looted by bandits or savaged by demons, blood and bodies in the street, houses charred and smoking. All these buildings stood intact, neat-thatched and clean. No destruction, only death.

Not everyone had died as peacefully as the boy. She saw clawed faces, blood crusted beneath their nails. Wide-eyed, rictus-mouthed, hands raised to ward off blows.

Something moved in the shadows beneath a house and she started, reaching for her blade. Only a dog. The animal whined and barked, then bolted past her toward Asheris and the soldiers. One woman crouched, offering a hand. The dog whined again, but finally let her stroke his head.

Isyllt turned away from the soldiers. "Deilin Xian."

The ghost appeared beside her, barely more substantial than the tattered fog. She snarled as she saw Isyllt. Then she looked around and her face slackened.

"Is this what you would have done to your great-granddaughter?"

"No," the woman whispered. "Never this. The madness was on me, but I only wanted to feel again, to be flesh again."

"Who did this?"

Pearlescent nostrils flared. "My kin, my compatriots. Those of us who fell fighting the Empire."

Isyllt gestured to the corpses. "And this is so much better than the occupation?"

Deilin glared, then shook her head and looked away. "I don't know."

"Where are they now, your murderous kin?" The whole village reeked of ghosts, so strong she could hardly feel Deilin standing beside her.

Again the ghost sniffed the air. "Gone, mostly. But fresh corpses attract spirits."

A soldier shouted, and Isyllt turned.

A corpse sat up.

She'd seen corpses stir before, as muscles stiffened or bloat swelled—this was nothing so innocent. A dead woman stood, moving with an eerie marionette grace. Her eyes gleamed like pearls in her death-bruised face. The dog growled and began to bark, rust-and-black ruff standing on end. Isyllt dismissed Deilin with a hasty word.

When the dead possessed the living, an exorcism might put things right. When ghosts or spirits possessed dead flesh, the result was not puppetry but a terrible melding. The result was demons.

A soldier fired and missed. The next man didn't; the demon staggered but didn't fall. The wound didn't bleed.

"Do you have spell-silver?" Isyllt shouted. The answer became clear as the soldiers fired at more corpses, none of which stopped moving. She drew her knife, a bone-hilted kukri. Silver inlay traced the hilt and blade, wrapped the weapon in spells.

The nearest corpse twitched and lunged for her legs. The blade bit deep, jarring against bone. The demon shrieked as smoke curled from the wound. Her boot caught it in the face with a crunch. Isyllt yanked the knife free and swung for its neck. The demon screamed again; the next stroke caught its larynx and the cry became a gasp.

The third stroke opened its neck to the bone. Flesh crisped and blackened. Isyllt planted her boot on its head, forcing its face into the mud as she wedged the knife between vertebrae and sawed. She felt the spinal cord sever, both through the blade and in the rushing chill as the spirit left the flesh.

Gulping air, she staggered away from the mangled body. The corpse was harmless now, the spirit dissolved; demons only had one chance at life.

Another clawed for her, nails raking her outflung arm. She buried the knife in its gut and twisted. Nothing close to fatal, but it screamed as the silver burned. The stench of bowel filled the air as she tugged the blade free; ropes of blood clung to the metal, thick and sticky as jam. Someone else was screaming, high and unceasing.

"Fire!" she shouted at Asheris. "Fire will stop them!" The screams ended in a gurgle; pistol shots echoed.

She kicked the demon's legs out from under it, wrestled it to the ground. Easy with the newly wrought, still clumsy and awkward. An old demon was nothing she ever wanted to meet again.

This was butcher's work—when the corpse fell still she pushed herself up, wiping at the mud and blood splattered on her face. The air smelled of roasting flesh.

Half a dozen bodies smoldered on the ground, while another handful writhed and flamed and shrieked. The soldiers huddled back-to-back while Asheris set demon after demon alight.

What came after the butchery was worse.

One soldier was dead, another badly mauled. Isyllt eased the woman's pain and checked the wounds as best she could. Corpse-bites always festered, but sometimes worse traces lingered. When she finished, the woman's comrades carried her off for proper treatment and returned with a barrel of salt from the closest village.

One by one Isyllt and Asheris searched the houses for demons or survivors—of the latter they found a few: an infant in her cradle, a toddler hiding under his bed, a dog nursing a litter, two cats, and a caged bird. Whether the ghosts took pity on them or they were simply too small to be worth eating, Isyllt couldn't say.

When all living things were out of a house, Isyllt circled the building with salt and Asheris burned it to the ground. He was one of the most skilled pyromancers she'd ever seen—fire answered him instantly, burned clean and fast, never a stray spark to threaten them. Even by the fourteenth house, when sweat ran down his face and strain washed his skin gray, the flames never faltered.

She salted the charred remains as well. The reek of death and witchery clung to everything, seeping into the soil. The crops had already spoiled from the chill. The village was as dead as its inhabitants; no one would rebuild here soon.

Xinai found the first ghost-marker late the next afternoon. Bones and beads woven around a wooden frame, dangling from a branch. A ward and a warning—it marked cursed land, haunted by spirits and the hungry dead. Even with Shaiyung beside her, Xinai had no desire to meet another gangshi, or any other incorporeal predator. They climbed higher into the foothills to avoid it, though that left them edging beside the mountain's wards as well.

They were perhaps a third of the way around the mountain; she'd never ventured so far northeast before, and nothing was familiar. Riuh only shook his head when she questioned him, and soon they were both cursing under their breath as they stumbled through the brush and over craggy hills. Xinai snarled at Riuh nearly as often as he spoke, only to apologize a few minutes later. After an hour of this he gave up talking, and Xinai cursed herself for not remembering the potion that put off her courses.

The mountain towered over them, blocking the sky. Once or twice when they broke through the tree line, she smelled the smoke and sulfur stench of the burning cauldron. The jungle spread out all around them, dipping and swelling over the hills, rising to meet the eastern mountains. Shadows floated across the canopy as clouds drifted east, where they thickened and shed their rain.

As dusk came on, Xinai was cursing in earnest. They'd passed three more ghost-wards, a greater expanse of unclean jungle than she'd ever seen before. Twilight chased purple shadows across the hills and the light was nearly gone. And as they circled east, the diamond's pulse began to fade.

Finally she stubbed her toe once too often and sat with a snarl, flinging a stone down the slope. Riuh turned back, eyeing her so warily she wanted to throw rocks at him too.

"If you want to stop, we should go down again." He gestured toward the shadow of the woods below.

"So the ghosts can kill us and the kueh peck our guts out? Not that it matters, when we're going the wrong bloody way!"

Riuh's eyes narrowed, but Xinai waved him silent. Her jaw slackened as a thought kindled. She pushed herself up, scrubbed sweat off her face, and clambered down the rock-strewn slope in the direction they'd come.

"What is it?" Riuh asked as he caught up.

The fourth ward she'd seen hung in front of them, rattling softly. She frowned at it, knelt to examine the rain-soft earth beneath the trees. Just enough light left to see without a charm. "Ha," she muttered. "Look."

Riuh crouched beside her, looked past her pointing finger toward a line of kueh tracks. No more than a day old; she could smell fresh droppings somewhere close. They'd passed half a dozen such tracks, but it had taken her this long to realize what was wrong.

Riuh stared, frowning. "They pass the wards."

All the tracks they'd seen crisscrossed the line of markers, wandering in and out of the blighted spot. Kueh, like tigers and dogs, had no love for ghosts.

"Those motherless dogs—" Riuh shook his head, nearly laughing. "False wards?"

"The wards are real enough, but I wonder how much blight there really is behind them."

"I'm fool enough to find out if you are."

She glanced up at the shadow of the mountain, the

stars blossoming all around it. "In the morning. A little foolishness goes a long way."

The western sky caught fire and lined all the clouds in orange and violet as Isyllt and Asheris returned to the Khas. Weariness dragged at her limbs, slumped her aching shoulders. Asheris hadn't spoken since they left the village, and she had no will to draw him out. The fierce exultation of the fight was long drained from her, leaving only a sick hollowness behind.

She sent Li away and drew her own bath, shedding her filthy clothes on the bathroom floor and sinking into the warm water with a grateful breath.

When she'd scrubbed dried mud and gore from her hair, she drained the cooling water and refilled the tub, then reached for her fallen coat and pulled the wrapped mirror from her pocket. She could all but hear Kiril's chiding voice—good mirrors were expensive and hard to replace at a moment's notice.

"Adam," she whispered, trailing her fingers across the surface; water streaked and beaded in the wake of her touch.

A moment later an image resolved, the mercenary's face focusing in the glass. His skin was pasty, eyes bruised, green vivid behind purple-shadowed lids.

Isyllt let out a breath she hadn't realized she was holding. "What happened to you? And where are you?"

A smile twisted his mouth. "The local wildlife. But Vienh promises the worst has passed." Isyllt raised a brow at that, remembering her missing scarf, but she knew Adam wouldn't trust carelessly. "She found me a smuggler's cache to hide out in for a while," he went on. "You look more comfortable. Not to mention cleaner."

She snorted, tilted the mirror upward. "It's very pleasant, for house arrest. But I think someone will try to kill me soon."

"Who?"

"An assassin posing as an apprentice mage—maybe she really is both. The Viceroy uses her to clean up messes."

"Then you've got more than one problem. The Dai Tranh has someone in the palace posing as a servant, and they're planning some entertainment during the execution tomorrow. Anhai's maid helped frame you, and it sounds like she wants a more permanent solution now."

"Lovely. Something to look forward to. What's her name, the maid?"

"Kaeru—I don't know the clan. The other woman's I didn't catch."

"Good work. Have you heard about what happened in Xao Par Khan?"

"I've been keeping my head down today. What happened?"

"Ghosts attacked, killed everyone, but I don't know why. Let me know if you hear anything useful."

"What do you want me to do tomorrow if trouble happens at the execution?"

"Stay close and watch. If I have to run, I'll try to meet you at the docks by sunset. I should go. Be careful."

"You too."

She broke the connection and his face faded into black. The water had cooled, and her fingertips were wrinkled. She ached for sleep, but instead she combed her hair and dressed and went to find Asheris.

He answered the door in a robe and loose trousers,

the smell of soap and water still clinging to his skin. The hollow look around his eyes lingered.

"Are you all right?" she asked.

"Just tired." He sank into a chair. "Some things I can't quite grow used to." He waved toward the dinner tray on the table. "Tea? I'm afraid it's cold."

"That's all right." Isyllt poured a cup, swirled bitter black liquid around for a moment. Leaves eddied and swirled against porcelain; a pity she'd never been much for divination. After a moment she set it down again and rose to pace beside the window. "You need a proper team of necromancers."

"I know. The Emperor has other priorities."

She paced another circuit, pausing as she passed his chair. His robe hung open, and for the first time she saw his collar clearly. Gold wire looped and whorled around his neck in delicate vining tendrils. Tiny rubies gleamed like drops of blood. She followed the twisting lines, but didn't find a clasp. She raised a hand, stopped before she touched him.

"What deserves such a prison?" The power of the diamond whispered against her hand, a rhythm she didn't recognize. Something strange about the feel of it.

Asheris turned, caught her hand and kissed her fingertips. This kiss was neither chaste nor courteous. Heat spread from his lips, shivered the length of her arm. He stood, still holding her hand, and warmth lapped over her.

"What are you doing?" Her voice wasn't as steady as she would have liked.

"What do you think I'm doing?" His other hand traced the angle of her jaw, tilted her face up.

"I think you're trying to distract me."

"Is it working?"

He kissed her; she didn't stop him. The taste of his magic spilled over her tongue. The strangeness was there too, some subtle flavor she didn't understand. She leaned in, mouth opening, free hand rising to cup the curve of his skull.

He flinched from her touch and pulled away. Her pulse beat in her lips.

"I'm sorry." He took her left hand carefully, not touching the ring. "Not this, please. Not after . . ."

She looked down at the diamond, black and still now, no fire in its depths. She might demand the same of him, but the bruised look on his face stopped her. Beyond foolish, but she was tired of being alone. She twisted the ring free, slipped it into her inside coat pocket and offered him her naked hand.

"No ghosts." That was a lie and they both knew it; their ghosts were always with them.

He kissed her fingertips, her palm, and pulled her close. The lamps flickered and died as he led her to his bed. For an hour or two, at least, they might banish them.

Isyllt woke with a start, reaching for a weapon that wasn't there. The bed was empty and cold, and the room as well. A draft gusted over her, teasing gooseflesh across her skin and tightening her breasts.

She reached down, found her clothes where she'd left them and checked her pocket. Her ring was still there; she slipped it on, shaking her head at her own stupidity. At least the diversion had been pleasant. She pressed her face to the pillow and breathed in the scent of sweat and spices.

Isyllt rose and dressed, followed the humid draft into the sitting room, where the balcony door stood open. Rain hissed against the leaves, dripped over Asheris's bare shoulders as he leaned out into the night. A shining rivulet snaked down his back, soaking into the waist of his trousers. He scrubbed a weary hand across his face and flung droplets away.

She bit her lip and nearly turned away. She knew that tired antipathy—she'd seen it in Kiril a dozen times, in her own reflection. But mercy was so rarely an option, for yourself or the enemy.

"Lie back and think of the Empire?" she asked softly.

Asheris turned, scattering water. In the darkness his skin was nearly purple. "I'm sorry," he said after a pause.

"For what? Not wanting me?" She smiled wryly; it stung more than she liked to admit. "You counterfeit it rather well."

"I've had practice."

She remembered Jodiya at the ball and glanced away. She didn't have the luxury of regrets right now.

"Are you planning to kill me?" she asked, catching his eyes.

He arched an eyebrow. "I wasn't—should I be?"

"The Viceroy has condoned my death. It seemed like a wasted opportunity back there."

"Ah." He stepped inside and latched the door. Steam drifted off his skin as water dried. "I have no orders to harm you. Not yet."

"If you want to take the initiative, now would be a good time."

He smiled. "It would be inconsiderate to wake the house. Besides"—his smile twisted—"I'd rather test my leash as far as I might."

She swallowed half a dozen questions. Pressing him too far wouldn't serve her now. Instead she turned, deliberately giving him her back, and fetched her shoes and stray underclothes from the bedroom.

"Will you attend the execution tomorrow?" she asked.

His lip curled. "So I am bid. There will be blood and death to go around this season."

And likely more than he realized. But warning him of tomorrow's attack was more leash than she cared to test.

"Good night." She left him in the dark and returned to her own cold bed.

CHAPTER 14

The execution began at noon.

Isyllt gathered with the other spectators around the dais. Councillors mostly, she guessed, and other bureaucrats who worked at the Khas. Some observers from the city had been allowed in, and servants lingered on the skirts of the crowd, shifting nervously. The sky was gray in the lull before the afternoon rains.

Asheris stood with the Viceroy and executioner on the dais; Isyllt had never seen him in an Imperial uniform before. His face might have been a wooden mask.

The prisoners knelt on the stone—two men and a woman, stripped to the waist, their hands bound to posts behind their backs. They didn't speak; one man kept his eyes closed, while his companions stared defiantly at the crowd.

When the last of the noon bells died, Faraj stepped forward to face the prisoners. His voice, however, was pitched to reach the crowd.

"Bai Xian, Yuen Xian, and Thuan Xian-Zhu. You are found guilty of conspiring against the Empire and the Khas Maram and murdering Khas soldiers. In addition, you have been implicated in the destruction of Imperial property, and the attacks on Amina Abbasi's shop on Market Street and the Floating Garden, which resulted in the deaths of over thirty citizens of Symir. The sentence for these crimes is death. But you've been offered leniency if you renounce your allegiance to the terrorist organization called the Dai Tranh, and I'll extend this offer once more. Will you repudiate these murderers and help us bring peace to the city?"

The woman, Yuen, spat on the stone. The others remained silent.

"Very well." He turned to the crowd. "Before the sentence is carried out, is there anyone present who would speak, either for or against the condemned?"

The silence stretched, not even a muttered word to break it. But as Faraj drew breath to speak again, footsteps crunched on the gravel path and a murmur rippled through the crowd.

"I'll speak."

Spectators cleared the path to admit Jabbor Lhun. Two Sivahri flanked him and soldiers with drawn weapons surrounded them all. The three wore honor-blades at their hips and gray sashes at their waists. A pattern of tiger stripes decorated their bare upper arms—ocher paint on Jabbor's dark skin, black on his companions'.

Isyllt bit down an annoyed sigh. All their plans would be for nothing if the Tigers got themselves killed or arrested on some foolish point of honor.

Faraj blinked, but recovered quickly. "And who do you speak for? More terrorists and murderers?"

"The Jade Tigers are no murderers and you know it. I speak for the Tigers, and also for Clan Lhun, since we are denied a seat in the House of the People."

"Clan Lhun may claim its seat whenever it chooses to swear the council's oaths. You stay apart by your own choice. But why are you here? Do you intend to defend the condemned?"

"I don't condone the actions of the Dai Tranh when they cost innocent lives, but I know that these people were arrested days before the attack on the festival. If you mean to condemn them, perhaps you should choose crimes they might've had the chance to truly commit."

Yuen Xian bared her teeth in an ugly smile. Faraj's lips thinned.

"They have admitted their involvement with the Dai Tranh, and the Dai Tranh's with these attacks. They choose to protect their compatriots and endanger the lives of still more innocents."

"But their blood won't undo the damage done, nor heal Sivahra's wounds, will it?"

"No, but perhaps it can ease the pain of some of the victims' families." He raised a hand when Jabbor would have replied. "If you wish to continue this conversation, Mr. Lhun, you're welcome to bring it before the council. We certainly have matters we'd like to discuss with you. But today, sentence has been passed and will be carried out."

The soldiers tightened their circle around the Tigers, weapons steady. Faraj signaled the executioner and the man drew his sword. A kris-blade, long and waving; patterns rippled like water along the steel.

The swordsman stood behind the first prisoner, aimed the sword at the valley above the man's collarbone. Down through the lung, into the heart—it would be a clean kill, at least, if done properly. The watchers held their breath.

Faraj lowered his hand, and the swordsman thrust. The prisoner gasped and shuddered but didn't scream. A bubble of blood burst on his lips. The executioner twisted the blade and tugged it free. The man wavered on his knees for several heartbeats, crimson spilling in waves down his chest, then toppled over. Blood washed over the dais, seeping between the stones.

The swordsman wiped the blade with a cloth, but rust-colored stains clung in the patterned grooves. He moved behind Yuen and raised the sword again.

And fell with an arrow sprouting from his chest.

Someone screamed and the crowd scattered. Shots cracked from a rooftop and Asheris seized Faraj, hauling him off the dais. A wall of shimmering air enveloped them. Isyllt ducked against a tree trunk, dodging fleeing spectators. Arrows rained with the bullets, but more accurately. A councillor fell in front of her, a feathered shaft through his throat.

One of the soldiers beside Jabbor fell too, his face shattered by a bullet. Another stabbed at Jabbor, but the Lhun woman gutted him before the stroke could land. Cursing, the Tigers fought their way free and ducked behind a row of hedges.

Isyllt crouched, ready to run toward them, but movement on the dais distracted her. Yuen Xian had slipped her bonds and claimed the executioner's sword. She freed her clansman, then turned on Asheris and Faraj. His shield would stop bullets and arrows, but could it turn a blade?

Run, Isyllt told herself, *run*. But she kept watching. Even if she shouted, she doubted he'd hear her over the chaos. Yuen raised the sword.

And screamed as flames encased her. The sword fell with a shower of sparks as she stumbled back and dropped to the blood-drenched stone, trying to roll out the flames.

But an instant's distraction was enough to cost Asheris his shield. Another pistol fired and he fell.

And Isyllt, cursing herself for a fool, bolted toward him, ducking behind the edge of the dais. Faraj crouched with his back to the stone, face drained ashen.

Isyllt grabbed Asheris's arm, hauled him into the dubious cover. Blood stained his left shoulder, spreading around the hole in his coat. Sweat glistened on his brow and his breath came short and sharp.

"Don't—" he whispered as she tugged torn cloth aside.

"Damn it, let me see." Not the heart, at least. She laid her hand on his shoulder, searching for death-echoes in the wound. Not that she could do a damned thing if it was mortal—

She sucked in a breath and watched as the misshapen copper ball melted and oozed out of the wound. His diamond pulsed and sparked in time with his pulse, but her own magic was silent. He carried no trace of death in his flesh.

"What are you?"

He only shook his head, that hollow look in his eyes again. Faraj frowned and grabbed at her arm, but Isyllt pulled free and ran. Gunsmoke hung in the air, along with the reek of blood and death. She glanced up, glimpsed crouching figures on the nearest rooftop before a bullet struck the path in front of her, kicking up dust and shards of gravel. She dove sideways, scrambling across the grass, nearly tripping over the dead councillor as she regained the shelter of the tree.

Jabbor and his Tigers were still pinned down across the path. They had no cover for yards if they ran for the main gate.

Leaves rustled behind her and she turned to find Li creeping toward her.

"Be careful," Isyllt hissed, beckoning the woman closer. She didn't see the knife till Li was nearly on her.

She caught the first stroke with her forearm instead of her neck; the blade traced a line of fire below her elbow. Isyllt drove her knee into the woman's ribs, falling back on her good arm. Li grunted, dodged a kick and lunged, driving Isyllt flat against the ground and knocking the air from her lungs. The sky darkened as Li leaned over her, knocked her left arm aside. She threw up her wounded arm to block the blow—

But Li wasn't aiming for her heart or her throat. The knife came down and Isyllt screamed as it skewered her left palm, nailing her hand to the ground. Her vision washed red and black; the weight left her chest, but she still couldn't breathe.

She didn't realize she'd lost consciousness till she came to at the sound of her name. Hands on her shoulders, dragging her up, and she gasped as bone grated on steel.

"Mother's bones." Jabbor crouched beside her. "Hold still," he said, reaching for the knife. "This will hurt."

She sobbed as he eased the blade free; metal slid past layers of skin and muscle and tissue, scraped bone. Blood pooled in her palm, ran down her wrist as she lifted her arm. She couldn't move her fingers. Li was gone and so was her ring.

"Where did she go?" She rose to her knees, cradling her useless hand against her chest. Blood soaked her shirt, dripped off her other arm as well. "Damn it, where did she go?"

"She ran," Jabbor said, gesturing toward the closest building. "We have to get out of here."

"I can't let her get away—"

"You think you can catch her like this?" He pulled her to her feet, holding her steady as she wobbled. "Besides, you were out for minutes—who knows where she is by now. We're leaving."

And he ran, dragging her along. Stumbling and cursing, Isyllt ran too, the other Tigers flanking them. She risked a glance back, saw soldiers closing on the rooftop. A suicide mission—or a distraction for something else?

As they reached the shelter of the pomegranate trees, another group of people broke from cover behind the eastern hall. Sivahri, and armed, but they bolted for the wall, paying no attention to Isyllt and the Tigers. One man held a child in his arms.

Four soldiers guarded the gates, nervous and distracted by the clamor across the grounds. As Jabbor and his people fell on the first three, Isyllt stretched out a bloody hand to the fourth.

"Help me," she gasped. "Please."

He hesitated for an instant, pistol half raised. Long enough for Isyllt's magic to wrap around him, to close cold fingers over his heart. He fell, gasping, brown face drained gray.

Jabbor cast a horrified glance at the man as they wrestled the locks open; he huddled on the ground, shaking and moaning—if he had that much strength left, Isyllt doubted he would die.

Outside, knots of people gathered on the sidewalks and alarm bells rang. A skiff poled toward the landing as they slipped through the gate, and Jabbor and the Tigers bolted for it. Isyllt followed, too slow, and wondered if they would leave her behind. Then someone shouted her name.

She spun, slipping on damp stone, and saw Adam waving from another boat. "Go on," she shouted at Jabbor, and ran for the other skiff.

The craft rocked as she stumbled aboard and Adam grabbed her arm, dragging her down. She cried out and fell, scraping her good palm against the wooden bench. The steersman poled away, face and hair shrouded in a scarf—Vienh.

"Blood and iron," Adam muttered, crouching beside her. He reached for her wounded hand, and she jerked away.

"I met your other assassin."

"Is she still alive?"

"Unfortunately."

"Show me where you're hurt, damn it," he said as she flinched away again.

She swallowed the taste of pain, nearly choked on it, and held out her left hand. Skin gaped—a perfect double-edged stab wound. A wonderful example to show a class of investigators. Some pale flashed amid the blood; tendon perhaps, or bone.

She started to laugh, high and shrill. Then Adam touched her hand and she passed out again.

Consciousness returned swift and cruel while they circled the canals of Straylight, making sure they weren't pursued. When Adam and Vienh were satisfied, they set out for Merrowgate, and the narrow waterway behind an inn. Not the Bride—Isyllt couldn't fault Vienh for that; she didn't trust her luck either.

Adam draped his cloak over her to hide the blood as they docked, held her steady up three flights of stairs to the room. The bleeding had slowed enough that she didn't leave a trail up the steps, at least.

"I need bandages and needle and thread," Adam said as Isyllt fell into a chair. "And clean water."

Isyllt bit her tongue while Adam cut away her ruined sleeves; when half-clotted scabs peeled loose she hissed. Her right arm was still bleeding, but it was nothing compared to the left. She could only stare at her curled hand, at the naked skin where her ring should be. Vienh returned with the supplies and Adam scrubbed his hands.

The water was tepid but burned like vitriol in her wounds. Adam cleaned her right arm first and opened a tube of ointment, nodding thanks to Vienh.

"I don't need that."

His eyebrows rose. "Humor me."

The cream smelled of tea-tree oil, sweet-sharp and faintly resinous. It also stung, and she glared at him while he smeared it on. The needle was a proper surgeon's tool, curved and razor-tipped; light gleamed and splintered off the tip. She wondered how many patrons the innkeeper stitched up. Adam's hands were steady as he threaded it.

Isyllt braced herself and swallowed. Her head ached, the edge of her vision too dark—more magic would only make it worse.

Her resolve lasted till the third stitch. Then the cold came, sweet and soothing. The throb in her temple became a spike, but instead of fire and wasp stings in her arm, she felt only the soft pop of skin, the slide and tug of the thread.

When he clipped the last knot, she tilted her arm to look. Ugly, thread black and stark against her skin and the red edges of the wound; at least the stitches were neat. Adam dabbed on more ointment, then bound her arm in bandages.

The pain had dulled to a queasy red blur by the time he was done. She stank of blood and sweat, and breathing ached where Li had landed on her ribs. All her luggage was at the Khas.

"Now this," Adam said softly, reaching for her left hand. The concern in his voice was no comfort. "Have you numbed the pain?"

She shook her head and quickly regretted it.

"Good. I need to know where it hurts."

Tears leaked from the corners of her eyes as he tested each finger, put gentle pressure on her palm. She could move her thumb and her first and last fingers, but the middle two curled uselessly, and she whimpered when he touched them. The nearly healed cut from the exorcism had torn open again, a four-rayed star cupped in her palm. Her hand felt too light without the diamond.

"I think a bone is cracked," he said at last. "And the tendon's severed."

She swallowed, lips pressed tight; for a moment she thought she would be sick. She'd seen enough dissections

to understand the worst of it. The physicians at the Arcanost might repair such an injury, but it had to be done
quickly. Nearly a month of water lay between her and Erisín. And she still had work to do.

"Pack it," she said at last. "Pack it and splint it and
wrap it tight."

Adam nodded and reached for the ointment again.

The markers didn't entirely lie. Traces of ghost-blight lingered in the woods: barren patches of earth and withered
trees, patches of sickly grass. Xinai felt spirits flittering
through the jungle around them—curious, cautious, but
not malevolent. Whatever evil had happened here, it was
long cold.

The worst scare came when they finally crossed a kueh
trail before the bird had left it. Xinai looked up, and up,
and found herself staring at a sharp, curving beak. A male,
by the brilliant blue neck and crimson wattle. A dark bone
crest curved from the top of its beak to the back of its
skull. It rasped a loud *kweh* and flared its wings—black
on the outsides, bronze shading to dark gold beneath.

Xinai's breath caught as one golden eye fixed on her.
Claws longer than her hand scratched the earth. Her hand
tightened around a knife hilt, but could she draw faster
than the bird could kick?

Before she had to answer, a freezing wind whipped over
them. The kueh shrieked and flapped, hopped backward
awkwardly before it turned and bolted into the brush.

Xinai's blood tingled, stabbed pins and needles. She
let out a shuddering gasp and pried her half-numb hand
off her knife.

"Ancestors," Riuh hissed. "Is that a ghost?"

Xinai grinned past him, where Shaiyung faded from sight. "Don't worry, she's with us. But you can walk ahead for a while."

Lingering excitement sped them up for a while, though they finally forced themselves to a steadier pace. The diamond pulsed against Xinai's chest, and she knew they were going the right way now. The sun had begun its westward slide when Riuh caught her arm and drew her to a halt.

"What is it?" she whispered.

"Look." He pointed toward a broken vine, a thread snagged in tree bark. "There are men about. We'll rush straight into them if we're not careful."

So they edged south till the diamond's throb slowed, and crept in slow and soft. Once or twice they heard men passing nearby, but Xinai's charms and Riuh's stealth held up. Soon she heard voices and distant splashing. The trees thinned and they crouch-crawled through the brush till they reached the edge of the woods.

Now Xinai began to sense something, a creeping sense of wrong that she hadn't felt at the markers. The nape of her neck prickled and she felt Shaiyung's icy discontent, but her mother kept quiet as they crept on.

The ground sloped into a valley, and a broad, lazy river unwound below them. One of the many veins of Sivahra that flowed to meet the great artery of the Mir. She didn't know its name, but all lesser rivers were Gai—the mother's daughter.

Buildings lined the shore, solid enough to have stood for years. Locks of wood and stone enclosed stretches of river perhaps a hundred yards long, the water between them brown and silty. People stood in the river, a dozen for every stretch, scooping mud into loosely woven baskets. Every so often one would pull something out of the mud, rinse it clean, and tuck it into a bag. For a moment Xinai thought they were fishing, but what fish or crab was so valuable it needed armed guards lining the shore?

The men and women on the shore wore forest garb, the mismatched styles that had become common among the people of the lowland jungles. Mostly Assari, but not all, skin ranging from teak to honeyed cream. No uniforms, no badges or colors, but she recognized the way they moved, their circuits and posts, the watchful ease with which they stood. Mercenaries. Or soldiers.

The diamond throbbed against Xinai's chest, and slowly she realized what she was watching. The taste of blood filled her mouth; she'd bitten her lip. Her jaw ached from clenching it.

She'd expected something worse. Scars carved in rock, caverns full of glittering stones, chained prisoners with picks and shovels. From above these looked like children, searching streambeds for polished pebbles or blue crabs for stew. But these must be the missing prisoners—they'd gone to the mines after all, just not the mine the Khas claimed.

"There are ghosts down there," Shaiyung whispered in her ear. "On the far side of the river. A lot of them, all unsung." Her face was grim and ghastly as ever, but her voice cracked with anger and sorrow.

The air chilled and the shadows deepened around them; the sun had moved behind the mountain, casting the valley in a false twilight. Beside her, Riuh's face was ashen, his shoulders stiff.

"We should go," Xinai whispered, touching his arm; his muscles trembled with tension.

"This is where they all go. My father might be down there."

She glanced at her mother.

"I don't know," Shaiyung said in answer to the unspoken question. "And the ghosts are in no shape to help us—they're trapped, weak and faded."

Xinai shook her head sadly. "We could never take them, and you know it. Come on—we have to tell Selei."

A guard whistled and she flinched, but it was only the sign for the prisoners to come in. One by one they trudged out of the river, revealing rope hobbles barely long enough for a short woman's pace. The guards took their bags away and frisked them thoroughly, checking under their tongues.

One of the prisoners closest to the lock dawdled as the others left the water, leaning down as if to scoop more mud. From her vantage, Xinai saw he wasn't using his basket at all, but reaching for his ankles.

An escape attempt. Her breath caught; Riuh stiffened.

The lock below was empty. After that, the river flowed free. If he could only make it . . .

If he made it, could they help him? Should they? He'd only slow them down. Her hand tightened on her knife hilt.

The prisoner bolted. Xinai winced at the sound of splashing feet, at the shout of the guard. One, two, three, four strides and he was nearly at the lock. A guard drew his bow—the sound of a pistol shot would carry too far over the water.

He reached the lock. Riuh crouched on the balls of his feet, ready to run. The twang of a bowstring carried through the air. The prisoner arched into a dive.

And fell gracelessly as the arrow pierced his back. If he cried out, Xinai couldn't hear it. He surfaced, clawing the water, then sank again. Riuh let out a painful breath, as if he'd been struck.

Below them, the body drifted gently toward the last lock. Scarlet ribbons spooled into the current, dissolved into mud and brown as the guards ambled down to retrieve the corpse.

"Let's go," Xinai said, her voice hollow.

Riuh didn't answer, only stared at the guards, his face twisted with anger and pain.

"Let's go!" she hissed, tugging his arm. "We'll avenge them all, but not today."

He shook his head, braids rattling. After a long moment he moved, following her into the trees. She pretended she didn't see his tears.

He came to her in the dark that night, silent and trembling, his cheeks slick with salt. No icy touch of possession this time, only a tangle of pain and grief and need, of guilt and desire. She didn't push him away.

CHAPTER 15

After Adam had doctored her wounds, Isyllt cleaned up as best she could while Vienh went out for food. The room still stank like a surgery in spite of the cracked-open window. She felt better having an emergency exit, though she doubted she'd survive the two-story drop in her present condition.

"How much money do we have left?" she asked, trying to undo her shirt buttons one-handed and mourning all the clean clothes she'd abandoned in the Khas. She could sell the silver chains in her kit if she had to, but she carried nothing else of value.

"Enough for a few days here or a cheap passage home. Sleeping-on-deck cheap. I hope you don't need anyone bribed."

"At this point it'd be easier to kill people." Her fingers slipped off a button for the third time and she swore.

Adam's smile was a ghost in the deepening gloom. "It usually is."

"They'll have someone watching the embassy by to-morrow. At least the supply ship is already on its way." She cursed foreign assignments and buttons silently. "I have to get my ring back."

"Are you sure that's smart?"

"Losing it in the first place was stupid enough. I'm not leaving without it." She fumbled another button and snarled.

"Need help?" Adam asked, nearly smiling.

Pride fought pragmatism and lost soundly. "Yes, damn it."

She watched his nimble calloused fingers and swallowed a laugh. He caught her expression and his lips quirked as he undid the last button and helped her slip the remnants of the sleeve off her left arm. Her linen undershirt was stiff with dried blood and sweat—it itched, but not so badly that she'd rather be naked.

Adam turned toward the door an instant before someone knocked. He eased the latch up, double-checking before he opened it wide enough for Vienh to slip in. She carried bamboo cartons of food and—saints bless her—a change of clothes. Isyllt's stomach clenched at the smell of curry.

Dusk bells tolled slow and sonorous as they ate, and Vienh lit the room's single lamp. Isyllt was halfway through a carton of rice and lentils when Adam tensed again. A heartbeat later someone else knocked. Isyllt swallowed a mouthful and glanced at Vienh—the smuggler shook her head sharply.

"I wasn't followed, I swear," she whisper-hissed when Adam glared at her.

He stood, easing a dagger from his boot as he edged toward the door; the quarters were too close for swords.

Isyllt thought of her knife safely packed across the city and swore under her breath even as she edged out of the door's line of sight.

"Please let me in," a familiar voice asked softly. "I'll attract more attention standing out here."

Vienh drew her knife and moved behind the door. Adam glanced at Isyllt. "Only one," he mouthed. She nodded slowly, and he reached for the latch.

Siddir slipped in—cautiously, when he saw Adam's blade. The mercenary checked the hall quickly and shut the door. Siddir pulled a scarf away from his tousled curls. Isyllt tensed, waiting for soldiers' footsteps, for the brush of hot magic, but none came.

Siddir smiled at her expression and bowed, stopping when Adam's knife drew closer to his throat.

"They'll charge more if you make a mess in the room, you know," he said.

Isyllt started to cross her arms, but thought better of it. "How did you find me?"

Siddir cocked an eyebrow. "I am a spy, after all. I wanted to talk to you without the whole Khas looking on."

She gestured toward the hard wooden chair. "So sit and talk."

His gaze slid along her bandaged arms. "Did that happen at the execution?"

"Yes. You were there?"

"I was, but I didn't feel the need to be in the thick of things. Luckily for me."

"What happened? Is the Khas looking for me?"

"The Khas is a bit preoccupied at the moment. Nineteen people are dead, not counting the Dai Tranh—three councillors, the rest bureaucrats, servants, and soldiers. And it turns out the attack may have only been a distraction."

Isyllt retrieved her food, nodding for him to continue.

"While all the shooting and dying was happening, more rebels kidnapped the Viceroy's daughter. Lady Shamina was injured in the fight. Faraj is . . . distraught. I'm afraid recovering you won't be the first thing on his mind."

Isyllt swallowed and blinked. The man fleeing with a child—Murai. "Have they made demands for her return?"

"We've heard nothing."

She cocked an eyebrow. "We?"

Siddir smiled. "A figure of speech. As I told you, my loyalty is not to the Khas."

"Where is it, exactly?"

"To the Empire." His smile stretched at her expression. "To the Empire, but not to Rahal."

She set the curry down again. The pressure in her head had become a stabbing pain above one eye. She rubbed her temple, wincing as the movement tugged stitches.

"Would you please just tell me what the hell is going on?"

One brown cheek dimpled as he nodded. "The Emperor's dreams of expansion are no secret in Ta'ashlan, but not all the Senate supports him. The Senate has consistently refused to increase taxes for military spending. But that doesn't seem to be stopping Rahal. The money keeps coming in—never fast enough to be conspicuous, but enough that some senators have become suspicious."

Isyllt reached for her cup of ginger beer and wished it were something stronger. "And they think it's coming from Symir."

"I'm almost certain of it. But we're not sure where. At first we thought he was skimming from the tithes, but the Khas's records balance—far too neatly, for a known hive of graft and corruption. Something's happening off the books, but I don't know what."

It was Isyllt's turn to smile. "I do. But," she continued as Siddir cocked his head, "how will this be of any use to me? Giving the Empire a legitimate source of wealth will do nothing to keep Assari armies away from Selafaïn shores."

"Expansion is not the will of the people in Assar. Rahal has supporters amongst the generals and the arms-makers, of course, but too many families still mourn those who died in the Ninayan campaign, or in Iseth, or here. Assar is large enough—there are things we want from Selafai, but another vassal country isn't one of them."

"And you think proof of this embezzlement would be enough to stop the Emperor?"

"Yes. Some of the senators are ... willing to take steps."

She pressed her tongue against her teeth, tasted ginger-sweet and treason. If he was lying, she couldn't tell.

"Sivahra has a diamond mine. The Viceroy is smuggling the stones out in private ships."

Across the room Vienh stiffened, lips parting. She subsided without speaking, though.

Siddir blinked. "Well. I've been underestimating Faraj, it seems, if he's kept something like that a secret. I wonder where Rahal is selling them." He shrugged the question aside. "We need proof."

"I think I know where to look. I'll need to speak to my contacts."

He nodded. "I encourage haste. If the situation here

continues to deteriorate, the Emperor will send troops, and everything will become more complicated."

"I have another question for you, my lord, while we're being so forthcoming. How well do you know Asheris al Seth?"

He didn't blink, quite, but he stilled for a heartbeat. "Ah. Yes. Once, I knew him well. We went to the university together. We were friends." The word came out too quickly, too blandly. "He had no designs to be an Imperial agent in those days. He was a middling mage at best—a lot of talent, but little dedication, more interested in carousing than serious study. His connection to the throne was too remote to concern anyone, and mostly he was left to his own devices."

"But?"

"Seven years ago, something changed." He frowned, smoothed his face again. "I still don't know what it was. He joined an expedition into the desert—a spirit cataloging trip, very ordinary. Al Najid was with them as well. When they returned, no one heard from Asheris for several months, and when he finally emerged he was . . . different. More focused, more reserved. More powerful. It wasn't long afterward that he began to rise in the Emperor's confidences."

Isyllt swallowed, her stomach cold. Seven years of feeding off a bound spirit. A spirit powerful enough to make a man immortal. Yes, that might change someone. Her left hand tightened before the pain stopped it. No doubt his fear of death was real enough, even if his distaste for bindings was a lie.

He would come after her. It was a secret worth protecting. He knew the taste of her magic—her magic and her skin. At least, she thought bitterly, no one could track her by her ring.

"How can I reach you?" she asked Siddir.

"I have a box at the Imperial Post. Leave word there, and I'll get it within the day." He started to rise, glanced at Adam to make sure the way was free of blades before he finished. "Thank you, my lady."

"Thank me when this is over and I'm still alive. I'll leave a message when I know more."

When Siddir and Vienh had gone and Isyllt had arranged to send word to Zhirin, she sat down to finish her cold dinner. There wasn't an inch of her that didn't hurt between her forehead and feet, and her stitches itched. It wasn't safe to sleep, but she couldn't fight it much longer.

"Sleep," Adam said. "I'll keep watch."

"To hell with it," she muttered, sitting heavily on the bed. "I'm not running anywhere else today."

Slats creaked as she lay down. The mattress smelled of mildew and old sweat; she wondered about fleas. By the time her eyes closed, she'd stopped caring.

The alarm bells began at three-quarters past noon, shattering the stretched-thin peace that filled the Laii parlor. Zhirin stumbled over a line of verse, dropped the book she'd been reading from. Fei Minh's cup rattled against her saucer.

Zhirin cursed her cowardice—she should have attended the execution, though the thought had turned her stomach. But her mother disdained public bloodshed, and Zhirin had allowed herself to be convinced to stay home, to speak of nothing and read poetry aloud when neither of them had the nerve to voice their accusations and concerns.

Zhirin stood, and Fei Minh followed.

"No," her mother said as Zhirin turned toward the door. "Don't even think about it. Stay and wait for the criers."

Her spine stiffened at Fei Minh's tone, but Zhirin had never been much good at rebelling. And it was no use running anywhere if she didn't know what was happening. Instead she nodded and hurried toward the bathroom.

Water splashed into the basin, rising quickly to the brim. She stilled the surface with a pass of her hand and pushed her nerves away. "Jabbor," she whispered to her rippling reflection.

No image came. He was beyond the river's sight. Isyllt's name brought no response either, nor did Faraj's. Zhirin bit back an angry hiss, rinsed her hands in ritual ablution before unplugging the drain and sending the water back to the river. She dried her hands and returned to the parlor, and the volume of Laii clan poetry.

The criers started an hour later. Zhirin and her mother stood on the front step and listened to story after story—the Dai Tranh had attacked the Khas; the Tigers had stormed the execution; the Viceroy had been shot; Asheris had been shot; the Vicereine had been attacked; the Vicereine's daughter had been attacked. Zhirin's stomach twisted tighter and tighter at each new rumor—no matter how wild, all agreed that the Tigers had been at the execution. But no one could agree on who was truly dead.

The rain drove them inside before the dusk bells, and Fei Minh helped Mau with supper while Zhirin paced the front hall. Someone knocked at the door as they laid out dishes. Zhirin hurried to answer it, fingers knotting in the hem of her shirt. Surely the Khas would send a message to her mother. Surely Jabbor would let her know what had happened—

A young mehti girl stood on the doorstep, rain dripping off the hood of her oilcloak.

"I've a message for Zhirin Laii."

She swallowed. "I'm Zhirin."

The girl's eyes narrowed as she glanced through the open door. "Isyllt wants to meet you."

At least someone was alive. "When? Where?"

"At dawn, at the Bridge of Splinters."

Zhirin tightened her jaw to keep her mouth from falling open. If Isyllt had left the Khas— "Do you know what happened today?"

The girl shook her head. "Only rumors. What answer should I give her?"

"I'll be there. Wait a moment." She ducked into the tradesman's parlor, fished a few pennies out of the tipbox. The girl palmed them neatly and they vanished into a pocket. "Thank you. And tell her . . . Never mind. Just tell her I'll be there."

The girl nodded and hurried down the steps.

"What is it?" Fei Minh asked as Zhirin shut and bolted the door.

"Only Vasilios's housekeeper sending a message." Her voice caught on his name, but at least she had reason enough for that. "She wants me to help dispose of the house tomorrow." Fei Minh might not be swayed by sentiment, but the proper disposition of wealth would move her.

Her mother frowned, and for an instant Zhirin thought she would argue. But all she said was, "Dinner's ready," and turned back to the kitchen.

Zhirin followed her to the table, hoping food would clear away the taste of lies.

Zhirin woke with a start, darkness pressed tight against her window. She'd told Mau to wake her well before dawn, but she was alone, her door latched.

She jumped as a pebble rattled against the shutter, then let out a breath. She threw off the covers, wincing as she caught her toe on the edge of a rug, and hurried to the window. Easing the latch open, she waited a few heartbeats to be sure no more rocks were inbound before she leaned out.

Jabbor crouched on the wall between her house and their neighbor's. For an instant relief was so sharp in her chest she thought she'd cry. Shaking it off, she closed the window and pulled on clothes. She paused in the hallway, listening carefully, but her mother still slept. Sleep charms, at least, were easy to manage.

The garden was a walled-in square behind the house, shaded by a pair of spice-fragrant cassia trees. In the center a fountain welled—or hiccuped, now; she'd never gotten around to fixing it. Dwarf kheymen slept beside the water, their bodies barely as long as her hand, tails sharp as whips. Their eyes flashed gold and green as she padded across the damp mossy flagstones, but they didn't move. Her parents' room overlooked the garden, but that hadn't stopped her when she was fourteen, sneaking out with Sia. She looked up anyway, to be sure the curtains hung straight and still.

Jabbor waited in the shadow of the wall, apparently unhurt. Zhirin thanked all the waters silently. She breathed in the smell of his clean sweat as he took her in his arms, salt and cedar and drying rain.

"What happened?" she asked, pulling away sooner than she would have liked.

"I went to the execution."

She folded her arms under her chest. "Why?"

"Because it's our right to speak out, and what use is that if no one will? If the Dai Tranh had tried talking before burning, things might be different."

"You could have been killed!"

He shrugged. "I nearly was, and the Khas wasn't the worst of it."

She turned away, paced to the edge of the fountain. "Why didn't you tell me?"

"You would have worried."

"And I wasn't worried today, hearing the bells and not knowing what happened? Listening to criers say you were dead?" Her voice rose, and she forced it down again. The fountain choked and gurgled.

She drew a breath, exhaled the scent of damp stone and cinnamon. No use in being angry about it now. Instead she propped a knee against the fountain, damp soaking her trousers as she dipped a hand into the water. Only a fraction of the Mir's rush and depth, but it still soothed her. The problem was easy to find—a buildup of sand and clay in the narrow pipe. A bit of pressure, a gentle push, and the debris broke apart and washed away. The fountain gave one last hiccup, then began to splash rhythmically again.

Jabbor smiled, shaking his head. "Sometimes I forget what you can do."

She sighed. "Everyone does, don't they? That's what I'm good for."

"I'm sorry." He shook his head. "I don't mean it that way. I know how you've helped us. I know what you've risked."

"Not all of it, you don't." She cut him off. "First, tell me what happened today."

"I went to the execution to speak, but the Dai Tranh came too. They started shooting and everything went to hell. They attacked your foreign witch too. She escaped with us, then left with her own people. I've heard rumors about deaths and kidnappings, but I don't know what's true or not, yet. None of the Tigers were hurt. I saw the mage al Seth fall, but I don't think he's dead."

She thought of Asheris swallowing an inferno and shivered. "No, I suspect he's hard to kill." She scrubbed her wet hand against her thigh. "I found out what's happening with those diamonds." Her eyes darted toward her mother's windows again, and she didn't look away until she was done telling him about the diamonds, and her mother, and Jodiya's threats. As she fell silent, the midnight bells began to toll—once, twice, thrice, deep and solemn.

"Ancestors," Jabbor swore when the last echo died. He caught her arm, tugged her gently into the shadows. "Come with me. The Tigers can keep you safe. We can be in the jungle before dawn."

Zhirin succumbed to temptation for a moment, leaned her head against his shoulder and let his warmth soak into her. "I can't." She straightened, stepped back. "Not tonight. I have to meet Isyllt tomorrow."

"Zhir— Leave it. At this rate her supplies won't come in time and the city isn't safe. The Dai Tranh and the Khas will be after her."

Her jaw tightened. "Then she'll need my help, won't she?"

"This isn't a game!"

"No." Her chest tightened at his expression. "Was I ever a game piece to you?"

He opened his mouth, shut it again. "Not at first. When I first saw you, you were a pretty girl, a girl I wanted to walk with, to flirt with. Then I found out who you were, and . . . yes. Yes, I thought of what you could do for us, and decided it was worth the risk. But I swear, Zhir, I won't use you. I won't be like the Khas that way, like the Dai Tranh."

She stretched onto her toes to kiss him. "I believe you. But I'm still staying. You don't have anyone else to overhear Faraj's plans."

"I'm sorry I underestimated you."

She flushed. "It's not bravery," she said, forcing her voice light. "I don't want to sleep in the jungle."

He laughed and bent to kiss her again. It was harder to pull away this time.

"You should go," she whispered. "I need some sleep before dawn. Can I leave word in the usual places?"

"I think so." Heat soaked her arms where he held her. "Be careful, Zhir."

"You too." She kissed him again, a quick brush of lips, and fled back inside.

PART III

Deep Water

CHAPTER 16

Bright chimes faded as dawn crept damp and gray through the streets of Merrowgate, replacing nocturnal business with diurnal. From the front of a narrow tea shop, its windows opened wide to catch the breeze, Isyllt watched shopkeepers unroll awnings over the sidewalk, set out crates and barrels. Children wheeled carts of fruit and bread onto the bridge and sat on the warped wooden railings, legs dangling as they called to passersby. Others crouched with fishing lines on the slick steps of the canal.

A cool morning, but Isyllt sweated and shivered in turns beneath her cloak. Her magic fought off any infection that crept into her blood, but the battles left her feverish. If she had the luxury of half a day's sleep, she'd hardly notice it.

Her back itched with drying sweat and paranoia—she twitched at every sudden footfall, every flickering shadow, but moving made her harder to track, and people in Merrowgate seemed to make a habit of minding their own business. No one's head turned at another cloaked figure. With any luck, the men's clothes she wore—all that would fit—might fool a casual glance. Adam had laughed as she bound her breasts, but Zhirin, at least, had looked twice before recognizing her.

The girl returned to the table, carefully holding three bamboo cups. Ribbons of steam twined and tattered as she set them down and turned back to the counter for milk and honey. Isyllt cradled lacquered wood between her gloved hands—hiding bandages now. Not much warmth seeped through, and her left hand stung, but the gesture was comforting.

"What now?" Zhirin asked. Soft, but not furtive; casual—the girl was learning.

"I have to find my ring. And who knows, maybe that will lead me to Murai as well."

"Do you think that will change anything? If you bring her back?"

Isyllt shrugged. "I don't know. Perhaps they'd send me home in chains on an Imperial ship, instead of killing me." She still hadn't told anyone about Asheris, though she couldn't say exactly why she felt the need to keep his secrets. Or why his lies still stung when she thought about them.

"Will you try to help her?"

Somewhere on the street a child laughed and she thought of the girl standing on the edge of the volcano, face flushed in delight at Asheris's magic tricks. No child deserved to suffer for their parents, or for their country, but they always did. "If I find her." She'd seen what happened to people who tried to live for everyone but themselves—most often they ended up dying for nothing. "If

not, the more distracted the Khas is right now, the better."
She couldn't help a quick glance toward Adam, but he sat
silent as a statue, his eyes turned to the street.

Zhirin's lips thinned and Isyllt waited for the recrimi-
nations, but the girl only stirred her tea, adding milk and
honey till it was the same shade as her skin. "How will
you find the ring?"

"If I'm close enough I'll feel it. But for anything farther
than a building away I need to cast a finding. For that
I'll need space, a map of the area, and a stone—probably
quartz. Another diamond would be better, but I doubt I'll
find one of those in the market."

"No—" Zhirin paused, frowning. "Do you remember, was Vasilios wearing any rings when . . . we found
him?"

Pressing her tongue between her teeth, Isyllt tried to
remember all the details—the cold flicker of the witchlight, the old man's discolored face, one gnarled hand
curled against the carpet . . .

"I don't think so," she said after a moment.

"His hands swelled in the rainy season." Zhirin's voice
caught, throat working as she swallowed. "He sometimes
took his rings off when he wasn't working. They might
still be in the house. I'll check."

She was quiet for a moment and the sounds of the street
rippled over them, the muted rattle and clatter from the
kitchen. "Jabbor wants me to go with him. Into the jungle.
He thinks he can keep me safe."

Isyllt sipped her drink. The shop used a lot of cardamom; the taste spread rich and bittersweet across the back
of her mouth. "Do you think that?"

Zhirin's mouth twisted. "I don't know. I would have,

only a month ago. But I think you're right—I can do more here. I hope so, at least."

"Do you know any more about the next shipment?"

"Not the schedule. But the ship is the *Yhan Ti*, docked southside at the seventh berth." She stared at her milky tea as if she meant to scry it, set it down barely tasted. "I'm going to the house. Is there anything you need, besides the stone?"

"Money, or anything I can easily pawn in the market."

The girl's forehead creased, but she nodded. "If I get a mirror, can I use it to contact you?"

"Yes. Just say my name. I'll hear you."

"All right." Zhirin pulled a purse out of her pocket, stacked brass and copper coins on the table. "I'll talk to you soon."

Adam raised his cup as the girl left the shop, throat working as he swallowed. "Do you think we can trust her?"

"I don't have much choice. She may crack eventually, jeopardize the mission for foolish idealism. But she's clever and we're running low on allies."

He nodded, a crease between his brows. "What now, then? I don't want to stay on the street."

"No. I think we should have a talk with Izzy."

Red ward-ribbons covered the front doors of Vasilios's house, but if the house was watched, Zhirin couldn't tell. She straightened her shoulders; she wasn't a fugitive, and she had as much right to be here as family. She still ducked around to the back.

The kitchen door had been warded, but the cord hung loose now, the latch undone. Zhirin slipped inside, not brushing the rope, and kicked off her shoes. The floor was dusty, smudged and dappled with footprints and dripped water.

She paused inside the threshold, listening hard, and nearly jumped as something white moved at the corner of her eye.

"Mrau," said the cat, leaping onto the kitchen counter. Zhirin pressed a hand over her hammering heart and laughed. "Gavriel! You know you're not supposed to be up there." She bit her lip as she realized there was no one left to care what counters or shelves he climbed. She stroked his cream-colored head and he leaned into the touch, rumbling loudly.

"I'm sorry I forgot about you," she said, scratching between his shoulder blades. "You can come home with me today." She glanced down at his bowls, frowned to find them full of clean water and fresh meat.

"Who's been taking care of you?" she asked softly, but Gavriel only butted his head against her arm. Had the police thought to do it? Conscientious burglars?

She checked to be sure the ground floor was empty, then crept upstairs. By the time she reached the second floor, she knew she wasn't alone. No voices or footsteps, but a prickling down her back, a tingle of *otherwise* senses. She drew a silence around her with a whisper.

The second story was empty too—she shuddered as she passed the library where her master's body had lain—but when she reached the third she heard someone moving quietly in Vasilios's private study. Her pulse echoed in her ears as she crept toward the door.

Then she recognized Marat and sighed aloud. The woman spun, hand dropping to her trouser pocket. Zhirin raised a hand.

"I'm sorry. I didn't mean to startle you."

The old woman recovered quickly. "And I didn't expect to find you here, child. Have you brought the executors, then, to dispose of things?"

"No. I just wanted to look through the house." Her eyes slid to the silver-chased box in Marat's other hand. Zhirin recognized it instantly—her master's jewel coffer. She swallowed; stealing from the dead was ill-luck indeed. Would her luck be any better?

"If you need money, I'll make sure you get it. I haven't gone over the estate records yet, but—"

She stopped as Marat chuckled.

"I'm sure you would. You always were such a thoughtful child."

Zhirin flinched from the ugly mockery in the words. "What did I do to you?"

"Nothing. You've never done anything, and that's the problem. Not that I could expect much from someone raised by your Assari whore of a mother."

Zhirin stiffened, cheeks burning. "You don't know anything about what I do."

"What, because you run around with the Jade Tigers, you're a revolutionary? It's not that easy."

"No." The word came out nearly a whisper. "It isn't."

Marat's face didn't soften, but her voice gentled. "Go home. Or better yet, leave the city. Go with your lover and spare yourself judgment for your mother's crimes."

"A woman stealing from the dead has little room to cast stones. Give me that box."

Marat's hand tightened on the silver coffer. Her other emerged from her pocket, fingers wrapped around the hilt of a knife. "Go home, girl, or you'll end up like your master."

Her hands began to tingle, and Zhirin swallowed sour spit. "It was you, wasn't it? You killed him."

"He should never have involved himself in Sivahra's problems. Foreigners bring us nothing but trouble."

"So you murder them?"

"Leave it alone." Marat started toward the door.

Zhirin didn't move, though fear and shock flooded her. "Put the box down." She didn't know how she managed to speak with her pulse so thick and fast in her throat.

Marat's blade flashed toward her face and Zhirin ducked, grabbed for the woman's wrist like she'd seen knife-fighters do. Fighters stronger than she—Marat pulled away easily, and the knife traced a line of heat across the edge of Zhirin's hand. She gasped and jerked away, but didn't step aside.

With a curse Marat shoved her and Zhirin lost her balance. She kicked as she fell, tangling her feet in the old woman's ankles. Marat stumbled across the threshold, went down hard on her knees. The silver box clattered across the tiles—the sound was dull and distant through the roar of blood in Zhirin's ears.

Marat tried to stand, gasped and fell again, one knee popping loudly. Pain twisted her face as she turned and lunged for Zhirin. The old woman's weight drove the breath from her lungs and she barely threw up an arm in time to keep the blade from her throat.

Even three times Zhirin's age and injured, Marat was stronger. The knife crept closer and closer, and her arm trembled and burned. She clawed at Marat's face with her wounded hand, but did little more than smear blood on the woman's cheek. No weapon in reach.

No—she had the river.

She'd never reached out to the Mir in fear before—

the strength of the response shocked her. It rose through her like a wave, the power of rain and river and relentless tides. Her bleeding hand tightened on Marat's face—flesh and blood, earth and water.

Marat coughed, narrow shoulders convulsing. Moisture seeped between her tea-stained teeth, trickled from her lips, splashing Zhirin's face, and the pressure on the knife eased. She coughed again, choked. The woman jerked away from her grasp, knife falling forgotten as she reached for her throat.

Water leaked from around Marat's panic-wide eyes, dribbled from her nose and mouth. Not tears, not saliva— silty river water. Zhirin scrambled up, staring in horror as the flood kept coming. Marat tried to speak, but liquid bubbled up instead, a rushing torrent that soaked her clothes and spread across the tiles.

It felt as though she took an hour to die, choking and writhing and vomiting water, but doubtless only moments passed before the old woman lay still. Water flooded the hallway, trickled over the edge of the railing and splattered against the floor below. Zhirin could hardly breathe and realized her hand was pressed against her mouth hard enough to ache. The smell of blood and river water filled her nose, coated her tongue, and she turned away to vomit up her breakfast on the study's expensive carpet.

"Forgive me, Lady," Izzy said, "but you're being a fool."

Isyllt wished she could argue; instead she shrugged. Sweat crawled against her scalp and the stink of oil and salted fish unsettled her stomach. Adam stood at her back, and Vienh at Izzy's elbow—the heat of four people and the lamps was stifling in the Bride's cramped storeroom.

"Have you ever seen a city rioting?" the dwarf asked, leaning forward. Lamplight gleamed in his eyes, shadowed a crosshatched scar on his left cheek. "I was in Sherezad in 1217, and nearly got caught in Kir Haresh in 1221. The cities burned, and ships with them. I knew captains who lost everything because they were too damned slow lifting anchor." He looked at her bandaged hand, cast a pointed glance at his own maimed arm.

"I won't lose the *Dog* because you don't know when to cut your losses."

Isyllt ran a hand over her face. "I can't offer you cash, but I'll see you compensated, I swear."

"A dead woman's promises are worth dust in the desert."

Her lips curled, hard and sharp. "Even a dead necromancer's?" Izzy swallowed, but she didn't have the heart to toy with him. "If I die, my master will honor my bargains."

"I would rather keep the *Dog* than trust in the honor of spies."

Her hand twitched and Izzy's eyes narrowed. But threats were useless, and she wasn't going to kill him for being sensible. Saints knew someone should be. She looked at Vienh.

The woman frowned, ran her tongue over her teeth as if she tasted something sour. "Must I choose between my captain and my family's honor, then? I'll repay the debt, but I'll be little use without a ship."

Izzy turned, tilting his head back to glare at her. "You'd leave the *Dog* so easily?"

Vienh folded her arms under her breasts. "She saved my daughter's life, Izzy. What do you want me to do?"

Adam unhooked two gold rings from his ear, untied a leather pouch from his neck. "If you need cash—" Metal glittered as he tossed the rings onto the table. An uncut amethyst followed with a quiet thump.

Izzy snarled, baring a gold tooth; Adam's gold vanished off the table. "Rot your eyes. One more day." He turned back to Vienh. "You know how much I value you, but you'll be first mate of charred boards if we're not lucky." He swung down from his chair and left the room as fast as his short legs would carry him.

"I'm sorry," Isyllt said to Vienh when the door swung shut.

The woman shrugged, though her jaw was still tight. "Not your fault, is it? Sivahra might be a lot better off if no one cared about family or honor. But you'd better do what you can before sunset tomorrow, or I may be rowing you to Selafai on a stolen fishing skiff."

Before Isyllt could reply, her mirror began to shiver in her pocket, a tingle of magic that raised gooseflesh on her arms. She pulled back the grimy silk wrapping and Zhirin's splotchy red-eyed face rose in the black glass.

"Are you all right?" Isyllt asked, eyebrows knitting.

The girl rubbed a hand against her nose. "I'm not hurt. I have the ring, and I found out what happened to Vasilios." She glanced down, jerked her head up again. "I need— I have to do something with a body."

Isyllt and Adam exchanged a glance. "Wait there. We'll come as soon as we can."

She broke the spell and wrapped the mirror. "Corpses before lunch—this will be an interesting day."

Vienh fell in beside them as they left the bar, and Isyllt arched a curious eyebrow. The smuggler's grimace might have been meant as a smile. "I'm coming with you. Izzy's angry with me anyway, and everyone else thinks I'm a traitor to one cause or another—I might as well do something to earn it."

The swamp was thick with midges, the whining clouds enough to overwhelm the charms they wore. Zhirin waved and slapped, scratched stinging welts on her wrists and face. More insects bothered Adam and Isyllt—she wondered idly if it was just her own eucalyptus perfume keeping the worst away, or if their paler skin was more attractive. A breeze might have cleared the midges away, but too much magic could draw unwelcome attention.

Silty water slopped against her thighs, squelched between her toes. A pity the Dai Tranh didn't have a convenient city hideout, but Isyllt's spell had drawn them out of Symir, past the expensive houses and estates on the Southern Bank and into the thick mangrove swamps that lined the bay. Mostly fisherfolk lived here, in houses high on stilts to avoid the grasping tides and houseboats anchored beyond the trees. Such a simple place to hide, but effective—all the news of the rebels centered around the Xians and the Lhuns, northern forest clans. Who paid attention to a few mud-fishers in the south? Zhirin wasn't even sure whose lands these had been.

Clouds hid the moon and stars and they risked no witchlights, only a shuttered lantern carried by Isyllt's sailor companion. Zhirin moved carefully, avoiding submerged root-spears and crab-traps. Fish and snakes brushed past her; larger creatures swam lazily in the bay, and she kept one *otherwise* ear trained on them. The cold and hungry minds of eel-sharks were a welcome distraction from her own bruised thoughts.

"Are we there yet?" Vienh muttered, crawling around a thicket of roots. The sailor took point while Adam trailed behind, the two mages slogging in between.

Isyllt touched Vasilios's ring where it hung against her chest, and Zhirin clenched her jaw. A white diamond set in gold—it was hers if she wished to claim it. She couldn't decide whether she wanted to keep it in remembrance of her master or toss it into the depths of the bay. At least he'd kept no spirits bound in it.

"Not yet," Isyllt said, "but the pull is stronger. We're getting closer." She held her bandaged hand against her chest, away from the water.

Zhirin curled the fingers of her own wounded hand. It only hurt when she thought about it, didn't even need stitches. She'd cut herself worse on broken shells in the river. But the shells hadn't been trying to kill her.

How did you grow used to that? When did people become nothing more than threats? The necromancer had offered quiet sympathy but hadn't tried to hide her relief—one more enemy exposed and dead. Never mind that the enemy had been an old woman whom Zhirin had known for years. She clenched her fist; the scabbed cut cracked and burned.

Vienh paused, waved for silence and checked the lantern shutter. Isyllt and Zhirin moved closer, sloshing as quietly as they could. Ahead, the trees gave way to a narrow finger of water. A house stood on the far side of the inlet, shuttered and dark.

Isyllt touched the diamond and frowned, then turned toward the bay. "What's out there?" she asked, staring into the dark.

Zhirin squinted but saw only shades of black. She dipped her hand into the water, stretched out better senses. The bay welcomed her in, dark and soothing. Roots and weeds, salt and silt, the soft tickle of fish and crabs, the growing depth and pull of the sea. The sinuous undulations of eel-sharks and sharp, clever thoughts of nakh. And there, not too far from the shore, the weight of a boat, its keel digging into her skin. Delicate shivers rippled through the hull as people walked the decks.

Reluctantly, Zhirin eased out of the water's embrace, retreating into the stifling solidity of flesh. "A boat. Maybe a houseboat. There are people aboard."

Isyllt frowned, hand on Vasilios's ring. "That's it. They're there."

"So we swim?" Adam asked, sounding none too thrilled with the prospect.

"Be careful," Zhirin said before anyone could move deeper. "There are sharks in the bay. And nakh." She frowned. "A lot of nakh."

"Lovely," muttered Vienh.

"What are they doing here?" she muttered, half to herself. Nakh always swam in the bay, but she'd never heard of so many schooled together. Not since the attack at the festival, at least.

"What should we do?" Isyllt asked. Gratifying, to be asked so seriously, not to be treated as an apprentice, but it meant she had to think of a clever answer.

A solution came to her quickly—it wasn't exactly clever, but she couldn't think of anything else.

"I'll distract them," she said, before she could think better of it. "Wait a moment, then start swimming." She unbuttoned her blouse, hung it over a tree branch.

The night wasn't cold, but gooseflesh prickled over her arms.

Isyllt's eyebrows rose, but all she said was, "All right."

Zhirin hoped it was confidence in her abilities, not callous disregard for her life.

She tugged off her shoes too, set them dripping beside her shirt. *Mother*, she prayed, *watch over your idiot child*. Mud shifted like gritty silk between her toes. A few steps and the water closed around her ribs. Her chest swelled with breath as she slipped under.

She hadn't thought when she dove into the canal after Isyllt at the festival, only acted. It was much easier that way. She let the fear slip away in bubbles of air.

When she couldn't touch the bottom or break the surface with an outstretched hand, she called light, the sickly blue-green illumination of fireflies and fish-lures. It spread in tendrils around her, clung to bits of debris. A beacon. Blood seeped from her bandaged hand, dark threads unwinding.

An eel-shark glided past—the light slid across its wedge-shaped head, fringed gills and long, writhing tail. Its eyes flashed in the glare. In the distance, she heard the others begin to swim, clumsy mammal strokes. The shark heard it too.

"Stay," Zhirin said, filling the word with power. Its air bubble didn't float away but hung shining by her face. The shark circled, keeping to the edge of the light.

She felt the nakh coming a heartbeat before she saw them. Pale shapes emerged from the murk, triangular faces gleaming amid clouds of hair, tails shining with dark rainbow scales and iridescent fins.

Have you come to play with us? The words shivered

through the water, echoed inside Zhirin's head. *Or to feed us?*

"What are you doing here?"

We like these mammals. A tail flickered in the direction of the boat. *They feed us well.*

"They're murderers." The ache in her chest grew with every word.

What care we for mammal deaths? One of the nakh glided closer. Her—though Zhirin could only guess at gender—face was bruised.

"If these mammals betray and kill their own so easily, do you think they'll be more loyal to you?"

That gave them a heartbeat's pause. Zhirin's lungs burned, and she eyed the nakh's fluttering gills with envy.

I remember you, the nakh said. Her face glowed on the other side of the light, eerily beautiful even with the dark swelling on her cheek. *You chased us off the kill.* One long, webbed hand rose to toy with glowing bits of debris, rolling them across her knuckles like a coin-trick. Zhirin tensed for an attack.

But— The nakh flicked a luminous leaf with one clawed finger, watched it twist in the current. *You've come to us to speak. The others have never done that.* The eel-shark circled, bumped its triangular nose against the creature's hand. She stroked its head carelessly. Like a dog, but dogs weren't larger than their masters, and had far fewer teeth.

"I'm afraid I can't stay and talk much longer." The words slipped silver and shining from her lips, and the urge to breathe in was nearly overwhelming.

The nakh grinned, baring nearly as many teeth as her pet shark. *No. But I'm curious—you say these mammals*

*we aid now will turn on us. Would you offer us sweeter
promises?*

"I won't offer you men to eat." The image of Marat's
body rose behind her eyes, wrapped in sheets and spells,
weighed with garden stones, sinking into the canal. She
forced it down. "But if you let me and my friends come
and go tonight unharmed, I'll treat with you however I
can."

You'll speak with us here, below?

"I swear, by the River Mother."

The nakh cocked her head, eyes flashing white as she
blinked. *Very well, river-daughter. You and yours may
pass freely tonight, and you'll come to us again.* She patted the shark on the head and it turned, gliding silently
toward deeper water. *We know the taste of your blood, if
you lie.*

The nakh twisted away, vanishing into the black. Zhirin knew she should wait, make sure it wasn't a trick,
but her chest ached too fiercely. She kicked up, broke the
surface with a choking gasp. She floated for a moment,
spitting bitter water and letting the pain in her lungs
ease. Then she swam for shore.

It was a nice night for a swim through shark-infested waters. The water was cool but not icy, the tides gentle this
far into the bay. Isyllt concentrated on swimming quietly
and following the tug of the stone, trying to ignore the
blackness all around her, the memory of the nakh's cold
touch.

She whispered spells of silence but winced each time
her arms broke the surface too loudly. Her breath rasped
in her ears, and she didn't know how anyone could fail to

hear them coming. Even Adam's stealthy grace deserted him in the water. She forced herself to swim with both arms, though instinct wanted to cradle her injured hand against her chest; the real damage was bad enough, without letting the working muscles stiffen. Her hand throbbed and the stitches burned, but numbness would cost her precious reaction time.

She felt her diamond clearly now. Its presence shivered sharp and cold in her head—someone was using it.

The boat's lights came into view—lanterns hooded and shutters drawn, but drips and scraps still escaped. A low wide-bottomed craft, the deck mostly enclosed. Figures moved in the shadows of the eaves.

"How many?" Adam asked, treading water beside her.

She listened for heartbeats, felt several. The effort of keeping her head above water distracted her too much for an accurate count.

"At least seven, but probably more." He swore softly. "This is where you're supposed to tell me that you've faced worse odds before," she whispered.

Adam snorted. "I have, and usually ended up half-dead."

"As long as it's only half."

Vienh swam closer. "The sentries aren't patrolling, just standing on the deck. Whoever's in charge should flog them. If you can be quiet, we'll go up the anchor chain."

"You've done this before," Adam said.

"Of course not." Vienh's grin flashed in the darkness. "I'm an honest smuggler." She glided toward the ship, and Isyllt and Adam followed as quietly as they could.

They found the anchor on the far side of the boat—

Isyllt could never remember port from starboard—its chain descending from a gap in the railing. The rail was only a yard or so above the water, but the slick, curving hull would be nearly impossible to climb without being heard.

With barely a splash, Vienh hauled herself up the chain and eased over the rail. When no one raised the alarm, Adam followed. Isyllt hooked bare toes into the links, keeping her weight on her legs and steadying herself with her good hand. Rust scraped her palm, tore a fingernail; the chain pinched an already blistered toe and she grimaced. She nearly lost her balance at the top, but Adam caught her arm and heaved her over the railing.

They crouched in the shadows for a moment to catch their breath and listen. The walls were tightly woven wicker on wooden frames, the roof thatched. Shards of light glowed in a golden filigree. Without the distraction of the water, Isyllt felt the sentries nearby, and the cold pulse of her ring. And the bitter chill of the dead.

"Three guards on each side," she said, "and at least three others inside. And ghosts."

The diamond throbbed against her chest, tugging gently sideways. After a heartbeat Isyllt realized her ring wasn't moving, but a new diamond had entered the range of her spell. Another mage was coming.

"Hurry," she whispered. "We'll have company soon."

Something cold brushed her cheek and she started, but it was only a drop of water. A moment later the clouds opened and rain sighed down, rattling against the roof.

"At least we're already wet," Adam muttered.

"Somebody's coming," hissed Vienh an instant later.

Isyllt wrapped them in shadows just as a man stepped

around the corner, humming softly to himself. It didn't seem these Dai Tranh expected trouble.

Adam's knife gleamed as it left its sheath and Isyllt caught his wrist. "Don't kill." If whoever had her ring knew how to use it, death would alert them immediately.

He nodded, uncoiled from his crouch as the guard turned away. Three strides and he crossed the deck, reversing the knife as he brought it down. The pommel struck the man's skull with a dull thump and his knees buckled. Adam caught him as he fell, dragged him against the rail.

They slid down the wall facing the bay. The drumming rain covered the slap of wet cloth against flesh. The sentry at the far end of the deck didn't notice as they slipped inside the first unlocked door. It led to the helm and an open sitting room.

"The cabins will be in the back," Vienh said, nodding toward the hall on the right. She drew her knife and took a lantern off its hook.

The floor swayed gently beneath them as the wind gusted. Vienh went first, Adam watching their backs. Vasilios's diamond all but hummed as they drew nearer to its sister-stone. This close, Isyllt could feel the ghosts in her ring moving restlessly in their prison. And another ghost, free of the stone. Deilin.

"Be careful," she murmured to Vienh. "Your grandmother is here."

The smuggler cursed under her breath.

Light spilled from under a cabin door, along with a woman's voice. Vienh's shoulders stiffened.

"It's Kaeru."

The woman spoke in Sivahran, too low for Isyllt to fol-

low. It sounded like a one-sided argument; then she heard
Deilin's death-hollowed voice answer.

"What are they saying?" she asked.

"Kaeru's talking about a girl, and about how they
need someone. Whoever she's talking to. I can't hear the
response."

Beyond the door, Isyllt felt the old woman's heart, still
strong, and Deilin's icy presence. And someone else, alive
but not strong.

The voices rose. "It's not right," Deilin said.

"You must. We need you."

"She's a child—" She broke off, and Isyllt sensed the
dead woman's attention turning toward them.

Isyllt's jaw tightened. "Murai's in there. Let's go."

Vienh nodded, passing the lantern to Isyllt as she drew
back. The door cracked under the force of her kick, flying
inward and rebounding against the wall. The smuggler
caught it as she stepped inside.

The scene was all too familiar. Murai lay still, wan
and feverish, and Deilin stood at the foot of the bed.
Kaeru sprang back as the door opened, the black diamond
gleaming on her gnarled hand.

"It was you all along, wasn't it?" Vienh said. Lamplight rippled along the length of her blade. "You let her
through the wards. You let her take my daughter."

"Better than wasting Xian blood in another generation
of collaborators and mongrels."

"We took you in!" Vienh gasped, sagging against the
door, one hand rising to her throat. The ring glowed in
Kaeru's hand.

"Don't—" Deilin said, but the old woman ignored
her.

Isyllt pushed Vienh aside, forced her way into the cabin.

"Company's coming," Adam called from the hall.

The lantern kept her from reaching her knife, so Isyllt swung it instead. Distracted by her magic, Kaeru didn't dodge fast enough; the lamp struck her jaw with a wet crack and slipped from Isyllt's hand to shatter on the floor. Tendrils of burning oil licked across the wood.

The old woman fell, clutching her face. Vienh coughed and moaned; someone shouted in the corridor. Isyllt crouched, prying Kaeru's hand away from her bloody mouth and twisting the ring off her finger. Deilin lunged just in time to vanish into the stone.

Isyllt fumbled her ring onto her right hand, sighing as its comforting chill swept through her. Fire crackled at the walls, singed the bottom of the bedsheet. Murai tossed but didn't wake.

"So the child is a Xian as well?"

"Her mother was, before she became an Assari whore." The words came out ugly and slurred and Kaeru spat blood. Her jaw was already swelling. A knife flickered into her hand as she sat up and Isyllt rocked backward. "We won't let them take any more of our children."

Vienh's boot caught the woman's wrist, sent the knife spinning.

"No. I won't let you take any more of ours." The smuggler's blade sank into Kaeru's throat. With a twist, she pulled it free. A crimson bubble burst on the old woman's lips as she sank to the floor.

Steel clashed in the hallway. "Can I kill them yet?" Adam shouted.

"As many as you like." Isyllt pushed herself up; the swaying of the deck rippled her stomach uneasily.

Vienh wiped her blade on her wet trousers and sheathed it. Dodging around the spreading flames, she scooped Murai into her arms. "Bastards," she hissed. "They dosed her with laudanum." She glanced at the door, where Adam fought someone in the narrow corridor, then nodded toward the shuttered window. "That way."

Isyllt ripped the shutters open and tore aside the net curtains. The stink of scorched blood filled the air as the flames spread toward Kaeru's body. Clumsy and cursing, she clambered out the window, conjuring witchlight against the dark. Vienh passed Murai's limp form through, then turned to help Adam. By the time both of them scrambled out, the flames were high enough to hold the Dai Tranh at bay.

"Company," Vienh said, pointing toward the bay, where ship lights approached. "The Khas?"

"Probably."

The smuggler slipped over the side, surfacing to take Murai. As she dropped into the water, Isyllt prayed that Zhirin had taken care of the nakh.

The ship burned slowly in the rain, but it burned. By the time they neared the shore, the flames scattered gold and orange across the bay. Isyllt stumbled through the root-choked shallows, stubbing toes and scraping ankles as she hunted for her shirt and shoes.

"Here."

Light flared and Isyllt threw up a hand. Through her fingers, she saw Zhirin holding the lantern. The girl hooded it again quickly.

"Someone's coming." She nodded toward the innermost end of the inlet, where light flickered amid the trees.

Both diamonds shivered, and Isyllt clenched her hand around her ring. A mage was coming, and she could guess which one.

"Is she all right?" Zhirin asked as Vienh emerged, Murai in her arms.

"She will be, I think, but she needs to be warm and dry."

"Let's go," Isyllt said, tugging on her shoes. Lights shone nearer now, and footsteps rustled the weeds.

They hurried into the trees, but they'd gone only a few yards when Isyllt stopped with a gasp. Pressure like an iron band circled her chest, tightening as she tried to move. It eased as she stumbled back a pace.

"What's wrong?" Adam asked.

"A spell." She swallowed when she wanted to spit. Something this strong needed a physical component, but doubtless she'd left enough stray hairs on pillows at the Khas. "I can fight it, but I'll slow you down. Easier to go back and face the caster. Go on."

Adam's eyebrows rose. "Lousy time to get yourself killed."

Isyllt ignored him and turned around, drawing in a grateful breath as the tightness in her chest eased. Vasilios's diamond thrummed against her chest, then lay still as she banished the finding with a thought. Cold rushed through her as she drew power from her ring, leeching strength from the trapped dead. The night became sharp-edged and clear, all her aches and blisters fading away.

Asheris waited at the far end of the inlet, golden witch-lights hovering around him like a second entourage. The first wore Khas uniforms and aimed their weapons at her.

"Is that your doing?" he asked, gesturing toward the burning boat. "You've saved us some work, then. Though

I'd have liked more survivors to question." His spell closed around her and she couldn't move as he crossed the muddy ground and caught her arm. His hand burned her bare skin and his diamond glowed against the dark like a captive star. Maybe it was. "Where's Murai?"

"I don't know."

"You're not a very good liar."

"Not like you," she said, lips curling.

He blinked. "What do you mean?"

She wanted to slap the look of honest confusion off his face. Instead she focused her power, preparing to strike at him. But if she broke free, could she dodge the soldiers' bullets? "When you said you didn't believe in binding spirits. I actually thought it was true."

His grip tightened and she couldn't stop a squeak of pain. "What makes you think," he whispered, "that I was the one who did the binding?"

Light gleamed in his eyes like flame behind crystal, and a shadow flared around him, black and burning. The strength of it nearly staggered her.

"What are you?"

The light dimmed until only the man remained, rain-drenched and regretful. "Not free. I'm sorry—this is not my choice."

Isyllt rallied her wits and her magic, but before she could strike a voice carried through the damp air.

"Asheris!"

His grip didn't loosen, but he turned toward Zhirin. The girl paused at the edge of the light, Murai cradled in her arms.

"Which do you want more—Isyllt, or your master's daughter? She's drugged and half-drowned. She needs help."

His chest hitched sharply. His magelights flickered, and shadows twisted across his face. Isyllt gasped as he let go.

"You keep dangerous company, Miss Laii. Set the girl down and get out of here. Let them go," he told the soldiers. The compulsion on Isyllt crumbled and she stumbled away, clutching her scalded arm to her chest.

"How—"

"I've run out of leash," he said softly. "If I find you again, I must kill you or return you to the Khas. Try not to be found."

The look on his face brought a sharp lump of pity to her throat. She swallowed it down and fled into the swamp.

CHAPTER 17

They stumbled into the Storm God's Bride a few hours before dawn, slipping in the back to avoid the lingering patrons. Isyllt expected Vienh to send them away, but instead she gave them a room upstairs and left. Isyllt was grateful for both reprieves.

She nearly collapsed on the bed, but rallied enough energy to ward the room and strip off her damp and filthy clothes first. Her right arm itched and throbbed from wrist to elbow, and her left hand was stiff and near-useless. The red print of Asheris's hand circled her forearm, blisters bubbling where the tips of his fingers had dug in.

"Cute trick," Adam said, inspecting her arm.

"I'm lucky he decided to talk first and incinerate me after." She moved her hand, wincing as the burn stretched and stung. Mud crusted in the creases of her skin and flecks of leaf and dirt clung to her. She could feel the fever rising again as her magic and body strove to fight off whatever filth was in the bay.

Adam slipped out, returned a moment later with water, clean towels, and a bowl of crushed aloe. Isyllt fumbled with a damp cloth for a bit before he took it from her and cleaned the burn.

"We need to find that ship and get out of here."

Isyllt nodded, staring at the scuffed planks beyond her toes. She needed to leave. Especially if the thought filled her with such ambivalence. Her work was dangerous enough without worrying about the men trying to kill her. If she lost her focus, she'd end up like Vasilios.

"You won't prove anything by killing yourself," Adam said softly, smearing cool sap over her arm.

She frowned, then chuckled wryly. She might be a fool where Asheris was concerned, but at least it distracted her from being a fool over Kiril.

"We wait for the ship," she said. "It's the best we can do—wait and pray that Siddir can accomplish what he claims."

"Pity we keep killing the people we were supposed to help." Adam wrapped the burn loosely and knotted the bandage.

"They tried to kill us first." She leaned against the wall; the room was swimming, and she couldn't bring it into focus. Maybe she could blame the fever on the question that rose to her tongue. "Are you just going to leave her?"

Adam shrugged, lips tightening. "She made her choices. What's the use in arguing?"

"No use," she whispered. Her eyes sagged shut. "No use at all."

He caught her as she slumped, eased her onto the mattress. His hand tightened on hers, a fleeting sympathy, and then sleep pulled her away.

Zhirin came home aching and tired, weary to the bone in the absence of the night's fear. As she eased the door shut and locked it, she noticed a light burning in the kitchen. Mau was up very early, she thought for an instant, but no.

Her mother was waiting for her.

"It's true, isn't it?" Fei Minh said. She sat at the table, a cup of tea at her elbow. Dark circles ringed her eyes and shadows lined the weary creases on her face. "You're running with the Tigers."

Not tonight, she almost said. But there was no point in childish equivocations. "Yes."

Her mother shook her head, unbound hair sliding over her shoulders. More silver threaded the ink-black than Zhirin remembered. "I prayed that Faraj was wrong, that you wouldn't be so foolish." Her eyes narrowed. "You're going to get yourself killed!"

"If I'm killed, it will be to protect your schemes. I'm lucky I'm not in the bottom of a canal already."

Fei Minh's lips pursed. "Zhirin, please. I understand that you want to help, but this isn't the way. Look at how many are dead already—look at what happened at the execution."

"That wasn't the Tigers. And do you really think paying off the Emperor is any better?"

"It doesn't end in bloodshed."

"Really? Do diamonds grow on trees, then, and fall like mangoes? Do those prisoners who disappear spend their days picking gems in the shade and drinking hibiscus tea?"

Color rose in Fei Minh's cheeks. "I don't know which is worse—your misplaced idealism or your insolent tongue. I've worked for our family's future longer than you've been alive. Just because you're infatuated with some forest-clan mongrel with more mouth than sense, don't presume to tell me what's best for my clan or my country. I should have shipped you to the university years ago, if this is all your Kurun Tam education has been good for."

If she'd been any closer, Zhirin might have slapped her. The impulse made her hands tingle and stung her cheeks with anger and shame. Her mother hadn't struck her since she was five, and she'd never contemplated striking back.

"Mira—" She forced her hands open, stepped farther into the room. "Please, I don't want to fight with you. Everything's gone so wrong, so ugly."

Her mother's face softened. "Oh, darling. I know." She rose and took Zhirin in her arms, pausing as she touched her damp clothes. "What have you been doing?"

She considered a lie for an instant, but what was the point anymore? "Rescuing the Viceroy's daughter."

The look on Fei Minh's face was almost worth everything that had happened tonight. "You aren't serious— Ancestors, you are. You found Murai?"

"Yes. She's safe, I think. I sent her home with Asheris."

"My daughter . . ." She pulled Zhirin close, heedless of damp and filth. "I'm very proud of you, then, even if you've been terribly foolish." She drew back. "I doubt there's much Faraj wouldn't forgive you now. Just stay at home, out of trouble, and everything will be fine."

They were the same, Zhirin realized, her mother's schemes and her own. Both born of a blind and desperate hope that if they only did enough, did the right thing, everything would work out. She blinked back tears and swallowed the words that she needed to say.

"Yes, Mira," she lied. It grew easier and easier. "I'm home now, and everything will be all right."

Fei Minh smiled and caught a yawn with one delicate hand. "It's been a long time since I stayed up till dawn. Shall we make some tea and see if we can manage?"

Their fragile conviviality lasted through tea and breakfast. Mau arrived just in time to save the day's bread from Zhirin's inexpert baking; if she was disconcerted to find her cousins giggling and silly from lack of sleep, she hid it well.

The respite ended with a messenger's knock less than an hour before the dawn bells. Fei Minh answered the door, but Zhirin heard enough of the murmured conversation to send her heart to the bottom of her stomach. The *Yhan Ti* was leaving dock.

A moment later her mirror—carefully replaced after she'd bathed and changed—shivered in her pocket. She ducked into the hall to respond, but by the time she pulled it out the bronze was empty and silent. She whispered Isyllt's name, but there was no answer. A second time, and a third, and still nothing. Something was wrong.

"What is it?" Fei Minh asked when she returned to the kitchen.

She swallowed. No use in pretending any longer. "I have to go."

She ignored her mother's angry questions and demands as she tugged on her shoes. As she opened the door she paused and risked a backward glance. "I'm sorry. I'll be back when I can." *If I can.*

Isyllt woke to a sharp knock on the door and the jangle of her wards. The bed creaked as Adam leapt up; her skin prickled with the sudden absence of his warmth. She scrubbed gritty eyes, but it only made them ache more. It felt as if she'd only slept a few hours, and from the darkness beyond the shutters that was probably true. Sweat dampened her hair, pasted her undershirt to her skin, and her burned arm itched fiercely.

Adam eased the door open and Vienh slipped in, rain dripping from her oilcloak.

"The *Yhan Ti* is leaving port," she said, "bound for Assar. Izzy's ready to slip dock, and your friend Bashari is waiting on the *Dog*. Come on."

Isyllt stumbled up, groping for her still-damp clothes while Adam tugged on his boots. It took her three tries to pick up her shirt and her hands shook as she fastened the buttons. If the saints were merciful, she could sleep on the ship.

The hall was dark, only one lamp by the staircase left burning. Isyllt dropped to the back of the line, pulling out her mirror. Zhirin was probably asleep. She whispered the girl's name as they started down the stairs. An instant later, she heard a loud crack in the common room, followed by a heavy metallic clang. Adam paused and Isyllt nearly ran into him.

"What was that?"

A thunderclap shook the room, shivering the stairs and throwing them against the wall. She lost the spell and her grip on the mirror. Isyllt grabbed for the rail, gasped as she hit it with her bad hand, and fell. The rush of pain drove away the last fatigue-fog. Smoke billowed, reeking of gunpowder.

"Bombs!" Vienh shouted; her voice was distant and hollow through the ringing in Isyllt's ears. "Out the back."

Doors opened along the hall as they scrambled back, wary faces peering out. Another explosion echoed and someone screamed. Down the narrow stairs to the door behind the storerooms, but when Adam unbarred the door and flung it open a bullet shattered the wood inches from his shoulder.

Through the gloom of the rain-soaked alley, Isyllt saw a red handprint on the opposite wall. Vienh swore as they retreated from the door.

"Dai Tranh! It's an ambush."

Smoke eddied from the front of the bar, and orange light flickered at the end of the hall. Through the fire, or into the bullets.

"They'll be waiting in front too," Adam said, checking his pistol.

A shot cracked before she could answer. Isyllt ducked—in truth more a startled stumble—and saw a masked man crouching on the other side of the door. He fired again and Vienh slammed into her, knocking her down. Isyllt landed on hip and elbow, eyes blurring from the pain. Adam fired back and the man vanished.

They ducked into a storeroom and Isyllt called witchlight. Vienh gasped as she slouched against the wall. Red spooled down her right arm, feathering across her linen sleeve.

"Not bad," she hissed as Isyllt reached for her. "Just grazed."

Isyllt touched her arm anyway to be sure and promptly jerked her hand away with a curse.

"Lead bullets. Bastards." Isyllt shook her head. "They're not Dai Tranh."

Adam pulled out his mirror, used it to glance around the doorframe before he leaned out to shoot. "How do you know?"

"The Dai Tranh used copper bullets at the execution, even though they were shooting at mages. And they used rubies to blow up the other buildings, not powder grenades."

"Can we solve this somewhere else?" Vienh snapped as she pressed a fold of sleeve against her wound.

Another blast shook the front of the bar; a lamp fell from its hook and shattered, splattering the floor with oil. The building would collapse on their heads soon. More shots sounded in the hall and someone screamed. Adam took another look through the mirror.

"They're shooting anyone who comes down."

Isyllt crept closer to the door. The air tasted of blood and smoke and approaching death. She risked a glance outside, saw a man's sandaled foot and a thread of blood leaking across the floor. A bullet splintered the doorframe above her head and she jerked back inside. A moment later her ring chilled as the wounded man died.

"We're going to make a break for it soon," she said to Adam and Vienh, "but I'll be distracted, so cover me."

She reached into her ring, letting the cold wash away her fatigue and pain. Her magic crept out in icy tendrils, licking toward the corpse, oozing into his cooling flesh. It wasn't something she liked to do—most people didn't understand the difference between a demon and a corpse controlled by a necromancer, and didn't care to learn the particulars before they started screaming. But this might be the best opportunity she had before the building came down.

Magic settled into dead flesh, save for the ruin of his chest and the lead ball lodged there. But she didn't need his heart. She felt the body like a glove on ghostly hands. And like a glove, it moved when she flexed those hands. The man rose clumsily, driven by memory and will.

"Ancestors," Vienh whispered.

A shot struck her stumbling shield and she flinched from the ghost of the impact, but the corpse only shuddered.

"Let's go."

Adam and Vienh fell in close behind her, in the dubious cover of the dead man. The walking dead discomfited even trained soldiers, and the assassin outside was no stauncher. He stumbled back with a cry as the bloody corpse staggered toward him, and fell with a gurgle as Adam's bullet caught him in the throat.

Isyllt paused at the doorway, forcing more of her awareness into the body. Through rain and death-blurred eyes, she saw more people crouching on either end of the alley. Also masked, like no Dai Tranh she'd seen. A bullet flew past her puppet's head; another hit his shoulder, splattering congealing blood.

To their left, the alley led to a narrow canal—to the right, the street. The light had paled from coal to iron. How long would Izzy wait for them, with Siddir already aboard?

"Take the left," she told Adam. "Kill as many as you can, then get to the docks. Don't wait for me."

"What?"

"I'll distract them. Find the stones and make sure

Bashari doesn't try to double-cross us. Come back and find me and then we can get the hell out of here."

"And if you're dead?"

"Then go back to Erisín and tell Kiril what's happened. It will be his problem then."

He balked a heartbeat longer than she expected him to. "Can you manage a distraction?"

Isyllt grinned, cold and sharp, and stroked her ring. "I think so."

"I'll find you."

She nodded. "On my mark." The dead man turned to the right and stumbled down the alley. Her ears still rang, but she heard the assassins' frightened shouts and smiled. She reached deeper into the diamond, calling the cold till tendrils of mist writhed around her. "Ready—"

And she called the ghosts. They burst free like a whirlwind, faces ghastly and misshapen. Two flew shrieking toward the canal and the others turned right. A scream echoed down the alley.

"Go!"

Adam and Vienh bolted. A heartbeat later Isyllt stepped into the rain. Two of the killers broke and fled at the sight of the raging dead. One vanished toward the street, but a ghost caught the second and he fell, screams turning to choking gasps.

Deadly as they were, ghosts couldn't stop bullets, but animating took more concentration than she cared to spend, and she wasn't skilled enough to make her corpse-puppet truly dangerous. Isyllt let him fall. Only a few more yards and she could reach the street—and pray a dozen more false Dai Tranh weren't waiting there.

The last assassin held her ground, pistol steady, not flinching as a ghost shrieked past her. Warded. She was veiled, but her graceful walk was familiar. Faraj's pet killer had come out to play.

"Odd," Isyllt said, "I've never seen a Dai Tranh with blue eyes before. Put down the pistol and I'll put down the ghosts. Don't tell me you don't like to get your hands dirty." She spread her arms, witchlight flickering around her fingers. Magic ached in her bones, a relentless, empty cold that reached deeper than the grave.

Jodiya's shoulders shook in a silent laugh. Slowly, she lowered her pistol.

And flung the grenade she held in her other hand.

The fuse kindled in midair, burning unnaturally fast. No chance to outrun the explosion.

Instead, Isyllt caught it. She hissed at the pain in her left hand, at the precious fraction of fuse being consumed. As soon as iron touched her skin, her magic began to work. Rust blossomed across damp metal, corroding at preternatural speed. Within heartbeats the iron shell crumbled in her hands, black powder hissing to the ground. She turned her head just in time as the fuse caught the last of the gunpowder and sprayed her with sparks.

Her hands twisted with the pain of it, but she bared her teeth at Jodiya. "Again?"

The girl raised her pistol, but before she could fire the water rushing through the gutter rose, uncoiling like a snake charmer's asp. The water serpent struck Jodiya hard enough to send her sprawling, then dissolved with a splash.

"Come on!" Zhirin called from the end of the alley.

Smoke poured from the ruin of the Storm God's Bride, but Isyllt only spared it a glance. Someone shouted as they bolted across the street and down another alley, but she couldn't tell if it was another assassin. No one appeared behind them as they ducked through Merrowgate's back streets.

"Good timing," Isyllt said as they crossed a canal.

"You're lucky traffic wasn't worse," Zhirin gasped, her cheeks flushed dark. "I heard you call me and then you didn't answer." She slowed, pressing a hand against her side. "Who was that?"

"Khas assassins trying to pass themselves off as Dai Tranh." Her lungs burned, one more little agony to join the chorus. "Where are we going?"

The girl paused, frowning. "Out of the city."

In the wake of the attack, ferries stopped running from Merrowgate to the Northern Bank—no one wanted to be accused of helping Dai Tranh escape. Wrapped in spells of distraction, Zhirin and Isyllt fled to Jadewater, where they found a skiff willing to take them across. No simple charm could keep Isyllt from being memorable up close, though—pallid and sunken-eyed, with fierce red burns scattered across her cheek and singed hair frizzing around her face. She moved like an old woman, left arm cradled against her chest. Zhirin felt as though she should help her aboard the boat but couldn't nerve herself to do it; she'd watched iron dissolve in the woman's hands, and the bitter scent of the magic clung to her still.

The skiff had no top and they were rain-drenched and shivering by the time they reached the shore, docking at the closest jetty in Lhun lands. As they moored, Zhirin counted out coins—she had enough for the passage, but if she paid extra to keep the ferryman's mouth shut she'd have little left. She should have refilled her purse while she was home.

"Let me," Isyllt said as she dithered over the bribe, and scooped the coins out of her hand. Zhirin fought a flinch at the necromancer's cold touch. Isyllt handed the money to the pilot with a whispered word. The man's hands closed on the coins and his eyes dulled, mouth slackening.

"Hurry," Isyllt said, climbing onto the dock. "It won't last long."

Zhirin glanced over her shoulder as they hastened away, saw the man stir and shake his head in confusion.

"Where now?" Isyllt asked. Rain dripped from her hair and her teeth had begun to chatter, which Zhirin didn't like; it wasn't that cold.

"We need to find Jabbor," she said. "The Tigers can find us a safe place." If she said it confidently enough, perhaps it would be true.

The sun climbed behind its veil of clouds as they walked to Xao Mae Lhun and the Tiger's Tail. Morning chill gave way to tepid stickiness, but Isyllt didn't stop shivering. Zhirin bought them hot tea doctored with brandy and paid the bartender to take a message to the Jade Tigers. For all of Jabbor's promises, she wondered what his reaction would be when she came penniless with a hunted foreign spy at her side. Only days ago such doubt would have been unthinkable.

They waited in a dim corner of the bar. Isyllt drowsed, her face splotched and damp, and Zhirin chewed her lip.

This was a terrible time to pass out, especially since her own eyes ached and she wanted so badly to lay her head down. The bartender shot her pointed glances every so often, but she couldn't afford much more to drink and it would only have gone to waste anyway.

The noon bells died before the door opened and a familiar shadow stepped inside. Zhirin kicked Isyllt under the table as she rose, trying to keep the desperate relief off her face. She held herself straight, even when Jabbor grabbed her shoulders.

"What happened?"

"Isyllt was attacked. We need to get out of the city. Does your offer still stand?"

"Of course it does." But his eyes narrowed as he glanced at Isyllt. "She's sick."

"All the more reason to get us to a safe place quickly."

He sighed and nodded. "Let's go. Can you walk?" he asked Isyllt.

"Of course." But her hand was white-knuckled and trembling on the back of her chair as she rose, and Zhirin wondered how much farther she could go.

A pair of Tigers she didn't know waited outside, flanking them as they moved through the village. Rivulets of mud ran down the narrow path, twisting and eddying around stones.

They headed northwest toward the sloping mountain road, but by the time they reached the outskirts of the village Jabbor was frowning. "We're being followed." He turned a fierce glare at Isyllt, and Zhirin flushed.

Turning, she found three hooded figures closing on them. Jabbor shoved her behind him, hand on his knife-hilt, but their assailants already had pistols drawn. The middlemost pulled aside her veil, baring long brown hair.

"You're right," Jodiya said, gun pointed at Isyllt. "I do like to get my hands dirty. But I like getting the job done even more. And now you've made this even more convenient. Lucky for me Asheris is soft."

"And lucky for me you talk too much."

Jodiya spun, but her companions kept their guns steady. Zhirin's lips parted in shock.

"Mother?" she gasped, before she could stop herself.

Fei Minh stepped closer, a pistol in her manicured hand. "Really, dear. Did you think I was going to let you run off like that without someone to keep an eye on you?" Her escort fanned around her, weapons drawn. Zhirin gaped more when she recognized Mau among them.

"You wouldn't dare," Jodiya said. "You're Faraj's creature."

Fei Minh's eyebrows rose in the shadow of her hood. "I'm a politician and a merchant—you think I don't know when to hedge my bets? And you might consider a milder tongue, under the circumstances."

Jodiya's lips twisted and she whistled once, high and sharp. Zhirin tensed and Jabbor's arm stiffened under her hand, but Fei Minh only laughed.

"I'm sorry, but the rest of your men won't be coming."

Jodiya's jaw clenched; a raindrop trickled down her cheek and dripped from her chin. "What next, then? Shall we stand here until all our guns are too damp to fire?"

"Or perhaps you should put yours down. You're outnumbered."

"Yes, but you or your daughter might die with us if you shoot. Will you risk that?"

Zhirin's fingers tightened on Jabbor's sleeve, and she felt leather beneath the cloth. She loosened her grip, holding her breath as a knife dropped silently into his hand. Beside her, Isyllt shifted her weight. One of Jodiya's companions began to tremble faintly.

Fei Minh drew a breath, perhaps to answer. Zhirin felt a prickle of gathering magic and tensed just as a shrill, icy shriek cut the air.

Guns thundered and Jabbor pushed her down as he launched himself at the closer assassin. Zhirin slipped and hit the ground with a splatter of mud. Someone shouted; someone else fell. She scrabbled out of the road, hands skidding across wet grass—water everywhere, but too scattered to answer her. She looked back to see smoke fade into the rain and the last assassin fall as Jabbor broke his knee with a kick. The knife flashed as the man went down, and he didn't rise again.

Stories spoke of heroes fighting from dawn to dusk, but in truth it happened so fast she could scarcely follow. Four bodies sprawled in the mud—Jodiya, her men, and one of the Tigers whose name she'd never learned.

"Idiot girl," Fei Minh muttered. Zhirin wasn't sure if she meant her daughter or Jodiya. She tucked her pistol inside her coat and picked her way around puddles till she reached Zhirin.

"What are you going to tell Faraj?" she asked, taking her mother's hand.

"I'll think of something. Or perhaps nothing at all— murder is an ugly business, after all, and one can hardly

be surprised when an assassin finally makes a wrong
move."

"Mira—"

Someone shouted, and past her mother's shoulder she
saw Jodiya stir.

"Watch out!" But her shout was swallowed by a pistol's crack. Fei Minh's lips parted in shock and she stumbled into Zhirin's arms. She threw a clumsy arm around
her mother and flinched; the moisture soaking her back
wasn't rain.

"Mother!"

They both fell to their knees. Fei Minh gasped, mouth
moving, but Zhirin couldn't hear the words over the roar
of her heart. Blood slicked her hands as she tried to
stanch the wound, but already her mother was crumpling
in her arms, her grip on Zhirin's hand falling away.

She might have screamed, but she couldn't hear that
either.

People were shouting. Jabbor knelt beside her, trying
to tug her away. Isyllt rose shakily from beside Jodiya's
still form. Mau fell to her knees beside her mistress,
mouth working. Water rolled down Fei Minh's face,
soaking her hair and tangling in her lashes as her eyes
sagged closed. Zhirin could hardly see through the blurring rain.

Jabbor's words finally began to make sense. "We have
to go, Zhir, now. We have to go." She couldn't fight as
he lifted her up, could barely keep her knees from buckling. Rain ran down her face, hot and cold, washing the
blood on her hands rusty pink.

"Go," Mau said, her voice harsh and cracking. "Get
out of here. We'll deal with this." Mau tugged a ring off

Fei Minh's limp hand and pressed it into Zhirin's. Her fingers curled around it reflexively, blood smearing the gold. She couldn't draw breath around the pain in her chest, as if the ghost of the bullet had passed through her mother and struck her.

"Come on," Jabbor said, tugging her away. "I'm sorry."

They only made it a few yards before Isyllt collapsed onto the rain-soaked road.

CHAPTER 18

Even unconscious, a trained necromancer was never truly helpless. It certainly felt that way, though, as Isyllt watched Jabbor carry her limp body into the forest. She was lucky he didn't leave her in the mud, especially since Zhirin was in no condition to argue for her safety.

On the other side of the mirror, Sivahra's forest rose thick and dark. The sky was a low ceiling of gray and violet clouds, twilit gloom. Spirits chattered in the trees and the breeze twisted through the leaves in silver and indigo ribbons, beautiful and disorienting.

Vertigo struck quickly, the familiar dizziness that came of casting her spirit free. On its heels came the wild rush of freedom, the longing to run and fly unfettered by meat. It was the most dangerous part of ghostwalking, more dangerous than any lurking spirit—if she abandoned her flesh too long, she might never return to it. She held on to the echo of her heartbeat until the urge passed. At least, she thought bitterly, as a ghost she had two good hands.

At the Tigers' safe house, Jabbor carried her inside and laid her body on a bedroll, less gently than she would have liked. The living glowed blue-white with heat and life, distorted as if she watched them through water. Her own flesh was clearer and dimmer, the light drawn in. She hadn't realized how awful she looked, blue as milk and hollow-eyed. She could return to her body, perhaps even wake, but she needed rest and this might be the safest place to find any.

Zhirin sank onto a pallet in the far corner. Jabbor tried to speak to her, but she wouldn't answer and after a moment he left her alone, closing the bamboo door behind him. When he was gone, she began to cry.

Isyllt turned away from the girl's grief. She'd known Jodiya wasn't dead but hadn't acted in time. And while it was true that she'd been so exhausted she could barely walk, that wasn't a particularly good excuse. Not one Zhirin would want to hear, at any rate. Even the memory of the assassin's heart stilling beneath her hand was a hollow one.

She made sure her pulse was steady and wrapped her body in webs of wards. She needed to rest her spirit as well as her flesh, but not just yet. And she didn't want to fall asleep listening to Zhirin's tears. The diamond flared as she touched it with spectral fingers, but the girl didn't notice.

Deilin Xian appeared, lips curling. On this side, the ghost was clearer and more solid than the living. A frown replaced her snarl when she saw Zhirin. "What's happened?"

"Khas assassins killed her mother."

Pity looked quite ghastly on the dead woman's face.

"Leave her to her grief," Isyllt said. "Walk with me."

They stepped through the wall, a queer scraping sensation that Isyllt always hated, and emerged on a narrow walkway. The building was set on stilts and wrapped around a broad and towering tree. Lights flickered among the branches, green and gold firefly flickers.

"What are you doing?" Deilin asked as she followed Isyllt over the rail, landing silently on the leaf-strewn slope below.

"Looking around. I thought I'd take a native guide." It was all she could do not to spin around like a child; the absence of weariness and pain made her light-headed.

"You're in my world now, necromancer. Do you think you could best me so easily here?" More curiosity than threat in the question and Isyllt turned to face her, taking in the honor-blade at Deilin's hip, the easy warrior's grace of her stance. She was younger than Isyllt had first thought, perhaps thirty-five when she died. A bullet beneath her right breast had killed her; the wound bubbled and slurped when she spoke and her face and hands were tinged blue. Not a quick or easy death.

"I think I'd win," Isyllt said at last. "But it wouldn't be easy. And if that happened, I'd never let you out again. Do you want to risk it?"

Deilin smiled; she was lovely when she wasn't frothing mad. The resemblance to Anhai and Vienh was clear. "I won't warn you if I do."

Isyllt smiled back and turned her eyes to the forest sloping around them. "What do you call this place?"

"The Night Forest. The unsung dead remain here, with the spirits."

"Where do the others go?"

"East, or so we're told. The songs and offerings carry

them to the cities of our ancestors, on the far side of the mountains."

"But not you."

Deilin shrugged, one hand on her knife hilt. "I wasn't given to the Ashen Wind. The Assari left my corpse to rot, and scavengers have long since eaten my bones. I might have walked, climbed the Bone Stair, but the way is long and dangerous and I was afraid. Even if my granddaughters were to sing me on, my wounds will never heal. And I doubt they would, now."

The soft bitterness of the last turned Isyllt's head. "Why did you do it?"

Deilin didn't answer for a moment and Isyllt wondered if it was worth compelling her to answer. In the silence, she heard the soft, wet sounds of the woman's ruined lung flopping inside her chest.

"I don't know," she said at last. "I wandered in the forest so long—I was already half mad when Chu Zhen found me." Dark eyes flickered toward Isyllt. "Kaeru, she called herself to you. She was the last of the Yeoh clan, or at least of those who didn't sell themselves to the Assari. We were close as girls, but she fled south when her family died and I married soon after.

"She found me only a few seasons ago—I hadn't realized so much time had passed till I saw how old she'd grown. She told me of the city and the Khas and the Dai Tranh, how we lost more children and warriors every year, to death or despair or the lure of Assari decadence. She told me of my granddaughters, and my half-blooded great-granddaughter. And the more she told me, the madder I grew, till my blood burned and all I knew was the need for flesh, for revenge." She touched her wound absently; the blood faded from her fingertips as she pulled them away.

"It's anathema, of course, for the dead to possess the living, but no worse so than for children to forget their ancestors. I remember thinking that, just before Chu Zhen broke the seals and summoned me into the house. Then the madness took me and everything was blood and hate until I woke up in your stone prison."

Isyllt's hand tightened around the ghostly reflection of her ring.

"You argued with her, though, on the boat."

Another shrug. "It's anathema, and I was calmer then. Being bound gives one plenty of time to think."

"What do you think about?"

"Revenge."

Steel hissed and Isyllt spun, turning just in time to watch Deilin's knife sink into her gut. It burned like ice, colder and cleaner than living pain. Deilin bared her teeth as she twisted the blade.

Silver-blue light spilled from the wound. Not blood, but life and magic. It hissed and steamed down the blade and Deilin jerked her hand away as it burned her fingers. The hungry ground swallowed what fell.

Isyllt touched the hilt and grinned. Light surrounded the phantom blade, dissolving it, absorbing it. An instant later, blade and wound vanished, leaving glowing drops on her fingers. Deilin gaped and Isyllt laughed.

"Not so easy, I'm afraid." She reached out and touched the ghost's face with a whispered word of banishment. Deilin vanished with a curse on her lips.

With the woman gone, Isyllt let go of her bravado and staggered to one knee, grunting with pain. Leaves crisped and crumbled where her unblood struck. Kiril's voice rose in her mind, the echo of long-ago lessons. *Take care of your soul as well as your flesh, or you'll find yourself with neither.*

Pride drove her to her feet, pride and the too-close growl of a spirit-beast drawn by the smell of shed magic. She reached for her heartbeat, and in the space of one found herself beside her body.

Zhirin slept, her face stained with tears. Some priests taught that death was an end to pain, but that was a lie. Sleep, at least, might keep it at bay for a time. Isyllt sank into her weary, aching flesh, bound herself with blood and bone, and let the darkness take her.

Xinai and Riuh made better time on the way back, marching through much of the night and finally reaching Cay Lin near midnight five days after they'd set out. Her legs ached to dragging from the pace she'd set and cramps twisted her guts—the sight of the ruined walls filled her with bittersweet relief. Perhaps Selei would be asleep, Xinai half hoped, and she could deliver the news in the morning.

But when the guard escorted them to her makeshift house, a light glowed inside. Xinai didn't recognize the broken building and didn't try to recall who had lived there so many years ago. Selei sat cross-legged on a bedroll, maps spread in front of her and the remnants of a meal set to the side. The old woman looked up as they entered and Xinai frowned—Selei might have aged years in the days they'd been gone. Unhappy lines seamed her face and her eyes were sunken and red-rimmed.

"Grandmother?" Riuh knelt in front of her. "What's wrong?"

"More of us dead." She shook her head, hair tangled and streaked with ashes. "The Khas attacked a Dai Tranh boat last night—no one survived. One of my oldest friends was aboard. My sisters, my cousins, my friends . . . So many of us fallen. Nearly a generation lost to Assari blades, or living clanless and alone in the city."

Xinai knelt beside Riuh and took the old woman's hand. So fragile and light in hers, and she swallowed around a sudden tightness in her throat.

Selei smiled, brief and bitter. "But grief is a luxury I shouldn't indulge in yet. You found it."

"Yes." Xinai stripped the diamond charm off her neck, and only manners kept her from flinging it into the fire. She dropped it on a map instead. "On the eastern side of the mountain. They fish the stones from the river. It's as you feared—prisoners die there and rot unsung."

"Father might still be there," Riuh said. "Or his ghost. We have to find out."

Selei shook her head sadly. "This is greater than one family's grief."

"What, then?"

Her mismatched eyes narrowed, gleaming in the firelight. "We destroy the mine."

"How can you destroy a river?" Xinai asked.

"I don't know yet. We'll find a way." She slid a map out of the stack. "Show me where it is."

Xinai leaned forward to mark the spot with a smudge of charcoal. "They've hung ghost-wards all around, but they're only a distraction." She fought a grimace as she rocked back on her heels; she'd begun to bleed.

Selei stared at the map, at the sinuous curves of the river and the sharp lines of the mountain. One thin, calloused finger tapped Mount Haroun slowly. "I don't think we'll need to worry about that."

The Ki Dai gathered at dawn. Xinai had never been introduced to the rest, or even known their names, but it wasn't hard to guess—all those around her wore charms or witch-marks, and a chill followed them, greater than any one ghost. Shaiyung kept close, till Xinai's arm tingled with cold.

A few protested at first as Selei laid out her plan. It was madness. If the mountain erupted, it would easily destroy the mine and the Kurun Tam mages responsible for it, but the jungle was sure to burn as well. But the more Selei talked, the more sense it made. The Assari had bound the mountain with magic as they'd bound the land with steel and stone— what better way to teach them the strength of a free Sivahra than to unleash the fire they tamed? The forest would grow back, unlike all the clansfolk who had died in the mines.

Soon the assembled witches nodded to the argument, and murmurs of assent rippled through the crowd. Their breath hung in shimmering plumes.

When the gathering dispersed, she escorted Selei back to her makeshift house. The fire had left her, and the old woman seemed frailer than ever, leaning on Xinai's arm as they walked.

"I need you to do something for me."

"Of course."

"I'll be on the mountain tonight, to make sure the bindings break. When you're done with the wards, join me at the eastern rim of the cauldron."

"Are you sure that's safe? It's a long climb—"

Selei snorted. "I'm not infirm yet. And I'll have warriors with me, don't worry. But I want you there as well. And your mother."

"We'll be there."

"Thank you." The woman's fingers squeezed Xinai's arm. "I'm glad you could be here for this. The more clans we have, the stronger we are."

"Not much of a clan, are we?" She shrugged a shoulder toward Shaiyung.

"You don't need to take the gray yet. You're still young. More than one clan has been renewed from a single scion."

Xinai chuckled. "Those stories were more heartening when it wasn't my womb needed for the renewal."

"It isn't so bad. And I think you'll find no few men willing to help you."

"Now you sound like my mother."

They passed a cooking fire and the smell of pork and curried lentils wafted around them. Smoke stung Xinai's eyes and for an instant it was like looking through time. People moved in Cay Lin, cooking and talking, walking between the houses. She almost thought she heard a child's high laughter. But was it the past she saw, or the future?

She shook her head and the illusion vanished, leaving only warriors breaking camp in the iron dawn.

Zhirin drifted in and out of sleep, surfacing at the sound of voices or footfalls or the clack of a tray, only to sink again. Dreams waited for her, circling like nakh in the deep—bright dreams and dark, ordinary and terrifying, till she couldn't tell what was real.

Eventually she woke, blinking till her eyes adjusted to the darkness. Her head felt stuffed with wool, sticky and dreamsick. She sat up with a wince, neck popping; her right arm tingled from being pinned against the floor. Rain rattled softly against the thatch roof.

She rubbed her face, pausing at the salt and snot crusted on her cheeks and lips. Rust-colored crescents darkened her fingernails and the heavy heron-ring gleamed on her hand. The bird's topaz eye glittered coldly. A sick, hollow feeling opened in her stomach, and for a moment she thought she might vomit.

Cloth rustled and she started before recognizing Isyllt's pale face in the gloom. The necromancer sat against the far wall, a blanket draped over her shoulders.

"There's food," she said softly, nudging a tray with her foot.

Zhirin shook her head, swallowing sour spit. "What time is it?"

"Just past dawn."

She touched her head, frowning at a strange lingering tingle behind her eyes. "You spelled me."

Isyllt shrugged. "I thought you needed it."

With unsteady hands, Zhirin poured a cup of water. The first swallow eased the taste of salt and sleep and reminded her of her aching bladder.

"Are you all right?" Isyllt asked.

Zhirin's hands tightened around the cup till she was surprised the clay didn't shatter. "I'd rather not talk about it," she said. It came out harsher than she intended, but she didn't think she could stand either pity or heartless pragmatism at the moment.

The door scraped open and she flinched, slopping

water over her hands. Gray light washed the room and she squinted as a woman leaned inside.

"You're both awake? Jabbor says I'm to look after you. Do you need anything?"

Zhirin clenched her fists so she couldn't see the blood under her nails. "A bathhouse?"

The woman nodded. "Follow me."

The Jade Tigers' compound was a collection of thatch-and-bamboo buildings bounded by thorny canebrake and a rough stone wall. Zhirin didn't recognize the forest, nor could she remember the twisting paths they'd taken to get here. She couldn't remember much of anything after her mother—

She buried the thought deep, concentrating on the sway of the Tiger woman's braids as they walked. The jungle offered her no comfort, and the river was faint and far away. The rain had slackened, but water still dripped from the trees and ran in muddy channels down the sloping ground.

The bathwater was cold but clean, with soap enough to wash away the last of the mud and blood. Zhirin scrubbed her hands raw before she was satisfied. The woman, Suni, found them clothes and ointment for Isyllt's wounds. Zhirin watched in pity and horror as the necromancer changed her filthy bandages, burns and stitches stark and ugly against white skin. The clarity of her ribs and hip bones made Zhirin regret skipping breakfast.

After they dressed, Suni took them back to the room and found tea and fresher food. Zhirin forced herself to eat rice and jackfruit; wasting away with grief wasn't something she could afford to do, not until they were truly safe. She wasn't sure she could even imagine that anymore.

They were free to roam the camp, Suni assured them, but Zhirin was happy enough to stay inside. Isyllt was content with silence; she doubted Jabbor would give her that luxury.

Neither, as it happened, would fate. No more than an hour had passed before voices rose outside and the door opened again.

"A council is gathering," Suni said. "Jabbor says you're both to come."

The rain had returned, drumming on the roof of the long council chamber. Benches and mats lined the edges of the room, and nearly all of them were taken. The gathered spoke in restless mutters, half drowned by the rain. Zhirin braced herself for Jabbor's pity as she sat beside him, but his face was grim and he only squeezed her hand quickly. Voices rose in anger and curiosity when the Tigers saw them.

"Who are they, Jabbor?" a man called, not quite a challenge.

"Some of you have met the Lady Iskaldur," he replied. "She offers us aid from Selafai. And more of you know Zhirin Laii, first daughter of Cay Laii."

She wasn't first daughter anymore, she realized, but silently thanked Jabbor for the omission. She didn't think she could recount the story yet.

Jabbor cut off the next question with a raised hand. "This isn't the time. We have something more important to discuss now. Are we all here?" he asked the guards at the door.

"As many as could be found."

"Bring her in."

An expectant hush settled over the crowd. The door

opened and Kwan Lhun entered, an armed escort at her back. Her eyes narrowed as she saw the gathering.

"Damn you, Jabbor. Must we make a circus of this?"

"Tell them."

Whispers rippled through the room and Zhirin leaned forward. Kwan had been close in Jabbor's confidences for as long as she'd known them, high-ranked amongst the Tigers. To see her under guard was unsettling; her hip was bare where her kris should hang.

Kwan snarled, then shook back her long hair and drew herself straight. "For years now, my cousin Temel and I have been doubling for the Dai Tranh."

Voices rose and Jabbor shouted them down.

"We believed the Tigers too soft," she continued, staring at the wall behind Jabbor. "Too willing to compromise and dance with the Khas, too unwilling to take the measures necessary for Sivahra's freedom." Her gaze shifted to Jabbor, and Zhirin beside him. "I still believe that."

Jabbor smiled, though tension tightened his jaw. "I know all about my shortcomings, Kwan. Get to the point."

Zhirin swallowed, trying not to fidget on the hard bench. She'd always thought that Kwan's dislike for her was half born of jealousy; her cheeks stung as she realized her own childishness.

"The point," Kwan said, biting off the words, "is that I no longer stand with the Dai Tranh. The Tigers may be soft, but the Dai Tranh goes too far, and means to go further still."

She turned to face the room, one hand reaching for her absent sword hilt; she tucked her fingers into her belt instead. "The Dai Tranh found a diamond mine in the forest on the far side of the mountain. The Khas has been harvesting soul-stones for years, using Sivahri prisoners."

Voices rose again, louder and angrier. Jabbor couldn't quiet them, but finally Kwan shouted them down.

"That's right. And that's the fury you should feel—but Selei Xian has let her rage madden her. She means to sabotage the mountain itself and let its fire destroy the mine and the Kurun Tam. The others won't gainsay her."

"What?" Zhirin's voice carried in the stunned silence, and her cheeks burned. Kwan turned to face her and she rallied her wits, pushing herself to her feet. "Never mind the madness of it—they'd burn their own lands as well—but the mountain is warded."

Kwan smiled. "Oh, yes. But we—they—have someone inside the Kurun Tam. Did you think you were the only one, little mage? They know about the wards and how to destroy them. The plan is insanity, but I believe they could do it. That's why I'm here. Lhun lands will burn, and that I cannot allow."

Zhirin sat, catching Jabbor's arm to steady herself. The one thing taught above all other lessons at the Kurun Tam was respect for the mountain. Vasilios had shown her text after text from the Assari histories, painstaking illuminations of the volcanoes found in the southern empire and the devastation they caused when they erupted.

The council became an ocean of angry voices, and she used the confusion to explain the conversation to Isyllt. By the time she'd finished, Zhirin couldn't tell who was yelling what.

"Enough!" Jabbor finally shouted, his voice carrying from floor to rafters. "Whatever the arguments, do we at least agree that burning Sivahra is . . . ill-considered?"

The Tigers nodded, a few snorting at his dry tone. "Kwan, how much time do we have?"

"They'll move tonight. I imagine they'll stage a distraction for the Khas first. And there's more. You've heard the rumors of the White Hand? Well, they're true. The Dai Tranh witches have recruited the unsung dead to fight for them."

Another silence filled the room and Jabbor spoke before it could erupt. "Then it's lucky we have a necromancer with us, isn't it?"

After breakfast, Selei divided the warriors into groups. The Ki Dai, living and dead, would go to the mountain—it would take all their witchcraft to break the wards. The rest would provide distractions to keep the Khas and the Kurun Tam busy.

Riuh frowned as they were separated, but Xinai was glad of the reprieve. Between her cramps and the task ahead of her, the last thing she needed was him lingering at her side, or her mother's smug and knowing glances.

As the witchless groups began to slip away, a warrior pulled Selei aside for a whispered conversation. A Lhun, Xinai guessed from his nose and broad cheeks. Not many other clans had joined the Dai Tranh—Lhuns and Khans, a scattering of clanless. And her.

As she stared at the broken walls and empty houses of Cay Lin, it was hard to share Selei's optimism. The thought of babies was foreign, and for all of Riuh's affection, she had no desire to marry. Not even Adam had made her think of family, and there had been a time when she'd imagined spending the rest of her life with him. Not that a mercenary's life was often long.

Not that a revolutionary's was any longer.

Worry about it later, she told herself. If they survived the night.

Selei finished talking to the man and shooed the last stragglers out of camp. When they were gone, she turned to the Ki Dai.

"We've been betrayed." She raised a hand to forestall questions. "Not to the Khas, I think, but the Tigers will know what's coming."

Mutters rippled and died and witches exchanged glances. "Do we change the plan?" asked Phailin.

"No. If the Kurun Tam gets wind of it, we won't get another chance so easily."

"Do you think they'll try to stop us?" someone else asked, a boy barely old enough to wear a kris. "The Tigers, I mean."

"If they do, be merciless. They've had opportunity enough to join us, to hear the truth. We can't let their weakness stop us now."

The boy's throat bobbed as he nodded.

CHAPTER 19

Zhirin marked the wards on the Tigers' maps, but after that she was useless as they prepared for battle. She wasn't as helpless in a fight as she'd once thought, but she had no gift for strategy. Isyllt stayed with the council, leaving Zhirin to retreat to their room, where she rubbed her mother's ring till her fingers ached and watched the light change as it slipped down the wall.

Jabbor came later in the afternoon, and now his face held all the pity and concern she'd feared. He eased the door shut and sat beside her, not quite touching. His warmth and familiar wood-sweet scent would have been comforting, had he not obviously had something to say, something that left him awkward and nervous.

"What is it?" she asked, after a few moments of listening to him draw breath but not speak.

"I—" He swallowed. She'd never seen him so nervous. "I know how hard a time this is for you. I'm sorry."

She swallowed an unkind reply—his parents had died when he was young. Maybe he did know.

"Thank you," she said instead. "And thank you for taking us in."

He shrugged it aside and took her hand, his broad palm engulfing hers. "Zhir, I know this isn't the best time, but . . ."

"You want help from Cay Laii? I'll do whatever I can, but I need to talk to Mau—"

"No, no." He cut her off as her chest began to tighten at the thought. "I mean, yes, we'd welcome any help Laii can offer, but that's not what I want to ask." His hand tightened on hers, and the heron ring dug into both their flesh. "Zhir, would you marry me?"

She opened her mouth, closed it again, and turned to stare at him. A lattice of light fell over his face, caught splinters of gold in his eyes. "Are you— You're serious."

"Yes. When this is over. If I don't get killed by the Dai Tranh or the Khas." His lips twisted. "Not the best marriage offer, I know, but will you consider it?"

Would she? Dizzying, to realize that the choice was hers alone. She'd always assumed her mother would make a match for her when she finished her apprenticeship, had considered it as inevitable as the tide. But now she had no mother, no master. And now that the Khas knew her loyalties, she had no one to hide from anymore.

Jabbor watched her, brow creasing as her silence stretched. A month ago his proposal would have left her giddy.

"I will," she said at last. "I mean, yes, I'll marry you. But I need time, Jabbor. First Vasilios, and now my mother, and I don't know what Clan Laii will say—"

"Of course, of course. I don't want to rush you. I just wanted you to know how I feel, before—"

She nodded and leaned in to kiss him. He wrapped his arms around her and she sank into his warmth. But the cold, hollow feeling in her chest wouldn't go away.

The Ki Dai left Cay Lin before dusk, changing their route in case the Tigers were waiting. The gibbous moon had already risen, a milky ghost through the clouds. Xinai and Phailin had spent the day making charms, weaving owl and night-heron feathers with night-vision spells. They'd turned to nightjars when they ran out of larger birds, but every witch and warrior with them could see in the dark now. Safer than smuggler's lanterns, though they carried those as well.

They could never reach all the wards in one night, but hopefully they wouldn't need to. If they could destroy enough of them, the circuit would be sufficiently weakened for Selei's invocation at the cauldron to work. Or so they prayed.

Xinai tried not to stare at the sullen glow of the mountain as they worked.

She ended up teamed with Phailin and the young boy who'd been reluctant to fight the Tigers. The wards closest to the Kurun Tam were their task.

The boy, Ngai, might have been too young to shave, but he knew his witchcraft. The three of them picked at the web of magic until it weakened, then dragged the post from the earth. The spell made a sound like a snapping silk cord as it broke.

They grinned when the first ward fell, but by the third they were sweating from the effort as well as the humidity, and worked with silent frowns. Closer and closer to the walls of the Kurun Tam they moved, scanning the jungle as they crept from post to post. Through gaps in the trees, Xinai saw a plume of smoke smudging the sky over the city, nearly lost in the low clouds. The first distraction was under way.

They were close enough to the Kurun Tam to watch the second begin.

She heard the warning shout first and looked away in time. A heartbeat later flame blossomed inside the walls. Glass buoys filled with oil made lovely firebombs. The flames had spread by the time they ripped down the last ward. Shouts and cries and the screams of horses carried from the courtyard.

"Give the signal," Xinai said, "then let's get out of here." Bowstrings twanged from the walls and pistols cracked.

Trembling and sweaty, Ngai unhooked the lantern from his belt and scrambled up a tree, flashing the light when he cleared the canopy. Though it would be a wonder if Selei would see it against the larger blaze growing nearby.

"Aren't you coming with us?" Phailin asked as Xinai waved them away.

"I have to meet Selei. Get to safety or join the others."

The girl nodded and dragged Ngai into the cover of the forest.

Xinai looked up at the moon—nearly midnight. It would all be over by dawn, one way or another. She shook off her fatigue and began to run.

Even with Kwan's warning, they arrived too late to save the closest ward-posts. Those along the mountain road had been uprooted, their spells unraveled. Scraps of magic still flickered around the carven posts; Zhirin thought she could have repaired them if they'd had the luxury of time.

"There aren't enough of us for this," Jabbor muttered.

The Jade Tigers had gathered perhaps a hundred warriors tonight—they guessed the Dai Tranh to have twice that, though how many were in this White Hand, no one was certain. The Tigers split up to cover more ground and could only hope the Dai Tranh didn't travel in larger packs.

Sweat dripped down Zhirin's back as they climbed, pasted her borrowed shirt to her skin. She took a certain grim comfort in Isyllt's ragged breathing and sweat-drenched face; at least she wasn't the only one not used to so much exercise.

As they drew closer to the Kurun Tam, Zhirin felt movement in the trees around them. Humans, which might be other Tigers or cautious Dai Tranh, and the quicksilver flicker of spirits. And colder flashes that she thought must be ghosts. Isyllt's ring glimmered softly, and the necromancer scanned the woods as they climbed.

They heard the shouts before they crested the last hill and saw the flames. As they scrambled up the slope, Zhirin gasped. The fire burned inside the Kurun Tam's walls.

"Are they mad? Attacking the hall—"

"It's another distraction," Isyllt said. "Damn me for not seeing it sooner. Breaking the wards isn't enough—they mean to wake the mountain. They'll have someone at Haroun's summit, waiting for the others to finish."

Jabbor swore. "What can we do?"

"You and the others stay here, try to salvage as many wards as you can. I'm going up."

"Why?" Jabbor asked coldly. "Why do you care? Why not just run?"

Isyllt shrugged, her pale face impassive. "Because I'm trapped on this side of the river too, and I don't want to die for the Dai Tranh's zealotry. Zhirin?"

She only hesitated a heartbeat. "I'm with you."

She thought Jabbor would argue, steeled herself against it. He let out a breath and shook his head. "Go on. Be careful."

From the southern road came the sound of horses. "The Khas is here," Jabbor said. "Maybe they and the Dai Tranh can kill each other off neatly and leave us to clean up." He leaned in and kissed Zhirin, soft and quick. "Hurry."

She'd ridden to the mountain dozens of times, but never walked there, let alone run. Her sandals chafed her feet raw, and she didn't know how her legs kept moving. She thought she glimpsed someone in front of them, but it was hard to be sure through the darkness and flicker of the wards. The posts glowed fiercely, not their usual soft light; Zhirin doubted that was a good sign.

The ground sloped steeper and steeper as they neared the stair, and they scrambled and slid with every step. She heard hoofbeats again, close behind, but the riders would have to abandon their horses to follow any higher.

They hit the stairs and ran faster, despite stubbed toes and burning thighs. Someone was definitely climbing ahead of them, and they were gaining now.

"Wait!" Zhirin's breath failed and she had to shout again.

The person paused, a slender silhouette against the witchlights.

"Xinai!" Isyllt called.

Another few steps and Zhirin recognized the mercenary. White as bone in the cold light, eyes lost in shadow. Isyllt's ring blazed and Zhirin glanced around as if she might see the ghost.

Steel gleamed in Xinai's hand. "Stay back." Her voice was rough, cold as her blade.

Isyllt hesitated, one foot on the next step. "Don't be a fool, Xinai. The mountain isn't some little spirit you can tame. It's not like the nakh."

"Go, necromancer. This is none of your concern. Consider your life a gift for bringing me home."

Isyllt's breath hissed through her teeth. "You're possessed."

"No, just reunited. Leave, before I decide to take that ring away from you."

Zhirin looked from Xinai to Isyllt. She had to stop this, but her mouth was too dry for words.

Footsteps scraped on stone below, and the tension broke and reformed. Isyllt cursed. Then golden witchlights blossomed all around them as Imran and Asheris climbed onto the landing.

The five of them stared at one another for a long moment, then Xinai bolted. Not up the stairs but down, dodging lithely around the startled mages.

"Kill the necromancer," Imran said to Asheris. "I'll take care of the Dai Tranh."

Zhirin looked at Isyllt, whose face was a mask in the eerie light.

"Go on," she said, calm and brittle.

Zhirin hesitated for a heartbeat, but her courage broke and she fled down the path after Imran and Xinai.

She caught up with them at the next landing. Xinai's daggers gleamed, and Imran's magic hung around him thick enough to make Zhirin's skin tingle. He didn't spare her a glance, but a tendril of power licked at her.

"Go home, girl," he said. "And for Vasilios's sake, I'll spare you."

Zhirin barely saw Xinai move before a dagger flickered toward Imran. Only to clatter to the stones a yard shy of its target. He gestured in turn and Xinai stiffened and stumbled, one hand rising to her throat.

Zhirin stared as the woman's face darkened, her own hand lifting in unwitting accompaniment. She could help Isyllt while Imran was distracted, or climb to the crater and try to stop the Ki Dai. The mercenary had chosen this.

But she couldn't walk away. People had already died tonight, ancestors only knew how many, Dai Tranh and Tigers and whoever else was unlucky enough to be in the way. More would doubtless die before dawn. But she couldn't walk away from this.

"Leave her alone." Her voice nearly broke.

Imran frowned and glared over his shoulder. "I told you to go." He'd probably never had an apprentice talk back to him before; it nearly made her laugh.

"And I told you to let her be. Killing her won't stop the others. Worry about the mountain."

"Don't dictate priorities to me, girl. The rebels are the danger here—and after tonight, we won't have to waste our time with them any longer."

She didn't argue, only drew her magic to her. The incredulous look on his face was almost worth what was sure to be her quick demise. The river was too far away to answer her here; instead the mountain churned hot and angry at her back.

Imran fought like a classical duelist, his body straight and still behind layers of wards while his magic spun sharp as daggers around him—Zhirin was surprised he didn't call a halt till they could find seconds and draw circles. She wasn't strong enough to face his spellcraft head-on. Instead she dodged and wove, threw illusions and ribbons of fog to distract him while she twisted away from his assaults.

Magic dizzied her—for an instant she was quicksilver speed, elusive and untouchable. Then a gust of wind sharp as a blade sliced her cheek, and another tore her sleeve and the flesh beneath. The air thickened in her lungs and her throat tightened when she tried to draw breath. Her magic broke against his and rolled away as the pressure in her chest grew. Drowning on dry land. Her knees shook, but the vise around her throat wouldn't let her fall. The night splintered into shards of black and red.

Then the grip vanished and she collapsed, knees cracking the stone hard enough to make her sob as air rushed into her aching lungs.

Imran stumbled and fell as well, groping toward his back. As Zhirin's vision cleared, she saw Xinai's knife hilt standing out of his shoulder. She and the mercenary stared at each other while Imran swore and bled on the stones.

Then he began to scream.

Isyllt stared at Asheris with *otherwise* eyes. Now that she knew how to look, she could see the truth. Such a simple disguise, but effective. Few would think to look for demons in the Emperor's palace.

"They bound you." The words left on a wondering breath. "They bound you in flesh and stone."

Asheris nodded. "And they bound me well. I will do as I'm bid. I cannot free myself, and I must kill anyone who tries to free me. And even if I were rid of the stone, the chains of flesh cannot be broken—I am anathema now, demon. My own kind will never take me back."

"There must be a way—"

He spread his arms, gave her a mocking bow. "Lady, you're welcome to try, since I must kill you anyway. I won't be as easy to stop as an animated corpse." His smile fell away. "I'm sorry. This is not my will."

She barely called her shields in time to stop the wall of flame that crashed over her. Heat and chill shattered each other. She flung witchlights in his face, but he batted them away like gnats. He was stronger than any other demon she'd fought; he was stronger than her. They might duel for a time, but eventually he'd wear her down.

She sent a ghost shrieking toward him—it couldn't harm him, but he flinched. She closed the distance between them in three strides, slammed her shoulder into his chest. His flesh might not age or die, but it still functioned; the air left his lungs in a grunt and he stumbled back. Isyllt kept close, ripping his coat as she clawed for the collar.

It was ensorcelled, of course. Layers of spells wound the thick work-hardened wire, shielding and strengthening and reinforcing.

She expected him to throw her off, braced against the blow, but he only wrapped his arms around her, gentle as an embrace. Why fight, when he could burn her to ash?

Letting her ring hold the shields, she concentrated on

the spells on the collar. It was cunningly wrought—a pity she couldn't show it to the Arcanost. Three different mages had layered the wards, each style reinforcing the others' weaknesses. She found a loose end and tugged, but the spell only unraveled a little before catching in another knot. It would have been a lovely puzzle if the air in her lungs weren't already painfully hot. Sweat dripped from her face, slicked her hands and blurred her eyes. Asheris murmured something in her ear, but she couldn't hear the throb of her pulse.

Abandoning finesse, she called the cold. Too soon since she'd last done it; a shudder racked her. Her bones ached, and the force of it scraped her veins like glass splinters. But it answered. Death, decay, the hungry cold that waited for the end of everything, spiraling through her like a maelstrom. She tightened numbing fingers in the collar's loops and whorls.

Asheris shuddered now and caught her shoulders. His magic rose to answer hers: a sandstorm, a whirlwind, smokeless flame. Two faces hung before her—the man's, and a fire-crowned eagle. She closed her eyes before it dizzied her.

Her spells were failing. The heat bit deeper; her hair was burning. But the spells on the collar died too, slowly corroding beneath the entropy in her hands. Asheris caught her left wrist, gave a raptor's shriek of rage and pain. She smelled her skin crisping, but she was already numb.

"Stop," Asheris gasped. "Please."

He was more powerful than she, but not more powerful than the force she called. Storms stilled, flame smothered, and in the end even stars chilled and died. She could stop his undying heart.

But she'd die first. Ice within, fire without, more than her fragile flesh could withstand. If she left herself open to the abyss too long, it would claim her.

The last of the ward-spells dissolved, leaving nothing but gold beneath her frozen fingers. Gasping, she broke the channel. The pain of it made her scream and she might have fallen, but her hands were locked stiff around Asheris's throat. He cried out too and stumbled, and they both fell to their knees.

"Please," he whispered, "please—"

She had exhausted her magic. His fire would burn her, and she had nothing left to stop it. But she wasn't dead yet, and gold was soft.

"I'm sorry," she whispered back, raw and ragged. Then she kneed him in the groin as hard as she could.

He groaned and tried to curl around the pain, but she forced him back, driving her knees into his stomach and tugging at the collar. Blood slicked her hands, hers and Asheris's, as wire bit their flesh. Her vision washed dull and spotted as she began to feel the pain, but she held on, shaking like a terrier with a rat in its jaws. Metal twisted, bent, broke. Strand after strand. She sobbed with the pain, tears and sweat and blood from a bitten lip splashing Asheris's face.

Snarling, he pushed her off and backhanded her across the face, sending her sprawling on the stones. She choked on her own tears and curled into a pain-riddled ball. She couldn't stand, could only lie shuddering and wait for the death stroke.

But Asheris didn't spring for her, only rose to his knees, trembling like a blown horse. One hand clutched his throat as he choked and gagged. She might have crushed his larynx. As blood filled her mouth and her cheek began to throb, she couldn't quite care.

Then she felt the pain in her hands, and something else. Gold twisted around her claw-hooked fingers, gleaming beneath the blood. And in the palm of her ruined left hand lay a blazing diamond.

She forced herself to her knees, peeling the wire out of her hands; blood welled in the cuts, dripped to the ground. She and Asheris stared at each other through witchlight and shadows.

"Destroy the stone," he gasped. "Imran wears its twin—part of me is still bound in them. I can't do it, please—"

The pain on his face made her look away, pain and desperate hope. She couldn't stand to hear him plead again. But she had no way to even chip such a stone, let alone shatter it . . .

She turned, clumsy, and stared at the orange light glowing from the mountain's cauldron. Diamonds were forged in the earth's fire. That would be enough to melt it.

She stumbled to her feet, knees buckling. Her arms were nothing but pain from fingertip to shoulder, and her face was already swelling from the blow. But she could still walk.

The stones shuddered beneath her feet. Beneath the keen of the wind she heard shouts and sounds of battle. The Dai Tranh must have broken the wards. They needed to be away from the mountain as fast as they could.

So she, like a fool, was climbing up it. It made her laugh, till her hand cramped around the stone and she whimpered instead.

The lake of fire was higher than it had been, great bubbles of flame bursting on its surface. The stench of sulfur and burnt rock choked her. She crouched on her knees at the lip of the crater, afraid to stand against the wind.

She spared a heartbeat to stare at the ruined collar. Still beautiful, rubies like drops of blood amid the mangled gold, the diamond rich and flawless. He was a demon and she meant to free him. She'd never be able to stop him again if he turned on her.

Only a heartbeat's hesitation and she flung the stone away, into the cauldron. She didn't see it land, but flames belched high and bright. And from the landing below came a fierce raptor's cry.

She turned, scrambled down the stone till she reached the steps. And stopped as Asheris rose in front of her on four burning wings. His eagle's head turned, watched her from one blazing eye. Even Assari friezes couldn't capture the beauty of the jinn.

He alit on the step below her and the light died, leaving only the man. His clothes were torn and filthy, skin lusterless beneath blood and sweat, but his throat had healed.

"Lady, it is done." He offered her a hand and she took it, but when their fingers touched he flinched away. He stared at her right hand, her beringed hand, and for an instant she wondered if he would send her into the volcano as well, to free the bound ghosts.

Instead he turned her hand over, frowning at the blood, at the fingers hooked with pain. Then he caught her left, baring the blackened, blistered mark his hand had burned into her wrist.

"I'm sorry. I wish I could heal you—"

She smiled crookedly. "But that's not what either of

us is made for, is it? Perhaps you could help me off this mountain instead."

"It would be my pleasure."

The ground shook again when they reached the landing and they stumbled.

"This is bad, isn't it?" Isyllt asked.

Before he could answer, footsteps slapped against the path and Zhirin stumbled up the stairs. Witchlights flickered around her and she raised a hand in warding when she saw Asheris.

"It's all right," Isyllt said. "We're not killing each other anymore. What happened?"

The girl gaped an instant longer, then shook her head. Blood ran from a cut on her cheek, spotting her shirt collar. "Imran is dead. He burned, and I don't know how—"

Asheris smiled, cold and cruel. "Backlash. A pity I wasn't there to watch."

"But," Zhirin went on, "Xinai got away. And I think they've broken too many wards."

His bloody humor fell away. "Yes. The mountain is waking." He tilted his head, listening. "It's been waiting such a long time."

"Can you stop it? Like you did at the warehouse?"

He shook his head. "This fire is greater than I could ever quench or contain. All we can do is get away."

"But the Kurun Tam, the villages, the forest—"

"Are all going to burn. I'm sorry. Imran would have done better to send me after the Dai Tranh while there was still hope of stopping this."

The mountain rumbled, a roar building beneath their feet.

"We're not going to make it down, are we?" Isyllt said.

She didn't feel like running anyway. It was hard enough staying conscious.

"We wouldn't, no." Asheris slipped an arm around her waist. "But we're not going down." He held out his other hand to Zhirin. "Miss Laii?"

Zhirin stared. "What—"

"Come on," Isyllt said as she began to understand. She grabbed his waist, abused fingers clutching a handful of silk. "Zhirin, please, let's go."

The girl took his hand, let him pull her close.

"Hold on," he said. And uncased his wings.

Zhirin shrieked, short and sharp, as they rose. Isyllt slipped, her hand nearly useless, but his grip tightened.

"I won't let you fall."

His wings blazed against the night. Isyllt felt their warmth, but it didn't burn her. The mountain fell away in a dizzying spiral, a burning eye in the black stretch of forest; Symir glittered in the distance. They moved into the low clouds and her skin tingled as the damp touched her burns. For a moment there was nothing but wind and mist, the taste of rain and the delta spreading out beneath them. Zhirin made a soft sound of wonder and delight.

Then the mountain exploded.

Xinai fled before the mage stopped screaming, leaving the Laii girl to stare as he burned and writhed. She avoided stairs and sorcerers altogether, scrambling across the crags instead. The rough pitted stones scoured the skin from her hands but were easy enough to climb. Light leaked over the lip of the cauldron, sullen even to her colorless night-eyes. She could imagine the red glow easily.

A touch of a charm lent her a burst of speed; she'd pay for it the next day, but now she needed the deer's grace. Her mother's presence surrounded her like a cloak of ice, chilling the sweat that ran down her back.

She thought she heard a shout below as she reached the edge of the crater, but couldn't tell who it came from. With any luck the mages would all kill one another.

Crouching against the wind, she ran. The light was brighter now, and she kept her eyes averted. As she neared the northeastern side of the crater she heard Selei call her name.

The old woman waited a few yards down the slope, a pair of Dai Tranh warriors keeping watch. The wind was gentler there, though it still whistled sharply over the rocks.

"The mages are coming," Xinai gasped, sinking to her knees in front of Selei. She let her night-eyes fade. "We need to hurry."

Selei nodded and turned to her guards. "Leave us. And hurry down—I don't know how quickly the mountain will wake."

"What about you, Grandmother?"

"I know what I'm doing. Don't worry about me."

They nodded unhappily and started down, leaving behind a wooden box. Xinai could feel the magic humming inside it, hot and violent. The rubies, soon to be reunited with the mountain that charged them.

"You'll have to leave soon too," Selei said. "But I wanted to see you again, before this ends."

"What—" Her mouth opened, closed again. A queasy chill settled in her gut. "No. You can't—"

"It has to be done, and this is the price." She shook her

head. "I'm tired, Xinai. I've lost so many—my brothers and sisters, my childhood friends, even my children. I don't want to end my days a dowager, a burden on the clan."

"You're no burden! You lead the Dai Tranh."

"But not for much longer, I think. I may be a clever old witch, child, but even witches' wits dull with age. I want to have a death that means something. That buys something."

"Why not a life that means something?"

"I think I've had that." She took Xinai's hands in hers. "Don't you?"

Xinai nodded. Her eyes prickled, pressure building behind her nose. "What about Riuh? You're all he has left."

"Look after him for me, then."

Selei's face blurred as Xinai blinked angrily. She couldn't talk her out of this. "I will," she choked. "I promise."

"I wish you could have been mine by blood as you've been in my heart. But Cay Lin is lucky to have you." She untied two charms from around her neck. "Give this to Riuh," she said, tapping the larger. "This one is yours. There'll be nothing left for the rites, but if you and he would sing for me when this is over . . ."

"We will."

A tongue of flame uncoiled from the crater, washing the night carnelian and gold. The mountain was a hot pressure against all of Xinai's senses, scraping her raw.

"It's time," said Selei. She knelt and took up the box of rubies. "The wards are failing. You should go."

"I can't let you go alone."

"This will be a bitter enough victory—don't make us lose another warrior to it. Run, child."

Scrubbing her eyes, Xinai turned and started down the slope. Rocks slipped and scattered under her feet and tears blurred her already strained vision. She looked back once, saw the old woman picking her way carefully toward the top of the mountain, silhouetted against the cauldron's glare.

The first tremor threw her down and she slid cursing through rock and brush before catching herself. She kept her footing through the next, but the path was treacherous.

She was scarcely a quarter down the slope when the night shattered into flame and ash.

CHAPTER 20

Zhirin was so busy staring at Mount Haroun that for an instant she didn't understand where the roar was coming from. Then the sky blotted dark and Asheris twisted up and sideways, his impossible wings shredding the clouds. She screamed, gasped as his arm tightened around her ribs. She clutched at him as they spiraled farther away from the mountain, land and sky spinning around them.

When they paused again she saw what had happened. The cauldron hadn't erupted, but one of the hills flanking the mountain had burst open, spewing smoke and ash. The plume rose before them, past them, blotting out the stars. Sparks flashed in the column like blossoms on a tree. An instant later she cried out again as cinders and ash rained over them.

Asheris cursed and turned, shielding them with one set of wings while the other beat frantically against the thickening air. Zhirin choked on the stench of sulfur and char; grit crunched between her teeth.

Craning her head and shielding her eyes, she saw lava leaking from the shattered mountain, incarnadine blood pouring down the southwestern slope. Flames flared gold and vermilion around the flow. The forest was burning.

The air cleared as they gained distance, though the smell was still thick. Asheris turned and they watched in horror and amazement as the mountain shuddered and split again. A new rift opened on Haroun's main slope, spitting fire and rock. Lava spilled from the cleft, rushing down the hills.

To her *otherwise* eyes, a many-headed serpent writhed free of shattered rock, hissing his hundred-tongued fury into the sky.

Zhirin wasn't sure how long they hung there, coughing on the acrid fumes, watching the mountain rip itself apart. Her lungs and throat burned and tears leaked down her face.

"We need to land," Asheris finally said, turning away from the devastation.

The air was clearer to the east; the worst of the ashen cloud rolled west, toward the bay. Toward Symir. Useless to think about that now, she told herself. There was nothing she could do.

Asheris's wings stretched wide and they wheeled downward in a narrowing gyre. The river glittered beneath them. He was landing near the dam.

He touched the ground as gracefully as any bird, but Zhirin stumbled as soon as he let her go. A rock bit her foot and she frowned—she'd lost a sandal somewhere in the sky. She took a step, then kicked off the other. When she turned, his wings had vanished.

"What are we going to do?" she asked.

He shrugged, steadying Isyllt with a hand on her elbow. "Stay out of the way until Haroun's wrath is spent."

"But Symir is going to burn!"

"There's nothing we can do to stop that now."

She turned away, gritting her teeth in fear and frustration. Even the river's nearness couldn't soothe her now, though it steadied her, eased the drain of spent magic. She could see the gray bulk of the dam upriver, the sharp-toothed mountains behind it blotting out the stars.

"The dam," Zhirin said. Her voice sounded odd and distant, like a stranger's. "If we release the dam, the river can help stop the fire."

Asheris shook his head. "Then the city would flood and burn. It would only add to the destruction."

"You always speak of the mountain as though it lived. Do you think the river is any less alive?"

"Fair enough. But men bound the river as they did the mountain. What makes you think the Mir would help us if it could?"

She smiled slowly. "Because I've asked."

Without her charms, Xinai would have died a dozen times on the mountain. As it was, her spells were all but exhausted when she reached the foothills near the Kurun Tam. Her muscles screamed, pushed to their limits, and falling rock and ash left her bruised and burned; her lungs felt scoured raw despite the scarf over her face.

The pillar of smoke blotted out the sky, hid the coming dawn. Lava writhed down the slope like red gold worms, consuming everything in its path. It would be on them soon.

People moved among the trees, gawking like her. She

didn't know if they were Tigers or Dai Tranh or Khas, didn't have it in her to care anymore. They'd all be just as dead if they didn't run.

She might have stood and stared until the fire took her, but the earth shook again and Haroun belched another gout of smoke and sparks. A moment later the rain of stones resumed. A black rock the size of her head landed a yard away, shaking Xinai out of her daze.

A hand closed on her arm, yanking her toward the cover of the trees before another could crush her. Phailin's face was streaked with soot and blood and her mouth worked soundlessly. An instant later Xinai realized that the girl was shouting, and she was the one deaf.

The road, already softened by rain, was murderous now. Mud slid away in sheets from the steeper slopes, and branches and sometimes whole trees blocked their path. A horse passed them, only to founder and fall, crushing its rider as it rolled. Xinai was glad she couldn't hear man or animal scream.

The ash thickened, worse than rain; a stone struck Xinai's shoulder, wringing a gasp from her burning throat. She stumbled, slid, scrambled up again. *Just a little farther*, she told herself—they were almost to the ferry. Her sweat-drenched scarf smothered her and she clawed it away from her mouth. Her lungs hurt so much already she didn't care about the ash.

The slope eased, trees thinning. Almost there— Another tremor and she hunched, arms around her head to ward off falling stones. Phailin slipped and crashed into her and they both went down in a tangle of limbs and mud. Xinai tugged at the girl's arm, but she didn't move. She pulled her a few feet, then paused as she saw the black blood glistening across Phailin's face. Xinai touched the wound, and jerked her hand away when shattered bone shifted under her fingers.

Hands on her shoulders, pulling her up, turning her. She could barely stand, or focus on Riuh's face. He was shouting, voice sharp with fear, but she could only shake her head and gesture angrily at her useless ears. He flinched when he saw Phailin, jaw working as he swallowed. He took Xinai's arm, dragging her toward the dock. Her knees shook and she wondered if he'd have to carry her to the boat.

Then a familiar chill settled into her flesh, driving back the pain and filling her with unnatural strength. She knew she should protest, but it was too much relief to let someone else move for her.

Even through half-numb limbs, she felt instead of heard a roar building behind them. They turned just in time to see a wall of mud and trees sweep down on them.

The Sajet Dam curved across the river like gray veils, two tiers of stone where the Green Maiden Falls had once cascaded. Zhirin had seen the waterfall only in pictures, or in her dreams. Towers rose on either side of the water, their western faces carved into colossal statues of women—the ancient Assari queens Sajet and Anuket, though she had always thought of them as the River Mother and one of her reed-maiden daughters. The towers were home to guards and engineers and the mages who siphoned energy from the surging water. Walkways fringed the walls like lace, arching over the rushing spillways.

The earthquakes had already weakened the foundations. A hairline fissure spread down the lower face of the dam, slowly leaking threads of water. As they drew closer, she could make out people moving on the walkways and tower balconies.

When they were within range of normal eyes, a man ran from the northern tower. He looked around, probably for horses—Zhirin wondered what he would have thought if he'd seen them land. "Lord al Seth, what's happened?"

"The mountain has woken. Take your men and get out of here. Symir isn't safe—keep to the Southern Bank and avoid the wind from the west."

"But the dam—"

"There's nothing you can do for it now, and the earth may keep shaking. I'll look after the dam."

They waited as both towers emptied. The already skittish horses would have nothing to do with the causeway, and the guards finally released those stabled in the northern tower.

"Are you sure about this?" Asheris asked as they watched the evacuation. Isyllt had barely spoken since they landed, only stood in a weary daze, her mangled hands held against her chest.

"Can you think of any other way?"

His silence was answer enough.

When the last of the guards had vanished on the other side, Zhirin stepped onto the causeway across the top tier. The roar of water through the sluices was deafening and she felt the force of it shivering through the stones beneath her feet.

The river was different here. The Mir she knew was soft-voiced, relentless but gentle, deep and dangerous but not angry. The water behind the dam raged and surged, pushing against her prison, constantly searching for a way out, a way free. She tasted of stone and snowmelt, carried dizzying images of falls and cataracts, of soaring mountains and jagged crags and the distant lands beyond them.

Zhirin closed her eyes and listened, let the river's voice fill her, let her intentions spill out. She wasn't sure how long she stood there, but when she opened her eyes again the eastern sky had begun to gray and she knew what she needed to do.

"I'm no engineer," Asheris said when she returned to the bank, "but I think we can manage to open the floodgates."

Zhirin shook her head. "It's not enough. She wants freedom. Can you break the dam?"

He and Isyllt looked at each other, dark face and white wearing identical frowns.

"I can find the faults," Isyllt said at last, "but I'm too weak to do much else." Her mouth twisted at the admission.

Asheris smiled wryly. "Show them to me and I can exploit them. This is a day of breaking bonds."

"And everything else," muttered Isyllt, touching her swollen lip.

Zhirin stood in the center of the causeway while Asheris and Isyllt went about their work. She couldn't bear to watch the plumes of ash in the western sky, the rain of cinders; instead she bent her head and let the river's dark thoughts fill her.

She knew what was needed. What was demanded. It was a much lower price than the mountain had claimed. And when she thought of her city burning behind her, of Jabbor's forests, it was easy to agree.

He would understand, she thought. And even if he
didn't, this was better. Her love of the river was older than
her feelings for him, older than her desire for the cunning sorceries of the Kurun Tam. Still, she was glad she'd
known both. Even glad she'd met Isyllt, when she thought
about it. Gladder still to know that she wouldn't grow as
cold and heartless.

She searched in her purse, found the wooden comb
Suni had given her. It took a moment to free her braids;
ash and bits of leaves fluttered loose. As soon as the teeth
touched her hair the water answered, waves rising and
strengthening. Somewhere in the churning depths in front
of her she felt spirits stir, glimpsed pale mottled faces and
long weed-green hair.

Sister, they called. *Sisterdaughtermotherriver.*

"We're ready," Isyllt called soon after. "Get clear."

"No." The strength of her voice surprised her. "This is
where I need to be."

She saw understanding in their faces. "Are you sure?"
Isyllt's voice was much gentler than she'd ever heard
before.

"You don't have to," Asheris said. Not arguing or
pleading, and she was grateful for it.

"No. But this will be best."

The lake surged and roiled, waves crashing against
stone, high enough that their spray slicked her face. The
voices of the reed-maidens filled her head.

"I'm ready," she told them. "Do it."

Asheris and Isyllt clasped hands, and she felt the magic
gathering beneath her. She waved once in farewell, then
turned back to the waiting water.

"Mother," she whispered, and wasn't sure if she meant

Fei Minh or the Mir. Her hands tightened on the railing, rust scraping her palms. No, that wasn't the way. She inhaled a damp breath, blew out her fear as the lower dam crumbled with a roar.

The causeway shattered.

She raised her arms and opened them to the oncoming wall of water. It hurt for an instant, as the impact broke her limbs, drove shards of rib into her lungs, but the river took the pain.

The river took everything.

CHAPTER 21

Dark and fast, the river runs, thick with flotsam—jagged stone and bits of iron spinning in the current before they sink into the mud; a girl's shattered body; a daughter's soul cradled in her mother's arms. Water rushes over the banks. Spirits ride the surge, ecstatic in their freedom.

The river rages, decades of anger unleashed, tempered by a daughter's grief, a daughter's hope. A daughter's bargain.

The mountain shakes, heaving the river in her bed, undoing centuries of patient carving. Fish and snakes writhe in upthrust mud; slime glistens on bones and stones hidden for hundreds of years. The water tastes of ash, of hot stone, of blood and brimstone.

Boats snap their moorings and capsize, throwing screaming passengers into the roar and rush. That part of the river that was a girl mourns each snuffed and broken life, but knows she cannot save them all. Mud rushes down the flanks of the shaking mountain, adds its weight to the flood.

In the city, canals burst out of their banks, water sweeping over streets and sidewalks. A bull kheyman washes onto the steps of a house, roaring his outrage. The earth trembles and a bridge shudders and gives way. In the Floating Garden, potted trees break their tethers and bob away, shedding leaves and branches into the hungry current. In Straylight, buildings groan and slide, bricks and mortar raining into the floodwaters. In the harbor, the sea already churns, vexed to tempest by the earth's upheaval. Caught between wave and flood, docks splinter, ships founder and sink. Bayside windows shatter under the onslaught, doors burst from their hinges. The water snatches people off quays and sidewalks and drowns all their cries and prayers.

But it hears those drowning prayers too.

Throughout the city fires are doused, but rocks and cinder still rain, and wave after wave of ash blots out the sky. Buildings crumble beneath the weight of ejecta, piling stone upon stone over their unlucky occupants. If it cannot burn the city, the mountain means to bury it, to wipe out all trace of those who in their hubris bound it.

And that, the river decides, will not happen. Not to her namesake, this curiosity of men nestled in her delta, the home of the daughter who set her free. The daughter prays; the mother listens.

And as the mountain renews its offense, the river rises and enfolds the city in her arms.

Dawn never came.

From the tower beside the ruined dam, Isyllt and Asheris watched the mountain burn. Ash drifted past the window like gray snow. Eventually she slept, lulled by the roar of the river and the warmth of Asheris's shoulder. When she woke her head was on his thigh and the darkness hadn't brightened. The murk hid the mountain, giving only the occasional sullen flash of orange. The sky to the south was the yellowish gray of necrotic flesh.

"What time is it?" Her voice was a croak, throat raw and lips cracking. Her eyelids scraped as she blinked.

"Afternoon," he said, his own voice rough. "Or it ought to be."

Golden witchlights blossomed over their heads, driving away the gloom. Dirt smeared Asheris's face and clothes and itched on Isyllt's skin. When she scratched her cheek her nails came back black with grime; it dulled her ring, hid the diamond's fire and clogged the setting.

Her left arm was numb, wedged between her and the floor. Her elbow creaked when she straightened it, and the rush of blood to her ruined hand made her eyes water. But it didn't hurt as much as it should. Wincing, she eased her tattered sleeve back. The print of Asheris's hand circled her wrist like a shackle gall, char-black and flaking in the middle, seeping raw flesh beneath. The edges were pink and blistered, hot and painful enough leave a sour taste in her mouth, but she couldn't feel the worst parts. At least the ashen air had clogged her nose enough that she couldn't smell the burnt-pork reek of it.

She'd seen burns like this before, knew the infection sure to follow in one as filthy as this. She might have another day before the fever set in. The bandage on her palm was foul with blood and soot, and she didn't want to imagine the state of that wound.

"Wait here," Asheris said and left the room, brushing futilely at the dirt on his coat.

Another tremor came while he was gone, rumbling softly through the stones. Isyllt tensed as dust sifted down from the ceiling, but nothing else gave way. He returned a few moments later with a length of linen and a brandy decanter.

"The pipes are broken," he said as he crouched beside her. "No clean water."

She picked up the brandy, smearing the glass. "Is this for the burn or for me?"

Asheris frowned, lifting her arm carefully to peer at the burn. "Internal application would be better, I think."

He took the bottle from her and doused a corner of the cloth, wiped his fingers clean. She sighed as the smell filled the air, caramel-sweet and stinging the back of her nose. The sting was worse when she took a sip, not just in her sinuses but in the tiny cracks and cuts in her lips. The first swallow went down bitter with blood and char; the second numbed her tongue and coated her throat in sweet fire. Reluctantly, she set the bottle down after a third drink. The alcohol and the rush of the waterfall only reminded her how thirsty she was.

Asheris wrapped the burn loosely and rigged a sling. His eyes glittered in the witchlit gloom. Not the copper-red flash of an animal's, but a crystalline sparkle like a flame behind amber.

"Who are you, really?" she asked as he tied the last knot.

"I'm Asheris, now." He rocked back on his heels and raised a hand, palm up. "This is more than just a prison, or a skin. I have his memories, his loves, his life."

"And before?"

"This tongue couldn't pronounce my old name, and it's lost to me anyway." He chuckled. "We were well matched, Asheris-the-man and the jinn I was. I doubt their trap would have worked as well otherwise. Both so very curious, so incautious. The Emperor's mages plied the man with wine and the jinn with incense, but it was that curiosity, that desire to know the *other*, that bespelled us long enough for their chains and stones to bind." He touched his throat, rubbed the unscarred flesh.

Isyllt didn't look at her ring, but she felt its weight keenly. "What will you do now?"

His smile sharpened for a moment. "Find some old colleagues. Imran wasn't the only one who cast that spell. And I worry they may have tried it again."

An army of bound jinn. Isyllt shuddered at the thought and Asheris nodded. "I won't let them. After that—" He shrugged. "I don't know. But first, I think we should leave the tower. The earth hasn't settled yet—you slept through several tremors before that last, and I suspect more will come."

He rose, taking her elbow to help her up. "Zhirin's bargain did something. The river has woken. Whether it was any help to Symir, I don't know."

Isyllt stared at the darkness in the west, the sifting ash, the flare and flash of cinders. "Shall we find out?"

They wrapped their faces before they stepped outside, but that couldn't stop the smell of smoke. Looking back at the tower, she saw how lucky they'd been— the stones at the river's edge had crumbled and the tower leaned toward the cliff. Cracks spread across the queen's carven face, bits of hair and cheek fallen away.

Another good quake and the whole thing might topple over the falls.

They walked at first, either out of prudence or some unspoken respect for the black-burnt sky. But the closer they grew to the Northern Bank, the harder the way became. The earth had shifted—what had been the reedy banks of the Mir were now cliffs taller than a man, scattered with stones and still-warm ash. The corpses of trees littered the ground, half buried in debris. The once-gentle river thundered below. Nothing green remained.

When the ashfall rose to calf-height, they had to stop. Isyllt's ring had begun to chill, and she could see only a few yards into the murk, even with their witchlights. Sweat ran down her face and she scrubbed it away with her veil.

"I suppose there aren't many people around to notice," Asheris said to himself. An instant later his eyes flashed, and his four wings unfurled, shining gold and cinnabar. Isyllt's breath caught at the sight.

She stepped in close, hooking her good arm around his neck. It might be easier if he carried her, but she balked at the thought of being cradled like a babe in arms. Instead he tightened his arms around her waist and bore them up. She winced at the strain on her shoulder, then forgot the discomfort as the draft of his wings swirled the ash away and let her see the land below.

The Mir had shifted her bed yards to the south, leaving a swath of sooty mud bare. Gray froth tangled on the current, churned over the now-rocky bank. As they moved south she saw the remains of villages, streets buried under dust and cinders, thatched roofs burned away and beams like bones rising from the slag. Her ring chilled till her right

hand was as numb as her left. The ferry landing and the
hill above it were gone, washed away by mud and ash—
nothing remained of the dock but a few charred splinters.

It was harder to breathe here. The ash fell thicker and
the air reeked of alchemy—sulfur and salt spirits and salts
of ammonia. Tears ran down her cheeks and she couldn't
stop coughing. Her exposed skin prickled painfully. Asheris didn't falter, but his eyes reddened and watered and
she could see the tightness of his jaw even through the
veil.

"We can't go much farther in this—"

He broke off, eyes widening, and Isyllt turned to look
below them. She drew in a wondering breath and quickly
regretted it as she began to cough.

They had reached the city. But where she expected to
find another smoldering ruin, instead a shimmering dome
of water rose.

Asheris sank slowly, landing on a spur of stone outside
the wall. "She woke the river," he whispered.

"She bought a miracle."

The dome flowed in an unceasing cascade. It washed
over their boots, soaked their trousers. Ash slid away in
silver streams as soon as it touched the water. Asheris
pressed a cautious hand into the wall, drew it back wet to
the elbow and somewhat cleaner.

"I think we can go in."

The pressure was enough to sting as she stepped
through, but not much worse than a strong shower. They
emerged drenched and gasping. Isyllt tugged her sodden
veil aside and scrubbed her face with it, wrinkling her
nose at the stains. She coughed and spat gray phlegm. Her
throat ached, lips parched and tongue thick, but she didn't

want to risk the water, however miraculous. At least the air within was cleaner, thank the saints.

Thank Zhirin.

Symir hadn't escaped entirely. The streets were strewn with rubble and stones—from both collapsing buildings and great porous black boulders that must have come from the volcano. The ground was slick with black mud, and bodies lay broken amid the debris. But the death-chill eased; there were survivors here too.

The streetlamps were out, but the gloom brightened. The water itself glowed, she realized, a subtle witchlit iridescence. Silver-green light and ash-shadows rippled over the ground and broken walls, washed everything unreal, dreamlike.

"Where should we go?" She wasn't sure why she whispered, except that the shining vault of water reminded her of a cathedral.

"To the Khas, I suppose."

"Did Faraj know, about you?" Their boots squelched as they walked, cloth slapping against flesh.

"I don't think so," he said after a moment. "He knew something, knew that my service was not entirely willing, but I doubt Imran or Rahal would have entrusted him with the truth."

They passed a few survivors. A woman crouched in the rubble of a house, keening softly. A man kneeling beside an overflowing canal, a child's body limp in his arms. They didn't stop; there was nothing either of them could do.

As they neared Jadewater, voices rose over the constant rush of water. Glancing at each other, they turned toward it. The bridge was still intact, though cracked in places. The temple district had flooded knee-deep, nearly swallowed by the black pool that had been the Floating Garden. At the steps of the River Mother's temple, a crowd gathered, voices raised in grief and wonder. One of the ivy-crowned domes had fallen, but the building was otherwise sound.

The Khas hadn't fared so well. Its walls stood, gates open, but the Pomegranate Court was a ruin of fallen trees and muddy ash, and the dome on the great hall had caved in. The council dais was buried, and several councillors with it; guards tried to dig the bodies out but seemed too stunned to be effective. A few of them looked at Asheris with eyes wide and hopeful as hungry dogs, but he only shook his head sadly and turned away.

They found Faraj amid the rubble of the west wing, Shamina huddled lifelessly over Murai a few yards away. Isyllt swallowed the taste of char and started to turn, then paused. The chill wasn't deep enough.

"Help me," she said, crouching awkwardly beside the Vicereine. The woman's skin was as cool as the air, her muscles locked in place. The jade-gray light painted everything cold and deathly, but Murai's flesh was still warm.

Asheris knelt beside her and helped pull the corpse aside. Beneath her mother, Murai lay bruised and unmoving, but her breath rasped faintly and her eyelids twitched as Asheris checked her for broken bones. She didn't wake as he lifted her.

"There's nothing left here for any of us," he said softly.

As they passed the gates, something moved in the flooded water plaza, a long shape twisting into the shallows where the steps had been. Isyllt tensed as a nakh raised its pale upper body, tail lashing. She groped for a knife she didn't have, but the creature lifted one webbed hand to stay her.

"Your companions are at the docks," it hissed, needle teeth glinting in the dull light.

"Thank you," Isyllt said after a moment of surprise. "But why are you telling me?" A fading bruise mottled the creature's face; she wondered if this was the one she'd met in the canal.

Black eyes flashed pearlescent as the nakh glanced toward the ceiling of water. "The river-daughter asked me to. She's been waiting for you."

The river-daughter. "Zhirin."

The nakh shrugged, a disturbingly liquid ripple of bone and flesh. "She has no need for mortal names now." It grinned a cold shark grin. "You have her protection here, witch. Come swim with me in the bay."

Isyllt smiled back and nodded toward her bandaged arm. "Sorry. Not today."

"I'll be waiting." Then the creature flung itself backward and vanished into the deep rushing water.

The destruction in Merrowgate was even worse. No building she saw had escaped damage, and some were in ruins. The Storm God's Bride was rubble now, and Isyllt shook her head sadly at the sight. Survivors huddled in doorways, watching her and Asheris warily or staring blankly ahead. The docks were gone, nothing but shattered wood and debris. A ship's mast canted out of the churning gray water, her shredded sails snagged on splintered spars. The rest of the craft was lost under the bay, and under the shining aqueous wall.

Some survivors moved about, searching the ruins for signs of life. She recognized Jabbor and the woman who'd spoken at the Tigers' council; the weight in her chest eased a fraction.

Jabbor's skin was dull and gray and he carried himself stiffly, but otherwise seemed unhurt. He blinked when he saw her and brushed a hand across one eye.

"What happened?" His voice was raw and stretched-thin and she knew he wasn't asking about the mountain.

"She went into the river. To save the city. She chose it."

He seemed to shrink for an instant, then straightened and raised his chin. "I heard her voice. We were going to die in the mudslides or the river, I was certain, and then I heard Zhir's voice and the flood carried us here."

He stared at her and Asheris, and the bitterness was clear in his eyes for a moment. She could hear the unspoken question—why them? Why them and not the woman he loved. He didn't say it aloud, and she was glad; she had no answer.

"Excuse me," he said, turning away. "I have to help. There are so many—"

They walked on, leaving the Tigers to their grief.

The nakh hadn't lied—farther on in the gloom sat three familiar figures. Her stomach chilled with relief as Adam rose and turned toward her. He and Siddir and Vienh all seemed unhurt, if tired and ghastly wan in the watery light.

Adam grinned. "I told them you'd show up." He raised an eyebrow at Asheris, and she nodded—safe.

Siddir was staring at Asheris as well, and Isyllt remembered the brittle tension between them at the ball, the glossed-over history. But before either man might speak, Vienh stepped between them to look at Murai.

"The Viceroy's daughter?" She laid a careful hand on the child's forehead; Murai still didn't wake.

"Her parents are dead, and I don't know of any other family. Perhaps in Ta'ashlan . . ."

Isyllt swallowed as she realized who wasn't with them. "Your daughter?"

Vienh's smile chased away the weariness on her face for an instant. "On the *Dog*, with my sister. I took them over as soon as I found them, but Adam insisted we wait for you." She followed Isyllt's glance toward the shrouded bay. "Izzy's out there. The water's too rough to come close. Nowhere to dock, anyway."

"And the diamonds?"

The woman's humor died and Siddir shook his head angrily. "We caught the ship," he said, "but they sank the stones before I could get them. All this destruction, and I still don't have the evidence I need."

"Don't worry about that." Asheris's smile was slow and predatory. "I anticipate changes in the Court of Lions very soon. My employment with the Emperor is over," he added to Siddir's raised brows.

"We should go," Vienh said. "The mountain isn't finished. We'll take you all as far as Khejuan, and you can find your own ways from there."

Asheris nodded. "Thank you, but I'll go my own way here. Will you take her, though?" he asked, nodding toward Murai.

The smuggler frowned but extended her arms for the child.

Isyllt looked at Adam and found him scanning the ruined streets, a frown twisting his mouth.

"I'm sorry," she said softly.

He shook his head, snorting sharply. "No. I thought I smelled her. Damn this filthy air."

"Are you sure?"

In answer, he took a step toward a rubble-strewn alley, then another. Isyllt reached for his arm, but he broke into a loping run before she touched him. Her ring sparked fitfully on her outstretched hand. She exchanged a glance with Asheris, then hurried after Adam.

The diamond burned brighter as she crossed into the shadow of the alley. Not just death—a ghost. She heard the wet rustle of cloth as Asheris followed her. The cold thickened as they turned a corner, scrambling over a fall of brick and beams. The chill, the hunger in the air, reminded her of Par Khan.

On the other side of the collapsed wall she saw Adam, a slender shape beside him. It took her a heartbeat to recognize Xinai—filth crusted her skin and clothes, flattened her hair to her skull. Beneath the mud and blood her face was sickly pale, eyes wide and black. One arm hung limp at her side; the other reached for Adam.

He knew—Isyllt could see it on his stricken face. He knew the woman in front of him wasn't his partner. Maybe he even knew what she wanted. He clutched his sword-hilt, tendons sharp-etched with tension, but he didn't draw, didn't pull away from the touch that would suck out his strength.

"Adam!"

They both turned. Adam shook himself like a dog and staggered back. "Xin—"

"No," Isyllt said, climbing clumsily over the pile of brick. "It's not. Who are you?"

"Her mother." The voice was ghastly, rough and hollow and cold as shattered glass—a wonder it didn't draw blood.

Isyllt laughed. "Does every ghost in this country want to eat their children?"

Xinai's lips peeled back from her teeth. "She would have died if not for me. She needs me."

"She needs rest and a surgeon. Not a leech." She unfocused her eyes, looked *otherwise*. Xinai's life was faint, nearly overshadowed by the darkness. If she died possessed, the demon would have her. Something pulsed an ugly red against her chest—one of her charm bags, its colors woven into woman and ghost.

"You don't know what she needs, necromancer."

Isyllt drew a deep breath and stepped closer. "Maybe not, but I know what you need. Adam."

And thank the saints, he understood. The ghost turned, still clumsy in her meat-puppet, but he was already on her, pinning her arms and holding her while she shrieked like a scalded cat. He gasped, blanching as she began to suck the heat from his flesh.

Isyllt lunged toward them, off-balance with only one arm. She stumbled, scraped her palm on the wall as she caught herself. Clumsy and cursing, she fumbled through the charms around Xinai's neck till she found the one that stung like ice. The ghost screamed and writhed as she ripped it free; for an instant Isyllt saw the shadow of a knife-gash bleeding down her throat.

She couldn't bind the ghost, not without her name, but she could break the connection to Xinai. Her diamond blazed, a cold light that sliced through the shadows but didn't lessen them. Her bones ached as she called on the abyss again. Her fingers cramped around the pouch.

This spell was nothing compared to the diamond collar. Leather stiffened and cracked. Thread rotted. A lump of rust-stained wood splintered, till nothing was left but a pile of silver dust on her palm. She tilted her hand and that too was gone.

Xinai slumped in Adam's arms and he staggered, both of them sinking to the ground. The ghost remained, bloody and wild-eyed, flinching away from the nothing that Isyllt wielded, the darkness that swallowed even the dead.

For a moment she contemplated it, reaching out for the ghost, unraveling all the skeins of memory and madness and desire that held wraiths to the living world.

Instead she lowered her hand with a sigh. "What you need is to move on," Isyllt told the woman. "Go."

And like a gust of wind, she was gone.

"What did you do?" Asheris asked. His warmth lined her side as he leaned in. Cold sweat beaded on her back; the fever was coming on.

"Just a banishment. It's not permanent, but maybe she'll have time to think."

Xinai stirred, tears tracking through the mud on her cheeks. "Mira," she whispered, one hand groping at her neck.

Isyllt turned away. "Deilin."

The ghost appeared beside her. Her lips parted as she looked up at the dome of water. "What's happened?"

"Everything the Dai Tranh wanted, mostly."

Black eyes turned back to Isyllt. "What now, then?"

"I'm going home. You spoke of going east, of the Ashen Wind." She gestured to the gray ceiling. "The wind is nothing but ashes now. Will you try it?"

Deilin cocked her head. "Does that mean—"

Isyllt nodded. The words were only ritual, but she

spoke them anyway. "I release you. But for the love of heaven, leave the children alone."

The ghost nodded, then looked down at her wound—the bloodstain on her shirt was shrinking.

"Tell my granddaughters . . ." She shook her head with a rueful smile. "No, never mind. Let them be. Good-bye, necromancer." And then she was gone.

The ground shuddered softly and brick dust trickled from the broken walls. Adam stood, Xinai in his arms. "Time to go."

Vienh started to harangue them when they returned to the dock, but stopped when she saw Xinai and Adam's grim face.

"Will she live?" he asked Isyllt, easing her down.

She touched the woman's shoulder carefully. Bruises and scrapes, strained muscles, a broken arm and fractured ribs. But no damage to the heart, no poison in the blood. "I think so. She needs rest, medicine, but no miracles." She glanced up. "Are you going to stay with her?"

A muscle twitched in his jaw. "No," he said after a moment. "She made her choice." He nodded toward the Tigers. "They can look after her. And I promised to see you back safe." He glanced at her sling. "Or as close as I've managed."

She gave him a lopsided smile. "Close enough for government work."

"I'm not rowing you to Selafai in a storm-cursed longboat," Vienh shouted across the quay, kicking the boat in question. "Let's go."

Isyllt turned to Asheris. Her arm itched and she'd started to shake; her voice was dying fast and taking her wits with it. "If you're ever in Erisín—" she said at last.

"Yes." He smiled, took her hand and pressed a kiss on her filthy knuckles. "Or come to Assar. I'll show you the Sea of Glass."

"If it's anything like the mountain, please don't bother." She grinned, squeezing his hand. He didn't flinch from her ring this time.

His smile stretched and he leaned down to kiss her brow. "Go home, necromancer." It sounded like a benediction.

She couldn't wish him the same. "Good luck," she said instead. She turned toward the waiting boat and didn't look back till they'd crossed the river's shining veil.

EPILOGUE

The news beat them home. Only days after the destruction of Symir, Rahal al Seth, Emperor of Assar, was dead. He and several of his mages had burned when a palace laboratory caught fire. No one knew what had started the fire, but it was assumed to have been a spell gone wrong. It occurred during the demon days before the start of the new year—always an ill omen.

His half sister, Samar al Seth, would be crowned before the month was up, and already promised aid to devastated Sivahra.

Isyllt smiled when she read it. For a time she considered walking the labyrinth beneath the temple of Erishal and releasing the rest of the ghosts in her ring. Pragmatism won, however, and she settled for opening a bottle of Chassut red and toasting the embers falling in her hearth.

The physicians at the Arcanost opened her hand and stitched it up again full of silver pins. The damage was too great for even their most cunning surgeons, though, and she'd left it too long untreated. She retained the use of thumb and forefinger, but the two middle fingers curled uselessly and the smallest followed them, muscles already atrophying. She wore a ridge of scar tissue in the shape of a man's hand around her left wrist—that would last longer than the payment sitting in her bank account. She began to wear her ring on her right hand, and learned to wash her hair one-handed.

The pain and guilt in Kiril's eyes whenever he saw her might have given her a vicious pleasure only a month ago. Now they were just another little sadness. As Adam had said, what was the use in arguing?

The next courier ship came a month after the first and carried reports of the new Empress's coronation, as well as news of an investigation into embezzlement and financial mismanagement in the military. Several generals had hastily retired and the Empress had not yet replaced them.

The ship also brought a package for Isyllt, delivered by a ruddy-faced dockrat. After cursing and fumbling with the nailed crate, she finally produced a smaller box. She raised an eyebrow at the seal; not the Imperial stamp, but the crest of the family al Seth. This box was sealed with a spell and the latch lifted when she touched it. Inside the padded coffer were a note and a velvet pouch.

I hope this finds you well, she read.
My situation here has much improved, in light of recent events. The new Empress has offered me a position, and I think I shall accept it. I cannot re-

turn home, but the City of Lions is not so unpleas-
ant when it isn't my prison. You asked me once if I
could give up our profession—the answer, it seems,
is no. We are as we have been made. I'll be certain
to tell Her Majesty to give me more necromancers
on staff.

Enclosed is a token of my gratitude—only a pal-
try one, for what you've done, but more becoming
than the scars, I think.

Your friend,
Asheris

Isyllt opened the bag and laughed as a stream of opals poured free, gleaming with iridescent fire.

ACKNOWLEDGMENTS

More people than I can count offered help and support during the course of this book. Just a few include Elizabeth Bear; Leah Bobet; Jodi Meadows; Jaime Lee Moyer; everyone in the Online Writing Workshop and its Zoo; all my blog readers who endured my cursing and struggling; the circulation department of Willis Library; my husband, Steven, who survived at ground zero; my fabulous agent, Jennifer Jackson; and my equally fabulous editor, Dong-Won Song. Thank you!

extras

orbit

meet the author

Amanda Downum was born in Virginia and has since spent time in Indonesia, Micronesia, Missouri, and Arizona. In 1990 she was sucked into the gravity well of Texas and has not yet escaped. She graduated from the University of North Texas with a degree in English literature, and has spent the last ten years working in a succession of libraries and bookstores; she is very fond of alphabetizing. She currently lives near Austin in a house with a spooky attic, which she shares with her long-suffering husband and fluctuating numbers of animals and half-finished novels. She spends her spare time making jewelry and falling off perfectly good rocks. To learn more about the author, visit www.amandadownum.com.

interview

Prior to becoming a published author, what other professions have you had?

I've been a book buyer for a medical bookstore and a library supervisor, and spent years as a retail minion. I'm currently dayjobbing as a bookseller in a used-book store, which isn't at all a bad way to spend eight hours of a day.

When you aren't writing, what do you like to do in your spare time?

Besides selling other people's books, I make jewelry and rock-climb (outside whenever I can, but mostly indoors). I've tried gardening, but that turned out to be depressing for me and deadly for the plants. My next hobby may be something involving sharp objects, like knitting or crochet.

Who/what would you consider to be your influences?

My mother read me Tolkien, Lewis, Le Guin, and L'Engle as a child, and they carved permanent channels in my brain. Later on I discovered Lovecraft and binged on horror novels, and now magic and monsters are pretty much my favorite things. My favorite modern writers are Elizabeth Bear, Barbara Hambly, and Caitlín R. Kiernan.

Besides the literary influences, I've always loved to travel, and I get a lot of inspiration from visiting or reading about other places.

The Drowning City *is a novel with an amazingly lush setting and unique world. How did you derive the idea for this novel?*

Several different ideas had been floating around in my head for a while: the character Isyllt, a spy novel, and second-world fantasy (I'd been working on several contemporary fantasies previously, and wanted a change of pace). And then in 2005 Hurricane Katrina came, and as I watched all the horror and ugliness and heroism and grief, I thought of the title *The Drowning City*, and all the disparate ideas started to come together. Which makes me feel a little like a vulture.

In writing the novel, were you particularly influenced by your time living in Southeast Asia?

Having lived in Arizona and Texas since I moved back to the States, I really miss rainy seasons. So as soon as I had a book with monsoons, a South Asian–inspired setting seemed perfect. The most specific influence on *TDC*, though, was in the scene with the pigs. That was something I heard too often, living up the hill from a pig farm on Yap.

Do you have a favorite character? If so, why?

Definitely Isyllt. She's one of my oldest characters, and survived an unfortunate juvenilia project that will otherwise never see the light of day. She can always be relied on to run straight into dangerous situations—or crawl into them in the dark—and otherwise get herself in trouble, which I've discovered is the most useful thing a character can do when I'm trying to plot a novel.

What can readers expect in* The Bone Palace*?
Intrigue, heartbreak, and more forensic necromancy. And vampires, though not the oversexed variety.

As a debut author, what has been your favorite part of the publishing process?
Seeing my cover art! Book covers have fascinated me ever since I started to read, and even the bad ones are often very entertaining. That I really like the preliminary cover art for *TDC* is just an extra helping of awesome.

introducing

If you enjoyed THE DROWNING CITY,
look out for

THE BONE PALACE

The Necromancer Chronicles Book Two

by Amanda Downum

In the Sepulcher, death smelled like roses.

Sachets of petals and braziers of incense lined the marble halls and scented-oil lamps burned throughout the long vault, twining ribbons of rose and jasmine and myrrh through the chill air. Meant to drown the smell of blood and rot that crept out of the corpse-racks in the walls, but death couldn't be undone so easily. The raw, coppery scent of recent violence teased past the sweetness, creeping into Isyllt's sinuses as she studied the dead woman on the slab.

Blue-tinged lips parted slightly, expressionless in death, but the slash across her throat grinned, baring red meat and pale flashes of bone. Barely enough blood in her to settle—some clotted like rust in brass-blonde hair, pasted damp-frizzed tendrils to her cheeks. Her clothing had already been removed, faint lines down her ribs showing where corset stays had pressed into flesh. Her garments, cut away by competent, uncaring attendants, were likely shelved in an oubliette of an evidence room upstairs.

Isyllt crossed her arms under her breasts and shivered beneath her long black coat. "Where did you find her?" Her breath trailed away in a shimmering plume; spells of cold etched the stones.

"In the Garden, in an alley just after dusk." Khelséa lounged against the frescoed wall between corpse-drawers, her orange uniform coat garish against pale green. Vines and leaves swirled across the vault—the builders had tried to make the room cheery, but no amount of paint or plaster could disguise the death that steeped these stones. "She was cold and stiff when we got there."

Isyllt frowned at the dead woman, brushed a finger against a lock of yellow hair. A prostitute, then, most likely. A foreigner too, from the coloring—Vallish like Isyllt, perhaps, or Rosian. Refugees crowded tenements and shantytowns in the inner city, and more and more turned to the Garden for work.

Isyllt pressed gently on the woman's jaw, and it opened to reveal nearly a full set of lightly tea-stained teeth. Her elbows were still stiff, and her knees immobile. Rigor had only just begun to fade. "A day dead?"

"That's our guess. It was raining when we found her, and she was soaked, but there were hardly any flies. And the alley is visible from the street—she couldn't have lain there all day."

"So dumped. Why call me?" The Garden was the Vigiles Urbani's jurisdiction, unless the Crown was somehow involved, or the crime was beyond the city police. And while pride insisted that the Vigiles' necromancers weren't as well-trained as the Arcanosti or Crown Investigators, Isyllt knew they were perfectly competent. She bent over the white stone table, examining the wound. The knife had nicked bone. "What can I tell you about this that you don't already know?"

"Look at her thighs."

The woman's legs tapered from flaring hips to gently muscled calves and delicate ankles. No spider veins or calluses on her feet—chipped gold paint decorated her toenails. Flesh once soft and supple felt closer to wax under Isyllt's careful fingers. Death whispered over her hand, lapped catlike at her skin. The cabochon black diamond on her right hand flickered fitfully, ghostlight sparking in its crystalline depths.

She ran a gentle hand between the woman's thighs, tracing the same path as a dozen customers, a dozen lovers. But this time there was no response, no passion real or feigned. Only stiffening muscles and cold flesh.

No wounds, no bruises. No sign of rape. No violation but that of the blade.

"What am I—" She paused. On the inside of the left leg, near the crease of the groin, she touched a narrow ridge of scar tissue. More than one. She pressed against stiff flesh to get a better look. Old marks, healed and scarred long ago. Teeth marks. She found the same scars on the other leg, some more recent.

Very sharp teeth. Isyllt shivered; she knew what such bites felt like.

"Do you think this had anything to do with her death?" She kept looking but found no fresh wounds.

"Maybe." Khelséa reached into an inside pocket of her coat and pulled out a folded piece of silk. "But this is why I called you."

Isyllt stretched across the dead woman and took the cloth; something small and hard was hidden in its folds. She recognized the shape of a ring before she finished unwrapping it.

A heavy band of gold, skillfully wrought, set with a sapphire the size of a woman's thumbnail. A rampant griffin etched the stone, tiny but detailed. A master's work. A royal work.

"Where was this?" A knot colder than the room drew tight in her stomach.

"Sewn inside her camisole, clumsy new stitches. Her purse was missing."

A royal signet in a dead whore's clothes. Isyllt blew a sharp breath through her nose. "How many know?"

"Only me and my autopsist." Khelséa snorted. "You think I'd wave something like this in front of the constables?"

Isyllt stared at the ring. A woman's ring, but no woman alive had the right to wear it. She looked down at the body. A sliver of blue iris showed beneath half-closed lids, already milky. "What was her name?"

"Forsythia."

Not a real name—at least she hoped it wasn't. Not many mothers branded their daughters with a prostitute's name at birth.

Isyllt dipped a finger into the gaping wound, licked off coagulated blood and fluids. Khelséa grimaced theatrically, but the captain's nerves and stomach were hard to upset.

Cold jellied blood, bittersweet and thin with rainwate.
No trace of illness or taint, nothing deadly save for the
quantity spilled. The taste coated Isyllt's tongue.

"Forsythia. Are you there?"

No answer, not even a shiver. Isyllt listened till her ears
rang, but heard nothing. Her power could raise the corpse
off its cold table and dance it around the room, but no
ghost lingered to answer her questions. She sighed. "A
clean crossing. They never stay when you need them to.
She might be wherever she was killed, though." She nib-
bled the last speck of blood from under her fingernail.

Gently she pushed back Forsythia's kohl-smeared
eyelids. *Rain*, she wondered briefly, looking at the ashen
streaks, *or did you have time for tears?* Her reflection
stared back from death-pearled eyes. She rested her fingers
on the woman's temples, thumbs on her cheekbones; the
black leather glove on her left hand was stark against pale
skin. The woman's soul was gone, lost on the other side of
the mirror, but memories still lingered in her eyes.

Isyllt hoped for the killer's face, but instead she saw a
sunset. Clouds glowed pink and orange as the sun sank
behind the ragged skyline of Oldtown, the colors burned
into Forsythia's mind. The last thing she saw was that
jeweled sky fading into dusk, then a sudden pressure of
hands and blackness. Much too quick for death, even as
quick a death as this must have been.

Isyllt sighed and looked away, the colors of memory
fading into the white and green of the mortuary. "She was
grabbed off the street, somewhere in Oldtown. Maybe the
Garden." Death must have come not long afterward; she
hoped the woman hadn't suffered much. "What else do
you know?"

"Nothing. There was nothing but rain in the alley, and no one saw anything." Khelséa rolled her eyes. "No one ever sees anything." She pushed away from the wall, shaking back her long black braids. "Do you have any magic tricks for me?"

"Nothing entertaining." Isyllt turned toward the back of the room, where tables and benches were set up for students and investigators. "Will you bring me gloves and surgical spirits? And a dissection plate."

The captain opened a cabinet against the wall and removed thin cotton examiner's gloves, a bottle, and a well-scrubbed tin tray. "What are you doing?"

"Testing for contagion. Someone touched this before she did." She sat down, stripping off her left glove. Her scarred and claw-curled hand, bandaged or gloved for nearly two years, was corpse-white beneath. She tried to ignore it as she scrubbed her hands with cold spirits; she was mostly comfortable with only seven working fingers by now. She wiped down the tray as well, then tugged on the white gloves and set the ring on the tin. Already contaminated, of course, but every little bit helped. It was much easier to test for transference—be it of skin, hair, blood, or energy—with a suspect at hand, but she could also tune the ring to react to the presence of anyone who had handled it recently, and even seek the person out, at close enough range.

Closing her eyes against the bitter-sharp alcohol fumes, she touched the ring lightly. She could have managed a more sterile space in her own workroom, but this would serve. Tendrils of magic wrapped around the gold, resonated through the stone. Mages used sapphires and other such gems to hold energy—the cut and clarity of this one made it ideal for storing spells.

The taste of the spirits crept over her tongue, stinging her palate as it sharpened the spell. Alcohol, like her magic, was clean of living things, anathema even to disease and crawling necrophages. Against its stark sterility, any contagion should shine clear.

Isyllt opened her eyes and leaned back, wrinkling her nose at the mingled stink of spirits and roses and death. Witchlight glimmered in the sapphire's crystalline depths, then faded into blue. "There. Let's test it." She stripped off the cotton gloves and touched the ring with her bare hand. The light flared again briefly at the familiar skin, and the spell shivered in her head. She let the essence of the alcohol erase the contamination, and it stilled again.

"Now you," she said, holding the ring out to Khelséa. Another shiver and flare at the captain's touch, and again she let the memory of it vanish. Now the stone should react only to whoever had held it before Forsythia. She found a spare silver chain in the exorcist's kit in her pocket, and slid the ring under her shirt. It settled cold between her breasts, warming slowly between cloth and skin.

"Do you need anything else?" Khelséa asked.

Isyllt ran a hand over her face. "A night's sleep. Other than that, no. I'll tread lightly. More vigils hanging around would only attract attention."

Khelséa snorted and tugged her orange coat straight. At least her dark skin let her wear the Vigiles' distinctive shade well. "What's one more death in Oldtown, after all?"

"Eight for an obol." Their boots echoed in unison as

they started for the stairs, leaving the dead woman on her slab.

Outside, the night smelled of autumn rain, and wet stone and cobbles glistened under the streetlamps. Ink-stone was a quiet neighborhood after midnight, scribes and bureaucrats long safe in bed. Shadows draped the columned facade of the Sepulcher, hiding the faces of the owl-winged gargoyles who crouched on the roof. Isyllt felt their unblinking granite stares as she descended the broad steps. Sentinels of the Otherworld. A carriage waited in the street, the driver half dozing, horses snorting rest-lessly. Isyllt breathed deep, letting the night wash away the smell of blood and roses.

"I saw your minstrel friend in the Garden tonight," Khelséa said with a grin. "Maybe I should take him in for questioning."

Isyllt snorted. "Is that the only way you can start a con-versation with a man?"

"Better than calling them from their tombs." The cap-tain unlatched the carriage door and held it open. "Let me know what you find. I'm sure it will be interesting."

Isyllt smiled. "This job always is." She pulled herself into the carriage and Khelséa shut the door. The horses' hooves clattered against the cobbles as they carried her across the city.